SONG OF THE WOODEN SPARROW

ISABEL TUTAINE

GOLDEN BRIDGES
PUBLISHING

SONG OF THE WOODEN SPARROW

Published in the United States by Golden Bridges Publishing 2024

Library of Congress Control Number: 2024944771

ISBN (Print): 979-8-9907356-4-4

ISBN (ebook): 979-8-9907356-5-1

CONTENTS

1

THE DEVIL'S PUSTULES

Ghana, 1894

The crimson flush under the miner's dark skin indicated he was running a fever, and the guarded way he bent his limbs to sit suggested his joints were swollen. Leah suspected he had one of the many contagious jungle fevers, some of which only the natives had names for, and immediately placed him in isolation. She hoped he did not have smallpox because not everyone at the field hospital was vaccinated, not even now.

Then she continued tending other patients, intermittently looking in on the miner, who seemed to be getting worse by the hour. She would later relish the steady pace of that afternoon before the chaos took over.

Two days later, Nurse Akua came running after her. "He's crying blood! Blood! From his eyes!"

Leah looked askance at the nurse. No one cried blood. But Nurse Akua was not prone to overstatements, so Leah rose calmly from her chair, determined to hold whatever she was thinking at arm's length until she could investigate the circumstances for herself.

When she examined the miner, she found that his slight rash had developed into enormous blisters, even in his eyes. Not only were his eyes bleeding, but he was vomiting violently, unable to keep down anything, not even water. With a piece of gauze, she pressed a pustule on the man's arm. The fluid shifted from side to side, but the pustule did not break. It looked to be filled with...blood? This was not a version of smallpox she had seen.

"Please get Dr. Titus Maays," said Leah. She wanted her husband to look at this phenomenon.

THE NEXT MORNING, Leah stepped out of her tent into a gritty cloud from a pit the laborers were digging. She tripped and almost fell into one of two trenches that had already been dug, one on each side of the main hospital tent.

"What are you doing? What are these trenches for?" she asked Jabari, the foreman of laborers. She pointed to the pit. "And what is that for?"

Jabari, tall and wide and always lumbering at an even pace, said in his sonorous voice, "The pit is to burn things. This trench, for Ghanians. The other, for whites."

"Why?"

"The devil's blisters have arrived."

"You were spared," said Leah, taking Jabari's facial scars as proof that lives could be snatched from any illness, even smallpox. "And you shall not get smallpox again, having caught it once."

Jabari shook his head. "This is not smallpox. I have heard about this. Pray to your gods. Wear gloves."

"Jabari, this is a field hospital, not a graveyard," Leah snapped. She tended to lose patience with people who gave up on those who were merely sick.

"It will become a graveyard," Jabari said in his deep, prophetic voice. "Everyone will be covered with the devil's blisters. You will see."

A few days later, Nurse Akua broke out in rashes that within days turned into purple, bloody pustules the size of quarters, just like the miner's. Her liver enlarged to the point where Leah could see the organ bulging against the abdomen without having to press to feel it. Her joints were so swollen she could not bend her arms or legs.

Within the week, several other nurses and one doctor developed rashes. Now Leah experienced her first tingle of serious concern. She wasn't surprised that whatever the miner had was contagious but was taken aback at how rapidly it transferred from person to person.

Then the deaths began, commencing with the miner's. Most died during the crepuscular hours, an observation Leah thought to investigate but abandoned when people began dying faster than clocks could tick. One week later, time between deaths ceased to exist. Patients were dying faster than she could move from bed to bed to pronounce them dead and pull bedsheets over their faces. At record speed, one by one or in small clusters, almost everyone turned into a patient, then into a corpse waiting to be buried.

The pit Leah once thought unnecessary now burned day and night. No sooner did a person die than the laborers descended like ravens on the bed in which the person lay. They hauled the body to a trench. They moved everything that had touched the body to the pit—bedsheets, pillows, compresses, bandages, clothes, shoes, invalid feeders, bedpans, mattress, bed frame—and set it on fire. The laborers worked in shifts around the clock, and none was ever idle when awake.

Leah had never pegged Jabari as melodramatic until he took it upon himself to inform persons who came to claim the bodies of relatives that they could not leave. Even with that mandate, most sneaked out during the night.

As rumors of people elsewhere developing blisters drifted back to the compound, Jabari held a whispered conversation with one of the laborers before sending him into the forest to get help. The laborer fled in fear, but he sent back men who carried rifles. Those men stayed outside the compound, clear of the infirmary, with orders to shoot at anyone coming in or trying to get out.

Leah tried to take comfort in Jabari's militant restrictions. They were necessary to prevent Ghana, if not all of Africa, falling to this plague. Still, the restrictions felt like a noose around her neck. She now understood plainly that she was here to take care of survivors or die with the rest. No other options were available.

Occasionally, Leah would hear a gunshot, but no one with a bullet wound was ever brought into the hospital. In fact, no one entered or left the compound once the men with rifles surrounded it. Jabari never granted any exemption, to the degree that Leah began to worry that Jabari might have her shot if she tried to leave.

ON THE EVENING Titus came into the tent after his shift, Leah felt a strangeness in how perfectly still he stood by the tent door. She knew by the late hour he had to be exhausted, although to her, he always looked handsome. She smiled at him from across the room where she sat nursing their William.

His distance seemed so premeditated she momentarily wondered if everyone had finished dying and he was about to announce that they could go home. Then Titus raised his shirt and revealed the rash across his abdomen. Pressing their William against herself, Leah instinctively rose and stepped toward him.

Titus held up his hand and backed away. "I shall continue working as long as I can."

"But, Titus—"

"I have caught it! There is nothing more to be done. My only hope is to survive it." Knowing full well that no one had yet survived the disease that putrefied people's bodies while they lived, Titus let out a sob. "Keep yourself and William safe, my love."

Weak kneed, Leah slipped back into a chair, pulling her arms around William to protect him, as if such a gesture could. She was so stunned she could not form thoughts.

There was nothing she could do. She couldn't sneak out with William because they were surrounded by Jabari's armed men and beyond that by dense Ghanian forests that could not be traversed without a guide. She couldn't even walk across their tent to comfort Titus.

A trickle of grief ran through her as she watched through the tent flap in a state of suspension while Titus made his way back to the infirmary, where one more infected body would not make a difference. She knew he planned to continue as a doctor until he became a patient, and then...

Falsely calm, Leah drew water to ease William's fussiness from the heat with a bath before she put him to bed. She set out his change of clothes, neatly folded beside the wash basin, and pulled off his linen gown, struggling against his little flailing arms and legs. She became immobile, holding the linen gown in midair, when she saw the rash, more red than pink and speckled with white heads, across his torso.

At that moment, Leah developed an abrupt intimacy with death she had never experienced, despite having recently seen so much of it. She screamed to ascend elsewhere on the sound of her voice. She screamed to make her soul disperse and to make the world end. She screamed, offering to exchange her life for Titus's and William's because even if she survived, her life would not be worth living.

2

INTO THE SMALLNESS OF THE WORLD

Six months later

Port of Edith's Bay, Maine, USA

Leah was not deceived. The carriage ride from the port of Edith's Bay into West Edith's Bay would replace four months of ocean swells with four hours of frost heaves that were hardly less violent. The thinly padded carriage seats did nothing to alleviate her travel aches, and she gave in to slumping against a window that rattled against her head.

Occasionally, she looked out the window to check for progress and fretted. The place she sought might not be there anymore. Or it might have changed so much it would not match what she thought it was. Or perhaps she had changed and it would disappoint her. For her serenity, she wanted to find it exactly as she left it, to slip back into it exactly as she had once belonged in it, however absurd her wish was.

After miles and miles of pastures and trees that all looked alike, the first orchard of gnarly apple trees came into sight and nudged her soul. Leah sat up. West Edith's Bay started where orchards began. As the hills of apple trees rolled across the carriage window, she held her breath and eventually pressed her lips into a tiny smile.

The carriage slowed to enter the town, and she leaned forward to catch glimpses of the general store and the post office. From the lack of new buildings, she suspected the population still held at around five hundred, counting stray dogs. She grabbed her black bag when the carriage came to a full stop and clutched it against her chest while the coach master dismounted and, a moment later, opened the door.

Cold air and light startled her like a splash of water. A sliver of West Edith's Bay stood before her like a slice of earth at an archeological site. On orange dirt loomed a dark brown building with a handsome sign: Carpentry and Fine Cabinetmaking. Above the building stretched a strip of stark, unwelcoming gray sky. The sliver of the town had all the glory of unbuttered toast.

This was West Edith's Bay, a landbound offshoot of Edith's Bay, the bustling port town, just as she remembered it. March was always cold in West Edith's Bay, often followed by summers that did not fully yield to heat. Leah placed her hand on the coach master's arm to steady herself and stepped out of the carriage feeling that she was hatching from an egg into a new life.

The coach master lugged a sack of mail to the post office and took off as efficiently as he arrived, leaving her alone with her two trunks and a suitcase. Leah sauntered around the trunks, disheartened that her aunt and uncle were not there to greet her, but for all she knew, she probably arrived before the letter she sent to them from Ghana.

With her black bag in hand, she walked to the general store to find a child who would take a message to her uncle. She didn't think twice about leaving her luggage on the street. No one in West Edith's Bay ever stole anything.

The general store was packed. Leah tucked her tummy so she could move through the customers and shelves cluttered with practical things—ink bottles, hand lotions, penknives, cans of varnish, tins of oil, sewing threads. The glittery row of penny candy jars on the counter tempted her. She had left Edith's Bay without having breakfast to catch the early carriage.

The street door opened just as she stepped up to the counter to vie for the proprietor's attention, and a man covered in sawdust crossed the floor, drafting the odor of Klein's Disinfectant Solution for Topical Wounds. The history of the spill was clear in the blotches on his shirt and pantleg. He took his place by the counter beside her, shedding some of the wood shavings that nested like highlights in his coarse, brown hair. Leah glanced out the store window at the Carpentry and Cabinetmaking sign.

The carpenter plopped his forearms on the counter and grimaced as he hung his head. With one hand he clutched a sock saturated with blood. With the other hand, he clutched that hand by the wrist.

He raised his head and, in a tenor that rose above the buzz of the crowd, called, "Mr. Hoburn! Bottle of Klein's. Sir. And bandages. Please."

The proprietor froze in mid gesture. He exchanged looks with his wife before leaving her in charge of the counter and reaching into a shelf to toss a box of bandages on the counter. Methodically, then frantically, he rummaged through another shelf.

Then he stepped back and fidgeted as he disclosed, "We're out of Klein's, Mr. Shay."

The carpenter fixed a look on Hoburn that made the proprietor cringe. The din in the store softened as people turned their attention to the two men.

"Alcohol? I got alcohol. Works just as good." Hoburn slid an amber bottle across the counter, as if feeding a wild animal through the bars of a cage. "We'll be sure to order Klein's this week."

The carpenter looked away from the proprietor, exuding dissatisfaction like a fog. He clutched his bloody hand and turned to leave.

Leah stepped toward him. "I can look after that, sir. If you will permit me."

The carpenter turned on the heel of one foot and took his time looking her over without speaking.

She swung her black bag on the counter. "I am a doctor. I can help you."

"A doctor!" cried Hoburn. He dropped a tin of snuff in front of a customer and slapped his hands on the counter to peer at Leah. "A doctor? You ain't by chance Utterance Cobb's niece, are you?"

Leah nodded, welcoming the proprietor's acknowledgment.

"Well, I'll be! They said you went off to study medicine and got married. And then to Africa! Imagine that! Now here you be again. A lady doctor! Why, I'll be blessed! Dr. Haloway'll be tickled pink. You going to introduce us to your husband and boy?"

"They are deceased," Leah said with clinical bluntness. The question always caught her off guard and stopped time. She could not answer quickly enough to prevent the topic from disquieting her.

Hoburn stood with his mouth open until his wife nudged him with her elbow. He blinked at her, apparently unable to interpret the nudge.

The proprietress glared at him and said to Leah, "We are sorry for your losses, dear."

"Thank you."

The proprietress looked over her blue dress. In her head, Leah took a moment to practice saying that she hadn't had time to buy a mourning gown because she was tending to patients. In truth, she had never wanted one, preferring to slip through people without calling attention to herself because condolences never comforted her.

To avoid a conversation with the proprietress, Leah turned to the carpenter. "With your permission, sir."

She took his hand and opened his fist the least amount possible to look under the bloody sock. Hoburn jerked his chin upward at the sight of blood and drew a sharp breath through pursed lips. The carpenter clenched his fist and pulled back his hand.

"Come, now. Let me see." Leah pulled back the carpenter's hand, stroking the back of his fingers until he relaxed his fist. She pinched each fingertip to study how the color flowed back. "Please move your fingers. Slowly."

The carpenter moved one finger at a time in a cautious wave. Determining the injury was below the ring finger he hesitated to move, she bent his fingers around the sock and looked up confidently without releasing his hand.

"It is not so bad." Leah turned to Hoburn. "Is there a place to wash?"

"Well, um—" said Hoburn and ran out of words.

The carpenter grabbed the box of bandages from the counter. "Pump out back, ma'am."

Hoburn continued to bounce his gaze between Leah and

the carpenter until the carpenter glared at him. The proprietor jumped to the task and escorted them out the back of the store into a courtyard.

Chickens flapped with excitement in a coop when Leah stepped outside with the carpenter. In the center of the courtyard stood the water pump she sought, with a bench to one side. When Leah took off her cloak despite the spring chill, Hoburn stood by the door as if on guard.

She waited for him to express whatever was on his mind, but Hoburn retreated into the store. Leah wasn't sure why he left the back door open in such cold.

She resisted the urge to brush the sawdust off the carpenter's arms when she rolled up his sleeve. As she pulled a bar of soap from her medical bag, her patient gave the pump lever a half dozen powerful pushes with his good hand until the water came gushing out. He had been evaluating her, she knew, by the amount of attention he was devoting to pumping water.

Leah worked up a thick, medicinally scented lather. "Now, let's see that hand."

The carpenter gave the lever a gratuitous pump and tossed the blood-soaked sock aside. She clasped his wrist with authority to deter his temptations to pull away. As she cleaned the gash, she explored his hand, finding broad, flat-tipped fingers that resembled the leaves of succulents, and an index finger with an odd curve.

She concluded the washing by wrapping his hand in a linen towel from her bag and led him by the wrist to the bench. Once seated, Leah pulled a bottle out of her bag with *Whiplash's Tonic* pressed into the dark green glass and soaked a piece of gauze with the acrimoniously scented liquid. The carpenter wrinkled his nose.

"With your permission." Leah slipped his arm under hers against her torso.

The impropriety of her gesture often confused men into making vulgar comments or advances. She prepared herself to redirect the man's thoughts, but the carpenter simply twitched and pressed his lips together.

"You shall feel this," she warned and pressed the gauze against the gash.

The carpenter jerked from the bloodcurdling sting for which Whiplash's Tonic was renowned. She plunged her elbow into the crook of his to prevent him from straightening his arm and flipping himself over the bench. A moment later, Leah removed the gauze and rotated his hand to inspect the cut as he wiped his eyes. It now looked insignificant, a thin line of clotted blood that did not appear as if it could cause any discomfort at all.

"Excellent. You shall not need stitches," she declared with satisfaction and bandaged his hand. "I am sorry about the sting. The tonic cauterizes and frequently negates the need for stitches, even if it makes patients squirm."

"Didn't. Squirm. Ma'am." The carpenter stood and shook out the cuff to his injured hand in a cloud of sawdust.

She was certain his intent was to singe her off the face of the earth with scorn, but she stood, striking a straight-backed military pose. Her eyes barely came up to his shoulders.

"No sir, you did not squirm. If I had a lollipop in my bag, I would certainly award it to you for your bravery."

She almost laughed at how wide-eyed he became and turned away in an effort not to offend the poor man. Leaving him to sort himself, Leah resumed packing her medical bag, tight with every conceivable item she might find useful during a medical emergency.

She glanced up again to find her patient with downcast eyes and arms crossed over his chest. When he rubbed his face with his uninjured hand, she stopped fiddling and faced him with concern.

"Be deserving that, ma'am. Please forgive me."

She now considered him in a new light. She seldom got apologies, except from mothers for their uncooperative children. He stared at her without blinking as she accommodated the bottle of the unkind tonic and clipped the worn bag shut.

The carpenter pulled out his wallet. "Mighty mess for a little cut. How much is it, ma'am?"

"Oh—nothing. Nothing at all. Hands bleed profusely. You should be fine. Please change the bandage daily to prevent infection."

"Mighty grateful, Doctor."

His easy acknowledgement of her as a doctor caught her off guard. She sometimes treated people for weeks only to still be mistaken for a nurse. Or worse, a patient would demand that she summon a real doctor—meaning a male doctor. Even Titus's colleagues teased that he called her Doctor only to keep peace in the household.

Leah slipped on her cloak and picked up her bag. By now she was cold, and she suspected her patient, in shirt-sleeves, was colder. Without further discussion, they headed back to the general store.

"I'll fetch Mr. Cobb for you, ma'am," he told her when he paused to allow her to enter the building first. "The Hoburns'll let you stay until they come for you."

With that, he strode down the center aisle as if hiking through an open field instead of a crowded store. Men stepped out of his way with calculated casualness. A young woman in a stylish hat turned away from him with equally stylish disdain. The proprietress looked him over and swung her hip with a righteous coolness as she turned to tend to another customer.

Only the sheriff kept himself in the man's path, eyeing him as he plowed across the store, reeking of disinfectants. "What trouble you get in today?"

The carpenter swerved around the sheriff as if the man were a tree stump. Without answering, he pulled open the shop door and left.

In the wake of the path customers parted for the carpenter, Leah made her way to the front window of the store, feeling people's attention shift to her. She made herself as comfortable as she could on a crate. Traveling involved too much sitting in one place and waiting. Exhausted and hungry, she watched as the store emptied, grateful for the decreasing hubbub, until only the Hoburns remained, preoccupied with tallying the day's earnings and restocking shelves.

Eventually, a work wagon came squeaking and rattling down the road. Two familiar silhouettes jiggled on the wagon seat: Utterance, thin as a vanilla bean, and Martha, stout as an apple. Side by side, they resembled a pair of mismatched salt and pepper shakers.

Leah bolted out of the general store with a bare-bone thank you and goodbye to the Hoburns. Abandoning all pretenses of dignity and sophistication, she ran down the street, waving and calling, not caring that she looked like a tardy schoolgirl. Utterance halted the back of the wagon in front of her luggage, overshooting her by a few wagon lengths.

Leah turned to double back and found the carpenter

sitting on the back of the wagon, his feet dangling to the rhythm of the ride, and holding his injured hand in the other while he stroked the bandage. He had changed his stained clothes before heading to the farm. As the wagon slowed, he looked up and sat straight when he saw her.

They locked gazes until the wagon came to a halt, then he pushed off, limbs stretched for maximal balance before landing elegantly. A formality about his gestures suggested he was well educated, even if he wore tradesmen's clothes. For a moment, they stood in the road, staring at each other, then he turned and headed to the carpentry shop.

Leah expected him to offer to help with the luggage and be properly introduced. At the very least to bid goodbye to Utterance and Martha, who had given him a ride back into town.

She refocused at Martha's squeal as her aunt ran toward her with arms outstretched. They collided in a hug, revolving in a circle and almost knocking each other over. Leah's black bag fell to the road. Utterance picked it up and shook it gently before placing it on the wagon bed.

He came forward and tapped Martha on the shoulder as if breaking up a dancing couple. "You goin' make me wait in line?"

"Don't be silly, Uncle. Come here."

Utterance slipped his arm around her and gave her a long, sturdy hug and a kiss on the forehead. They were each other's favorite, and from this reserved manner of greeting, Leah discerned no one had deposed her. Finally among people who mattered, an inner tranquility spread within her, the likes of which she had not felt since leaving Africa.

"See you took your time a'comin'," Utterance said.

"Really, Uncle, you make it sound as if Ghana is next door."

"Heard you had a rough time over there. Glad you're here now."

"Well, yes..." Leah's voice faded as a whiff of sadness swirled around her, threatening to constrict her.

Martha tried unsuccessfully to align the twists in Leah's bangs. "You poor dear. We been worried sick 'bout you!"

"Thank you, Auntie, but it could not be helped."

Leah hugged her aunt again, sandwiching herself between her and her uncle. She kissed her uncle's cheek before the three disengaged from their embrace and began to load her luggage onto the wagon. They loaded the suitcase and the first trunk without travail, but she and her uncle had to put down the second trunk because its weight threatened to pull their arms out of their sockets. Leah wondered how all the porters had managed it so effortlessly.

"Dint occur to you I be old when you packed this one, did it?" said Utterance.

"It's mostly books. And some laboratory equipment. We can take out the books," said Leah.

"You got books 'bout old men's back troubles? Be needing them soon, I tell you."

A rattle from the carpentry shop door rang over the street when it opened and closed. Leah looked over her shoulder just as the carpenter began crossing the street to the wagon.

"Want help, sir?" he asked.

Utterance and Martha exchanged looks.

"I got it." said Utterance. He bent over the trunk and motioned for Leah to grab a handle.

"Be getting that. Ma'am."

Leah stepped away, wafted aside by the carpenter's commandeering tone and sensing that the very notion of refusing his help was unacceptable. She watched him wrap his uninjured hand around the iron handle and nod to Utterance. At an unspoken count of three, they lifted the trunk onto the wagon bed. The carpenter flexed the fingers of his good hand with a wince after he released the handle. Utterance shook out his arm.

"Come on." Martha put her arm around her. "Get in. You be real tired by now, dragging all them trunks with you, especially after all you gone through."

"Haven't been introduced. Ma'am." The carpenter's tone riveted Leah where she stood, as if he had not given her permission to leave.

She waited for the required formal introduction until the waiting drifted from awkward to embarrassing. Still wondering what had overcome her aunt and uncle, she bent her knees slightly, not quite into a curtsy.

In response, the carpenter bowed with full formality. "Duncan Shay, ma'am. Cabinetmaker."

"I am honored to make your acquaintance."

Utterance and Martha began talking at once, each jabbering over the other as Martha tugged her toward the wagon seat.

"She just come in—"

"Africa—"

"Ain't seen her in forever—"

"They got elephants there—"

"She be tired—"

"Real grateful you givin' a hand. Thanks," Utterance concluded artfully.

The carpenter wrinkled his brow as he sorted through their babble for her name. Leah could see he was not sure how to gracefully address the problem that it had not been mentioned. He did not seem the sort who would leave without the thing he'd come seeking.

She tested the carpenter's resourcefulness. "I thank you for your generosity, Mr. Shay."

"Welcome, ma'am," he said without hesitation and walked away to the shop under the Carpentry and Fine Cabinetmaking sign. He shut the door behind him, just short of slamming it, and flipped the Open sign to Closed.

3

____

THE HOUSE WITH PILLARS

Leah positioned the pruning saw against a dead limb and tipped back her head as if dipping her hair into cool, still water. Even when Utterance was directing migrant laborers, the orchard absorbed the men's voices as it did the cries of crows and hawks. Everything became part of the orchard's tranquility, and the orchard had a way of becoming everything.

Being out of Ghana helped her spirits, she had to admit. Everything in Ghana reminded her of her misfortunes, from the inescapable heat to the quivering greenery of the ever-present vegetation. The orchard coolness helped transport her—forward, she hoped—but she still had to be careful because at any moment she could trip and fall into her memories.

Fortunately, her arrival coincided with the start of pruning season, intense weeks of removing dead and weak branches before the trees broke dormancy. The year's farm-work schedule was loosely based on the four New England seasons but controlled in every minuscule aspect by the demands of the trees. Pruning gave her an opportunity to be absorbed into the workforce without having to feel profoundly about anything.

Martha wove her way toward her through mud patches, and Leah paused sawing while Martha leaned against the limb to prevent it from binding the saw. Leah's childhood pruning lessons had never left her. She'd thought of amputations in medical school as prunings to distance herself from what they really were.

"Leah, you ain't been back in town. Dun you need nothing? Saw some cloth at the general store that looked real pretty."

"I have dresses, Auntie. Thank you."

"Ah! They be out of style. Just 'cause them cannibals cain't tell the difference dun mean we here dun know better."

Leah tightened her lips and forced herself not to argue with Martha about calling Afrikaners cannibals. She doubted anyone in West Edith's Bay had ever seen an Afrikaner or would know what to think if they did.

"Perhaps some wool," Leah finally said. "I am short of wool dresses. Not much use for wool in Ghana, as you know."

"You cain't wear a wool dress to a dance, Leah. You be melting on the floor."

"Auntie, I am not up to any dance—"

"Well, you ain't staying home alone and moping on the night of the dance, that be for sure. Utterance ain't permitting that."

Leah looked toward Utterance, who was managing to keep himself a safe distance from the conversation. "Uncle has not said a word to me about any dance, Auntie."

"Well, he be going to. Soon. Besides, the dance'll cheer you up. Best we go to town tomorrow and look at some cloth for a dress. Dance be up mid-summer. That come up quick. Hoburn'll run out of cloth, and by the time you figure you be wanting to go, what'll you do if you ain't got a nice dress? Go in them old things? Better be all ready than full o' regret. That's what I say. Bring that branch with you when you be dun before the hand take the wagon down."

They mean well; they mean well, Leah chanted to herself to summon patience as she dragged the branch behind her to the wagon.

How could they not feel what happened in Ghana? To her husband? To her son? To her? Did they think it happened less because they weren't there to see it? Could they even imagine it? The notion that the world continued as if nothing were sacred to it made her think she had to sleep at night with her eyes wide open.

BY THE TIME pruning season ended, Leah felt guilty for wasting a trained physician's time on sawing branches, but she still felt she needed the absentmindedness of farmwork to clear her head. She didn't expect people in West Edith's Bay to understand that pausing would sometimes help get a person further in the end.

Martha began advocating that she help Utterance prepare some cuttings for rooting. The suggestion reminded Leah the orchard would absorb her into its relentless chores if she did not orient herself to accomplish what she wanted. When Utterance, who seemed to understand her growing restlessness, suggested she introduce herself to Dr. Haloway, she promptly made her way to town.

Dr. Haloway lived in a staunch white house with four Doric columns that marked his importance in the community and hinted at his prosperity. Within a circle of last year's dead asters, a modest sign with an arrow and the word *Office* directed patients to a side door.

Leah ignored the sign. She clanged the bell by the front door to distinguish herself as a visitor and smiled at the eye that looked at her through a slim part in the curtain on the side window. A frantic shuffle of footsteps and whispers followed, then so much quiet that she began to wonder if the inhabitants were pretending to not be home.

She was about to clang the bell again when Dr. Haloway cracked open the door. Through the slim opening, she made out an elderly man who, based on the bone structure of his face, might have once been a stunning specimen of masculine good looks.

"Good morning, Dr. Haloway," Leah said with her crispest professional demeanor. "Please allow me to introduce myself. I am Dr. Leah Maays, Mr. Utterance Cobb's niece. If you have a moment, I thought we might become acquainted, as we have a profession in common."

"Ah. Yes." Dr. Haloway opened the door another inch.

Leah smiled at Mrs. Haloway, who peeked through a doorway and scuttled away without smiling back. Dr. Haloway opened the front door barely wide enough for Leah to step through. He closed the door behind her and began walking to the other end of the house. Not knowing what else to do, she followed him.

"Please sit down," said Dr. Haloway when they entered his office. "In the future, we prefer that you come in through the office door. All the same, how may I help you? Are you feeling unwell today?"

Leah arranged herself on the chair as if sitting on a

pincushion. "I come in perfect health, Dr. Haloway, thank you. As I said, I thought I would offer the courtesy of introducing myself, as we share a profession."

"I see."

She hesitated. Dr. Haloway did not seem as tickled pink as Hoburn, the shopkeeper, had suggested he would be. She proceeded to her point. "My uncle tells me you often visit your daughter in Edith's Bay. I have come to propose that I cover for you when you are away."

Dr. Haloway leaned back in his chair and rounded his chest with a breath. "Mrs. Maays, West Edith's Bay has a very small population, and it is unlikely that it can support more than one physician. I am sure you understand."

"Yes, I do indeed understand." She was more troubled by having him address her as "Mrs." than by his proprietary manner. "I have no wish to impinge upon your practice. At the same time, physical law dictates that you cannot be in all places at all times. While I am in West Edith's Bay, perhaps I may step in during days you are not in town. And please feel free to call upon me during any emergency, should you need assistance. Please understand my intention is not—"

"Mrs. Maays." Dr. Haloway raised his voice just enough to silence her. "Allow me to come to the point so we may be efficient in our dealings. I must speak honestly, perhaps at the risk of offending you. That is, I do not accept that women have the fortitude to withstand the rigors of being a physician."

Leah girded herself. She almost rolled her eyes because already being a doctor never seemed enough proof for some men that she *was* a doctor. *Remain professional,* she reminded herself before speaking. "Then I suggest you become acquainted with my qualifications. I have just come from Ghana where I spent two years working at the—"

"Mrs. Maays, I mean no offense. I am sure as a woman you are very caring. But be advised, Mrs. Maays, that no one in West Edith's Bay is as desperate as Negroes for medical attention, with all the diseases they carry. Compared to the witchcraft they consider medicine, anyone is competent there. Here, we hold physicians to very high standards. It would be more becoming if you concentrated on succeeding in endeavors more suitable to the proclivities of womanhood—perhaps teaching or attending properly to husband and children," concluded Dr. Haloway as if they were discussing where best to go fishing.

Leah bolted to her feet with a force that made Dr. Haloway startle. "Being a woman and having worked with Ghanian doctors and nurses has made me profoundly comprehend that personal limitations have to do with the individual, not with God-given race or gender. Please take note that truly magnificent people are rarely afflicted with the self-inflicted limitations of small-mindedness. Thank you for your expedience, Dr. Haloway. I truly welcome it."

She marched out of Dr. Haloway's office and across his house to the front door, where she let herself out. Dr. Haloway would undoubtedly interpret her exit as overly emotional, but how could anyone be told her accomplishments were worthless without being entitled to anger? Where was his responsibility for her anger? Or did Dr. Haloway believe women walked around unable to pass up random opportunities to become upset?

Leah tried to ease herself out of her ire as she walked down the street, but the conversation continued rumbling in her head. Witchcraft as medicine! Disease carriers! Natural proclivities of—what was it? Ladyhood? And those extremely high standards of...of...small-minded people! Not the least tickled pink Dr. Haloway turned out to be. In fact, Dr. Haloway turned out to be quite an odious fool in pants.

What idiotic hubris and optimism, to think that anything had changed during her time away. What a fine job she did of assuming she finished fighting the battle by bedsides where men, too sick to raise their heads, would still make filthy suggestions when she examined them. And in the laboratories, where her male peers jeered when she held an organ to discuss it. Had she cooked the same organ with onions, they would have eaten it and lavished her with praise.

Her sorrow overflowed and intertwined with her anger as she felt the sensation of William dying in her arms, so infected he barely looked human... Titus shortly thereafter...

Did Dr. Haloway not understand how quickly a plague could spread? Sixty-four people in five weeks. Patients, doctors, nurses, laborers...everyone! No one could work fast enough. Every moment burst like an explosion with news that someone else had died—explosions she hoped at the time would end her life but didn't. She survived, never having caught whatever it had been. She became the unlucky one among the fortunate.

Leah diverted into the alley beside the general store where Hoburn stacked empty crates, her rage coming in flares. A barely controllable urge to check her body for rashes and pustules overcame her. What if she had carried the disease to West Edith's Bay? As unlikely as that seemed after so many months, she still gasped at the idea. Although the possibility was gone from her body for certain, it seemed entrenched her mind.

She kicked a crate out of her way, only to have it break

open and spill rotting cabbage leaves all over the alley. A mouse scampered out of the leaves.

The shadows of two men walking by the alley slithered over her as they passed. Leah clamped shut her eyes. All she needed was for one of them to tell Dr. Haloway she had been crying in a pile of Hoburn's rotting cabbage leaves.

As always, she questioned why she survived. Dying would have been easier. She stopped short of beginning a sob, knowing she could cry forever if she began. The stench of rotting vegetables from the broken crate almost made her gag. She blinked into the skimpy light that filtered between the buildings.

In a world full of fools—that's where she lived. Dr. Haloway was just another one. There was never a shortage of fools, and no medicine yet discovered was known to cure the affliction.

She wiped her face with the heel of her palm and felt a familiar exhaustion wring her as she braced herself to run the errands Martha assigned to her. That much she could do, even in her current state. She smoothed her dress to finish composing herself and marched out of the alley, up to the door of the general store, and hauled it open. For a moment, she could not recall what she needed to buy, but she stepped into the store with a presence that might have blown everything off the shelves.

"What's wrong with you?" asked Martha, who was chatting over the counter with the Hoburns.

"Nothing." Leah could not even imagine how to explain to Martha what had just happened.

Mrs. Hoburn and Martha shared knowing glances, although Leah never understood what they thought they knew. Hoburn nodded to her and turned his attention to sorting receipts. They all looked out the window when an impressive carriage with polished brass bells came to a stop in front of the store.

A woman wearing astonishing, large mutton sleeves began emerging from the carriage like an elephant from a rabbit hole. The skirt of her fancy dress impeded her graceful exit because it was dense with lace, ruffles, cloth rosettes, and ribbons that snagged on the door as if trying to prevent her from leaving. When the bustle appeared, it was so wide and extended that Leah imagined serving lunch on it as if it were a table.

To accommodate her gargantuan hat through the carriage door, the woman waggled her head from side to side so the fans of feathers and flowers could emerge undisturbed. She waved a silver-handled walking stick as she tried to lower herself onto the ground, but her flailing rendered the cane useless. Assisted by her driver—a diminutive, white-haired gentleman dressed like a prince in pale-blue velvet livery—she managed to step down, whacking the driver across his shins with her walking stick several times and almost blinding him with its tip.

"Who is that?" Leah whispered to Martha.

"Mrs. Groth. She be from the city. She funded the new schoolhouse," Martha whispered back. "Let's get Utterance's boots. We'll come back later and get the rest."

Martha exchanged more knowing looks with Mrs. Hoburn. But before she and Leah could leave, the woman's driver opened the store door, and Mrs. Groth—or, rather, her enormous dress—blocked their exit.

"Mrs. Cobb! How lovely to see you. Good day, Mrs. Hoburn, Mr. Hoburn," she called out.

Martha gritted her teeth, but Mrs. Groth was already waddling down the aisle toward her, thrusting her bustle from one side to another. Hoburn followed her, bowing to pick up objects that the woman's bustle brushed off the shelves and catching a bottle of hair tonic just before it shattered on the floor.

Mrs. Goth stood before Martha and demanded, "Do you intend to introduce your niece to me, Mrs. Cobb? Or is she a secret?"

Mrs. Groth might have tossed a lighted match on Martha, judging by how Martha jumped. "Mrs. Groth, this be Miss Leah. Leah, Mrs. Emma Groth. My niece."

"I am happy to make your acquaintance," said Leah, unable to remember the last time anyone called her "Miss Leah." Apparently, Martha never adjusted to Mrs. Maays—a change that happened without her presence—much less to Dr. Anybody, a change Martha still preferred to think had not happened.

"How very lovely to meet you, my dear." Despite her sweet tone, Mrs. Groth looked her over as if evaluating a cow. "I've been wanting to speak to you because I heard you spent time in Edith's Bay. Did you notice whether Farrar's Department Store had new walking sticks? This one has worn uneven. Or perhaps you can recommend a craftsman who can make a new one."

Unable to make sense of why someone would ask a total stranger whether they had gone looking for walking sticks, Leah answered as neutrally as she could. "I did not visit Farrar's. Perhaps the carpenter in town is qualified."

A slight sound, part whoop, part gurgle, came from Martha. Leah and Mrs. Groth turned to her. Mrs. Hoburn ducked behind a shelf. Mr. Hoburn sank below the counter.

"Pardon," said Martha, changing colors with embarrassment.

Without moving her head, Mrs. Groth rolled her eyes, now slick with slyness, from Martha to Leah. "Do you mean

Duncan Shay? That murderer and thief? I would rather fall and break a bone than engage that man!"

Leah suppressed a full-blown body spasm into a tiny twitch she was certain was not lost on Mrs. Groth. The carpenter was a murderer and a thief? The man whose hand she tended alone in the courtyard? Who offered to compensate her on the spot? Who apologized and addressed her respectfully as "Doctor"? Leah looked around. Neither Martha nor the peeping Hoburns looked likely to negate Mrs. Groth's statement.

Gold chains slithered from under Mrs. Groth's neck wrinkles as her voice filled the store as if she were delivering a soliloquy from a stage. "Yes, he's robbed banks and killed men in ripe, cold blood. In front of witnesses, no less. A shameful creature, he is, having been in a penitentiary as well. Albeit not for long enough. Murderous heathen! Take my advice: Being alone with him is the best way to ruin yourself. If not out and out be ruined *by* him."

"Leah been to medicine school. She be a doctor," said Martha, placing her hand on the small of Leah's back and shoving her forward, as if to justify why Leah had been alone with Duncan Shay, a rumor that seemed to be now running all over town like a loose horse.

"A doctor! A lady doctor?" cried Mrs. Groth a little too loudly. "You must mean a nurse, Mrs. Cobb."

"I am a fully qualified doctor. I minister to anyone who is ill," said Leah, resenting being spoken about in third person as if she were not present.

"Even men?" Mrs. Groth pressed her hand against her chest. "How scandalous!"

Leah curtsied and turned to leave. "Please excuse me."

"Where you goin'?" snapped Martha.

"Mrs. Groth has declared me scandalous. It would be deplorable if I wasted any more of her time. Or mine."

She assumed Hoburn was aiding in her escape when he rushed from behind the counter to open the store door, but behind the door was an elderly gentleman on a makeshift crutch. Leah stepped out of his way as he hobbled to the counter, where he paused to rest and rub his sore armpit. She abandoned plans to depart and approached the man as if drawn by magnets.

"Good afternoon, sir. I am Dr. Leah Maays."

"I heared 'bout you," said the man, avoiding eye contact with her.

Mrs. Groth rolled her eyes and scoffed. Martha glared at her and retreated into a corner.

"Utterance Cobb's niece," Hoburn added. "Mrs. Maays, this is Tom Pratt. He grows pears in his orchard."

"My uncle mentions your pear trees with great admiration," said Leah. "Of your foot, he might not be as envious. Come sit on the cutting table, and with your permission, I shall have a look at it."

Without waiting for an answer, Leah slid herself under his shoulder. The man's surprise ran through her body, although he hobbled with her to the cutting table, where she sat him and lifted his feet onto it. Leah tucked his ankle under her arm and pulled his boot, modifying the strength of her tugs to his grunts, until it popped off and flew out of her hand to reveal a massively swollen foot.

Tom let out a yowl. Without pause, Leah peeled off his sock and pushed him down on the table. She slipped a bolt of muslin under his head as a makeshift pillow before turning her attention back to his foot and pressing her finger in several places against the swollen skin.

"How revolting," muttered Mrs. Groth, just loudly enough for everyone to hear.

Hoburn and Tom exchanged looks as Leah put her palm against Tom's sole and pushed the foot by less than an eighth of an inch. Tom half sat up, howling in pain.

"I come for a poultice!" he demanded while swatting at Leah.

"A poultice shall do you no good, Mr. Pratt," said Leah.

"What's wrong with a poultice?"

"Your foot is broken. Right at that bruise. Not to worry, though. I can set it for you."

"You? Set my foot?"

"Rest assured, Mr. Pratt, I am highly qualified."

She tolerated Tom's troubled silence a bit longer before playing her best card. "Dr. Haloway is very competent, I am certain. However, he will charge you, and I shall not."

"You say you setting it for free?"

Leah grinned. Doing things for free had a way of getting people to try things they'd never consider if they had to pay. Well, if that was what she had to do now, she would do it.

"Yes. If you incur the price of the plaster and materials, which Mr. Hoburn surely has, I certainly shall."

"Well... Dunno. What you think, Hoburn?"

"I highly encourage you to take your foot to Dr. Haloway —if you ever want to walk again," said Mrs. Groth.

People's eyes shifted between Mrs. Groth and Leah. Leah retained a neutral expression. She was not going to get into a cat fight about her competence with an abhorrent creature like Mrs. Groth.

Hoburn shrugged and said as if proof of something, "She's Utterance's niece, Tom."

"Well..." said Tom. "Might consider it. If for free."

"I assure you I shall not charge you. Please fetch the

plaster, Mrs. Hoburn. I am not sure where it is," said Leah before Tom could change his mind.

Dr. Haloway could be damned if he thought she was incompetent. She would prove her qualifications, even if she had to advertise her work on a foot cast.

Mrs. Hoburn went about gathering the things Leah requested from the corners of the store while Hoburn rummaged in the back room for a real pillow to put under Tom's head. Leah mixed the plaster and organized the splints.

When everything was prepared, she handed Tom a little vial of opium syrup. "Please drink this, Mr. Pratt. It will be somewhat effective against the pain but shall not last long."

She watched him down the syrup and waited, keeping her attention on the man's eyes as he relaxed into a daze. "Mr. Pratt, I am going to set your foot now. You might still feel some pain."

"Reckon... I be..."

"Then let us begin." Leah tucked Tom's ankle under her arm. "On the count of three. Ready? One. Two. Thr—"

Leah poked her finger into the darkest bruise while pushing his sole with her other hand. Tom let out a sharp groan. His arms jerked up and came bashing down on a bobbin tray, sending bobbins flying in all directions. Tom fell limp on the cutting table as Mrs. Groth, Martha, and the Hoburns yipped in unison.

Leah reached for a splint. A moment later, she began applying the bandages and plaster as Tom drifted into a nap now that the most painful part of the procedure was over.

As she applied the plaster, her bun loosened and sent her hair cascading down her back and over her face. She shook her hair back, knowing she could not touch it when her hands were encrusted with plaster. Mrs. Groth gasped as if Leah were advertising herself as a woman of the night by shaking her hair loose in public.

When finished, Leah wiped her hands as best she could on her apron and sat Tom up to give him sips of water. She left him sitting to go to the courtyard to wash her hands and took the opportunity to saw off the tip of Tom's homemade crutch so the height would not make his shoulder sore. And she remembered to twist her hair back into a bun.

As soon as the opium lost its effect, she and Hoburn helped Tom onto his wagon so he could drive himself home. Leah warned him several times that the cast was not fully set and not to put any weight on it. She ticked off on her fingers the activities Tom could and could not do, while insisting that he drive the wagon with his foot on the bench so the swelling would not increase. Leah looked on with satisfaction as Tom rolled his wagon down the street.

Take that, Dr. Haloway. And you too, Mrs. Groth. Women give life. There's nothing to stop us from also saving it.

Tom's foot would prove Dr. Haloway wrong in short time. Word would get out. Titus would have been proud of her.

"Oh! Oh! I have to pick up Utterance's boots before Granger closes," cried Martha. "I'll never hear the end of it if I come home without them."

Hoburn looked at his wife as Martha trotted off. "Might as well take this chance to go to the post office before it closes. Don't lock 'til I get back."

"We're now closed," Mrs. Hoburn said for the benefit of Mrs. Groth, and she held the door open for her to step out of the store. To Leah, she said, "Why don't you wait here for your aunt, dear?"

Once inside the store, Mrs. Hoburn acquired a glint of greed in her eyes. "That certainly was a grand finale for the day, wouldn't you say? Why, you sold plaster, splints, a wood heel, bandages, opium syrup, opium tablets, a wad of quilting wool, and a real pair of crutches that we still have to order."

The store door swung open before Leah could answer, and they looked up, expecting the return of the insufferable Mrs. Groth. Instead, Duncan Shay strode into the shop. Leah gaped at him, now seeing the bank robber and murderer in the hard lines of his face. Mrs. Hoburn slipped behind the counter.

Duncan stood before Leah, expecting what, she could not fathom, until he bent to pick up a bobbin from the floor and placed it on the counter.

"Ma'am," he said as greeting.

Leah pushed the bobbin toward Mrs. Hoburn and mumbled, "Thank you, Mr. Shay."

Mrs. Hoburn grabbed the bobbin and turned her back to Duncan to replace it in a case. Leah looked away. That he was a bank robber and a murderer annihilated her other thoughts.

"Saw Mr. Pratt leave in a cast. Came to see if the store's now selling broken bones, ma'am," said Duncan.

In the midst of the tension, Leah laughed out loud at his unorthodox interpretation of events. "Yes, I am certain somewhere in here there's a stack of broken limbs and malfunctioning organs. They certainly have everything else. What do you think, Mrs. Hoburn?"

The front door opened again because Mrs. Hoburn had yet to lock it, and two young men swaggered in, each with thumbs tucked into their belts. Mrs. Hoburn's frown almost went down to her knees. The round-faced one with squinty eyes nudged the other—apparently his sidekick—after he spotted Duncan. The pair made their way toward him.

"Good day, ma'am," said Duncan under his breath and moved to leave.

"We heard we got a new lady in town!" said the round-faced man. "Sure can use more beauty around here. My name's Cory. Cory Baines. This here's my friend Ogden Lapp."

Ogden grinned and wiggled his fingers in a way that made Leah certain he had more fingers than intelligence.

Duncan was almost out the door when Cory asked in a voice so loud the world could not help but hear, "Did you know, Mrs. Maays, they teach dancing in prison? And you sure need mighty pretty skirts to get picked!"

Duncan's skin turned sallow as the men broke out laughing. They snickered until Duncan turned and planted his heel on the floor with an ominous thud that made the pair shuffle away from him.

Leah backed into the shelf behind her, certain Duncan would send them flying through the store window with a single blow. Mrs. Hoburn cried out as Cory bumped into a barrel that held mops and brooms. He grabbed one of the sticks in an attempt to steady himself but pulled out a broom as he fell behind the barrel with a thump that made glass bottles clink. The broomstick clattered beside him. On his hands and knees, he scuttled out of sight behind a shelf. Ogden must have dispersed into thin air from fright because he was nowhere to be found.

Duncan picked up the broom and thrust it down like a spear. Leah slapped her hand over her mouth to stifle a cry, certain Duncan Shay skewered Cory with the broom. The thrashing in the aisle ceased. She listened. No thrashing. Where was the broom? It was not on the floor. It was not in Duncan's hand. Was it in Cory? With horror, Leah watched Duncan Shay back away from the aisle.

"Be back when you're not so busy. Ma'am," he said in a voice so low it rumbled.

In a few strides, he was gone. The store remained still. Leah exchanged looks with Mrs. Hoburn, uncertain as to which one of them would be the first to look down the aisle where Cory was, presumably, impaled with a broom. Without stepping forward, they both stretched their necks for a peek.

Cory popped up like a jack-in-the-box from behind the shelf, holding the broom over his head. Leah and Mrs. Hoburn shrieked.

Shaking with laughter, he tipped his hat to Leah. "Weez just having a little fun."

"Are you buying something?" shouted Mrs. Hoburn from behind the counter.

"Well, we thought—" Cory began with a smirk.

"Best you get out of here if you ain't. In fact, best you get out of here, period!"

Cory strolled out the door, imitating Mrs. Hoburn's mannerisms while sniggering. Outside, he met up with Ogden. They knocked elbows into each other's ribs and howled with laughter.

"Those men!" Mrs. Hoburn muttered as she watched through the window as Cory and Ogden walked down the street. "You watch out for all of them. They are a complete list of the wrong men in this town." She put her arm around Leah and walked her to the door. "Here comes your aunt, dear. I certainly hope you won't think poorly of us because of those three. We are perfectly respectable."

Leah reassured Mrs. Hoburn that her opinion of her or the store had not wavered because of the male visitors. She slipped into the dusk as Martha approached, grateful to leave the general store and still amazed that a fight that could have destroyed it had not taken place. Certainly, Duncan Shay had taken offense. He could have pounded Cory out of existence for the innuendo. Or skewered him with a broom.

Mrs. Hoburn, in her fit of self-righteousness, did not seem the least bit aware she needed to be grateful to Duncan Shay. Leah cautioned herself to be careful with her sympathies. She did not know much about Duncan Shay, and the few things she knew were unfortunate.

4

THE CHRONOLOGIST

Henry Moore often stood by the window in his office, taking enormous satisfaction in being the postmaster and telegraph operator of West Edith's Bay. The small town, often considered a pimple on the rear end of Edith's Bay, produced many things the world needed, and without his meticulous work, transactions would fall apart.

Because the Carpentry and Fine Cabinetmaking shop was across the street from the post office, Duncan Shay frequently walked across his window view, and Henry developed an obsession with him. The obsession began when he tried to figure out what about Duncan Shay made some women dissolve into giggles when he said hello to them.

Town folk thought Duncan Shay was aloof—not that Henry disagreed with that. It was just that Henry was as subdued in public as Duncan was, and no one ever considered him aloof. And despite said aloofness, Duncan attracted everyone's attention the moment he stepped into a space. The moment Henry stepped into a room was yet another moment when nothing changed, even if people noticed him.

Henry began investigating how Duncan moved. In front of a mirror, he practiced walking assertively, pivoting on the heel of one foot, standing to commandeer the space around him, glowering to silence a person. He even tried posing against the dresser with the languidness that sometimes made Duncan appear to be draped over railings and furniture.

Without exception, the mirror reflected an awkward idiot. At best, Henry felt he looked like a girl when he practiced being languid against his dresser and resembled a scarecrow when he attempted to stand sternly. Eventually he concluded he could not reproduce Duncan's gestures through practice. He doubted Duncan was even aware of how he moved. He just moved when he needed to move.

Try as he might, Henry could not remember the year Duncan arrived in town as a human being on two legs. Only after the nomadic harvest pickers left at the end of the season did Henry remember seeing Duncan on the common, shaping handles for shovels and pitchforks on a makeshift lathe.

Duncan's timing was perfect because everything breaks during a harvest and needs fixing after. The town hadn't had a local carpenter in several years, and Duncan satisfied a great need. He stayed until the ground froze under him, then left.

Rumors held that Duncan went back to Edith's Bay to work at a shipyard. No one expected him to come back, but in the spring, Henry looked out the window and saw Duncan setting up shop in the barn across the street.

Henry risked being one of Duncan's first customers when he asked him to level a cabinet kept stable with coins and pieces of cardboard under the front legs. Whenever the cardboard compressed or the coins slipped out, the cabinet tipped forward and spewed its drawers on the floor, never failing to scare the daylights out of Henry.

Henry expected Duncan to just sand down the stubby feet, but Duncan replaced the feet, so perfectly matching the curve and stain the repair was barely detectable. Afterward, people began bringing him broken things to fix as if they had been saving them for generations. Then they started asking him to build porches, fix roofs, and repair carriages, which he also did amazingly well.

Even in those early days, Henry remembered Duncan as a man of few polite words who never invited familiarity. When faint rumors about his wrongdoings drifted into town, townsfolk got jittery about Duncan's guarded manner. The Corwals were the first to unload their concerns in the post office when their daughter, Mary, developed a crush on Duncan.

"Just wait 'til he loses his temper. He'll start killin' again, I betcha," Mary's father predicted. "I need two stamps."

"Let me tell you, nobody wants someone with that kind o' past making grandchildren in our family. And certainly not with our daughter!" Mary's mother shook her finger at Henry, making him feel as if she were holding him responsible for the situation.

Henry nodded but did not say anything. He didn't think anything could be said to people who were hair-on-end scandalized that a man whose past consisted of murdering people and robbing banks was looking at their daughter who, in turn, did not have the common sense to not look back at him.

He had nothing against Duncan, who had done an excellent job replacing his cabinet's knobby feet and who otherwise kept to himself. If Duncan had a past, then, well, he had a past. West Edith's Bay didn't have a bank, so Duncan couldn't be planning to continue a career as a bank robber. Breaking into people's houses to steal their savings seemed easier than robbing a bank, but that hadn't happened either. And everyone who had been alive when Duncan arrived was still alive. Cory Baines, whom Henry couldn't stand, was much more unfavorable, and no one was minding him yet.

Henry also had nothing against Mary. Even if she was somewhat uninspiring, she was pleasant. He sometimes danced and talked with her, but not so much as to make her parents think he wanted to marry her.

At the annual church dance one year, Henry was about to ask Mary to partner with him when he saw Duncan heading toward her. At the time, he was still trying to emulate Duncan's style and stepped back to study how Duncan approached a woman.

With a flair of stately class and a brilliant smile, Duncan strode right up to Mary. He briefly acknowledged her parents and asked her to honor him by partnering with him in a square. Henry suspected Duncan just wanted to dance because he had not paid much attention to Mary until that moment.

At any rate, Mary immediately broke under her father's reproachful stare and said, "No thank you. I dun dance with thieves and murderers."

The flush of vibrant dancing and brilliant smile evacuated Duncan's face, and he swallowed like someone trying to drink a cup of sand. Duncan pivoted on one foot and walked out of the building. He did not return to the dance that night.

Henry considered extending a comforting word but was

afraid Duncan might feel mortified to have anyone acknowledge what happened. He did not ask Mary to dance that evening because he could not believe anyone could be so cluelessly cruel while turning down a dance.

Mary gave the dance to John Corwal, whom she later married, becoming Mrs. Mary Corwal. While Mary danced with John Corwal, Henry could hear her words spread like wildfire, giving those who did not already know about Duncan's past an opportunity to find out.

In the days that followed the dance, Henry swore Mary waited in every shadow for Duncan to leave his shop so she could apologize to him. Duncan always walked away the moment she began speaking. The last time she tried, he dispatched her to the depths of hell with a wave of his hand, never even making eye contact. He never acknowledged her again, and Mary began avoiding Duncan, even when he gave no sign of being aware of her.

"Man like himself should own up to his past and not slight Mary," Mary's mother told Henry the next time she came in to mail letters.

"Least he ain't got mad and kilt her for turning 'im down," said Mary's father.

"We count our blessings!" Mary's mother clutched her hands together and raised her eyes to the heavens as if her daughter's encounter with Duncan at the dance had been a close call with death.

Not much time later, Duncan could walk down the entire length of the main street without anyone returning his good morning. Almost overnight, townsfolk began treating Duncan as if he were some soulless automaton who barely existed. Henry was certain Duncan would leave town, but for reasons Henry never found out, Duncan stayed.

For several months after the dance, he rarely saw

Duncan outside his shop but could hear him ripping boards and running the lathe all hours of the day and night. Sometimes in the dawn, kerosene lamps burned bright, and the great shadow of his hand with a brush swept across the wall over and over.

One morning Henry rolled up the shade on the post office window and saw a massive armoire in Duncan's storefront window. Never in his life had he seen such a magnificent piece of furniture.

He adjusted his glasses to get a clearer view of the raised paneled doors with rich, sensuous curves and spectacular inlays of exotic woods. A pair of herons in bas-relief framed a full-length beveled mirror on the center door. Dragonflies with intricately fretted wings were destined to be in flight across the same mirror in perpetuity and seemed in constant motion with the play of light. Each curved drawer had an elaborately carved leaf for a handle, no two alike.

When the sun set that day, Henry sneaked up to Duncan's shop window with a lantern to have a closer look at the armoire. It was not just a piece to look at but something to be experienced. He was completely engaged in the majestic details of design and workmanship when the shop door opened and Duncan Shay stepped out.

Henry almost gagged on his heart. Duncan loomed over him like an obelisk about to fall on an ant, expanding his presence into every speck of space around him in a way Henry never figured out how to do. Duncan put his hands on his hips and glared.

"It's real—perfect," Henry croaked, feeling he'd been caught stealing silver spoons. "Like a forest that belongs in a castle. You know?"

Duncan kept his hands on his hips, but the sternness slipped out of his shoulders. The tension went from his face, and his eyes flashed astonishment. On a second look, Henry would have sworn Duncan had transferred his well-being to the armoire. He was as pale as freshly cut pine, and dark circles made his eyes resemble knotholes.

Encouraged that Duncan Shay had not bitten him, he added, "I just came to admire it. That's all."

"Thank you, sir. Mighty grateful." Duncan took a step back and took his hands off his hips. The space around him shrank back to common space.

"Well, um, sorry to disturb you. I'm going back now."

"Not disturbing me, sir. Look as long as you want. Thank you."

To Henry's surprise, Duncan went back into his shop. Henry took the gesture as a sign of trust, although everything he'd ever witnessed about Duncan indicated the man was always on guard. Henry knew if he ever saw someone looking in through the post office window at night, he'd want to know what that person was up to, but he was pretty sure he'd never confront the person head on as Duncan had done.

The armoire stood on display for several weeks while a stream of well-dressed men from Edith's Bay came to look at it. Then one day, Joey the carrier arrived from Edith's Bay. Without ceremony, Duncan disassembled the armoire into a stack of planks, drawers, and a sack full of bolts.

Joey took the pieces to Edith's Bay, and no one in West Edith's Bay ever heard about it again. Duncan presumably went back to turning handles for pitchforks and fixing milking stools, never again displaying anything he made in his shop window.

Henry found out about the phenomenal price the armoire eventually commanded because the negotiations went through his telegraph wire. Each time the price went up in the bidding war, he broke into a cold sweat. Never had he ever imagined there were so many people in the world who could spend many times his yearly earnings on a single piece of furniture.

From the armoire on, Duncan left his shop fewer and fewer times. He worked incessantly, from dawn well into the evening, all days of the week, including Sundays, and often throughout the night. Henry figured Duncan left his shop only when he ran out of food or to get his mail in the afternoon.

The shop window began accumulating pieces of furniture that no one could see because he covered them in dust cloths that in some lights resembled ghosts. When quiet fell upon the shop, town folk asked Henry what Duncan was up to, as if Henry could see through walls because his post office was across the street.

"Least when he be makin' noise we know he ain't throttling people like he dun before," someone eventually said.

Henry nodded without commenting, as he took to doing when someone said something about somebody else. He didn't know how many people Duncan Shay had killed and was unlikely to ever ask him. He knew he should be concerned about what the number was, but Duncan's gentle demeanor and expressions of respect toward him kept making him forget about being concerned.

Of course, Henry made a point to never provoke Duncan's formidableness. That was easy enough—don't ask him about himself. Sometimes he was tempted to tell people that if Duncan Shay killed as many people as town folk credited him with doing, every inch of West Edith's Bay would be lumpy with unmarked graves.

HENRY KEPT MONITORING Duncan's telegraphs and after several months, put together that Duncan was divesting from general repairs and building up a fine cabinetmaking business. At first he couldn't reconcile Duncan's methods because Duncan declined more orders for fancy furniture than he accepted, even when he was short of work.

Not that Duncan was lazy. He worked like twelve men when he had a commission. When he didn't, he pretty much cleared his shop out in an afternoon of anything that needed fixing.

Then, in a splay of envelopes Duncan dropped off one day when his business was going strong, Henry spotted a pattern. In disbelief, he shuffled the envelopes to look for exceptions. There wasn't one.

Henry sank into his chair as he realized Duncan did not accept a commission based on what was being ordered. He accepted a commission based on the return addresses that indicated well-moneyed parts of Edith's Bay, including a cuff of mansions overlooking the bay and two urban neighborhoods of brownstones that flanked the fancy shops in the center of the town.

Those areas were inhabited by the owners of the largest companies on the East Coast, including companies that made Edith's Bay's prosperity possible: the Van der Joost Ship Company, Strauss Investments Incorporated, Wirth Sails Incorporated, and Spark Canvas Company. The cuff around the Bay was also where railroad tycoons had summer houses.

Henry looked up from the envelopes in his hands to across the street where he could hear Duncan running the scroll saw. Apparently, Duncan Shay had a savvy for business most craftsmen lacked. He wondered where one acquired such savvy but already knew it was best not to ask.

By the end of that year, commissions from Edith's Bay, New York, Boston, Atlanta, and Philadelphia began coming through the wire and regular mail. A fever for Duncan Shay pieces overtook the very rich, who began claiming no house was complete without a piece by Duncan Shay.

One morning, Henry raised the shade on the post office window to see a sign hanging outside Duncan's shop: CARPENTRY AND FINE CABINETMAKING. Duncan had even put a little gilding around the letters. In the privacy of the post office, Henry thrust his fists in the air and cheered.

DUNCAN'S MAIL began perturbing Henry. All of it had to do with business—orders, bills, invoices, catalogs, payments. Henry never slipped anything that resembled a personal note into Duncan's mail slot, with the exception of multi-paged letters from a mysterious Mr. A. Lawry that came in envelopes with a route number and an "I of C" logo where the return address would normally be.

Duncan always smiled when he found one of these letters in his mail slot. He would tease it out from his other envelopes and squeeze it between his thumb and index finger as if evaluating a ripe fruit.

Henry got himself a map and looked up the route where I of C was supposedly located and found...open fields. He began looking for places that incorporated I of C anywhere in their identity. He asked other telegraphers but could not find anyone who knew what I of C stood for. He looked through every exchange index he got his hands on, but none listed anything resembling I of C.

Surrounded with dead ends, Henry abandoned sleuthing for whatever I of C was. For all he knew, Duncan

Shay might have hatched from a speckled egg in the middle of a hay field and been raised by crows.

Henry's theory that Duncan never got personal mail soon blew apart when Duncan received a gray envelope somberly addressed in black ink from I of C. The handwriting on it was different from the handwriting of Mr. A. Lawry. From the moment Henry put what was clearly a death notice in Duncan's mail slot, he became inexplicably frantic about how Duncan would react.

He began sorting mail to not be caught looking when Duncan flipped through his envelopes as he usually did and came across it. Duncan stopped walking across the post office. He pulled it out tenderly and stared at the sealed envelope while a sheen of tears formed over his eyes. Henry wanted to say something, but he didn't know what to say to a person who had sunk into grief so instantly and deeply over something he knew nothing about.

From that day on, Henry never again put a plump letter from Mr. A. Lawry or I of C in Duncan's slot. He probably wished harder than Duncan did that another one would appear.

EVEN AFTER HENRY thought Duncan could afford to move into a house, the carpenter continued to live in the space behind the shop, and the only domestic help he took on was a local laundress to wash and mend his clothes and linens. Supposedly, a single man did not need much room. Henry lived above the post office in a modest suite of four rooms, one of which he rarely entered. And he was just fine with that arrangement.

For that matter, Duncan did not seem to spend money

from his distinguished income. Occasionally, Henry stamped a letter from Duncan to a tailor in Edith's Bay, after which a box of work shirts arrived a few weeks later. Hiring a tailor to make work shirts was preposterous to Henry, seeing how easily work shirts ripped and got stained. Nobody cared how they looked because, well, work shirts always got ratty.

But then, every man had vanities, and he supposed Duncan Shay was no different in that respect. Judging by the fit, Duncan liked them plenty ample both in the shoulders and across the back, as if the man could not stand to be confined even within a shirt. However eccentric tailored work shirts might be, they were harmless and, as far as Henry could tell, Duncan's single vanity.

Most of the time, Duncan seldom came back from Edith's Bay with more than what he had taken. Occasionally, a wagon full of exotic wood planks would show up at Duncan's shop a few days after a business trip, and Duncan would help unload it, giving explicit instruction about where each board needed to go.

One time, however, Duncan took the carriage to Edith's Bay for business and returned on the finest horse anyone had ever seen. People claimed Duncan purchased it with money from the bank robbery, although Henry calculated Duncan was earning enough money by then to buy such a horse many times over.

By this time, Henry had developed a notion that Duncan could not exist outside of his business, shunned as he was on the streets. He imagined Duncan might one day walk out of his shop and fritter away like a dandelion caught in a wind.

5

THE BOOKSHELF

The lady doctor had not been back to town in over a month, but her oddities kept whisking through Duncan's thoughts. Her navy-blue eyes had an uncompromising quality that disquieted him. The twists of her unruly bangs hinted she had eccentricities. Just what, he wasn't sure. He couldn't say for certain that hair revealed anything about a person.

He had not known women were allowed to be doctors. If he hadn't been convinced he was losing a finger, he would have waited for Dr. Haloway. But his cut was healing and without stitches. Haloway always gave him stitches, and one time, a few popped and got so infected, he wasn't able to work for days. Still, he paid for not getting stitches with that bloodcurdling tonic she put on him. The very thought of it still made his arm hair rise.

When Hoburn asked to meet her husband and son, people said she answered coldly, but he thought she answered as if that was all she could manage. Very poor timing, but Hoburn could not have known. She wasn't dressed in black... A fresh widow in a blue dress.

And she tended his hand as if nothing horrible had ever happened to her, administering touches as impersonally as an accountant tends ledgers. Nothing in her manner encouraged familiarity, not even when she slipped his arm next to her waist. Of course, her corset prevented him from feeling anything feminine. Seemed corsets were always made of iron plates trimmed with barbed wire.

Duncan's thoughts moseyed back to the task at hand as he finished turning the last spindle of a bunch. He pinched the spindle in several places with a caliper to make certain it was consistent with the others. When he was satisfied with the dimensions, he looked long and hard out the window and scanned the street as he brushed off the wood shavings from his clothes. Confirming no one was walking on it, he scratched up a shopping list on a scrap of veneer. At the door of his shop, he paused before crossing to Hoburn's, which, to his relief, was as vacant as the street.

Duncan placed his list on the counter and nodded when Hoburn reached for it. Hoburn would have the box ready for him to pick up later. He turned to leave but stopped short when a tin of shoe polish rolled into the center aisle and spiraled against the wooden floor. It continued with a soft, metallic hum until it wobbled and clattered into silence.

Hoburn leaned over the counter and called, "Did you find it?"

Duncan's skin prickled when Leah stepped from behind a shelf. She swooped as if curtsying to royalty to pick up the tin but rose with a wobble that distracted from her poise.

Duncan glanced at his list on the counter and said to Hoburn, "Be waiting for that. Sir."

Hoburn launched into putting the goods on the list into

a wooden box while Duncan waited as Leah checked the tin for dents. She looked up, making eye contact.

"Ma'am."

"Sir." Leah matched his intentionally curt greeting with such precision he wondered if she was mocking him.

The tin slipped out of her hand again and rolled toward him. He stopped it with his foot, picked it up, and brushed it against his sleeve before holding it out to her. When she did not reach for it, he took her response as a rebuke for attempting familiarity and placed the tin on the counter with a sharp tap.

Leah approached the counter and, without touching the tin, began picking coins out of her purse. She pushed them toward Hoburn and asked, "How is your hand, Mr. Shay?"

Surprised she had spoken to him, he held out his fist, eventually unclenching it to display his palm.

"With your permission, Mr. Shay."

Leah took his hand in both of hers and tapped her thumb over the scar, still pink and slightly raised. She turned his hand and felt his ring finger as if to determine the source of its crookedness, then pressed a little harder where the finger curved, and she scowled. She released his hand to recount the coins on the counter.

Duncan closed his hand into a fist and withdrew it. "Still grateful, Doctor."

"You are welcome, Mr. Shay. May I ask if you make bookshelves?"

"Bookshelves?" She was asking him to make something for her? Realizing he sounded like someone who had never heard of bookshelves, he said, "What size, ma'am?"

"Four feet high by two feet wide, by twelve inches deep, please."

"That's very narrow, ma'am. You might want to have the

base wider so it doesn't tip over." From his shirt pocket, he took out a slip of paper and a pencil stub to take notes. He lowered his voice as he stepped forward. "What wood, ma'am?"

"Wood? Oh... Any. Bookshelf wood." Leah flipped through the latest copy of *Arthur's Home Journal* until an article caught her attention, and she began to skim it.

"Got ash, beech, rock and bird's eye maple, and cherry," Duncan recited. "Assorted Mediterranean fruitwoods, rosewood, bubinga, and other exotics, mahogany, walnut in limited amounts, pine in plenty but don't recommend it, oak—"

"Oak! Oak is fine. Oak is quite suitable. Thank you."

"Red or white, ma'am?"

"Unpainted please."

"Red oak or white. Nothing to do with paint, ma'am."

"Oh! I— I— White, please." She blushed, then laughed softly to herself as she shook her head.

Duncan glared at Hoburn when he peeked from behind the counter. Hoburn withdrew. Leah turned to wander down an aisle.

Duncan stepped into her path. "Plain or quarter sawn? Ma'am."

Leah tucked her chin and looked over her eyes at him. He imagined falling into her eyes as one would into a dark ocean.

"Forgive me, Mr. Shay. Only a joiner can find so many variations on a simple bookshelf."

"Not simple if it doesn't please you. Ma'am."

"Yes, you are in the right. You are being admirably thorough. I am sorry I mistook you for a pest. What other information do you require?"

He refrained telling her he was not a joiner but a cabinetmaker and took refuge in his notes, refusing to consider she had just called him a pest. "Four feet high by two feet wide by twelve inches deep. White oak. Don't care quarter sawn or not. That right, ma'am?" He looked at Leah again without bothering to push back the block of hair that fell over his eyes.

"Yes, that is correct," she answered, at once somber. "I leave the quarter sawn business to your aesthetic discretion. Thank you."

He tucked the pencil stub behind his ear. She was not so much trusting his sense of aesthetics as she was brushing him off—a sure sign she had been "informed" about him. But then, why ask him to make her bookshelves? The woman harbored many mysteries.

He hesitated before speaking again. "Carvings, ma'am?"

"No, thank you."

"No extra cost, ma'am. Comes regular with shelves. Recommend your favorite flower."

Leah tipped her head and looked at him from the side of her eyes. He put on a poker face.

"Pansies, thank you," she finally answered.

He nodded, scribbling a number on a scrap of paper before flicking the scrap toward her between his index and middle fingers. "That price suit you, ma'am?"

Leah pulled the paper from his fingers. He watched her eyes flicker over the number several times.

"This is very reasonable. Especially if it is to include carvings. And if I may add, you have exquisite handwriting, Mr. Shay."

Without acknowledging the compliment, Duncan folded his notes and tucked them into his shirt pocket. "About a week, ma'am. Be delivering it."

The store door shook open and in stepped Martha. The

moment she spotted him next to Leah, Martha began to babble. "We— Uh— We be running late! Time to hurry home!"

He was well aware that lateness had not yet been imagined in West Edith's Bay, which was so uneventful the only clockwork it needed was the rising and setting of the sun and the ripening of fruits. He glared at Martha until she looked away.

Leah picked up the tin of boot polish. "I am coming, Auntie. Thank you, Mr. Hoburn. Good day, Mr. Shay."

"Goodbye, ladies," called Hoburn.

Duncan did not say anything.

LEAH MEASURED Martha's wrath by the vigor she expended jerking around the basket she carried as they trudged up the hill to the orchard. Her aunt was the most transparent person she had ever known.

"Wears thoughts on her nose," Utterance liked to claim.

At the first semblance of privacy after they turned the bend, Martha broke into a tirade. "Ain't you got no sense, Leah? Dint you hear what Mrs. Groth have to say about him? She be difficult, but she knows things!"

"Auntie, what is this about the carpenter murdering people in cold blood and robbing banks?"

"We was going to tell you, but we dint want you coming here and being fearful."

"Don't be ridiculous, Auntie! I've lost my husband and my son. I've lived in other countries. I've crossed the ocean by myself. There is nothing here that can frighten me. And are you telling me the sheriff hasn't noticed a mad carpenter wandering about town, killing people?"

"Them robberies and murders happened in Edith's Bay. I ain't got details, but the sheriff said he came here right straight from the prison."

Leah opened her mouth but closed it when she realized the sheriff would be privy to such information and had no reason to lie. "Surely that cannot be the entire story, Auntie."

"Why you innerested in the rest of a story that starts with a murder and a robbery? 'Specially when he been in a prison? Leah, you need get yourself some sense. It be real simple. Dun talk to Duncan Shay. Ever. That man be dangerous. Sooner you know that, sooner we all sleep better. Dun you see how he looks at people? You think Hoburn goin' to keep quiet about you talking to him?"

"I was examining his hand."

"His hand! That was fine when you dint know better. Now you know better. Or should."

"I am a doctor. It's always fine."

"He can go to Dr. Haloway, like he always dun. Ain't like he ain't noticed you be a woman 'cause you told him you's a doctor."

Leah let this comment pass, hoping Martha would be less volatile when she changed the subject. "I got a job, Auntie."

"A job! Ain't we got 'nuff things to do at the orchard? I cain't believe Utterance told you to talk to Dr. Haloway and keep on with the same foolishness that almost got you kilt. Like losing your husband and baby wasn't 'nuff. Maybe that be all right for Africa, but here that doctoring'll get you ruined. You heard Mrs. Groth."

Leah filtered out Martha's voice. Her aunt spoke about Titus and William as if they were knick-knacks that got broken. Leah struggled to respond with sufficient simplicity that would not cause Martha to have another conniption.

"Rejoice, Auntie. Dr. Haloway and I are not working together. Mrs. Hoburn offered me a position. At the store. As a shopgirl."

"A shopgirl! People going to think we cain't afford to feed you, Leah. Not like we dun got things for you to do at the farm. Well, maybe Hoburn will give you a discount on cloth for your dance dress. That's coming right up in a few weeks."

Leah kept silent and plodded forward. The world was booby trapped with people who saw any alteration of convention as indecent—Dr. Haloway, Mrs. Groth, Martha. Fools in pants. Fools in skirts. Swarms and swarms of fools all around. West Edith's Bay had indeed not changed at all. She recognized its aspects all too readily.

She contemplated her options. She could use her medical degree as a bookmark and spend the rest of her life stirring apple butter. She could marry a local fellow, as was expected, although she could not even begin to image who that would be. Neither of these options allowed her to do what she really wanted to do, which was to be a doctor and heal people. That left one last option: work to become financially stable and leave. Again.

THE WEEK PASSED, and the bookcase did not arrive as promised. Perhaps the carpenter was disreputable after all and would never deliver the shelves. Leah was not concerned because she had not yet paid him, but she was a little disappointed.

She had not yet told Martha she ordered the shelves, and the more days passed, the more consumed she became with how Martha would react. Leah could not even explain to herself what possessed to do so in the first place—except, perhaps, to satisfy a gnawing curiosity about a man sufficiently violent to rob a bank and kill someone but not to start a fight after being insulted in public. The game was dangerous, but apparently, she could not refrain from playing it.

Too weary to continue worrying about her self-inflicted circumstances, Leah retired to her room after dinner to read the latest copy of the *Journal of the Society of Medical Academies* that had arrived in the mail. And there on the editorial page was a letter from Dr. Ernest Haloway, citing women's feeble constitutions, emotional instabilities, and inferior intellects as proof that they could not be doctors. He warned that allowing women to graduate with medical degrees did nothing for humanity and served only to encourage female delusions and vulgarity.

Vulgarity! Why all the women in town did not riot against Dr. Haloway was beyond Leah. She was more than well qualified to be a physician, having outranked most of her male peers, including her dear Titus, by coming in ninth in the class.

Even with that accomplishment, the university banned her from the graduation ceremony, refusing to even mention her name because she was not a man. A professor meandered around the campus until he found her in a hallway and shoved the diploma at her without even congratulating her.

At least Leah could still grin at the expression on his face when she said, "My heartfelt condolences for having drawn the short straw, Professor. May the rest of your day improve."

Titus was the only one who celebrated with her that evening. The rest of their medical cohorts attended a party at a gentlemen's club she was not allowed to enter. Titus gave her a gold locket, a bouquet of flowers, and a marriage proposal.

She accepted all three on the spot, knowing she might never have become a doctor if not for Titus's support, her oasis of sanity. With only a week left before they had to sail to Africa, they married the following morning.

Now she pulled out the locket from a drawer and opened it to see a dry petal from the bouquet. She could not bring herself to wear the locket anymore. It gave her no comfort, being too much from a past she could no longer access. She put the locket back in the drawer, wishing she could will her past away so she could step into her future, but grief had a way of clinging, even in her best moments.

Leah lowered her sight to the books that were piled in two stacks on the floor by the foot of the bed. In Ghana, she carried them under blankets to her tent through the stench, pyre smoke, and heat. She had intended to leave them in the safety of an embassy but brought the books home when no one showed interest in them.

Now she wanted to honor them with a bookshelf, even if the shelves were made by a carpenter with a disreputable past. The books were the most magnificent she would ever own. She could not afford them then or even now.

They included atlases of the human body, muscular and skeletal, with pages that unfolded into elaborate, hand-painted illustrations; reference books of symptoms; compilations of known cures; dictionaries of organs with lists of the diseases, symptoms, causes, and cures for each; recipe books of herbal and pharmaceutical cures, tinctures, and compounds. Usually only major medical institutions had such books.

She even had an illustrated book about the male and female reproductive systems and their maladies that the librarian at the university would not allow her to borrow. A professor told her that, out of respect for her, she did not have to take the examination for those body systems, but Titus checked out the book for her, and she insisted on taking the exam.

The professor made her take the exam in a separate room so she would not embarrass the other (male) students by having secular knowledge they were required to have. When she passed the examination with flying colors, the professor looked at her with distaste for the remainder of the semester, as if the only place a woman could acquire such detailed knowledge of reproductive organs was in a brothel. More of her pride should come from having survived such incidents with grace than from having graduated ninth in her class.

Her thoughts drifted to the bank robber and murderer. That he offered to include carvings for free made her suspicious. She thought of the contrast between how Duncan Shay commanded the space around him in the general store and how, like a child trying to remain in a spotlight, he tried to impress her with choices of woods. She wondered if the carved pansies would infuriate Martha and began to foster fantasies about slipping the shelves into her room through a window in the middle of the night.

THE FOLLOWING DAY, at Martha's unrelenting insistence, Leah spent a good part of her first pay on a cut of paisley cotton so she would have a new dress to wear to the annual dance in a few weeks. With the cloth wrapped in brown paper under her arm, Leah left the store at the end of the day to walk up the hill, hoping that making the dress would distract Martha from the shelves—if they arrived.

Halfway up the hill, the dry crunch of wagon wheels interrupted her thoughts. She made out Duncan Shay on the seat and took in yet another incongruity: The wagon was roughly hewn, but the horse that pulled it was a fine steed, an enviable riding horse with a rich chestnut coat that glistened from intense grooming.

Duncan stopped the wagon a short distance from her. He got off and stood resting one elbow on the wagon bed while inspecting the treetops against the sky. His languid posture and his work clothes had as much in common as the wagon and the horse, although Leah had never seen a work shirt of such excellent quality and cut.

He bowed his head when she approached. "Ma'am."

"Mr. Shay." So. He had manners. And had gotten a haircut. She curtsied to his bow, wondering why she expected this man to greet her formally when no one else in the backwater of West Edith's Bay ever would.

"Delivered your shelves, ma'am. Sorry for being late with them."

"Then I must compensate you." She reached for her money, remembering how promptly he had tried to compensate her for treating his hand. At this rate, she would be out of money before she got to the house.

"Be owing that to your uncle, ma'am. He paid me already."

"Oh, that is good. I would not want to keep you waiting."

"Thank you, ma'am."

Leah found herself questioning how he could be a murderer and a bank robber. He seemed very tentative at the moment for someone who almost incinerated Hoburn every time he looked at him. He could have taken her money after Utterance already paid him, but the West Edith's Bay community would probably never buy anything from him had he tried such a thing. Then why tolerate a murderer and bank robber...

Unable to bear the silence between them, Leah said, "I believe the store is in your debt that nothing was broken during that encounter with Mr. Baines and his friend."

"They're not worth bruised knuckles, ma'am."

"I agree, but they offend all the same, do they not, Mr. Shay?"

A sense of distance billowed from him, and Leah worried she had been too pointed.

"Yes, ma'am. They're good at that," Duncan said, sounding very raw.

She was relieved his response was fresh and unguarded. "Well, if it is of any consolation, please know I considered clobbering Mr. Baines for his behavior. It was deplorable."

Duncan lowered his head and squinted hard while his shoulders quaked. "Pardon, Mrs. Maays. Would appreciate it greatly if I can be witness when you clobber Mr. Baines on my behalf."

She burst out laughing, and Duncan smiled in full—a broad, even smile as rare as it was charming and brought the man's natural good looks to a peak.

Just as quickly, however, he became somber. "Be happy to give you a ride up, ma'am."

Leah considered accepting the ride and inviting him for coffee to study his incongruities in the safety of the house, but her smile seized when she thought of Martha. "Thank you, but— I am almost there. It would be more trouble for you to turn your wagon around. And I am sure you have other things to do."

He climbed back on the wagon with barely a nod. With

reins in hand, he eased the brake and, without addressing her again, rolled the wagon into a gentle motion and continued down the hill.

Leah continued her walk to the orchard, resisting the temptation to look back at him in case he was watching her. The joiner with whom she had just spoken and the thieving murderer of the town gossip seemed as incongruous as the horse and the wagon.

As she approached the house, she could hear Martha's voice coming through the window. "Utterance, that man's up here buzzing 'round on account of Leah! Ain't you got no sense left? Next time she wants bookshelves, you go on in the barn and make her some!"

With a thinness of spirit, Leah wondered whether the shelves were worth the turmoil they were causing. She really should not have ordered them, although it was too late for regret. She turned to face them with the morale of someone confronting a mistake, and her breath cut short.

The shelves were stunning.

For a moment, she did not even understand why. They were just bookshelves. She ran her fingers along the matched wood grains and over the sophisticated construction with unusual hidden joints that made the piece look as if it had been carved from one massive timber. The shelves swept up as if in flight, with a wider base incorporated into a magnificent, elegant curve.

The frilly clutter of flowers she expected on the frieze was not present. The frieze was simple, ornamented with an eyebrow curve and wide flakes of quarter-sawn oak. As she walked around the shelves to look at the sides, the pansies came into view, one on each side, each the size of a dessert plate carved in deep relief, reminiscent of pansies in Japanese paintings. Each one had a meandering stem that concluded in a shape suggesting a leaf but fashioned from the letters "D" and "r."

She could not flatter herself to think she had been Duncan Shay's muse. Such sophisticated design and expert craftsmanship were clearly habit, not an incidental inspiration. What Duncan Shay charged her for the shelves had been a pittance, perhaps worthy of utilitarian pine shelves with not much craft to them.

By now, she could neither see nor hear the wagon. She felt their transaction would be forever incomplete until she could express her appreciation to him for the exceptional piece he had not just constructed, but created.

The fringe on Leah's shawl ruffled when the front door swung open and out stomped Martha, her mouth open like a dark cornucopia of lectures. Leah thrust the package of cloth into her arms and began to rip the brown paper.

"Look, Auntie! I got the paisley. The purple one you liked, remember? Mrs. Hoburn said it will make my eyes look lovely for the dance. Come and look. Do you have thread? I didn't get any because I know you always have some..."

Leah unwrapped the package in Martha's face, blinding her with the brown paper and deafening her with its rattle and crunch as she made her walk backward into the house. In the hallway, Leah slipped her arm around Martha's shoulders and maneuvered her into the kitchen. Just before the kitchen door closed behind them, she saw Utterance stealthily bring the bookshelf into the hall and take it upstairs. Utterance always knew what to do.

~

LEAH SLOWED as she passed the carpenter's shop on her way home from Hoburn's the following day. Curiosity blazed within her after having taken an even closer look at the bookshelf Duncan Shay delivered. To her relief, the sign on the shop door was flipped to Closed, and Duncan Shay was nowhere to be seen.

She stepped up to the storefront window and looked in. Among the many large objects in the shop window that were draped with dust cloths stood a slender mahogany post with all the attributes of twisted cloth, including a calculated asymmetry of folds and wrinkles. Leah studied the post until she recognized it was part of a side table that rested upside down on a crate. The rest of the table was covered with a dust cloth.

Town talk held that Duncan occasionally made furniture to sell in Edith's Bay, but nothing of what she heard prepared her to see a table-part this extraordinary, not even the bookshelves he had made for her. The last time she saw furniture of this magnificence was in the Dutch embassy in Ghana. She continued to study the shrouded forms, trying to make out shapes, until the drafting table with Duncan Shay sitting at it came to her attention.

He was riffling the corner of a sketchbook as he tapped an eraser against the tabletop until it bounced out of his hand and landed on the floor. Seemingly exasperated, he ran his hand through his hair and, with his long fingers still over his eyes, looked up.

Leah prayed lightning would strike her to spare her the embarrassment of being caught watching Duncan Shay as if he were an animal in a zoo. She considered turning and fleeing when Duncan shot to his feet, banging his knee against the table and almost tipping the drafting chair. He lunged toward the door and opened it so forcefully that Leah jumped back.

"Mrs. Maays," he said, immediately composed.

Leah blurted the first thing that came to her mind. "The shelves you made are extraordinary. They are exceptional. The joints, the wood, the craftsmanship. I wanted to tell you they are exceptional. You have not been compensated enough for them."

Duncan steadied himself against the door frame and grew so still she wondered if he was even breathing. He finally drew an abrupt breath and declared with an impeccable, deadpan professionalism that contradicted his physical reaction, "Your appreciation compensates me plenty, ma'am."

He shifted to one side when a spindly yellow dog squeezed between his leg and the door frame. Ancient and arthritic, the hound swayed side to side without bending its knees to walk. It shuffled to Leah, led by its nose, and leaned against her, tipping her onto a bench. The dog rested his head on her lap, furling his enormous eyebrows into two velvety rolls, and nudged her hand.

Leah scratched his ears and, from habit, evaluated the cataracts in his eyes. "Why, you are a very old thing."

Duncan stepped outside and sat on the porch banister. He snapped his fingers at the dog. "Come here."

But the dog, probably also deaf, did not heed him. It breathed out a sound between a wheeze and a sigh and made itself comfortable with its head on Leah's lap.

"He's no bother, Mr. Shay. In fact, he's very sweet. Aren't you, boy? What's his name?"

"Old Dog, ma'am."

"Old Dog! You named him Old Dog?"

"Came old, ma'am. Hasn't gotten young since."

She couldn't tell if he was joking. "Well, I suppose they follow our example."

"Yes, ma'am."

She placed her attention on Old Dog to see if Duncan would continue the conversation. She could feel his eyes wandering over her, but when she looked up, his eyes were focused elsewhere, and his expression revealed nothing. He was quick.

Leah could not bear another long bout of silence with him. She stood and stepped around Old Dog's outstretched legs. When her skirts brushed against the dog, it paddled its back legs in a struggle to get up. Duncan slipped off the banister to raise Old Dog's hips.

Once the dog was on its feet, Duncan scanned the sky. "Be getting dark, ma'am. Might I have the privilege of walking you to your uncle's house?"

His offer seemed inevitable, but on the verge of saying yes, a walloping sense of caution rose within her. Rumors about robbed banks and murdered men began buzzing in her head. Surely not every person in town could be mistaken.

With his powerful display of anger toward Cory Baines fresh on her mind, she withdrew. "I thank you for offering, but I have not far to walk. Good evening, Mr. Shay."

6

THE CHAT

June always snuck up on him, Duncan admitted as he polished his black boots until they gleamed white shards when light struck them. He bathed, shaved, and dressed in his best white shirt and the black pants he usually wore to conduct business in Edith's Bay. He put on a black ribbon tie before hesitating about wearing the jacket. It was too formal for a country dance where most men attended in shirtsleeves. In the end, he slipped on the jacket and stood by the window, tapping his fingers against the sill, still trying to decide whether he should spend his evening in a less risky way.

When Utterance Cobb rolled his work wagon to a stop in front of the post office, Duncan stepped away from the window into a shadow. Leah jumped off without assistance the moment the wagon halted, her skirts flaring out to reveal a froth of lacy petticoats that quickly disappeared beneath the dark paisley of the outer skirt.

Utterance leaned over and spoke to her. Leah flicked her hand as if shooing a fly, while Martha tightened her face into a scowl. Leah patted Utterance on the back as he helped Martha down and said something that made him laugh.

The moment she turned away from her aunt and uncle, her face settled into disgruntled lines, and she trudged toward the church dance looking like a hostage who would rather be anywhere else. She smiled when spoken to but hunched into herself the moment others looked away.

Despite her tense body language, the familial gossamers that bound the figures prevented Duncan from looking away until the church door shut behind them. He leaned back. Waited until the fiddler inside the church began to play. Waited a little longer. Braced himself. Then stepped out and pulled the shop door shut behind him.

A CAGE CAN BE MADE from anything, thought Leah, trapped in a square with Charlie Hunt as the first side couple. Charlie was a highly touted, very eligible, benign bachelor who came complete with many acres of prime orchard land. But he was so inarticulate Leah had not been able to extract a complete sentence out of him. She took shelter from him in the dance, flowing through the square while Charlie stomped beside her until the fiddler ended his tune and Leah almost collapsed from relief.

Launching into animated small talk so Charlie would not have an opportunity to ask her for another dance, she planned how to get away from him. She headed toward an alcove, hoping Charlie would realize the ladies' room was just beyond the alcove and tactfully abandon her.

Then, like a bird darting out of branches, Duncan Shay stepped out from behind a pillar. He was dressed somberly in simple clothes of a superb quality she would not expect a carpenter to be aware existed, much less own.

"Mrs. Maays. Mr. Hunt," Duncan said, bowing his head.

"Mr. Shay!" Leah was too startled to say much more. She almost forgot to curtsy.

"Enjoying your evening, Mrs. Maays?" Duncan asked with supreme decorum.

"Ah...punch. Mrs...er...Maays?" asked Charlie.

The fiddler started up again, and Charlie pulled her into the nearest square before she could make excuses to leave. She felt Duncan's eyes on her as she honored her partner and then her corner. During the Right and Left Grand, she watched with fascination as Duncan began to cross the room, and person after person turned a back to him. Some women even yanked their distracted daughters out of his path as though they had blindly wandered into the tracks of a rushing train.

A chill crept through Leah as she realized Duncan Shay was being shunned. Mrs. Groth said he was avoided, although until now, Leah thought there was only a smidgin of truth in all of Mrs. Groth and her flamboyant skirts. Leah had heard of shunning but had never seen it happen and almost did not believe the practice existed.

She locked eyes with Duncan as she held out her arms to the dancers by her sides. She barely felt their pull as she circled with them. Charlie Hunt's hand landed on her waist again, and when she came out of the swing, Duncan Shay... was gone.

The set ended, and Leah concluded that two dances with Charlie Hunt were more than enough. A third would indicate they were planning to court, a notion she found revolting.

She looked around. Tom Pratt sat in a corner with a

group of his friends. She had removed the cast from his foot, and he was now walking with a cane, which he could soon abandon.

She smiled to herself when she caught sight of the Haloways. Word of setting Tom Pratt's foot had to have reached Dr. Haloway by now, and he would be more respectful to her. She already knew working with a sort like Dr. Haloway was a form of death, but perhaps she could stop him from planting doubts around town about her as a physician.

Leah turned to Charlie. "Thank you, Mr. Hunt. I would like to converse with the Haloways."

"Oh...Waltzes..." began Charlie.

Without waiting, Leah headed toward the Haloways, leaving Charlie in mid mumble. He scampered to catch up with her.

Dr. Haloway got up and hobbled away when he saw her heading toward him. Leah fumed as she determined Dr. Haloway would not endorse a female physician, not even with his presence at a social event. He was moving more quickly than if his underwear had caught on fire.

She reconsidered her options, trapped between Charlie Hunt and Mrs. Haloway, who sat like a ruby in the center of a gilded setting, waiting for her. Pretending nothing offended her, Leah graciously sat next to her and rested one foot on the rungs of the chair next to her so Charlie Hunt would not join them. They looked up at Charlie, waiting for an introduction.

"Oh... Ah... Dr... Mrs. Haloway, um, Miss um— Aah, Mrs. Maays. Oh, eh, Doctor..."

Unable to bear Charlie Hunt's incoherence, Leah turned to Mrs. Haloway. "Good evening. I should like to sit out this dance in your company, if it does not inconvenience you. May I ask how you are enjoying the evening?"

"Indeed I am, thank you. I trust you are as well?"

"Yes, very much. Thank you."

To Leah's relief, Charlie Hunt made his way back to the bachelors congregating by the back wall. She made plans to leave Mrs. Haloway after a few more sentences. She wanted to leave the dance altogether but was unsure what scandal might arise if someone saw her walking back to the farm alone. Certainly, Martha would have a fit.

Mrs. Haloway lurched forward as if vaulted from a catapult and peered into Leah's face. "Is it true you tended to Duncan Shay's hand? He's somewhere here."

"Well, I—" said Leah, uncertain whether Mrs. Haloway was asking her a question or accusing her of an indiscretion. Leah let her sight wander over the room, immediately regretting looking. Her glance might become gossip fodder.

She prepared an answer, by which she was willing to be judged. "I also set Tom Pratt's foot. It is my duty to attend to the injured."

"My husband is used to dealing with Duncan Shay. If he bothers you again, you can send him straight to Dr. Haloway."

"Mr. Shay needed immediate medical attention, and he was not a bother. If your husband had been present, I am certain he would have tended to him as well."

Mrs. Haloway's mouth fell open. She whispered as if reporting a hovering menace, "But, surely you've heard."

"Heard what, Mrs. Haloway? That Mr. Shay has no use for his hand?"

Completely undone, Mrs. Haloway jerked backward. "Sending him to my husband should prevent—incidents.

There is wisdom in prevention, don't you think, Mrs. Maays?"

"I prefer to be addressed as Dr. Maays, please."

"A young woman like yourself. Close proximity to womanhood can provoke such a man to regrettable actions. Regrettable for you, that is. I am sure he would find much delight."

Of this threat, Leah had not heard. She thought of the many opportunities she had naively given Duncan Shay to commit transgressions against her and unsettled herself.

"For a murderer, everything is possible, if not probable in time." Mrs. Haloway's kind smile turned into a smirk. "Miss Leah, as your aunt prefers to call you."

"Please excuse me," said Leah, finding Mrs. Haloway's slight unforgivable. Even "Mrs. Maays" carried more status than "Miss Leah," and Mrs. Haloway, who reveled in being the wife of a physician, knew that well.

Leah stood and turned to the dance floor but saw Charlie step forward from the sideline to intercept her. She whipped around and slipped out to the side steps of the church. On the landing, she leaned back with her hands on the banister, luxuriating in the solitude. At least Charlie Hunt had not followed her out. Perhaps he was not immune to hints.

She simply could not go back to the dance. She should not have allowed Martha to pressure her into going when she still felt so tender about William and Titus. She wondered if she could weather the dance on the landing. Perhaps she could walk circles around the church until the festivities were over and make appearances only between sets when no one could dance.

Through the windows, the lamps within the church cast large blocks of light across the landing, and people's shadows leapt in and out of them as they danced. Leah moved out of the light to shelter in a strip of darkness between two windows and tried to settle herself.

She could not understand why Duncan Shay was allowed to roam freely at a public dance, when he took advantage of women, robbed banks, and killed men. None of that made sense. She was surprised town folk had not met him at the church doors with pitchforks in hand.

She had danced with the sheriff, a gruff, authoritative man who nonetheless was devoted to keeping trouble out of the town. Certainly he would know about the dangers of having a person like Duncan Shay in town. His eyes were always on Duncan, and people said Duncan did not step out of line because of the sheriff. But Duncan Shay sidestepped the sheriff at the general store without displaying any deference or apprehension.

The landing shook beneath Leah's feet, and from the darkness emerged Duncan Shay. Mrs. Haloway's words dropped out of Leah's head into her stomach where they became fact, solid and indigestible. *Bank Robber. Murderer. Provoked by womanhood. Prison.* She half hoisted herself onto the railing, preparing to jump over it and flee, although the ground was a good five feet below her.

But Duncan came to a full stop several feet away from her. He bowed, overflowing with formality and propriety, then rested one foot on a rung of a rickety chair that was sometimes used to prop open the side door. He placed his forearm on his knee with an evenness Leah thought was rehearsed and found disturbing.

"Didn't mean to startle you, Mrs. Maays. Please pardon me."

The fiddler stopped playing, and in the quiet, Duncan seemed to have always been there as if left behind by the church builders. Still suspicious, Leah exhaled unevenly and grasped the banister more tightly.

"You all right, ma'am? Pardon me if I startled you."

Leah nodded, although her skin prickled. She was grateful the fiddler was not playing. If she called out, someone would hear her.

"Been watching you dance. Mighty accomplished, ma'am. Will you please honor me with the next waltz, Mrs. Maays?"

Leah adjusted her grip on the banister. Dance with a bank-robbing murderer? Her evening was now officially intolerable.

In sharp contrast to her jitters, Duncan maintained a perfect calm until his eyes began to cloud, his lips to tighten. His rehearsed casualness slowly seeped out of him until he drew himself to his full height and planted both feet on the landing.

"And when did you get scared of me, ma'am?" he asked, reverting to his harshness.

"I am not frightened," Leah lied.

"Weren't scared when you put all those stingy things on me." He held up his hand, displaying the beige scar across the palm. "Or in the store, when you called me a pest." Slowly he lowered his hand and clenched the back of the chair. "Or when you came peeking in my shop. Not sure what you expected to see. Ma'am."

"You must be frightened yourself. You are holding that chair like a lion tamer," said Leah.

"Your coldness roars. Madam."

Leah gasped at his insolence. What a fool she had been to have permitted these encounters in the first place. They simply could not continue. A person like Duncan Shay could only result in trouble. Surely not everyone in town was mistaken. Many had already warned her about what she could now see clearly on her own.

She stepped forward as forcefully as she could, hoping to walk around him without incident and reenter the church where she would be surrounded by people. To her surprise, Duncan hopped back, banging his shoulder blades against the clapboards. Less than a yard away, she could feel the swell of heat he gave off in the night coolness as his shoulders inched up and back.

In the moment during which they faced each other, she wondered what a man who robbed banks and killed men had to fear from her. Confidence suffused her as she realized she had the upper hand, even if she did not quite understand the game—and the game could be downright dangerous. She stepped back into the light of a window where she was certain people inside could see her and measured her words carefully.

"Please excuse me, Mr. Shay. I am a bit unsettled. I have been hearing talk that is not flattering to you, and I am wondering if it is accurate. I think it only fair to ask you because only you can tell me the truth."

Duncan peeled himself off the clapboards and stood with renewed self-possession. "You plan on believing me? Ma'am."

Leah's courage ebbed. She had not expected such directness from him. She shoved back her shoulders. "I do not know, Mr. Shay, but I am willing to listen to you."

Duncan exhaled with a force that might have blown her off the platform. She flinched.

Then, as if deflating, he slid onto the banister to sit. "That's fair, ma'am. Ask your questions. Please."

His complete compliance befuddled her and transfixed her with curiosity. In which direction was he going? She distributed her weight evenly on both feet to steady herself and, after forming the most concise statement she could in her head, spoke clearly to hear herself over the cush-cush of her heartbeat.

"Mr. Shay, I have heard you have robbed banks and murdered men."

His look turned so hard she could barely hold up under it. "Tried to rob a bank. Ma'am."

"Tried?"

"Was sixteen. Ma'am."

"Sixteen!" Old enough to be a man with all the foolishness of a boy. Leah forced herself to not get distracted. "And the—killing...men?"

"Yes, ma'am. Didn't mean to, but it was still my fault he died."

He took responsibility with stark, unwavering force, laying all his cards before her with a fierce honesty that enfeebled her. She'd been expecting him to spew a series of creative justifications for why killing a man while robbing a bank had not been his fault.

Duncan looked away, although his tone sought her. "Was by accident, ma'am. I shot him, and he died because I did, but it was still by accident. Not something that deserves forgiveness, but I can't undo it. Ma'am." He looked at her again. In the little time that passed, dark shadows had formed under his eyes. He looked exhausted as he rubbed the scar on his palm. "What else, ma'am?"

"I heard you were in a penitentiary?"

"Yes, ma'am. I was."

"For long?"

He hesitated, as if counting up the years. "It's always too long, ma'am."

"I am very sorry, Mr. Shay."

Duncan shifted on the banister as his body tightened. "What else, ma'am? Not something I plan to do again. Still sorry I did it once. So. What else? Ma'am."

"I heard about—something about—being—provoked by...womanhood?" Her voice rose into a near squeak.

He cocked back his head as his eyes widened. His mouth hung open for a moment before he recovered. "Don't follow you, ma'am. Frankly, be afraid to ask what you really mean by that."

Fatigued into demureness, Leah looked away. "Thank you, Mr. Shay. It was kind of you to answer my questions. I know this has not been easy for you."

"Get all your questions out of the way now, ma'am. Don't need you being scared of me. Not necessary. No matter what anyone says."

"Do you think you have answered everything I need to know about you, Mr. Shay?"

Duncan's harshness waxed and waned until he folded. "Probably not, ma'am."

"Then I think this suffices for one conversation. I thank you for your honesty, Mr. Shay."

He looked thrashed, but Leah sensed he would have answered her questions all night while hating each and every one of them—as well as her for asking them. She regretted that her questioning, in retrospect so clinical and compassionless, had only complicated matters. The tension that should have been removed now vibrated between them.

Duncan slid slowly off the banister to his feet. "Don't blame you for needing to know, ma'am. Mighty grateful you asked kindly."

His forgiveness flustered her and increased her remorse. "I asked to know the truth, not to cause you pain, Mr. Shay."

"Be important you not be afraid of me, Mrs. Maays.

Would appreciate it greatly. There's no need for it. I've caused no trouble here."

He wants friendship? Kindness? She could only assume, but Leah felt the weight of an obligation she did not yet understand.

The fiddler started up again with a country waltz. Duncan glanced through the window and back to her. Leah implored the universe that he would not ask her again to dance. She could feel him composing himself to ask.

To her surprise, the sternness went out of his stance, and he relaxed as if melting against a post. "Seems I forgot my manners, ma'am. Should have had a conversation with you before asking you to dance. Don't want to presume, but you don't look like you even want to be here."

"I should not have come. It's premature. I recently lost... my husband and son. I'm not the least bit ready...to be festive."

"I'm very sorry to hear that, ma'am. Maybe you should go home, if it's too much."

Is he going to offer to walk me home? She chose the lesser of two evils. "I think I need to stay. Much insistence has been exerted for me to be here. They think they are helping me get over my losses by having me do...cheerful things. They mean well."

Duncan nodded. "Think you're being very gracious about it, ma'am. Can't imagine how someone having trouble walking around is expected to dance. Suppose they can't help it, it being in someone else's mind."

Leah blinked, amazed to hear someone speak of grief as a main event—more than just a mere side effect of being widowed and losing a child. Duncan Shay seemed to have a heartfelt sense for how the weight of sorrow was not some-thing to be solved or overcome.

She was trying to find a tactful way of finding out how he came to such an understanding when the side door swung open, almost crashing into Duncan had he not been quick footed enough to step aside. Emma Groth tottered onto the landing, leaning on Cory Baines, the fool who almost started a fight at Hoburn's, and slamming her walking stick into the boards with each step.

Her skirt, layered with thick, satin ruffles over a hoop, swung from side to side like a cow bell that could knock down the church walls. The massive mutton sleeves made her look as if she carried boulders on her shoulders, and Leah was afraid to let her eyes rove over the low-cut neckline that revealed something akin to the cleavage two side-by-side pancakes might form.

"Mrs. Maays! We have been looking all over for you," Mrs. Groth exclaimed with the operatic wave of one hand. She maneuvered Cory between Leah and Duncan without acknowledging Duncan. "This is Mr. Baines, Mrs. Maays. Mr. Baines, you may have the honor of meeting Mrs. Maays. Mr. Baines has been expressing all evening how honored he would be to dance with you."

"Sure have, Mrs. Maays. I sure would like a go with you," said Cory.

Leah took in Cory's ingratiating grin and his oily, carnal greed. She would rather lose a foot than dance with him.

She smiled and curtsied. "I am honored, Mr. Baines. However, Mr. Shay has already reserved this dance."

Leah caught a glimpse of the wildness in Duncan's eyes before he slipped on a poker face that revealed nothing. Silently, he sidestepped Cory as if he had known about this arrangement all evening. He held the door open, and Leah entered the church by passing under Duncan's arm, leaving Emma Groth and Cory gaping on the landing.

Inside, the gaping continued as everyone turned to look at them. Duncan formally offered her his hand, palm down as if entering a grand ballroom. Leah placed her hand over his, now wishing she could extract herself from this situation because the pressure of everyone staring was crippling.

She kept in step with Duncan's dignified pace as if they were walking in a procession. He seemed to have some fine breeding in him that had not bled through all the way. Only the stiffness of his fingers under her hand suggested he was less than at ease.

At the edge of the dance area, he swung her out with a twist of his wrist and pulled her back. In the unbroken motion, Leah found herself with one arm outstretched, hand in his, and her other hand on his shoulder. He took a moment to find his place in the fiddler's music, then with a preparatory nod to her, stepped out with the lightness of a bird taking flight.

Arm outstretched like the bow of a clipper, Duncan maneuvered her with superb fluidity between other couples who were knotted in rotating patterns of jerky motions. Leah could feel him transfer into her the glorious umm-pah-pah, one-two-three of a fully orchestrated Strauss waltz from the reedy rasp of the country fiddler's rendition.

They went around the floor again before he adjusted his stride and folded her closer to his body, still leaving several respectful inches between them. Leah stared at the sheen of Egyptian cotton on his shirt, afraid to look him in the eye. After another round, she finally gathered her courage and looked up. This time, he did not look away.

The dance ended abruptly, as if the fiddler lost the last bar of the music, but Duncan brought her to a flowing stop before releasing her and bowing formally. Leah bowed deeply, sinking into the center of her dress, as if it were a full-skirted ball gown. Duncan's eyes sparkled like those of an immigrant recognizing a custom from his old country.

"Mighty grateful for the honor, Mrs. Maays," Duncan said as he escorted her off the dance area. "Taking you to your uncle, ma'am."

Leah looked to the sideline and saw Utterance trying to whisper comfort into Martha, who was wringing her handkerchief. Mrs. Groth had taken a seat near Martha, although Martha had not yet seen her.

Spotting the brewing melodrama, Leah said, "I prefer the Hoburns, please." Hoburn would at least be professionally polite in his shopkeeper's way.

"As you wish, Mrs. Maays," said Duncan with a relief that made his shoulders slump.

Everyone was looking at them and whispering, some without discretion at all. Hoburn rose tentatively when they approached and offered his seat to Leah. She slipped into the chair next to Mrs. Hoburn, avoiding her eyes.

"Well, well…Mrs. Maays. Didn't know this town acquired such a good dancer," said Hoburn, but his unblinking eyes were stuck on Duncan.

"Mrs. Maays has requested the honor of your company, ma'am," Duncan said to Mrs. Hoburn before turning to Leah. "Thank you, Mrs. Maays, for the honor. Mrs. Hoburn." He nodded to Hoburn. "Sir."

Without further ado, he walked away. No one moved as he made his way across the room in the humiliating silence. Even the fiddler, who did not know the petty histories of West Edith's Bay, knew better than to play until Duncan stepped outside and was swallowed by night. When the fiddler started playing again, the dance floor did not fill because everyone was still staring at her.

Bearing the discomfort of such scrutiny, Leah sat and

withdrew into herself. For once she felt the tension of the constant observation people applied to Duncan—staring at him while pretending he was not present, being aware of him without acknowledging him. She didn't know how he bore the pressure.

Now, that scrutiny was turned on her because everyone discerned Duncan Shay came for the sole purpose of dancing with her. And she had abided. What they had not seen was that he opened his vault of vulnerabilities for her to rummage through at her mere asking.

She might have had an insight at that moment had she not heard Martha charging toward her, crashing through people like wildebeest crossing a river. Utterance was barely keeping up with her. A foot or so in front of Leah, Martha flapped out a shawl that landed around Leah's shoulders with the weight of a rug.

"We need to go home," said Martha, huffing with effort. "Now. Right now."

Befuddled at her aunt's urgency, Leah looked around. Utterance stood beside her. When she looked up at him, he tipped his head and rolled his eyes toward the door.

Leah stood. Ah. She was the reason. Or, rather, dancing with Duncan Shay was the reason. Well, she could now leave the dance as she'd been wanting to do, although not in the way she had expected.

Martha herded her and Utterance to the wagon, where against the sound of the fiddler's happy screech, they rode away from the church in clenched silence. Leah knew this silence intimately. She first experienced it when she announced she was going to become a doctor instead of a nurse and again when she announced she was going to practice in Ghana with a man she had just married. The silence was the sound of massive, inflexible disapproval.

From the wagon, Leah watched Duncan's silhouette form against a shop window as if carved out of his personal darkness. What had she accomplished by dancing with him, except perhaps to disgrace herself and be unfaithful to Titus's memory? To encourage Duncan Shay with faulty hopes that she would now have to remedy? Duncan's silhouette disappeared as the wagon headed up the hill, yet Leah knew he was still watching.

IN HER BEDROOM, Leah tried to make out Martha's and Utterance's agitated murmurs through the wall as she changed into her nightgown. After their voices eased into barely discernible murmurs, Utterance left the room and padded down the hallway. Leah waited with her hand on the doorknob for him to knock and opened her door the moment he did. She stepped into the hallway.

"Leah, what was in your head? First you don't want to go to the dance, but the next thing we know is you dancing with Duncan Shay. Duncan Shay! Of all people! Not like there wasn't nobody else there."

"It wasn't charity, Uncle. He worked very hard for it. I asked him about his wrongdoings. He appeared to be very pained by them," said Leah.

"Better be. After all he dun. Martha tole me you knew already."

"Knowing something by Emma Groth is like knowing nothing."

"Know it by me, then. I know it reliable he robbed a bank and kilt a man and dun years in prison. And I know this to be God's truth. Now, he been real quiet in that shop o' his since then, and we like to leave him quiet. Truth be,

Leah, we knowed it was in him to do it once. We ain't want to know if it be in him again."

"But it was an accident. The shooting, I mean."

"No sir! First degree murder. Shot a guard plum in front of four witnesses. Nothing to dispute. They had to tackle him to get him. Sixteen, he was. Mighty young to start killing people point blank. Surprised he ain't been hanged for it."

"His remorse is sincere, Uncle. I am certain of that. I felt it."

"Ain't difficult to feel remorse after you been jailed for murdering a man. Pays right being wise in your sympathies. Stick to Charlie Hunt. You need give him a chance. Mostly he be shy. Henry Moore's a good one too. He got a reliable job at the post office."

"I'm just trying to figure out the truth, Uncle."

"Well, that be the truth about truth—that it be hard to figure out. You best stay out of Auntie's way tomorrow. Almost had to call all you doctors over when she seen you dancing with him. She ain't stopped muttering and festering since. Don't see me getting any sleep tonight. Then that creature, Emma Groth, set down next to her a-wanting to discuss it. I tell you, that woman reminds me of a giant spider with all those sticky webs she throws around."

Utterance pretended to shudder, causing Leah to swallow a giggle. He tried to scowl and resume his stern mood but ended up choking back a bunch of chuckles. They silenced one another by waving their hands as if to swat away the laughter so Martha would not find out that her unfortunate evening was the source of their amusement.

Utterance threw up his arms and padded back into his bedroom. Martha's bleating started up the moment he closed the door behind him.

They mean well. They mean well, Leah chanted in her head. Still, she found herself wishing she could sneak out into the orchard to howl like a coyote and release the corroding tension that had been gathering within her since she came home.

7

———

THE NEW CITIZENS

On the next work day, Mrs. Hoburn kept trying to discuss Duncan Shay, attempting different angles without much success because Leah did not intend to discuss Duncan Shay or their dance with anyone. As public as the dance had been, it still felt intensely private in a way she could not articulate.

"He must have been real desperate the day he came in with that bloody hand. Why, we were wall to wall with people like today," chatted Mrs. Hoburn as she measured out two pounds of dry beans while Leah scoured the shelves for a bottle of violet water a customer wanted. "His hand must be fine by now, is it?"

He thought he cut off a finger, Leah almost said out loud.

"Ain't no way to predict," Mrs. Hoburn continued, chatting into the air. "Sometimes it's just us and dust. Other times everyone in the world has to be here all at the same time. Violet water's over one shelf, dear."

Leah delivered the violet water to the customer and made her way to the cloth table to finish wrapping lace collars for someone. She continued tidying the cloth table until the smell of birth surrounded her. She looked up.

The next customer was round with child and had four boys clinging to her skirts. Based on the ages of the children, Leah calculated the woman must have been pregnant for the past six years. One child started to wander away, intrigued by something shiny on a shelf.

"Enoch! What I say? Stay by me. You know I ain't feelin' so good. Dun give me trouble." The woman pulled back the child and leaned in toward Leah, wincing. "I was wondering if you could, um—"

Already sensing what was happening, Leah leaned forward and whispered, "How may I help you?"

"Um—I haven't been feeling good. Dr. Haloway says it's —" She broke off her sentence in a wince.

"Come with me," said Leah, pulling the woman toward the back room. "Mrs. Hoburn!"

"Yes, dear, what can I help you find?"

Leah pulled Mrs. Hoburn to one side and whispered, "Mrs. Hoburn, this woman is in labor and going to deliver now."

"Now? Here?"

"Of course not, Mrs. Hoburn. We are going into the back room."

"Why don't you go to Dr. Haloway, Mrs. Corwal?" asked Mrs. Hoburn.

"He said it ain't time yet," said Mrs. Corwal.

"Mrs. Hoburn, please find someone to watch the children," Leah added. "They cannot be present."

The last thing Leah saw before she shut the door to the back room was Mrs. Hoburn with her mouth hanging open standing within a circle of children, some already beginning to cry for their mother. Behind the counter, Mr. Hoburn had turned into a set of giant eyes. Someone called out that he was going to fetch Mrs. Corwal's husband.

In the back room, Leah settled Mrs. Corwal on the table and helped her undress from the waist down. There was always the risk that someone would walk into the back room, which had no lock on the door.

"Have you just come from Dr. Haloway's?" asked Leah.

Mrs. Corwal drew a breath between pursed lips. "He said it wasn't time."

"How much time did he think you had to wait?"

"Few more weeks. Said the ba-ba-ba-by ain't turned yet." Mrs. Corwal gasped with a contraction. "Felt like time to me."

"Well, you are correct. It is time. Let us see what we can do. I am going to go wash my hands. I shall be right back."

Leah pulled a bedsheet from a shelf and dropped it over Mrs. Corwal to preserve her modesty. At least the woman had given birth before and knew what to expect. For that, Leah was grateful, seeing that birthing in the stock room of a general store was highly irregular.

Upon returning with washed hands, Leah pressed against Mrs. Corwal's abdomen to feel the position of the baby. The hardness of the baby's head was near Mrs. Corwal's breasts. Nearer the exit rested the softer tissue of the baby's bottom. Between extremes, she felt the knobbiness of the feet. Leah pressed against the abdomen again and was relieved when the baby kicked back. It was still alive.

To Leah's surprise, Mrs. Corwal was almost fully dilated. She must have been walking around town in labor. Leah poked her finger into Mrs. Corwal and felt the baby's soft bottom. Undeniably, the baby was breeched, and labor had progressed too far to turn it around in the womb, which might have been possible earlier.

"Please wait before you push again, Mrs. Corwal. Let the baby slip into position," said Leah. "Try very hard not to push."

A few more contractions later, Mrs. Corwal began to look exasperated. Leah checked the position of the child again. She waited for a twitch in Mrs. Corwal's mouth, which usually indicated the beginning of a new contraction. With her hand, Leah again checked the baby's position.

"All right, Mrs. Corwal. On the count of three, give it your all," said Leah. "One... Two... Three! Push! Push! Push!"

With a groan, Mrs. Corwal pushed. The baby's buttocks poked through the opening, followed by the left and the right legs flopping out like wet wings. Before Mrs. Corwal could have another contraction, Leah slipped two fingers over the baby's right shoulder and ran them along the baby's arm, whereupon the right arm slid out. She shifted the baby and did the same to the left arm. The head was still in the womb. So far, the baby's coloring looked fine.

"You have a baby girl, Mrs. Corwal."

Mrs. Corwal smiled. Leah remembered all the children she'd had with her in the store were boys.

Leah braced herself. She resisted the temptation to pull out the baby because so much of her was already outside. But she called on her patience, having already witnessed one child's neck broken and another rendered an idiot from being pulled out prematurely. Not to mention the damage to the mother. Releasing the head from the womb had to be done at a precise angle and with masterful timing so the baby would not gasp a lungful of amniotic fluids and drown. That was the most delicate part of a breech birth.

Leah rotated the baby and waited for the next contraction. The moment Mrs. Corwal changed her breathing,

Leah slipped her hands into position to finish removing the baby from the womb.

"When it comes, please push hard, Mrs. Corwal," she said.

The moment Mrs. Corwal pressed down in pain, Leah tucked the baby's head so that the face became exposed before she slowly guided the rest of the head out of Mrs. Corwal's body in accordance to the contraction. The maneuver took seconds.

Leah tensed as the child turned purple in her hands, although she knew purple newborns were not unusual. With mechanical calm, she wiped the baby's face and puffed a bit of air into her mouth while tapping her chest. She puffed again, turned the child belly down and slapped her back several times. *Breathe, breathe. Please breathe.* The baby stretched her arms in a wiggle, coughed like an old man, and let out a garbled screech.

Leah almost dropped her from the sense of relief she felt. "She is very strong. I shall give her to you in a moment, Mrs. Corwal. Congratulations!"

With more relief than joy, Leah held the girl at an angle that facilitated her coughing as she continued to pat her back. She rinsed the girl with water from a bucket she had remembered to fill when she went to wash her hands. The bucket was meant for animal feed, but Leah reasoned she could pitch the water and Hoburn could sell it with no one knowing it had been used for nobler means.

After cutting the umbilical cord and swaddling the girl in a bath towel from a shelf, Leah indulged herself by holding her. She could feel the warmth of the little body against her breasts. For a moment, she closed her eyes as her mind dozed in a memory of her William, and she reimagined his life. When she began to ache with sorrow, she flung herself into the present, speaking quickly to get out the words before she lost her composure.

"Congratulations, Mrs. Corwal. You have a healthy girl." Leah placed the baby on Mrs. Corwal's chest just as her placenta slid out, conveniently landing in the feed bucket and splashing bloody water all over the back room. "Please allow me to clean you up a bit."

"Thank you, ma'am."

"You're welcome, Mrs. Corwal. Please call me Dr. Maays."

"Yes, ma'am—Dr. Maays, I mean. Thank you."

"Your little girl is perfectly formed and strong. Please rest while I see if your husband is here."

Leah took off her bloody apron and slipped into the store's front room, where almost everyone in town had congregated. She identified Mr. Corwal by the concerned look on his face and the four boys who were using him as a jungle gym.

"A baby girl, Mr. Corwal! Everyone is fine. Please go into the back room to see your wife."

At this news, everyone in the store cheered, and a chorus of children went up. "Can we come, too?"

"Me too!"

"Mama! We want to see Mama!"

"Mama!"

"Where's Mama? I want Mama!"

Leah knelt before the children. "Your mama is fine and will be out very soon. And you know what? You have a baby sister!"

Amidst the children's mixed responses, she heard Dr. Haloway's stern voice behind her. "Mrs. Maays, you should have called me. Having Mrs. Corwal give birth here! You were fortunate she is used to birthing."

Leah took a moment to suppress the urge to slug Dr. Haloway before she calmly stood and faced him. *Remain professional.* "She came here directly from your office because she was told it was not yet time. Dr. Haloway, when a woman says she is in labor, it is best to consult her body, not a calendar. The baby was not premature. She was breeched. She has the vigor of being full termed. I suspect the delivery date was miscalculated, as clearly contraindicated by the parturition."

Leah walked away. She returned to the back room to clean up before the Hoburns wandered into the birthing mess. Word was out. It would travel with Tom Pratt when he abandoned his cane to walk on his own. It would travel when Mrs. Corwal strolled through town with her new little girl.

If they start coming to me, Dr. Haloway, it is because you make mothers feel incompetent for being in labor when it inconveniences you.

THE REST OF THE DAY, fortunately, remained uneventful. Mary Corwal's husband, John, left and returned with a wagon to take Mary and the children home. He also paid Leah in full that very day for assisting with the difficult birth. Leah left for the day feeling more satisfied than she had in months.

On the walk home, she did not expect a shadow to come rippling from under the Carpentry and Fine Cabinetmaking sign, down the shop steps, and prostrate itself across the road until Duncan stepped on it as if catching it by the foot. He held his hat by the brim in one hand. Leah slowed her steps until she stood before him, his presence seeming to block the entire road.

"Mrs. Maays," he said without revealing his mood.

Leah held her breath. She squared herself into a stance similar to his and dropped her voice to mimic his perfectly flat tone. "Mr. Shay."

"Mocking me, Mrs. Maays?" His eyes flickered with amusement.

"No sir," Leah said, practicing the deadpan expression. "I am trying to imagine what it is like to be you."

"Best you not, ma'am." Duncan brushed the brim of his hat with his cuff. "Store looked busy, ma'am. Didn't want to be a pest."

When he didn't specifically mention the birth, Leah abandoned her impersonation. "That was very considerate, Mr. Shay—not that you are ever a pest."

She glanced at his hat, knowing he was preparing to ask to walk her home. She could not ask him into the house. Even having him step onto the porch was questionable. The truth about his standing in the community hung between them, acknowledged in their awkwardness, while remaining unspoken.

She looked away, feeling flustered and inept. She could ruin herself if she did not keep him at arm's length. And, if things were not difficult enough, she might have to forfeit establishing a practice.

Duncan slipped on his hat in one fine gesture. He had that no-going-back somber look Leah often saw on surgeons just before they amputated a patient's limb.

"Will you value my company, Mrs. Maays?"

She took a moment to savor the many layers of his stark question. Duncan Shay was not a simple man. His calloused hands did not foretell his ability to commandeer a dance floor with such force and elegance. He made bookshelves with qualities found only in museum sculptures.

Leah tried to look into his eyes, which were now concealed in the shadow of the hat brim. He was used to inhospitality, perhaps expected it by now. Any man so taken off guard by kindness had to be. He would take whatever response she gave in stride if she gave him the dignity of being polite. She suspected he would withdraw respectfully, averse to causing a scene. Leah straightened herself and prepared her response.

8

THE GIFT

I f ever West Edith's Bay had a stretch of hot, muggy weather, it would come at the beginning of August and last a week or two. Everyone dreaded the heat, most of all Henry. He would try to cope by flinging open the post office windows to encourage breezes to visit. The few that did were hot and unsatisfying, carrying so much humidity that even envelopes stuck to his fingers.

He had eight letters left to sort into mailboxes when the clock struck twelve, which didn't surprise him because he'd been peckish for a while. Only when he finished sorting the remaining envelopes did he realize that more than lunch was missing. Duncan had failed to come for his correspondence. He came daily at 11:30 a.m. more reliably than the office clock pinged the hour, especially when Henry forgot to wind it.

Henry stuck his head out a window and realized he had not heard the usual sounds of woodworking at any time that morning. Duncan was not out of town because he had not put his mail on hold. Henry paced in the crowded office as he dithered. Duncan was not the sort to want disturbing, but his absence at his usual time was sufficiently concerning that Henry decided to depart from his usual practice and deliver Duncan's afternoon mail to his living quarters.

All you need to do is hand him the mail and leave, Henry reassured himself as he crossed the street. Halfway across, he saw the Closed sign on the shop door and debated going back to the post office or knocking on the door to Duncan's private living quarters in the back of the shop. No one he knew had ever knocked on the door to Duncan's home. There was probably a reason for that.

Henry paused at the back door, looked at the envelopes in his hand, and again considered going back without delivering them. After all, he was not required to deliver mail. People came to him for their mail.

Just say hello and hand him the mail, Henry told himself. He knocked rapidly and loudly to commit himself. He didn't know what to expect, but he felt his muscles tightening in case he had to turn and flee.

After a cacophony of hoarse coughs and slimy sniffles, the door swung open. Duncan stood in the doorframe, blowing his nose on a fine linen handkerchief. The eyes above the handkerchief immediately transformed from bleary to sharp.

"Sir," he said hoarsely.

"Just came to deliver your mail. And—and to check if you're all right. You usually come, you know, before lunch."

Duncan squinted into the sunlight. "Think I slept through it, sir."

"You need a doctor? I can get Dr. Haloway for you."

Duncan peered at him. "No sir. Thank you. Just a summer cold."

"All right. I'll leave you then. Oh, here. Your mail."

"Mighty grateful, sir. If you don't mind, can you please take these with you?" Duncan turned and slipped back into the room.

Henry took the opportunity to see what Duncan's personal furniture was like. He expected mind-boggling pieces—a four-poster bed with pillars carved like Egyptian snakes holding up an intricate canopy, a chest of drawers with gargoyles for feet, or a full-length mirror flanked with fretted wings. Even with all that mental preparation, Henry was not prepared for what he saw.

Duncan's personal furniture was made of hard pine two-by-fours without ornamentation or a single curved edge: a double bed, a washstand, a simple rod populated with tailored work shirts and a business suit, a wooden box with folded work pants, another box with folded undershirts. The wood was not even stained. Everything was clean and neat, except the top of a table that had collected a clutter of books, sketchpads, and drawing pencils.

The only luxury in the room was a gold watch on a night table that rivaled any watch Henry had seen to date. It was housed in a fine, French gold casing that confirmed Duncan spent his money with as much discernment as he accepted customers. The last thing Henry caught sight of before Duncan returned was a little sign on top of the chest of drawers: PRACTICE THE PRACTICE.

"Thank you, sir. Much appreciated," said Duncan when he returned with some envelopes.

Henry hoped his eyes were still in his head when he took the stamped envelopes from Duncan. He nodded and began walking down the alley, trying not to twist his feet in the ruts and dirty his uniform.

At the post office, he put his head down on his desk and closed his eyes, trying to reconcile what Duncan Shay created for the world and the furniture he'd made for himself.

He couldn't.

THAT ON SOME days Duncan looked tattered from dragging himself through town without being acknowledged inspired Henry to conduct an experiment. He bought two cinnamon buns and positioned the open bag on one corner of his desk. Then he sat in his chair and practiced not looking nervous.

Like clockwork, at 11:30, when the post office was usually empty, Duncan strode in cradling a sack of sugar in one arm and clutching a handful of replies in his fist. He rested the sack on a side table, as he did when he had goods from Hoburn's, and pulled up the chair across from Henry.

"Sir."

By now, Henry was used to Duncan opening each transaction with this formal greeting as if he were Duncan's grandfather. "Want a cinnamon bun?"

"Pardon? Sir?"

"I said, you want one?" Henry pointed to the bag. "I got two."

Duncan stared, first at Henry, then into the open bag. He tipped back into the chair, completely dumbfounded.

"Comes with coffee," Henry added, hearing his pot boil over. He got up to fetch the pot and two mugs, giving Duncan a chance to regroup. Henry had never seen a grown man be so stricken by an offer of a cinnamon bun.

When Henry returned, Duncan apparently recomposed himself. "Most appreciative, sir. Thank you."

Henry poured coffee into the two mugs and gave Duncan the one without the chip.

"There's sugar, sir." Duncan slowly gestured to the bag on the table.

"Thanks, but I'm used to mine black." Henry pulled out a spoon from a pencil holder in case Duncan wanted sugar for his coffee. Duncan did not touch the spoon.

Henry was careful not to make direct eye contact as he sipped his coffee. He pulled out a cinnamon bun for himself. He pushed the bag with the other one toward Duncan and waved his hand over it as an invitation for Duncan to help himself.

Duncan picked up the other bun and looked at it. "Thank you, sir."

Henry nodded and took a bite of his cinnamon bun. Duncan looked at his bun again. Glanced at Henry again. Bit into the bun. Chewed. Henry diligently observed the uneventfulness of the empty street while Duncan diligently observed him.

"So what you got?" asked Henry, timing his question to coincide with the moment Duncan swallowed the last bite of his bun. Quite frankly, he had concerns about what might happen if he kept Duncan out of his routine for too long.

"Several replies, sir," Duncan said on cue and began dictating as if cinnamon buns and coffee still did not exist.

At that point, Henry concluded the experiment had been worthwhile. Duncan Shay sat through it without being combative with his stares or manner, and Henry caught additional glimpses of a civility and a cautious tentativeness he had not anticipated.

Henry had long contemplated that Duncan was guarded to compensate for severe shyness. Now he discarded that theory for a fear that Duncan was very slowly becoming feral from neglect.

After Duncan left, Henry resumed working with the usual conventions and trivialities. He thought about his experiment without arriving at any sound conclusion. It left no residue on Duncan's behavior as he resumed coming to the post office as was his habit, behaving as was his habit.

That was why Henry was bewildered when one day the smell of cinnamon buns invaded the post office. He looked up from postmarking envelopes to see Duncan in the doorway, hesitating majestically as he clutched a small bag from the bakery.

Henry collected himself enough to smile as though Duncan were his long-lost cousin returning from the Nile. "Something smells good."

"Cinnamon buns, sir. If you have time."

Henry rubbed his hands together. "Time was made for cinnamon buns."

He waved Duncan in and went into the back room to start a pot of coffee. By the time he came back out, Duncan was already seated, and the bag of buns was open on the desk.

From then on, once or twice a week, he could expect to have a snack with Duncan. Without making formal arrangements, they alternated purchasing the buns. Sometimes Duncan brought him a pound of coffee.

They began having elaborate conversations over cinnamon buns about woods, geology, astronomy, telescope optics, clock gears and the mathematics that made them work, geography, history, food, horses, architecture, and how much a railroad spur would ease the transfer of goods to Edith's Bay. Eventually, Duncan began draping himself languidly over the guest chair instead of sitting on it as if he were a wooden plank. Henry cheered inside his head.

The highlight of his day soon became Duncan's daily visit. The best were the ones when Duncan brought items to mail because Henry loved exploring Duncan's genius in the things he made, like a walking stick with a handle carved into a rabbit's head. When Henry rested his hand on the handle, he discovered an ingenious trigger that allowed him to wiggle the rabbit's ears without anyone detecting his hand motion.

Henry burst out laughing with delight. Duncan even smiled. Henry walked around the post office, feeling stylish with the walking stick, wishing someone would come in so he could wiggle the rabbit's ears and get a response. He wondered how Duncan could make such an enchanting cane in solitude and not yearn for the experience of seeing people react to it.

After almost wearing out the ear mechanism, Henry relinquished the rabbit cane. He turned his fascination to Duncan's other item, a stationery box with a complex arrangement of slots, pockets, and drawers. These boxes were carpenter's versions of quilts, and Henry was sure this one had fetched a hefty price, just as he knew the rabbit cane had. Everything Duncan Shay made fetched a hefty price, and for good reason.

To Henry's delight, Duncan revealed a hidden compartment behind the drawers. Henry accessed the compartment several times, trying to remember if he had any possession that might merit being kept in such a carefully constructed, special, secret place. He loved secret places.

Finally, he remembered he was at work and checked his pocket watch. "Plenty of time before the last post carriage gets here. I'll get these out today."

"Just the cane, sir. The box is for you."

"For me?" Henry checked through the holidays in his head. It wasn't his birthday either.

"Yes sir," said Duncan, looking over Henry's desk, layered with pyramidal piles of papers.

"Good heavens! I cannot believe you are giving me this. Why, thank you. Oh, gracious heavens, it's—"

"Got some replies to go, Mr. Henry."

Henry sprawled in his chair and took a moment to recover from the second gift of the day, which was that Duncan had finally called him by his given name.

"Well, Duncan," he said gingerly, "that is one heck of a fine stationery box. I cannot believe you are giving it to me."

But Duncan was through with his gift-giving ceremony, and he took his place in the chair across from Henry to begin dictating. "Address to Mr. Emery Farrar. Farrar's Department Store, Incorporated, please. Cane fifty-eight rabbit head arriving US post..."

Between the blips of his telegraph, Henry slipped in glances at Duncan and the box, side by side across the desk from him. He was barely able to believe Duncan had made such an intricate, time-consuming gift with the sole intention of giving it to him, a postman who could never afford a Duncan Shay piece of any kind. Duncan Shay, it seemed, had a completely untapped reservoir of openheartedness no one even thought existed.

Through open windows, Henry often listened to Duncan's conversations with Joey the carrier. On this particular day, Duncan was crating a table shaped like a half circle with three straight, fluted, tapered legs. The tabletop was embellished with matched butterflied mahogany that gleamed like glass under a layer of shellac.

Nothing about the table was ornate from what Henry could see. Its beauty was in its proportions. Proportion could be studied through mathematics, but Duncan's sense of proportion, Henry was certain, came with his sentience.

Joey the carrier arrived a little late and a bit hungover. He waited patiently enough while Duncan fussed with the table, giving it an extra wipe and checking that no wax was caught in the leg flutes before slipping the table into a crate. He was about to screw on the crate lid when he took another moment to again wipe the butterflied mahogany top.

"What the hell you doin'?" Joey almost shouted. "You think whoever gits this ain't got a maid to dust it?"

Henry backed away from the window so they wouldn't hear him laugh out loud. For someone who took flak from no one, Duncan seemed completely at ease being harangued by a hungover carrier.

Shortly after the church bell struck eleven that day, Duncan dropped off a box of work shirts with a complaint to the tailor about skimpy gathers across the back and asked Henry to ship back the shirts. He dictated some responses to be telegraphed and flipped through his new correspondence to see if he had anything he could dispatch right then, but he did not.

Duncan was almost out the door when he turned and bounced one fist against his thigh. "Joey just called me finicky, Henry."

"Finicky?" Henry's eyes rolled over the front of the stationery box Duncan had given him. "Why'd he say that, you suppose?"

"Asked him to spread word I was looking for an assistant. He said I was too finicky for anyone to be my assistant."

"What you suppose he meant?"

"No idea. Not like I ever complain about his work. Don't know who's been complaining about me. There's the man who makes my hardware, but he needs precision in my specifications to make what I need. Not like I can tell him, 'Go make hardware,' and he comes up with what I need. There's a fellow at Ibsen's who complains I take too long to select my wood, but he's got to know good furniture can't be made from mediocre wood. Don't understand who else would think I'm finicky."

Henry pointed to the stationery box with his pen. "You think an unfinicky man can make a box like that?"

"That's not finicky, Henry. That's precision. Not the same. Like those shirts don't have precision in the gathers. They're all higgledy-piggledy."

"Well, he probably just used the wrong word," said Henry, as it dawned on him that Duncan was revealing a monumental amount of personal information about himself —not just that someone deemed him finicky but that he was disconcerted about it. Henry felt as if a geode had cracked open to reveal a cache of gems.

Duncan put his hands on his hips and raised one eyebrow as he looked down at Henry. "You humoring me?"

"No. Never. Wouldn't dream of it." Henry shook his head but grinned, knowing his amusement was not lost on someone as astute as Duncan. "It's just easier to imagine you being finicky right here in front of me than your tailor being, um...imprecise in Edith's Bay. Wouldn't be concerned about it one bit if I was you. No sir, I would not. Fact is, I'd take it as a compliment."

"Not finicky," Duncan muttered petulantly as he blustered out of the post office. "Sir."

Henry watched as Duncan tucked his correspondence into his coat to keep it from flapping and getting wrinkled and wondered whether Duncan, after so many years of guarded solitude and public disgrace, would ever realize the effect he was having in some circles. The little cinnamon-flavored kindness had evolved into a friendship with many rewards. And not all the rewards were made of wood.

9

THE DIFFICULT FLOWER

Martha was delighted when she opened the front door and found Dr. Haloway's nephew, Dr. Nathaniel Elliot, standing in front of it. He looked downright dashing as he emanated learnedness and polish. Cradled against his arm was an enormous, hand-picked bouquet of late-summer flowers, the sight of which made Martha swing open the door and boisterously shout, "Come in! Come in!"

Dr. Elliot appeared a bit taken aback by her enthusiasm, but he smiled, displaying even teeth that sparkled. He floated into the entry hall with great panache, carrying himself with a sophistication that Martha found intimidating, even though she thought it compensated well for his lack of chin.

"Good afternoon, Mrs. Cobb. I trust you are well? May I inquire whether Dr. Maays is accepting visitors today?"

"Why dun you come in the parlor? I'll call her down for you."

"I would be exceedingly delighted, Mrs. Cobb. Thank you."

Dr. Elliot breezed into the house like a cashmere scarf stretching in the wind. He looked perfect in the parlor, dressed in the formal style of city dwellers with a dove-gray morning coat, matching pants, and a silk brocade vest from which dangled a shiny, gold watch chain.

Martha hoofed to the foot of the stairs and shouted, "Leah! Leah? You got yourself a visitor! You heared?"

In her bedroom, Leah gritted her teeth. Martha's buoyant manner already told her the visitor was a suitor, one of several who had been coming by regularly. Any suitor had the effect of making Martha very happy and Leah very miserable.

For once Leah wished she had a mourning gown and an extra dark veil to wear so men would not want to court her. Her heartache was easing, but she had yet to meet a man who could supplant her Titus. Furthermore, she wasn't even interested in knowing if one existed.

She considered tying her sheets together and escaping through a window. Her contingency plan for dealing with unwanted suitors was to lose herself in the orchard at the first sign of a man coming up the hill. Utterance understood. She'd seen him go to the far side of the barn to kill time when he said he would look for her, then wander back to the house to report her still missing.

"Think she gone and turnt into an apple tree," Utterance often told suitors. Utterance, who always knew what to do, understood the folly of looking for someone who did not want to be found.

If evening was imminent, she doused herself with eucalyptus oil to repel mosquitos and insisted on sitting on the porch. The visitor would find many reasons to depart after the mosquitoes left him itchy and anemic. Although the visits were understandably short, Leah always felt dispro-

portionately wearied afterward. But evening was not imminent, and Martha had probably already chained this suitor
to a parlor chair.

She would welcome seeing Henry Moore, with whom
she had enjoyed several fabulous conversations full of
wicked humor and very bad puns that nonetheless made
them both laugh like fools. But after several visits, she was
certain the only thing that would ever fly between them was
platonic conversation. That suited her perfectly, but she
appreciated Henry probably wanted a bit of romance she
certainly could not provide.

Her throat constricted when she thought the visitor
might be Charlie Hunt. Maintaining a conversation with
him was nothing less than painful, as the man could not
construct a sentence before eternity ended. The last time he
visited, she read him poetry for an entire hour, sometimes
reading lines out of order to minimize his chances of understanding the verse so he would get bored enough to leave.
Alas, after an hour of bad poetry readings, he opened his
mouth to speak and stayed for another hour.

When Martha called her again, Leah began her trek
down the stairs to face whoever was waiting for her. She had
a dozen steps in which to make herself gracious while
praying viciously that Charlie Hunt would please, please,
please not be standing in the parlor. *Please!*

Partly down the stairs, she saw Dr. Elliot, and her dread
thinned with excitement. She was already familiar with his
fine mind from lectures she had attended, and she followed
the papers he published in professional journals. His well-
established reputation for brilliance promised a phenomenal memory that encompassed facts from the beginning of
time and a dazzling facility for logistical reasoning. It would
be scintillating to have a conversation with him—if he had

not merely come to evaluate whether she merited being a physician because of whatever Dr. Haloway put in his head.

Leah entered the parlor and curtsied to his bow, trying not to display her mix of excitement and reservation. "Good afternoon, Dr. Elliot. What an honor to see you."

"The honor is entirely mine, Dr. Maays." Ceremoniously, he held out the enormous bouquet. "For the enjoyment of you and your family."

Dr. Maays! He acknowledged her as a physician with no trace of disdain or amusement. Leah wrapped her hands around the bouquet with the same fervor she might have used to embrace Dr. Elliot at that moment. Perhaps he would set Dr. Haloway straight. About to lose her grip on the enormous bouquet, she dunked the unruly stems into a pitcher of drinking water Martha had set out on a side table.

"We thank you, Dr. Elliot," Leah mumbled as she tucked stray stems into the pitcher while the table wobbled because of a loose leg. With her handkerchief, she mopped the water off the top that spilled from the pitcher whenever the table swayed. In a second glance, she noted Dr. Elliot's fine stance, his long arms resting by his sides.

He smiled. "I would like to extend my condolences for your recent losses. I understand how difficult it can be. I lost my wife two years ago. She was a nurse as well as my assistant."

"Thank you, Dr. Elliot. You have my condolences as well."

"If I may, I would also like to present to you a copy of the paper I have just presented in Boston. It is a treatise about how sugars are diverted to the liver in patients with pancreatic diabetes and a prescription for a new treatment." He pulled some papers from his jacket pocket and held them out to her.

Leah took the papers, glad to shift away from condolences. "Diversions to the liver? Oh, this is indeed very new."

"I hope you shall find it immediately useful."

"I am certain I shall. Dr. Elliot, please sit down. May I offer you some cake and coffee? This translocation of glucose into the liver..."

Leah peppered Dr. Elliot with all sorts of questions. He, in turn, answered with generous detail. From that topic, they wandered into a discussion of dysfunctional capillary action during edema and into the alternative purposes of assorted biles. Then they swung back to debate the possibilities of what remained inconclusive from the pancreatic study that required further study.

At the end of the hearty discussion that to Leah was as medicinal as it was medical, Dr. Elliot slapped his hands together with glee. "Well, Dr. Maays, I can see by the nature of your questions that you have an extensive understanding of the human body."

"Pity if I did not by now, after all these years of practicing medicine, Dr. Elliot," she said dryly.

"Yes, of course. You know, I would benefit from having an assistant in my research. Would you be interested in such a position? Of course, the position would involve working with me, if you can tolerate that." He chuckled at his deprecating humor.

The magnificent offer caused something to sparkle within Leah, and for a moment, she saw all the doors in the universe swinging open for her. Suspended within the possibility, she and Dr. Elliot beamed smiles at one another.

"It is well known," added Dr. Elliot with a sweeping glance over her dress, "there is no substitution for competency, especially when accompanied by the charms you exhibit, Dr. Maays."

Leah's bubble of elation popped as she focused on Dr. Elliot's unexpected flirtation. He might have meant it innocently. Perhaps as small talk. She glanced at the flowers. Was he looking for a professional assistant or someone to court? Or some convenient combination of both? Would he be willing to publish his research with her name on it as well? Leah scanned the cover of the paper he had just presented to her. It had only his name on it. She could not remember whether his other papers shared credit with anyone else.

A knock on the front door usurped their attention and prevented Leah from having to answer immediately, as enticing as the proposition seemed. Almost blanching with trepidation, she wondered what she would do if Charlie Hunt was at the door. Leah exhaled with gratitude when Martha came bustling out of the kitchen to spare them the interruption.

Martha opened the door and immediately said, "She's busy now."

Leah relaxed. Even Martha could fathom that combining Charlie Hunt's inarticulateness with Dr. Elliot erudition would produce a chemistry that might exterminate her.

"Thank you, ma'am. Please tell Mrs. Maays I came to see her."

The soft tenor of Duncan's voice lifted Leah from her chair. An unanticipated relief flushed though her. She had not been able to put behind her refusal to allow Duncan to walk her home and had been inexplicably consumed with worry about having offended him. Each time she thought about their conversation, she concluded that nothing meriting remorse had passed between them, but she still carried feelings that something had.

"Please excuse me," she said to Dr. Elliot as she abandoned him.

In her urgency, she bumped into the wobbly side table, causing more water to splash out of the pitcher. Grabbing the doorframe to catch herself from tripping, she swung into the hallway, barely holding on. Her skirts swooshed around her as she and Duncan aligned their sight through the opening of the door Martha was closing.

"Mr. Shay!"

Duncan's pupils enlarged at the sound of her voice. He pushed his hand against the door, forcing it open and unintentionally bumping Martha aside.

"Mrs. Maays."

Martha turned her back to Duncan, blocking his entrance into the house and glared at Leah. "Ain't you busy?"

"Auntie, I am sure Mr. Shay would like to join us in the parlor. We have such good company today."

Martha gaped and did not budge. Leah stepped up to her aunt and lowered her voice. "Or perhaps we should ask Dr. Elliot to join us on the porch."

Martha opened and closed her mouth without emitting a sound while twisting her ire into her apron skirt. She closed her eyes, gave her head a tight shake, and stomped to the kitchen. On her way, she apparently recovered her ability to speak and, in scathing words that were not entirely inaudible, berated Leah for allowing convicts to roam freely in the house to steal things and kill people. The kitchen door slammed behind her with a definitiveness that made Leah's shoulders creep up.

Leah was only vaguely aware of her dry mouth when she turned to face Duncan. He was staring at the kitchen door, standing rigidly as if his body were holding up a wall of rocks that might bury him if he stepped forward.

"Please come in, Mr. Shay," said Leah as soon as she found her voice. Her mouth was parched, and she was afraid she was croaking. If Duncan could brave such a reception, he deserved the benefit of being received, although she would not be surprised if he turned around and left.

Extending her hand, she pretended he was already in the hallway. "May I please take your hat, Mr. Shay?"

Duncan hesitated before stepping over the threshold. Keeping one eye on the kitchen door, he handed Leah his hat, took off his jacket, and hung it on the coat rack. He bowed in formal greeting.

Leah curtsied. "I value your company, Mr. Shay, and I am glad you have come to visit. Please come into the parlor."

He answered almost inaudibly. "Mighty grateful, Mrs. Maays."

In the parlor, Duncan stepped around the flamboyant bouquet that obscured the side table. He took a moment to notice Dr. Elliot reposing behind it on the settee.

Duncan tensed. "Don't mean to interrupt your visit, ma'am."

"Not at all. Please join us. Have you met Dr. Nathaniel Elliot? Dr. Elliot, this is Mr. Duncan Shay, master carpenter and cabinetmaker. Dr. Elliot is Dr. Haloway's nephew from Boston. Dr. Elliot is visiting with them after lecturing in Edith's Bay."

"Sir." Duncan bowed his head.

Dr. Elliot stood and nodded to Duncan. "Please, Dr. Maays, feel free to attend to whatever Mr. Shay is here to fix. I shall be happy to await your return."

"Mr. Shay is visiting, Dr. Elliot, just as you are. Won't you please sit down, Mr. Shay?"

The men eyed each other, taking in all manner of the other's dress and insignias of social status. Duncan, unpretentious as a sparrow, wore a simple ribbon tie and was in shirtsleeves with rolled cuffs that revealed square wrists. Dr. Elliot was fully buttoned on all fronts and trussed up to his neck in a jacket, newly reminding Leah of a stuffed chicken.

She realized they would not sit unless she was seated and dropped herself into a chair, hoping that giving the men permission to sit would ease the tension. To her relief, Duncan settled into the rocking chair across from her. Dr. Elliot slipped back into the settee and in a sulk, crossed his legs away from Duncan.

By degrees, the meaning of the sulk settled into Leah. Until now she had not imagined their discourse about biles and pancreatic transmissions to the liver was any indication that Dr. Elliot was courting her. Their conversation had felt more of an informal interview for the position he had offered.

Leah turned to Duncan. "Coffee and cake, Mr. Shay?"

"Yes, please. Mighty grateful, Dr. Maays. You make the cake, ma'am?"

"I am afraid not. That credit goes to Mrs. Cobb." A massive sense of relief swept through her when Duncan accepted a slice of Martha's cake.

Dr. Elliot began fidgeting when Duncan reached down to pet the cat that wandered into the parlor and began rubbing against his ankles. Duncan put down the plate and picked up the cat, letting it stretch in his hand like pulled taffy. For Leah, everything was moving in slow motion, as if they were trapped in aspic.

"And what is your name, ma'am?" Duncan asked the cat.

"Ichabod," said Leah, amused that Duncan addressed the cat directly.

"See. You be man, not woman. No offense meant, sir." Duncan lowered the cat to the floor. As he looked up, he scanned Leah's dress and settled his gaze on her face.

Leah absorbed his look. Duncan Shay was a powerful man. His reserve held people at a distance, but his eyes, the color of dark caramels, hinted of a gentle forbearance. Under his gaze, she wanted to snap her fingers and make Dr. Elliott disappear.

When Duncan withdrew to bear the brunt of Dr. Elliot's assessing stare, Leah broke the silence. "Dr. Elliot has been regaling me with information from this most recent research. But I cannot imagine the topics being interesting to anyone who is not in the medical profession. I am afraid physicians are a very boring lot. Dr. Elliot, Mr. Shay is extremely well versed in period styles of furnishings and the properties of all sorts of woods, including red and white ones."

Duncan's eyelids flickered at the private joke about red and white woods from when she ordered the bookshelf. He pressed his lips together but did not quite form a smile.

Dr. Elliot leaned forward, addressing Duncan slowly and loudly as if Duncan did not fully comprehend language. "You, are, a, carpenter? Yes?"

"Master cabinetmaker, sir."

"I do not suppose that line of work puts you in contact with philosophers?"

"Read some dead ones, sir."

"May I inquire whether you are then familiar with Plato?"

"Some, sir."

"How extraordinary," said Dr. Elliot. He relaxed into the

settee and smiled at Leah. "I trust you have read Phaedrus, Dr. Maays?"

"Around the time Plato wrote it, I fear. It has been very long." *Where had Duncan read Plato?*

Dr. Elliot turned to Duncan. "Have you ever attempted to construct a bird from wood?"

"Not following you, sir."

"No, perhaps not. Dr. Maays probably remembers the part in Phaedrus where Plato writes that the wing is the corporeal element that is most akin to the divine because it can soar and carry that which naturally gravitates downward. Among philosophers there has been speculation that Plato once constructed a wooden bird in order to understand the soul."

Wanting to drift away from the topic of Plato's writings before everyone fell asleep from boredom, Leah said, "I am afraid I have forgotten the details of Phaedrus. Poor Plato, I thought I knew him well."

"Is Plato poor Yorick's cousin, ma'am?" asked Duncan.

Leah blinked at Duncan. She had not expected literary humor from him. Duncan was full of surprises! She struggled to control her laughter, born not so much from the joke as from delight.

Duncan leaned back in the rocking chair and drew a deep, slow breath as his sight settled again on Leah's face. Dr. Elliot rearranged himself in the settee and cleared his throat. Leah turned to him. She had forgotten about him.

"Wood bird, sir," prompted Duncan.

"How would Plato best construct a wooden bird so as to determine whether it had a soul? Could one determine that if it flapped its wings, it had a soul? I am speculating that you, knowing something of carpentry, might have some insight into this matter."

Duncan rocked back and forth. "You recall if Plato put hinges on the wings, sir?"

"Hinges on the wings!" Dr. Elliot snapped his fingers and laughed so hard he started to cough and had to cover his mouth with his napkin. "Is that your resolution? Very clever! That is indeed very clever, Mr. Shay. I see why Dr. Maays enjoys your company. Indeed, Plato himself would have benefited from your expertise in the construction of wooden birds."

Dr. Elliot's laughter turned into a high-pitched clucking that mortified Leah. She began to see the man as a complex jigsaw puzzle that was missing a piece. Perhaps several pieces.

Dr. Elliot's laughter withered into a hiccup before Duncan spoke again. "Souls need wings like they need belly buttons, sir. Won't find a soul in a wood bird unless it wants to flap wood wings. Then you best have hinges so it won't die from want. Sir."

Dr. Elliot flattened under Duncan's somberness. He put down his coffee cup to defend himself from Ichabod, who was stretching against his leg and about to claw his knee. Leah stood and clapped. The cat shot into the hallway, bumping against the side table with the bouquet and making the table sway dangerously as more water splashed out of the pitcher and trickled to the floor.

Leah grabbed the edge of the table to prevent it from collapsing and began to wipe the top with a napkin even as the table continued to sway and the pitcher to splash water. By now, the bouquet had become an enormous nuisance like a big, unruly dog that constantly sheds.

She grabbed another napkin as Duncan rose from the rocking chair and knelt beside her to reach under the table to the base of the leg. His cheek brushed lightly against her skirt as he moved his fingers until the table stopped sway-ing. Then he stood and dabbed the water droplets from the back of his hand with his handkerchief.

"Perhaps a larger vase is advisable," said Dr. Elliot.

Duncan cast a discreet side look at Dr. Elliot. He began brushing yellow pollen off his trousers.

Leah handed him the last clean napkin. "I am so sorry, Mr. Shay."

"No harm, ma'am. Thank you." He took the napkin from her and noticed the flower petals on his shoes. As he bent to pick them off, several other petals floated off his hair into his coffee cup.

Leah choked down another laugh. Duncan's hair, coarse as a crow's nest, was a repository of all matter of tiny things. "It is hopeless, Mr. Shay. Quite hopeless."

The bouquet was now a mass of ragged flowers, some looking quite bald after having shed their petals. Duncan bent at the waist and focused on a corner of the table. Leah followed his gaze in time to see a plump spider skitter up its thread into the bouquet. They exchanged glances. Leah shut her eyes and clamped her mouth to keep from laughing.

"Good to know you're brave, Dr. Maays." Duncan raised one eyebrow and sat down. He faced Dr. Elliot and asked with a scholarly seriousness reminiscent of the solemnity at funerals, "What makes hiccups, sir?"

Leah clenched her body to control a sense of hilarity that threatened to discompose her. She contemplated leaving the room to gather herself.

Dr. Elliot pulled himself together in a mist of self-impor-tance. "Hiccups result from the irritation of the phrenic nerve in the diaphragm causing the glottis to close upon the orifice in the tracheae, and such sound—acknowledged in the vernacular as the hiccup—is emitted involuntarily."

"Thank you," said Duncan without a trace of contempt. "Sir."

For a moment Leah thought he was going to ask Dr. Elliot about the origins of flatulence, but he turned his attention back to her. "Been thinking about getting a cat like Ichabod, if Old Dog doesn't mind, Dr. Maays."

"Old Dog is Mr. Shay's dog," Leah explained to Dr. Elliot. "He came old."

"I say, do you remember dissecting those old dogs in Surgical, Dr. Maays?"

Leah's amusement vanished. The very thought of Duncan imagining her dissecting Old Dog made her want to shrivel up and die. Between Martha's reception and Dr. Elliot's choice of conversations, she wondered why Duncan had not yet bolted out of the house through a window.

To Leah's relief, Utterance came into the hall, stomping the mud of the fields from his boots. He nodded absent-mindedly to all as he hung his coat but did a double take when he saw Duncan sitting in Martha's parlor.

Duncan stood. "Sir."

Utterance nodded to Duncan and looked toward the kitchen. Not a sound was coming out of it. "Be easier to rest after church if God 'membered to tell them animals it be Sunday and made them all not hungry."

No one said anything.

"Auntie in the kitchen, Leah?"

"Yes, Uncle."

"It be safe in there?"

Leah released a little smile. "Probably not, Uncle. I wouldn't chance it."

"Then I be going upstairs."

Duncan stepped forward. "I was just taking my leave, sir."

"Uncle, will you please keep Dr. Elliot company for a moment while I see Mr. Shay to the door?"

"Dr. Elliot knows what makes hiccups, sir," Duncan volunteered.

"You do?" Utterance fixed his attention on Dr. Elliot like a barn owl on a mouse.

Tears swelled in Leah's eyes from the effort to not burst with laughter. She wanted to kill Duncan for making her want to laugh so hard, but she managed to say, "Please allow me to walk you to the door, Mr. Shay."

At the door, Duncan self-sufficiently took his hat and swung his jacket over his shoulder before he held the front door open. Unable to resist his expectation, Leah stepped out. They stood silently to one side of the parlor window, listening to Dr. Elliot explain the causes of hiccups to Utterance.

"Hiccups are the result of an irritation to the phrenic nerve—"

"Frenic? Dint know that be considered a medical ailment. Like them hiccups. They always come frenic. Learn something new every day," interrupted Utterance.

"No, sir. The phrenic nerve. It is the nerve that—"

Leah slunk to the other side of the porch and released the laughter percolating within her into her hands. Duncan followed, lilting with the lightness of his step. He leaned against the porch railing as Leah leaned against the house wall and stretched his long legs until they touched the hem of her skirt.

"Dr. Elliot is really very intelligent. He's quite illustrious in his field," Leah felt compelled to say when she calmed herself.

"Haven't said a word against him, ma'am."

"No, indeed you have not."

"Believe a man should present himself, ma'am."

"I see you've read Shakespeare, Mr. Shay," said Leah to redirect their conversation.

"Had good tutors, ma'am."

Tutors? "Have you read Chaucer?"

"Pardon, ma'am?"

"I meant Socrates."

"Read him some, ma'am."

Duncan patted his jacket and pulled from a pocket a triangular obelisk about the length of his hand and held it out to her. "Dr. Maays, would feel honored if you please accepted this flower from me for your kindness in taking care of my hand that day."

Searing with curiosity, Leah took the strange object from him and studied the long triangular form. The piece seemed made from one piece of wood, and even when she turned it in the sunlight, she could barely make out the joints along the edges. After her finger found a wind-up key recessed into the base, she noticed the small brass clasp near the apex.

Eager to solve the mystery, she flipped open the tip of the triangle as she would a hinged lid. An elaborate spiral resembling a flower popped up and began to rotate while the sounds of a Strauss waltz tinkled into the air, each note as delicate as an iridescent soap bubble.

Leah ran her fingers over the mysterious, musical pyramid. She understood nothing of its abstract design, seeing only the exquisite beauty of its craftsmanship in which every part was balanced against all other parts. It seemed entirely from another realm. Her attention swung between the exotic music box and Duncan.

"Mr. Shay, Did you make this?"

"Yes ma'am."

"Did you design it?"

"Yes ma'am."

"What is this wood?"

"Purplehart, ma'am."

"How did you make this?"

"I—"

"There aren't any nails!"

"Japanese joints, ma'am. They're hard to detect."

Leah tapped the glowing surface of the wood with her nail.

"Tung oil, ma'am. Five coats," said Duncan.

"This is exquisite!" Leah looked at Duncan, for the first time catching a glimpse of the real mystery about him. "Thank you so very much, Mr. Shay. This is absolutely beautiful. But I believe the real gift is that you made it."

By now, Duncan's face was set and unrevealing in all its aspects. Only the slight tension in his voice gave him away as the waltz continued flitting into the air.

"Will you honor me with this waltz, Dr. Maays?"

Leah looked down. She could not completely declare his past had no implications. Yes, he acknowledged it, almost collapsing under the angst of having to discuss it. All on her asking. But it was still a past.

She had witnessed Duncan lose his color and set his entire body into denying himself the satisfaction of sending Cory Baines flying through Hoburn's window. Now she suspected Cory Baines was certain Duncan would not strike him. Duncan had also not presumed the right of way when she slipped his arm next to her torso to tend to his hand— no gentleman ever would, but not everyone was a gentleman.

And what was she to do about the affinity between

them? She trusted it. Such affinity, however ill-defined at the moment, seemed worth exploring.

From the small incidents Leah itemized, the origins of her remorse stepped out. Duncan had done nothing wrong to deserve her refusals. If anything, he had been more correct and respectful to her than many others in town and most at medical institutions.

Leah nodded and raised her arms as if posing to dance. Duncan slipped one arm around her waist. She lowered one hand onto his shoulder. He raised his other arm and waited until she placed her other hand in his. They looked at each other and, for a moment, stood in the music without moving.

10

THE GAME

As usual, Leah was going about her life in the most mistaken way possible. One would think all the things that happened in Africa would have cured her of poor thinking, but no, fumed Martha. The girl persisted in her foolishness.

According to Mrs. Hoburn, Leah was spending as much time in the back room doctoring as she did out front tending customers. Cory Baines had been coming in every day with made-up maladies until Leah suggested he take a cure designed to fortify men's strength. That the cure ended up being a mild laxative that kept him away for days did not comfort Martha one bit.

Mrs. Groth was already going around town claiming no wonder Cory Baines was looking forward to becoming familiar with Leah because Leah had permission to touch men everywhere. Why Mrs. Hoburn had not already fired her was beyond Martha. Mrs. Hoburn was not known to be tolerant of deviant women, and Leah was certainly carrying on like one.

Cory Baines was a fool, but at least he was not

dangerous like Duncan Shay, who'd taken to walking Leah home after work for the past month or more or since Leah had been fool enough to let him into the house. That pleased Martha even less. The man was not likely to give Leah the choice to not become familiar with him. Already several people in town had mentioned it to her—some in precautionary tones, others in an attempt to extract further information. Undertones and speculations marked all their words.

Leah was being ruined word by word, and the girl was so obstinate she didn't even see it happening. Or didn't care. Leah thought being a doctor excused her from behaving proper.

For a while, Martha sent Utterance into town, wanting to see if the talk might provoke him into some action. But men's talk was never about anything important, at best about hardware and the price of feed, at worst about politics. Utterance always returned as unperturbed and ignorant as when he left. And as a result of his inaction, Leah announced that morning that she was going riding with Duncan Shay.

Riding! And by themselves, no less, because Utterance said riding with young people would land him in a coffin.

God knew Leah could not be dissuaded by mere mortals from doing anything she wanted to do. Just when Martha thought Leah acquired some common sense, the girl eloped and moved off to Africa to live with cannibals and lions under a coconut tree. Then, having barely escaped with her life and a suitcase, Leah was now unsuitable for anything except cutting cloth at Hoburn's—when she wasn't in the back with diseased people. And being walked home by Duncan Shay. No wonder respectable men like Charlie Hunt and Henry Moore were terrified of her.

Today, Duncan Shay had the audacity to stop and continue talking with Leah right in front of the house, pointing at various corners and windows. Martha was certain he was using Leah to study the house so he could break into it some night when they were asleep to rob and kill them all.

He stood very close to Leah, and Martha had to restrain herself from marching out and flattening his skull with her cast iron skillet. But he bid Leah goodbye without any further advances and went away—smiling splendidly, no less. It was well known Duncan Shay did not smile, and Martha couldn't figure why Leah allowed him to pull such familiarity with her.

Leah looked just fine, all smiles and brightness, when she waved goodbye to him, but she went straight into the kitchen and washed her hands with a vigor that made Martha think it was best not to interfere with her. Even after they sat to eat, Leah remained unpleasantly short, with single-word answers.

Martha prepared herself, aligning all her arguments in case Leah again suggested inviting Duncan Shay into the house. That, Martha would not tolerate again. Bad enough he caught her by surprise and got in once. Vermin always had ways of getting into houses. Martha ran her arguments over and over in her head until she finally felt up to matching Leah's stubbornness, but Leah's question caught her completely off guard.

"When did Mr. Shay build the porch?"

"Dun matter," said Martha, battening down her hatches.

Utterance looked up from his plate. "He use't to pick apples when he first came here."

Why Utterance was saying this, Martha did not know.

She didn't want Leah knowing Duncan Shay had ever set foot in the orchard with their permission.

"Mr. Shay, a picker?" Leah put down her fork and looked into the distance.

Martha sighed. Nothing in the world required as much thought as Leah gave to everything. The girl spent her time rearranging common sense into nonsense.

"Use't to pick apples like a madman. Your Auntie and me use't to say we could still make the harvest if only him showed up. That right, Martha?"

Martha sloshed a ladle of stew into Utterance's bowl with hopes that he would fill his mouth and stop spouting foolishness. She slammed the bowl of pickled beets in front of Leah.

"Yea," continued Utterance. "That boy—well, been a while since he been a boy—probably wasn't one even then —he kept himself goin' on bruised apples and taters for a real long time. Lived in the woods 'til it got too cold. Use't to sneak in the bunkhouse on cold nights and make fires in the stove to keep himself from freezing. Dun know how he be doing now. Hoburn says he appear be doing fine. Pays his credit on time. Bought the old barn from him, too, and made it good again."

"Cider." Martha grabbed Leah's glass and filled it without waiting for an answer.

"Then one day—you 'member that day, Martha?" continued Utterance.

"No, I most certainly do not, Utterance."

"Well, one day he was collecting his pay, and he sat on the porch railing like was his habit when the whole thing gave way. Railing went out. Pillar went out. Roof came down. That whole section right there outside the parlor window? Bash! Right fortunate he ain't got himself kilt. Turns out we had ourselves a mighty wood ant infestation we ain't knowed about. Dun know how you can forget that, Martha. You was terrified when them things started flying."

"Ain't worth remembering, Utterance."

"Well, he just got up from under all that mess. Had scrapes and scratches all over himself. Purple goose eggs on his forehead. Real lucky he ain't got kilt. Know what he says?" Utterance chuckled. "He says, 'Sir, now that you darn near kilt me with your porch, you might well let me build you one that dun fall down all the time.' Then he declared himself a carpenter, said he had references and all. Showed me some of them, he did. Seemed like people liked his work. Well, we felt real bad, so we let him. Figure most men can build a porch half decent, and if he built porches like he pickt apples, we figured on having a new one in an hour."

"We dint know he was a coldblooded murderer back then," said Martha.

"I understand the death was an accident, Auntie."

"That's right, Leah. And all them witnesses that saw him killing and the judge, they all be feeble-minded, blind, deaf, and mute."

"Auntie, he told me—"

"Leah, you got a hard face and no bounds. What you be doing discussing that with him? What you be doing talking to him at all?"

Leah turned to Utterance. "How long did he pick apples?"

"Few seasons. Pickt apples the first year he got his shop going. Maybe the second too."

Martha snorted. "Apple-pickin' coldblooded murderer. Leah, you be a grown woman, but you got the common sense of a boiled carrot. You be mighty extra careful. I dun ever want Emma Groth a-coming to this house investigatin' why you been taken advantage of—or worse, why you ain't alive no more 'cause of him."

"Uncle, you don't think Duncan Shay is an evil man, do you?"

Martha interrupted Utterance's response by shaking her finger at Leah. "Good men don't go robbing banks and killing people. If you ain't read the Bible, then common sense should tell you that, if you got any!"

"That ain't ever going to be something for me to judge, Leah," Utterance managed to say.

"Uncle, you go out of your way not to like him. Don't deny it."

"Ain't that, Leah. Ain't that at all. To speak the truth, never had a problem with him. Worked hard. Never tried to cheat on his apple counts. Itemized every nail he use't on the porch. Even brought his own wood when he made fires in the bunkhouse, and you cain't blame a man for not wanting to freeze to death. He ain't be the first man to pick apples after jail. Thems come in plenty during harvest. But I ain't ever had one who kilt a man, mostly 'cause those get hanged. But just 'cause he got lucky dun mean there ain't something broke in there. Cain't control when that sort of thing rises up again."

"Utterance, don't be talking like a fool," warned Martha. "That man been in prison. What else you need to know? If he acts up again, chances be good Leah will be right there next to him, she will."

Leah straightened her back. "I think you should both know I shall always be an acquaintance of some sort with Mr. Shay. There's more to him than meets the eye."

"Yeah, I feared that," said Utterance. "I feared that. Been watching both of you for a while now. Well, Leah, you be a grown woman. Seen more of the world than me. But you be wise 'round Duncan Shay. You be real wise. I dun want no news from Emma Groth either."

"Common sense of a boiled carrot..." muttered Martha.

THE NEXT DAY when Leah came home from work alongside Duncan, she did not expect to see Utterance sitting on the porch. He was wearing what she considered the first omen of autumn: two flannel shirts of completely different plaids, one tucked into his pants as a shirt, the other worn over the first as a jacket.

Duncan's loose stride tightened the moment he saw Utterance. His hands became still and clenched as he drew closer to the house. By the time he stood in front of the porch, he had lost the lightness he'd had while coming up the hill.

Utterance folded the newspaper he'd been reading and looked over Duncan. "Evenin'."

"Sir."

"Hello, Uncle." Leah smiled. Perhaps she could slip Duncan on the porch for a visit. "Mr. Shay, would you like—"

"Leah, Auntie just mentioned she be needin' your help. You want to look in on her real quick?" interrupted Utterance.

Duncan shifted subtly and positioned his feet inches from the bottom step of the porch. Utterance glanced at Duncan's feet, and Leah knew he had not missed how Duncan shifted the onus of an invitation entirely onto him in the subtle move.

"Look! Crows chasing a hawk!" said Leah, pointing over

the fields to distract the men. How quickly things had gone wrong. She needed time to think.

Utterance and Duncan looked over the field at the little black crosses gliding over the apple trees until they disappeared amidst the forest trees. The tension broke a little, but Duncan's feet never moved.

Leah forced herself to smile. Everything was so difficult. If she pushed the issue and failed to get Duncan an invitation, the humiliation for him would be too great. The best way to spare him was to let him go.

She turned to Duncan as graciously as she could. "Thank you very much for your company, Mr. Shay. It was very kind of you to walk me home." *Was that too sudden?*

Duncan stepped away from the porch. He bowed to her before slipping one hand into his pants pocket and held up the other one in a gesture of farewell to Utterance.

Utterance relaxed into his chair when Duncan turned away. "You play checkers, Mr. Shay?"

Leah froze in mid-step.

Duncan turned. "Me, sir?"

"Well, I already know Leah dun play."

Duncan looked to Leah for guidance. Leah widened her eyes and twitched her shoulders into a tiny shrug.

"Yes sir, I play checkers," Duncan answered warily.

"You up for a game?"

Duncan placed one foot on the bottom step and stepped up, momentarily supporting his body's weight on one leg as if testing whether the porch step was booby trapped to collapse under him. Then he brought his other foot down and decisively climbed onto the porch.

"Oh, Uncle's very good at checkers. You are in for quite the challenge, Mr. Shay."

Leah gathered her skirt to sit down and join them. Utterance threw her a thunderous look with a small head shake. In response, Leah moved back. "Oh, let me check on Auntie first."

Duncan sat down without looking at her, and Leah recognized that whatever was coming was intended to happen without her. Duncan could block out bombs when something was important to him. Still reluctant to leave, she slipped through the front door, leaving it ajar, and came face to face with Martha holding Utterance's revolver.

"Auntie? What are you doing?"

"Your uncle wants a word with him. But a man like him can do in your uncle like a twig, Utterance being slow and all. If any trouble comes up, I'm going to slip this to Utterance through the parlor window. Duncan Shay be lucky I dun use it on him myself."

A furious boil-over hissed from the kitchen. Martha shoved the revolver into the parlor desk drawer, leaving the drawer open.

"You call me if there be trouble," instructed Martha over her shoulder as she ran into the kitchen. "Or give that to Utterance through the window."

Leah threw herself into a chair. The house was full of lunacy! She slammed the drawer shut with her foot.

She settled in to listen to the men's voices drift from the porch into the parlor through the open window and began to fret. Duncan had sealed his history so tightly nothing could pry it open without his rare consent, as she feared Utterance would try to do. She leaned forward to catch what she could of the conversation.

Utterance was pulling out a board and a bag of checkers from beside his chair. "Red or blue?"

"Doesn't matter, sir."

"Blue go first. I'll give you that. Two out of three?"

"Thank you, sir."

Utterance set up the board, and they began the first game. The first moves went swiftly with Utterance occasionally tapping a checker against the board with unnecessary loudness as he jumped Duncan's pieces. He announced the conclusion of the first game with a hearty and tactless, "Ha! See, you lost this one."

Leah peeked out the parlor window. Duncan sat with his palms on his parted knees, elbows jutting out, undeniably impressed. Utterance was setting up the board again. She picked up the chair to move it closer toward the window and catch more of their conversation.

"Mighty grand move, sir."

"Ain't it, eh?"

At least things were cordial, although not much talking had occurred. The second game took forever because Duncan, now familiar with his opponent, was trying to win. Leah was driven to listen, although by now she was so anxious she almost preferred not to hear.

"You be up for apple picking? Season's a-coming up fast," Utterance said pleasantly.

"Mighty grateful, sir, but not this year."

"Dun look like we need a new porch."

Duncan's chair creaked as he shifted to check the structure. "Not for a while, sir."

"How be your business? Hear Joey comes regular to your place."

"Strong, sir. Got more work than I can handle." Slightly more relaxed, Duncan jumped one of Utterance's checkers.

"That ain't got you nowhere," mumbled Utterance, now jumping two of Duncan's checkers. "You sell mostly in Edith's Bay?"

"Yes sir. Good market there."

"Where'd you learnt your carpentry? 'Member you showed me some good references."

Duncan paused to move a checker before answering. "Institute of Craft. Sir."

"Ain't heared of it. It around here?"

"Edith's Bay. Sir."

"That's 'round here. That where you grew up?"

"Good player, sir. Where'd you learn?"

"My sister, Ruth. Leah's mother, bless her soul. Ain't no one could beat her. Not even me. That girl was a ball of fire, just like Leah. She was younger than me. Figure I be teaching her things, but I learnt more from her. Figure I go before her, but that was different too. We finished raising Leah when she went."

"My condolences, sir."

"How 'bout yourself?"

Duncan remained silent, seemingly engrossed in developing a strategy. He slid a checker onto another square.

Utterance jumped the piece. "Who taught you checkers?"

"Brother. Sir."

"Older?"

"Yes sir."

Utterance glanced up at the little bits of hard silence slipping like wedges between Duncan's words. "Ain't usual to get that good on brothers. Who else you play with?"

"Mostly brother. Sir."

"No sisters?"

"No sir."

"You still play with him?"

The chair creaked as Duncan leaned forward. "You can just come to the point, Mr. Cobb."

Utterance slid a checker into place. "What point's that?"

"About Dr. Maays. Sir."

The edge in Duncan's voice was so hard Leah sat up and leaned closer to the window.

"What 'bout her?"

"Dr. Maays's safe with me, sir. No harm's ever coming to her from me or anyone else when she's with me. Be important you trust that. Sir."

Utterance's chair squeaked as he leaned back and matched Duncan's stare. "Figure I be needing to trust you on that one. Dun seem she be intent on giving up your company."

"Be mighty grateful you doing so, sir. Be easier on both of us. Dr. Maays's in no danger from me. Give you my word on that. Sir." Duncan fixed his eyes on the checkerboard. The silence between the two men stretched.

"Who goes, sir?" Duncan finally asked.

"Still your turn."

Duncan moved a checker. Without fanfare, Utterance followed with a few jumps, then swept the checkers off the board.

Leah almost toppled out of the window at the sound of checkers being gathered. She had not heard Utterance's victory cry. Perhaps he lost? Utterance never lost, but then, this game was not about checkers.

She tiptoed out of the parlor, looking toward the kitchen in case Martha came charging out in her lunacy, brandishing a cleaver. Leah slipped onto the porch where she found Utterance and Duncan taking a respite from each other by gazing at the apple trees.

She rested her hand on Duncan's shoulder. "May I ask how the games went?"

"Warned me well, Dr. Maays," said Duncan as he looked at Utterance. "Mighty hard player, sir."

"Nowhere hard as you, Mr. Shay." Utterance wrinkled his brow and seemed to let go of the matter between them. "Dun help your game you looking all over the porch all the time."

"Build some things on it different now, sir."

"What for? Still standing."

"You play checkers, Dr. Maays?" asked Duncan. He reoriented the board toward her. "You play as well as your uncle, ma'am?"

"I am afraid I play as poorly as Uncle plays well."

Duncan set up the board for another game, but within five minutes, most of her checkers were in his possession. She stuck out her tongue at Utterance when he covered his face and shook his head with mock shame.

Duncan raised an eyebrow. "Mighty charitable of you, Dr. Maays, letting me win that game."

"I couldn't win a game of checkers against a mouse. Not even if it figured out how to push the checkers on the board."

"Intelligent woman like yourself, ma'am?"

"I have other virtues, Mr. Shay."

"Yes, ma'am. Certain of that. But I suspect not many got to do with checkers."

With a new softness in his eyes, Duncan held the bag open as Leah dropped the checkers into it, stretching the drawstrings as if to play cat's cradle. She unwound the strings from his fingers, taking the opportunity to touch his hands. Duncan stretched his fingers until his hands quivered at her touch, then folded his hands in his lap.

His response reminded Leah of how a cat arches its back and made her wonder whether anyone ever touched Duncan. He still kept a respectful distance from her on their daily walks from the town to the orchard. They had not even held hands.

"You ride like you play checkers, Dr. Maays?"

"I am much better at riding, Mr. Shay."

"That's a relief, ma'am." Another raised eyebrow accompanied the dry humor.

The front door opened, abruptly releasing the smells of dinner over the porch. Martha stepped outside. She removed her apron and dried her hands on it until it was wrinkled beyond recognition, glaring at Duncan the entire time.

Duncan rose from the chair. "Evening, ma'am. Game of checkers?"

"I dun play checkers," Martha declared as if he had invited her to a game of strip poker.

"Sorry to hear that, ma'am. Fine game, sir. Thank you." He nodded brusquely to Leah as if he had run out of words.

"Thank you, Mr. Shay," said Leah, marveling at his graciousness in the light of her aunt's continuing rudeness.

A familiar blankness curtained his face, and stillness subdued the recent animation in his hands. Without another word, he stepped off the porch and began his solitary trek back to town.

Leah wondered what he thought when he entombed himself behind that blank expression. Did he suspend himself, safely disconnected, until he could walk away? And what did he do after he walked away? She looked through the window into the dining room where dinner was served and felt like a flea for not being able to invite him to the table as she would have anyone else.

When Duncan was sufficiently far away from the house, Martha took off her apron and went back into the house.

Leah lowered her voice. "How did the checkers go?"

Utterance filled his lungs as if breathing for the first time since Duncan left. "Never seen a man march right up and state an issue without a hint of mercy and be done so quick. Checkers be darned. That commands respect. But he's got bits, mostly having to do with that family o' his, that needs handling like raw eggs. I'd say he be real tender in those spots. Dun like discussing it one bit. He ever tell you what happened there?"

Leah shook her head. "I don't ask. He tells me what he can."

Through a patch of sparse trees, she watched little strips of Duncan. Her soul knew something about him the rest of her did not, something he had not told her, something the town gossip had not enunciated and the newspapers had failed to report. There was more to Duncan than met her eye, and none of it felt evil.

"You eating?" Martha called impatiently, as she held open the door. "It's getting cold."

"I'm coming, Auntie," said Leah, leaving Utterance on his own.

Duncan Shay was... Was... The thought frittered away the closer Leah got to it.

11
———

THE WORK SHIRT

On the days they went riding on the dry flood plain by the river's edge, Leah practiced patience while waiting for Duncan to reveal bits about his history. The bits turned up anywhere in a conversation like rum raisins in a cake, but she had to wait for them.

Riding side by side, they made their voices just loud enough to carry above the horses' shuffling and the river's burble. Their pace was luxuriously unhurried, as if eternity belonged to them, and they let themselves be lulled into a lavish sense of privacy.

"Your uncle's hills look prettier these days than the coffee farms in Kenya, Dr. Maays," said Duncan as he looked across the river at the hillside of Utterance's apple trees, where farm hands were picking the first fruits of the fall harvest.

"May I ask how you know about coffee farms in Kenya, Mr. Shay?"

"Visited once, ma'am. My father was a coffee merchant. Think this is prettier, though."

He seemed so comfortable delivering this statement,

Leah suspected he had planned to tell her long before he saddled his horse that morning. Having a father who was a coffee merchant explained much of his good breeding. Duncan had probably been raised to have all kinds of formal manners and good tastes that she did not know until she went to Edith's Bay Academy for Young Ladies, as her mother had arranged for her to be able to do after her death.

"Don't suppose your uncle would appreciate me looking at his trees with an eye for carving wood, Dr. Maays?"

"Oh, he wouldn't mind so long as your cabinets bore fruit after you made them. Were you helping your father with his business while you were in Kenya?"

"Was too young, ma'am."

"Did your brother go too?"

"Yes. Ma'am."

He began to emanate distance, as he always did when she asked about his family. Perhaps they had died in Kenya, just as Titus and William had in Ghana. Africa was full of illnesses, some so mysterious only the locals had names for them.

Leah changed the subject. "Before I went to the university, Auntie insisted that Uncle teach me to waltz. She said it was an Important Social Skill. Can you just hear Auntie saying that? Well! Uncle has no sense of rhythm. He had me thinking waltzing was some esoteric convolution I would never master. I could not make sense of the dance until I finally saw someone else dance it. I don't know why, but later when I took physics and the subject became difficult, I always thought of Uncle teaching me to waltz and how I learned it only by looking at it from a different point of view. Do you know, I had to argue mightily to get into the class because they did not think a woman could comprehend physics? Then they made me sit behind a screen because they thought a woman was too distracting to the men. Tell me, Mr. Shay, are men really so feeble?"

"Depends on the woman, ma'am. Suspect a woman who understands physics can bring some men to their knees." Duncan was now grinning to himself.

"How did you learn to waltz?"

Duncan looked up, fixing his gaze on the horizon. "Mother. Ma'am."

Leah looked away. She had asked the wrong question. Her vague understanding of Duncan included two rules: Don't ask much about his family. Don't ask about how he learned to work wood.

She found herself concocting an epic sea tragedy, an extravagant scenario during which waves churned with coffee beans as a clipper sank and everyone except Duncan drowned. He was rescued and sent to an orphanage where he was taught carpentry. That might explain how the son of a coffee merchant would end up in a trade.

When the path narrowed, Duncan dismounted first and placed his hands around her waist to steady her dismount. He hovered until she handed him the reins, after which he stepped away and busied himself with the horses.

Had he wanted to kiss her? Any other man would have done so by now. Tried, at least. He hadn't kissed her the day they waltzed on the porch, but they barely completed one minute of the dance before the music box ran out of music. He thanked her graciously, bid her a good evening, and left.

Cautious to the teeth, Duncan had yet to act, but the impulse was there. Yes, it was there. She could sense it when he was close to her. Or perhaps she was projecting her desires onto him.

They walked a bit down the path in silence before she spoke again. "You seem preoccupied, Mr. Shay."

"Me, ma'am? Why?"

"I am not certain. Sometimes I believe you are the divine source of all worry in the universe. I become concerned for you."

"You worry I'm worrying, ma'am?"

"Oh, you." Leah turned up her nose playfully and walked ahead. Duncan could not be rushed into revealing anything.

He kept a short distance behind her but eventually caught up. "You got preference for being called Dr. Leah, ma'am? Keep hearing that in town."

"Dr. Maays is my professional preference. But Dr. Leah is fine, especially in West Edith's Bay. As long as both are spoken with respect."

"Would honor me greatly if you addressed me as Duncan, ma'am."

Leah stopped walking to enjoy the moment. "I would be delighted, Duncan. Thank you."

Outwardly, he looked perfectly collected, a model of composure, but tension hardened his features. Duncan nodded briskly. With a gallant sweep of his arm, he invited her to continue walking.

"And will you please address me as Leah?" she asked when he seemed to have lost all hope.

Duncan unfurled a smile that cascaded throughout his bearing. For a moment, he tucked his chin and could only set his sight on her in glances.

"I would be mighty honored, Leah," he said with a staunch formality that did not distract from his smile.

Again, he gestured to resume the walk, although now he held out his hand so she could place hers in it. Leah smiled graciously but did not touch him, uncertain what she would feel if she did. Duncan gave no indication that he noticed and slowed his stride to match hers.

"Are you still searching for an assistant?" Leah asked after they walked a bit more.

"Hmm. Can't get anybody out here but dolts, ma'am."

"Perhaps you are being too picky."

"You too? Joey the carrier claims I'm finicky. Can't get Henry Moore to disagree with him. Now you."

"Well, how accomplished does a person have to be to do rough shaping? I think even I can make a square piece of wood round on a lathe."

"One showed me tenon joints you could squeeze a cow through. Another showed me varnish with streaks thick as frost heaves. Had one make the ugliest repair I've ever seen on a bucket. And showed it to me with heaping pride." Duncan shook his head. "Can't have that coming out of my shop, ma'am."

"Does a bucket repair have to be beautiful?"

"Shouldn't make the bucket look like it'll leak more than before it got fixed, ma'am. Work too hard to have some dolt ruin everything."

"Your pieces are truly exceptional, Duncan."

The path had forced them into single file, and Leah now looked behind her to find Duncan as she had been hearing him, throwing small branches and stones into the river. He appeared not to have heard her comment at all. Duncan rarely acknowledged compliments.

But a moment later, he said, "Just make furniture, Leah."

Leah twirled around and stopped. He put his hands on her shoulders to steady himself after walking into her.

"Duncan, please. Morris designs furniture. Limbert makes furniture. Montgomery Ward sells furniture. You.

Make. Beauty. You do not just make beautiful things. You create beauty, the quality itself! You are exceptional. Please accept it."

He looked as if she had just attacked him with a stick and then slipped on a poker face. He released her shoulders and stepped back, his eyes flickering over her lips.

Yes, he was thinking about it. He approached everything with such caution, as if things might explode on him. Very wary of explosions, he was, even those that were not much more powerful than an unexpected compliment.

To release the tension, Leah smiled and looked at him from the tops of her eyes. "A touch obtuse, but exceptional, all the same."

Duncan ducked into his silence. They resumed walking. With backward glances, Leah watched him evaluate the stone ledge until he spotted a large, flat rock—a perfect perch for one person. He sprang toward it, landing solidly, and swung his arms in circles until he found his balance. Then he tucked his fingers between the buttons in his shirt with great pomp.

Leah laughed. "Napoleon at the battle of West Edith's Bay?"

With a chuckle and a smile, Duncan stretched out his arm and began walking on the ridge with an exaggerated jaunt. He was becoming increasingly playful around her, something Leah would not have predicted from watching his reserved presence in town.

She still was not certain what she wanted from him. She was not thinking about Titus every day now, but when she did, she felt not the debilitating grief of the recent past but a sadness that he was absent. Her sorrow for William never quite went away, although it had subsided to the point that she could now see Mary Corwal's youngest without having her soul crack. Her sorrow for William might ease, but it would never cease. Titus, she would always love but with equal sorrow.

Duncan's attentions were pulling her into a space between grief and desire. Neither sentiment would let the other step forward cleanly. Her draw to Duncan marched shamelessly in parallel to her sorrow for Titus, and neither seemed as bothered by the other as she was made guilty by both sentiments.

The muffled splash of a deer crossing the river caught her attention. She called out and pointed in the direction of the sound, but Duncan was...nowhere. Neither were any deer.

Puzzled to find herself alone, Leah looked around. Then, hearing a splash, she ran up to the ridge and threw herself belly down over a stone so she could see the water. It tilted under her before it slid into the water, missing Duncan by a yard. Duncan was floating toward the middle of the river, sputtering and splashing while trying to get his bearings. Not an inch of him was dry.

"Duncan! Are you all right?"

He shook his hair out of his face, blinked wildly, and raised his hand to indicate he was unharmed.

"Your hat! Your hat!"

The brown suede hat bobbed between two rocks before the current whisked it away through small rapids. Duncan smacked the surface of the water. By his expression, Leah knew he was muttering vile words as he stood waist deep in the river, blinking and dripping. Leah climbed closer to the river's edge and held out her hand before realizing she was not on sure footing and was on the verge of losing her balance.

"You there to help me out or for me to pull you in?" Duncan called.

"Help you out, silly."

Duncan shook his head at her offer and struggled against the current for his balance. He sloshed downstream until he found stable footing and hauled himself up by some bushes until he rolled himself over rocks onto the bank. Shaking water from his arms, he staggered to where Leah waited, now convulsing with laughter. Duncan dropped to the ground and began pulling off his boots and socks.

"Oh, Duncan, you poor thing."

"Don't seem so poor you can't stop laughing at me, ma'am," he said with remarkably good humor.

"I do not lose my compassion when I laugh."

"Should have pulled you in when I had the chance."

"You are too much of a gentleman."

"Got a bit of scoundrel in me, ma'am." Duncan flicked his fingers, lightly splattering her with water drops. He emptied his boots away from her, then he looked himself over. "Oh, mighty mess."

"You'll get chilled if you don't take off your shirt. This is no time to be proper, I'm afraid."

"Be fine. Leah."

Goosebumps already covered him because autumn breezes caused chills in everyone, especially the wet. One boot tipped over much too close to the water, and Duncan rolled on his stomach to grab it, having already donated his hat to the river. A burst of autumn wind plastered his shirt against his back, and even through the thick folds of wet cloth, Leah saw dark welts that ran like fat cords down the length of his back.

Whip marks! Duncan had undergone a whipping?

Nothing else left marks like that. Her laughter ended in a gasp.

At the sound of her gasp, Duncan became immobile, holding the boot at arm's length over the river. In one motion, he rolled over, glanced at her, and clenched his eyes. He withdrew into the densest silence Leah had ever sensed, a silence that could roll the universe into a little ball.

She sat beside him and patted the blood from a scrape of brambles on his hand with her handkerchief. "Duncan, it's not you. It's that someone would do such a thing to you. It's not you."

Duncan gave no sign he'd heard her.

"I will slip my shawl over you. Please remove your shirt when you are ready. No one can see you here. Everything shall be discreet."

Even before he opened his eyes, Leah felt the density of his apprehension. By now, he was shivering incessantly, and any gust made his teeth knock. Leah draped her shawl over his shoulders and resumed sitting next to him. When the wind gusted again, he quaked uncontrollably. She looked away, knowing he had no recourse.

Duncan briskly undid the buttons and pulled off his shirt. He flung it into a patch of sunlight. From the corner of her eye, Leah watched him wipe his face with her shawl and swallow as if preparing himself for another whipping.

"Prison. Flogging. Inebriation. Ma'am." He spoke in a monotone, as if life had spilled out of him.

"I am sorry such ever happened. For whatever reason."

She hoped Duncan would accept her sincerity. In medical school, she'd had a rotation at a women's penitentiary that gave her a fine understanding: The only way out of a prison made of iron bars and granite was through the head—delusions, inebriation, opium, violence, suicide—

whatever was available. The squalor, shrieks, roaches, rats, smears of diarrhea in hallways left her in disbelief that such a place could exist in a society where one could buy a book of poetry one street away. At the time, she found herself asking not why the women were in the prison but why people were left to live under such conditions.

Exasperated by the unconscionableness of leaving whip marks on a man for life for something as fleeting as inebriation, Leah abandoned her proper posture. She stretched her legs straight as knitting needles, letting her feet splay, and slapped her skirt to crush the air out of the petticoats.

She chose her next words with great care. "I wish we had brought some coffee or warm cider. It would warm us both."

Duncan slowly turned his head and looked at her, eyes wide and unblinking. Leah smiled as best she could. To kill time while Duncan composed himself, she fished an inchworm out of the grass with a twig and waited for it to begin crawling up the stick. When it reached one end, she turned the twig and watched the inchworm begin its climb again. Duncan had yet to take his eyes off her.

"Look, Duncan. It's like a little toy." She nudged his arm. "Here, take it."

Duncan reached for the twig without taking his eyes off her. The tiny creature continued crawling when Duncan turned the stick.

"I wonder if it will realize it's just going around in circles but in a straight line. What small rewards for such diligence," said Leah to break the silence.

She took back the twig when Duncan held it out to her, fully aware that he had not stopped looking at her, not even during their brief study of the inchworm's diligence. She let the inchworm crawl off the stick into the grass, still under Duncan's unyielding observation.

Leah borrowed Duncan's tactic of looking into the distance. "When I was in medical school, I once went to a lunch with my colleagues, and the waiter refused to serve me beer, even though everyone else was drinking it. In kindness, Titus let me taste his. When they saw me take the sip, said colleagues began chanting loudly that the waiter served me beer because I was one of them. I was so humiliated. If Titus had not hushed them, I don't know how long it would have continued. And to boot, the beer tasted like something that leaked out of a horse."

By now, Duncan was studying her with such intensity Leah wasn't sure what he was seeing or trying to see. She looked at him directly.

He spoke immediately. "You prefer wine, ma'am?"

"I suspect any meal is improved with wine, but I haven't had any in centuries. You know, Auntie has concerns and all."

"Understand, ma'am," Duncan said without looking away.

Leah nodded, welcoming the lack of edge in his voice. His shift from good humor to despair had been so meteoric she feared he might jump back into the river to finish drowning. Reassured that Duncan had found a way back from wherever he had marooned himself, Leah patted his hand.

"Well, you must feel mighty silly now. Soaked to the bone and wrapped in a woman's shawl."

"Not my best moment, Leah."

"You'll survive this, too, Duncan. You will."

Their gazes lingered on each other before Leah looked down to quell her urge to put her arm around him. She did not want to do anything that might make him think she pitied him because Duncan was the most resilient person she had ever known. And probably the bravest, although she was certain he never felt heroic.

He had to fight to do what others did without thought, whether walking through town, entering a shop, or even speaking. How he worked himself up to go to the dance or visit her at the farm was beyond her imagination.

To keep him out of silence, Leah asked, "When you go to Edith's Bay, what else do you do besides buy wood?"

"Depends. Go to a symphony, walk through the ship-yard, ma'am."

"Do you visit friends?"

Immediately she knew she asked the wrong question. She berated herself as she watched Duncan clench his eyes as if impaled with a knife.

She prepared to change the subject, but an onslaught of fragmented knowledge began assembling in her mind. Her eyes quivered while the pieces fell into an explanation. She recalled a letter from Martha expressing her distrust of banks, especially after the bank in Edith's Bay had been robbed by a boy. For certain, Duncan Shay must have been that boy. The timing was just right, if he had been sixteen.

The Edith's Bay bank held everybody's money. Even Mrs. Groth and the Hoburns had money there. Most likely it had held Duncan's family's money and the money of the family's business associates.

If he killed a guard when robbing the bank, no one would ever have anything to do with him. Or his brother. Business associates would sever ties with his father. His mother would be excluded from social gatherings. As newly minted pariahs, they would be fortunate to remain in the good graces of extended family, and even then, not for all occasions.

The bits of knowledge assembled into a whole with a

rapidity that made Leah feel she was being flung through the air. She warned herself to tread carefully, but all she managed was not to grab Duncan by the shoulders and shake him.

"Duncan, tell me. Do you ever see your family? Do they know you are here?"

Duncan jerked his hand into the air as if to shield himself from flying knives. He began breathing rapidly, and the quick movement of his eyes under his lids suggested he was trapped in his mind, reliving whatever had transpired so long ago and unable to escape. He grew paler and paler as a sheen of sweat formed over his forehead.

Leah startled when he gasped and opened his eyes. He gaped into the distance, following an object she knew was not present. A deeper understanding settled on her. She had experienced moments with uncontrollable descents into a past that was happening again as if for the first time but where she could not change anything.

Now she could appreciate Duncan's efforts to reveal bits of his life in his constrained manner, one or two facts at a time. He did not speak of his past to hide it but because extensive mentions of it made him relive what were probably the bleakest, most traumatic moments of his life.

So. His family had abandoned him? Or perhaps outright disowned him. She wondered if anyone had ever expressed sorrow for his loss, or if he had been surrounded by people who thought he deserved the loss because of what he did. Did anyone even know he had lost his family, even if his family was still alive?

Leah rolled onto her knees and took his hand. He pulled away.

"Stop. I won't hurt you. Give me your hand."

She hesitated before taking his hand again but held it

when he did not resist. She stroked the wet hair out of his face.

"Duncan, please listen to me. I have people I can't see anymore. They're gone. It doesn't matter how they went. They're gone now. Right after they were gone, I wanted to drop dead but couldn't. I'm better now, but I still have days when my soul doesn't believe in light. I'm sorry the same has happened to you. I do not wish it on anyone. I am deeply sorry."

She felt him struggling to liberate himself from the silence, to crawl out of the sorrow into which she had just shoved him. Unsuccessful with words, Duncan pressed her hand against his forehead.

With the sound of river and wind around them, they rested against each other, restoring themselves in the solace of each other's understanding. Losses were losses, whether by death or abandonment. Sorrow did not distinguish.

The wind turned over Duncan's half-dry shirt and began rolling it toward the river. He leapt up to fetch it, dropping the shawl on the grass. Clutching the shirt in his hand, he looked around as he held the shirt in front of him. When she made eye contact, he squared himself and dropped the shirt by his side.

Leah bolted upright when she saw the asymmetry of Duncan's rib cage, marked by an elongated dimple where a pair of broken ribs had healed crookedly. She could not imagine the fear of being beaten so savagely or the loneliness of being abandoned to heal improperly. Duncan waited until she looked into his face again, then deliberately turned his bare back to her.

Leah scrambled to her feet. "Duncan, this isn't necessary."

"Would rather you look good now than be peeking forever, ma'am."

"I understand, Duncan. I do. But I have no plans to peek. I should hope there is more honesty between us."

She snatched the shirt from the grass and held it for him to slip into it. The doctor in her made a quick evaluation of the scars that shifted with his motions like snakes. With a clinical eye, she saw they had been inflicted with a metal tip that ripped through skin and cut into muscle. The puckers and discoloration came from severe infection and lack of suturing. She knew Duncan would never be able to stretch in some directions without aching from the scar tissue permanently embedded in his muscles.

The cruelty revolted her, but Leah snuffed her anger and willed herself into gentleness while Duncan shoved his arms through the sleeves. When he snapped the shirt over his shoulders, she stepped in front of him and slipped her arms around him, resting her palms over the cloth against his back.

Duncan flinched against her touch. Everything about him became locked and immobile. Feeling she was trespassing against his body, Leah loosened her hands against his back so he could step away.

"There will be no peeking, Duncan. There will be no gossip. Nothing changes between us because of this. I promise you."

When he did not move, she reached to smooth his wrinkled collar. Duncan clamped his hands over hers. Unintentionally she caught a glimpse of the elongated dimple between his ribs and felt ashamed she had aggrieved him beyond remediation.

Without releasing her hands, Duncan bent his head and

kissed her with a tenderness that was sublime. Even shadows bowed and disappeared.

12

THE RIFLE

When the harvest was going full blast, Mrs. Hoburn took orders at the counter for unimaginable amounts of food that farm wives cooked to make meals for migrant farm hands. Hoburn disappeared in the back room to supervise the men he hired seasonally to load the orders onto wagons that farm hands then drove back to the farms.

That left Leah in charge of running everything else in the store, from tending injured workers to restocking shelves to cutting cloth to running the cash register for small purchases. The few people in the store in no way reflected the amount of unceasing activity that was happening in it.

She was certain the few people in the store had lost their minds from overwork when Duncan came in carrying a rifle. They parted a path before him like the Red Sea before Moses. Some pushed their children behind shelves or barrels before taking cover themselves. Even Hoburn, who had wandered out to the front room, ducked behind the counter, pulling Mrs. Hoburn with him. A woman shoved

Leah aside and thrust her toddler under the cutting table before kneeling beside him.

Duncan, intense as he was, was not holding the rifle in any way he could shoot it, seeing that he had clicked it open. He held it by the hinge, so loosely balanced in his hand that it swayed when he walked. In a town where almost everyone owned a hunting rifle, Leah wondered who would think anyone could shoot a rifle in that state.

On a mission, Duncan did not seem to see anyone when he called out, "Mr. Hoburn!"

Hoburn's head appeared from behind the counter. "Uh —yes?"

Duncan pointed to the rifle. "Two shots. Please. Sir. Thank you."

Hoburn looked around and apparently drew his own conclusions. He stood and began to sort through little boxes of bullets under the counter as the few people in the store gasped. Mrs. Hoburn's head rose above the counter and a moment later, she stood. Duncan didn't to seem to absorb any of these interactions.

Leah waited as he approached the cutting table, where she still held a length of cloth in mid-air while being fully conscious that a woman and child were hiding under the table.

"Dr. Maays."

Calm as a stone, Leah lowered the remnant she was folding and rested her hands over it.

"Need to put down Old Dog, ma'am."

Leah's breath caught. She was fond of the ancient, sweet, smelly dog and wondered how Duncan could muster his gumption to put him down. But Duncan usually did whatever right was required, and despite his poker face, she could see the angst in his eyes. She nodded vigorously, afraid to speak in case she burst into tears—for Duncan, for Old Dog.

"Best I do it now, ma'am. Asked Mr. Moore to see you home."

"I can wait," she said without hesitating, amazed the Duncan could consider her wellbeing at that moment. "I shall wait for you to get back. At the post office."

"Might take an hour, ma'am."

"I shall wait for you."

Duncan looked away and lowered his voice. "I'd be mighty grateful if you did, Dr. Maays."

He returned to the counter to place some coins on it and dropped two bullets into his shirt pocket. Customers remained immobile in twisted poses as he made his way out the door without looking at anyone.

Leah continued to fold the cloth she held by swinging her arms like an orchestra conductor, first to stretch it out to its length, then to bring its corners together. After a moment, she looked up, wondering if any of the people in the store would ever move again.

She wished she had walked Duncan out. He deserved more kindness than anyone in the world, even if he was never certain he deserved it. She could have walked him through this forest of fools and made his passage a little easier. Leah kept her eyes on the freshly folded square of cloth and smoothed it as the woman under the cutting table stood and dragged out her toddler.

The same customers who had been terrified of being shot now gathered by the window to watch Duncan mount his horse. Some even stepped out of the store to get a better view of what he was doing.

Next to the horse, Henry Moore held the rifle and a shovel as Duncan, now burdened with a sling around his neck and shoulder that held Old Dog, put his foot in the stirrup and swung himself over the saddle without his usual ease. He patted the pocket where he put the bullets, then took the rifle and the shovel from Henry. He took off in a gallop toward the woods, now brilliant with autumn leaves.

In the store, Leah waited for the woman to come back and claim the cloth she had just folded. The once lively ambience was now subdued. More people were leaving.

"Ribbon?" Leah asked as if nothing of matter had happened because Duncan coming to the store and leaving was not of matter. Or should never have been.

"No, that's fine," said the woman before leaning toward her and whispering, "You got something for warts?"

Leah whispered back, "Do you want me to look at it? Just to make sure that's what it is?"

"No!" the woman said. "It's a wart. I know one when I see it."

Leah left the cutting table and came back with a little bottle of amber liquid. "Twice a day. Morning and evening. It will sting, but please persist. It cures it in about a week—much quicker than vinegar."

"Dr. Haloway said to use vinegar, but that vinegar ain't never worked for me."

"If it's not resolved in a week, please come back, and I shall have a look at it. Is there anything else?"

"Did you see the rifle? Wha' you think he uses it for?"

Leah squelched her desire to answer justly, knowing anything she said would be fodder for gossip. At last she said, "Mr. Shay does not own a rifle. Remember: twice a day, even if it stings. Thank you for your patronage."

Within the hour, the last handful of the customers cleared out, and Hoburn locked the front door. Mr. Hoburn consulted with his wife by the cash register while Leah swept the floor around the cutting table and made her way to the medicine shelf to take the daily inventory. Since she began tending to the sick at the store, medical supplies ran short almost daily because with a little guidance, most people could treat minor problems successfully.

Mrs. Hoburn finished the discussion with her husband and began to wander around the store, straightening merchandise every place she could. Something was wrong about the stiff way she was moving, and after observing her from the corners of her eyes, Leah found herself thinking Mrs. Hoburn was building up her courage to fire her because of Duncan's visit.

With one eye on Mrs. Hoburn, Leah realigned the jars of Thompson's Ointment and tried to formulate a plan, a reaction, an objection, a plea, a justification—anything. If she was let go today, anything she told Duncan would devastate him on the spot. He would see through whatever tactful explanation she could invent, and town talk would inform him of the rest because Mrs. Hoburn never refrained from gossiping.

Leah braced herself. Mrs. Hoburn was running out of merchandise to straighten, and soon she stood before the medicine shelf. Leah picked up the box of wraps she accidentally dropped and replaced it on the shelf, knocking vials of laudanum against one another.

She shoved the inventory notebook into Mrs. Hoburn's hands. "A very fine day, we've had, Mrs. Hoburn. We seem to be in short supply of everything already, although we restocked only this Monday. Why, just today, I sold seven packs of wraps, six jars of Thompson's Ointment, three bottles of Klein's, even a bottle of Whiplash's Tonic, and heaven knows how many bottles of rubbing alcohol. I already see a big gap on the shelf. Oh yes, and a bottle of wart remover. It's more efficacious than vinegar, and people like that. We don't sell that too often, but we did today. Which reminds me, I expect by tomorrow we shall also be out of laudanum because that's when Mrs. Groth comes in. And we certainly do not want to be out of anything she needs."

Leah capped her report with her most glorious smile, although her lips felt as if made of wood. Mrs. Hoburn looked over the notebook, then across the store to her husband, and withered with uncertainty. She held up the notebook and, with a twist of one brow, mysteriously communicated with Hoburn. Hoburn stared back, his eyes vacant.

"And if you think it best," continued Leah, "would you mind if I asked Mr. Shay not to come to the store with a rifle? It was plain to see it wasn't loaded, but I do not think such actions benefit the business. Do you think that would be appropriate, Mrs. Hoburn?"

Completely unnerved, Mrs. Hoburn looked to her husband again, but his eyes communicated nothing. He turned away and began to open a crate with a crowbar. Mrs. Hoburn glowered at him. She thrust the inventory notebook into Leah's hands before heading in Hoburn's direction.

Leah began to count the bottles of rubbing alcohol on the bottom shelf and had to count them twice to keep the number in her head. She clinked the bottles loudly so she would not have to hear Mrs. Hoburn's angry whispers with her husband.

Mrs. Hoburn's skirt came swishing down the aisle until she stood in front of Leah. "Yes. Please tell Duncan Shay not to bring a rifle into the store again. It was most unfortunate today. Thank you."

"I certainly shall." Leah rose to her feet, swaying with

relief. "I recommend increasing the amount of rubbing alcohol and Thompson's to be ordered. I will look at the cloth and lace tomorrow. I think more of the calico would be appropriate, if we can still get it. It has been very popular." Leah placed the notebook on the counter and slipped on her cloak. "I shall fill out the ordering forms first thing after I come in. Good night, Mrs. Hoburn, Mr. Hoburn."

Without waiting for their responses, Leah stepped out of the store. She listened for a gunshot from the east, although she suspected that part had already happened. The distance would have swallowed the sound on her behalf, leaving it audible only to Duncan.

The telegraph machine was blipping away when she stepped into the post office. Henry nodded his greeting and continued scribbling down the message. When the message ended, he tapped out a few blips of his own and filed the note in one of the many slots around him.

"It's always busy at the end of the day," said Henry as an apology.

"So I see." Leah looked around, trying to fathom the complexities of Henry's filing systems. She seldom came into the post office because Utterance or Martha usually picked up the mail. "I don't suppose there is anything here for me?"

"You can't tell by looking around. I'd have to send word to you. But no, there's not."

Leah nodded and turned her attention to the box made of many woods on one corner of Henry's desk that, like an altar, was surrounded by two inches of dust-free neatness before piles of paper began extruding from the desktop. Only Duncan could make a box like that. His trademarks of excellent craftsmanship and aesthetics were unmistakable.

Leah ran her fingertips over the dovetails as the telegraph began blipping again.

Henry was scribbling furiously, translating blips into letters when she spotted Duncan's horse tied to a post through the window. Duncan was heading back to the post office with the open rifle in hand. Leah was about to swing open the door when she heard someone shouting in a way that made her instead crack open the door and look through the slit. Duncan turned his back to the post office as Sheriff Wilkes came into her view.

"Shay! Heared you was strutting 'round with that rifle, scaring people half to death."

"My misjudgment, sir. It's not loaded."

"That your rifle?"

"No sir."

"Where'd you get it?"

"Henry. Moore. Sir."

"He know you have it?"

"Yes. Sir."

"Where you heading with it now?"

"Returning. It. Sir."

"That rifle better not be loaded."

Duncan held the open rifle out to Wilkes, but Wilkes did not take it.

"I dun allow loaded guns in town. Expect you to know that by now."

"Then check it. Sir!" Duncan released the Sir like spit into Wilkes's eye.

Wilkes grabbed the rifle and peered into the empty chambers. He snapped it shut and thrust it back at Duncan. Duncan snapped the rifle open and turned his back to Wilkes to resume walking to the post office.

"Dun you walk away when I be talking to you! Man with your tendencies ought be careful—"

Unable to bear the thought of having Wilkes henpeck Duncan, Leah swung open the door. Both men froze when she stepped out of the post office. Duncan resumed walking almost immediately. Wilkes continued to scowl until Duncan stepped into the post office and shut the door behind himself. He placed the rifle on the side table and the spare bullet next to it. Henry nodded in greeting while he finished taking a telegram. The telegraph began to blip again.

"Good heavens," muttered Henry and grabbed another sheet of paper.

Leah cupped Duncan's cheek. "Are you all right?"

"Yes, ma'am. Thank you." He looked at Henry, who was busy taking down the message, before pressing his cheek against her palm.

"Everything went well?"

"He went easy, ma'am." Duncan placed one hand on her waist and again glanced at Henry, who was still absorbed with taking the message. "Mighty grateful you waited, Leah."

Duncan closed his eyes and pressed his chin against Leah's temple. Eventually, Leah stood on her toes and, seeing Henry was still occupied, kissed Duncan.

DUSK WAS PASSING into night when Leah arrived at the orchard, riding double with Duncan on his horse. Utterance was pacing on the porch, arguing through the window with Martha, who was inside the parlor. As they approached,

Martha drew the curtains, although Leah could see her outline against the gathers of the cloth.

Utterance charged off the porch. "I was just about to ride to town looking for you!"

Duncan got off the horse and reached up to help her dismount, but Utterance came around the horse and pulled her down by the arm.

"We been worried sick 'bout you!" Utterance shouted at Leah. He glared at Duncan.

"Mr. Shay had to put down Old Dog, Uncle. I waited for him to return."

Utterance half shouted at Duncan. "You unnerstand— we was worried sick 'bout Leah?"

Duncan faced Utterance. "Promised you Dr. Maays would be safe with me, sir. Gave you my word. Sir."

For a moment, Leah wondered if the men would come to blows. She really could not imagine either of them fighting, but all the tension was there.

"Mr. Shay, will you stay for dinner?" she blurted.

Duncan looked, not at her, but at Utterance and held his look on him.

"Yes, Mr. Shay," she insisted. "Please stay for dinner. This has been an awful day. You need distraction and company." She turned to Utterance, feeling herself enunciate more and more precisely the angrier she became. "Uncle, Mr. Shay arranged to have Henry Moore walk me home so as not to delay me because he knew you would be worried. We are late because I insisted on waiting in town. Next time, I shall arrange to send you a message. Mr. Shay's behavior was exemplary and took into account my needs as well as yours."

Leah stopped, feeling herself getting lost in the logistical propriety of the situation. She pushed forth. "Uncle, Old

Dog wasn't a farm animal like the sow. He was like family. Maybe not to you, but to Mr. Shay he was. When Mama died after being sick for so long, you didn't just throw up your arms and say, 'Thank goodness that's over! Let's go pick apples.' When William and Titus died, I—"

Duncan put his hand on her shoulder, around the time her eyes began to fill with tears. Her accumulation of losses —her mother, her father, her husband, her son, people at the Ghanian infirmary—rolled into one molten grief. She realized, just as men were trained not to reveal emotion, so had she trained herself to prevent her medical associates from concluding she was hysterical.

As she wondered how men survived being eaten inside out by what they were not allowed to express, she gathered what was left of her thoughts and concluded gracefully. "It was I who chose to wait in town because that was what Mr. Shay needed. I am sorry I caused you and Auntie worry."

Utterance closed his eyes while his lips moved silently, whether praying or cursing, Leah could not determine. She didn't care either.

Finally, he stepped aside and snapped at Duncan, "Corral your horse. Come in."

Leah gripped the reins as Utterance turned to go back to the house, convinced Duncan would mount the horse and fly off after such a reception. But he took the reins from her, nodded, and headed off to the paddock with his horse.

When Leah entered the house, she did not have to see Martha to know she was beside herself at the prospect of having Duncan at the table. Martha was waving her arms and flapping her hands as she followed Utterance around the table while he set another place setting on it.

"Ain't no shortage of old dogs on this earth, Utterance!

You 'spect everyone who shoots one to come here for dinner afterwards?"

"Nothing bad happened, Girl."

"Course not! We ain't twiddled our thumbs long 'nuff for something bad to happen. Just you wait, Utterance! You ever think what we plan to do with ourselves when it does?"

"Nothing bad happened, Girl. Man just put his dog down and brought Leah home. Everyone be safe."

"Shooting a dog dun entitle him to eat here—"

At Duncan's firm knock, Martha and Utterance clammed up into a tight silence that was as revealing as their arguing. Leah opened the door and admitted Duncan, who took a step into the house as if wading through cold molasses.

He bowed. "Evening. Mrs. Cobb. Dr. Maays. Mr. Cobb."

Leah curtsied. "Good evening, Mr. Shay. Please come in. I believe dinner is ready."

Martha stomped to her chair and pulled it out with a loud scrape before plunking herself on it. Duncan drew out Leah's chair and helped her get seated. He waited beside her until Utterance gestured open-palmed to a chair, then sat.

"What wonders have you cooked tonight, Auntie?" Leah asked, trying to inject cheer into the heavy atmosphere.

"What the Good Lord gave us," snapped Martha.

Leah advanced quickly, determined to incorporate Duncan into the meal. "Will you please say grace, Mr. Shay?"

"Would be honored, Dr. Maays. Ma'am. Sir." He bowed his head and began the recitation. "We are grateful for this meal that sustains our bodies, for the beauty that sustains our spirits, for the solace of good company, and for fruition of our labors. For all, we devote our gratitude. Amen."

"Amen," repeated everyone except Martha.

"That was lovely," Leah said. "You'll have to teach it to me some day."

"Be happy to, Dr. Maays."

Leah took the pork chops from Martha as Martha handed the mashed potatoes to Utterance and took the bowl of carrots for herself. Leah almost served herself before realizing Duncan had not been offered any food.

She passed the pork chops to him as swiftly as she could in an effort to cover Martha's inhospitality. Utterance jumped when he realized the same and passed the potatoes to Duncan. Neither she nor Utterance had served themselves.

Duncan crossed the platters over, potatoes to Leah, pork chops to Utterance without taking anything. When Martha put the plate of carrots on the table, he served himself from it. Then he availed himself of pork and potatoes. Leah wanted to shrivel into oblivion from embarrassment.

After a prolonged and indigestible silence, Utterance finally spoke. "Been hearing rumors railroad might come out this way."

"Everyone was saying today it is going to happen. Mr. Hoburn is all in favor of it," said Leah.

"Might make his goods come easier."

"And it would be shorter than the time it takes to get to Edith's Bay by carriage."

They looked at Duncan in case he wanted to express an opinion. As soon as he looked as if he might speak, Martha grabbed the bowl of mashed potatoes and began to scrape out a serving, clanking and scraping the spoon against the bowl. Duncan looked back at his plate with the patience of a saint.

When Martha put down the bowl, Duncan swallowed a few times before saying, "Spur would be helpful, sir."

After another silence, Utterance began another conversation. "We was talking today 'bout getting the church roof fixed. Seems it's leaked long enough now. Coming down in streams, not drops, these days. Emma Groth says she be matchin' twenty-five cents of whatever everyone else raises. Dun know how she can afford that, but she be useful that way."

Another bout of silence fell over the table before Utterance spoke again. "Almanac's been falling short these days. I can't see how anyone expect to predict weather infallible for a whole year. 'Round here you cain't predict it for more than ten minutes 'fore you ain't infallible no more."

"How was it that Uncle Otis predicted the weather?" asked Leah. "He was very good at it."

And so went the rest of the conversation. Leah and Utterance continued to weave an insignificant chatter about rain and hay to counterbalance the dense silence between Martha and Duncan. The meal ended after everyone duteously ate small portions quickly and without pleasure. When Martha did not offer dessert, no one dared ask for it, even though Leah knew a pie was sitting in the kitchen.

They moved into the parlor, where Duncan perched himself on the tiny thumb-back chair like a giant spider on a pinhead. While he attempted to converse with Leah, Martha knitted furiously. Each time Duncan shifted on the chair, she paused her mad clicking, giving the impression that she might stab him in the thigh with a knitting needle. Tolerating as much tension as he could, Duncan stood to take his leave.

"Fine dinner, ma'am. Thank you," he said to Martha, keeping one eye on the knitting needle she clasped like a stiletto.

Martha responded with silence. She followed Leah and

Duncan to the porch behind Utterance, where Duncan peered through the darkness. "Borrow a lantern, sir? Don't want to lame my horse."

Utterance lit and handed him the lantern that was kept on the porch precisely for the business of moving around in the dark.

"Mighty grateful. Thank you, sir."

"You plan returning that?" demanded Martha.

Duncan's voice became like an iron bar. "Can bring it back tomorrow morning if you'll be needing it in daylight. Ma'am. Otherwise, can get it back when I walk Dr. Maays home tomorrow if that's fine by you. Ma'am."

Martha shirked back. "We'll make do."

Duncan's tone did not soften. "Thank you. Ma'am. Dr. Maays. Sir."

"Good night, Mr. Shay. Tomorrow will be a better day," Leah said without any feelings of hope.

"Best it better be, Dr. Maays."

He stepped off the porch and did not look back. Leah stepped forward, wanting to comfort him the way she had in the post office when Henry had not been looking, but Duncan disappeared into the darkness between the house and the barn, becoming a thin beam of light from the lantern. When only darkness was left, Leah went back into the house, where Utterance and Martha had resumed arguing.

"You're goin' to have to walk her home, Utterance. It ain't safe."

"Maybe she can work mornings. Sure Hoburn ain't mind."

"That ain't the point! You think Duncan Shay dun walk in daylight?" shouted Martha.

They fell quiet when Leah came in and stood by the

dining room doorway, for the moment despising them more than she had once despised some of her peers in medical school. "You've made your point, Auntie. Quite well. Thank you."

She walked up the stairs without hurrying to keep them within the scope of her anger, which was so great she half expected the walls of the house to bow out from its force. There wasn't anyone in West Edith's Bay with whom she was not angry—Martha, Utterance, Sheriff Wilkes, Mrs. Hoburn, the rifle, Old Dog. But mostly she was angry with herself, for having naively arranged for—indeed, forced— Duncan to be humiliated in the grandest way possible.

13

THE BIRD CAGE MINISTER

Even after several days, the dinner at the Cobbs' house was picking away at Duncan. Martha's reaction did not surprise him. Her mind was nearly impenetrable to new ideas, and when a new notion managed to move in, it seemed incapable of finding its way out.

The last thing he had expected was for Utterance to flare up and berate him. He liked Utterance. Utterance did not fear him, the trait he detested most in people, even if he had cultivated a patina that inspired apprehension. Having Utterance berate him was like having solace stolen from him.

He could do without Martha, but Martha was part of Utterance.

And they were both part of Leah.

Everyone was part of Leah.

Leah.

Duncan picked up a drawer and measured it by eye before setting it in a squaring jig. Martha could make him feel like a trespasser, no matter where on earth he stood.

Now he was feeling spineless for relying on Leah to compensate with her diplomacy, not that she could keep the tenuous peace for much longer.

In another month or so, it would be too cold for he and Leah to talk by the porch steps, the only place Martha grudgingly permitted his presence. Leah, stubbornly shivering in the evening chill, could make anyone believe frozen air was a prerequisite to a good night's sleep and a happy life. To have Leah inside his shop after dark would cause too much malicious gossip, and darkness fell early during winter.

He knew Martha was banking on a bitter, bone-snapping winter. She would rather have Leah freeze on the porch than allow him into the house. She would rather Leah walk a mile up the hill by herself in winter darkness than have him accompany her.

When the drawer squeaked, Duncan loosened the clamps he had overtightened in his frustration. No longer trusting himself, he took off the clamps and walked away, disgusted at not being able to solve the problem. Because *he* was the problem. All of him was the problem.

He sat on his drafting chair and rested his forehead in one palm, hoping for a moment of clarity, when his thoughts took off like wild birds bursting from a tree. What remained was a gauzy, flickering memory of himself in the last room he remembered of the penitentiary where he had once been known as Duncan Sassure.

Sweat gathered on his forehead as he recalled how pleurisy from the broken ribs made every breath he took feel like inhaling a flame. The infected cuts from the whipping throbbed deep into his back muscles even when he did not move. He wanted to close his ears the way he closed his eyes. He wanted to turn off all his senses one by one, followed by each of his internal organs until he ceased to be. He wanted to disintegrate and have a draft blow his dust into darkness. But pains kept snapping him into an agitated awareness—and into guilt. His father's money had kept him off the gallows, and here he was wishing for death.

After a week of solitary confinement, Duncan welcomed the sound of the cell door clanging open. The warden stepped in, and Duncan hoped a doctor was following him. Instead, a tangle of men poured into the cell and moved on him like an overbearing machine with many arms and legs.

Their hands fell all over him as they stripped him naked and tied him face down and spreadeagle on the cot with no regard for the pain from his broken ribs that now carried the weight of the rest of his body and pressed against his lungs. Duncan coughed with dry heaves from fright and disgust, his head spinning from pain and lack of breath, thinking whatever little bit of humanity he had preserved for himself would be taken from him right then.

But the men left as efficiently as they arrived. A man who smelled of peroxide and ether slipped into the room without making a sound. In the dimness, all Duncan could see of him were flashes of white cuffs and pale hands as he opened a surgical case lined with shiny scalpels. The man picked up one of the little knives and sat on the edge of the cot.

Duncan rattled the cot to get loose and called out, but the man stuffed a wad of cloth into his mouth. He felt the pressure of the man's fingers on his back and then the cut at the edge of a scab with the scalpel. Systematically, the man ran the blade along the full edge of each scab before applying a salt poultice to draw the pus.

The pain from the poultice was blinding, sending a fire through his entire body. By the time the man collected his blood-streaked instruments in a linen towel and left, Duncan was convinced the man had killed him and left him in hell.

HE SPENT an unmeasurable amount of time roaming through fevers with brief moments of awareness. When he finally became fully conscious, vague pains still commanded his body. He breathed more easily, although he still could not draw a full lung's worth of air. Jagged pain from his back muscles paralyzed him when he tried to move. He became still, bewildered to still be alive.

In the distance, a dim racket of hammering and sawing and of men calling to one another filtered into his attention. The fear that they were building a scaffold piqued his senses. He would not mind being dead, but the very thought of having to walk up to it or of being hanged in front of his family made his heart pound.

He moved his head as much as he could to look around. Brilliant light suggested he was no longer in the dank, echoing cells of the penitentiary. The room looked ordinary, with white plaster walls and windows that did not have bars. He sniffed. The place did not smell like a hospital. He had no idea where he was.

Through the open door surged a raging argument. At first, only the sound of anger filtered into the room, but as the persons came closer, Duncan could make out words, and eventually he thought he recognized his father's voice.

He kept his eyes on the doorway. The last time he'd seen his father was the day he'd been in court, where his father would not even look at him.

"There is much benefit to seeing your son, sir."

"I shall not."

"Sir, he is your son."

"Not by my choice, he's not!"

"Then, sir, why have you brought him here?"

"So he won't shame us all to hell! I shall not witness the family name hanging from a noose."

"Sir, you are already here. I strongly suggest you at least look in on him—"

His father let out a growl of swear words the likes of which Duncan had never heard. A moment later, his father marched into the room with a momentum that implied he owned the building and stood by the bed as if he also owned him.

Duncan willed himself beyond pain to throw himself across his father's chest. He found comfort in the familiar scent of tobacco and the asperity of his father's woolen jacket. When he opened his eyes, all he could see was the worn sheen on his father's lapel and for a moment, thought he was hugging the wrong man. Impeccable dress distinguished his father, who did not tolerate shabbiness of any kind. His father donated his suits to charity long before the cuffs frayed or the lapels became shiny.

With one hand, his father shoved him back onto the mattress and held him down by the throat as he spoke in a voice whose sternness could freeze a glass of water. "I've paid up your inheritance to get you here. And your brother's inheritance. The company is destroyed. Everything is gone. Your mother has not been able to leave her bed. There's nothing left for anyone, so you better learn to save yourself because I am through with you, you bastard!"

Duncan felt a shame so engulfing it had neither bottom nor horizon to bind it. Closing his eyes to contain his tears, he listened to his father stomp out of the room. The argument resumed in the hallway as the men moved away and continued until Duncan could no longer hear it.

The hallway remained deadly quiet until what sounded like a giant teacart rolled toward the door. A little later, a dwarf in a wicker wheelchair rolled into the room. Duncan cursed the devil for having a stupendous sense of the idiosyncratic.

"Praised be the Divine! We are ever grateful you are awake!" the dwarf called joyously as he rolled toward him. "Good morning, Mr. Sassure. I am Mr. Avery Lawry. How do you do? I did not expect you would be conscious, but we are indeed very grateful."

Duncan closed his eyes, unable to process what he saw. He listened to the dwarf's voice, which had the amplitude and depth of a regular man's voice.

"I am sure I need not point out your father is very angry with you, Mr. Sassure. His anger comes from fear that you are what you have done. I have assured him you shall acquire understanding, just as I assure you now that his anger is a form of his love for you."

Duncan peeked from under the covers. Mr. Lawry had yet to make sense to him. If his father loved him, he should just come in and say so, instead of...of...what he had said.

As if reading his mind, Mr. Lawry added, "Strangers do not become angry with one another, Mr. Sassure. People must know each other before they matter enough to one another to merit anger. Your father bribed the universe to keep you off the gallows, and then he bribed the universe again to make your case known to me. I am sure he shall forgive you in time because although he does not feel it now, he still has hope for you."

Thinking Mr. Lawry was mocking him with riddles, Duncan pushed himself to the other side of the narrow cot.

Mr. Lawry nodded and began to wheel himself out of the room.

"Where am I?" he called just as Mr. Lawry reached the door.

"Ah, good." Mr. Lawry pivoted and rolled himself back to the bed. "It is good you ask that question, sir. You are at the Institute of Craft. You are here, Mr. Sassure, not because of your father's bribes but because I believe the murder you committed was an accident and there are better things in you."

Astonished that someone believed he had any innocence, Duncan clutched the bed sheet under him so tightly that he pulled it off a corner. He opened his mouth to speak, but no words came out.

"However, you did intentionally put yourself in a position to kill a man and, thus, you did. We shall work on your understanding of that, sir, so you can have your life back. Rest now, Mr. Sassure. I shall visit you later." Mr. Lawry wheeled himself out of the room with the agility of a natural body.

Duncan fought to stay awake to keep an eye on the door through which two of the most important persons in his life had entered and left within a half hour. One was his father. The other was a little man in a wheelchair who believed the murder was an accident.

ANOTHER WEEK PASSED before Duncan could contemplate, even in the most minuscule and circumventive manner, that his father disowned him and was unlikely to return. He could not bring himself to conclude for certain that his father would not return, only that he was unlikely to do so.

Perhaps his mother or brother would come to see him. Perhaps they could convince his father to come by again.

Mr. Lawry visited every day, sometimes more than once. He never mentioned Duncan's father, and from fear, Duncan never asked about him.

After another few weeks, Mr. Lawry rolled into the room with street clothes balanced on his lap. Until then, Duncan had been naked except for the bandages around his torso. Mr. Lawry had offered him a night shirt, but Duncan could not raise his arms enough to slip it on.

Mr. Lawry placed the clothes at the foot of the bed and patted them enthusiastically. "Mr. Sassure, I believe you are well enough to meet your Peers. Please come outside when you are dressed, and I shall introduce you."

Duncan already knew about the Peers. They were the other men who slept in bunk beds in the large room across the hall that he saw when he slipped out one day, wrapped in a bed sheet, to look around. From the window of the room, he often saw them working, building porch-like structures that weren't attached to any house.

He waited until Mr. Lawry wheeled himself out of the room before he grabbed the pile and held each article before himself. Underwear. Mended socks. New pants. Worn leather belt. Shirt with a patch. Work boots with uneven heels. All ordinary, civilian clothes. He gathered the clothes in his arms and hugged them, rocking himself with his face pressed against them, feeling his humanity pour back into him. He had not worn civilian clothes since the day he went to rob the bank.

In the vestibule, Duncan eventually discovered a modest collection of pamphlets designed for visitors. Speckled with encouragements for contributions, the pamphlets revealed the wheelchaired Mr. Lawry subscribed to the idea that any incarnation of spirituality was valid as long as it guided a person correctly.

He promoted that moral understanding created its own set of beliefs—not the other way around—that would eventually root into a person's soul. Apparently, he did not subscribe to any known religious establishment, was loath to describe what he believed in, and never insisted that anyone believe in anything specific. Duncan wondered how anyone who did not believe in anything could have faith in something. But he did not comment.

After the ennui of the prison where nothing happened and men were left to rot, the constant swiftness of activities at the Institute of Craft kept him on his toes. Each day began at six a.m. Breakfast was followed by Discussions, as Mr. Lawry called the hour of reading and discourse. Most readings seemed like scriptures, although Duncan had never heard of them: *The Cloud of Unknowing,* Rumi, St. Augustine, *Upanishads,* Lao Tzu, Teresa of Avila, Hafiz, Hildegard, and numerous European philosophers.

The readings were short, most of them about a paragraph. As much as he could surmise, most of the readings had to do with the human spirit, its requirements, and how to fulfill those requirements. Mr. Lawry never asked Peers to believe in anything they read, only to understand the reading, even if they thought it was foolish. And there seemed to be no penalty for saying any reading was foolish as long as a reason was clearly articulated.

The rest of each day was taken up with carpentry. In the Barn, Duncan learned to make things out of wood. In the

Shed, he learned to put finishes on the things he made in the Barn. There was also a non-place, the grassless, muddy area he had seen from the window of the sick room, where the Peers erected foundations, porches, and other structures that they subsequently took down when others needed to learn the same skills. For anything else, the Peers returned to the living quarters—the House.

Mr. Lawry also lived in the House but in a separate annex where able-bodied men also stayed. Their purpose was to assist Mr. Lawry, supervise, teach, and maintain order when necessary. They were a quiet, forceful presence who could go from placidly leaning against a wall to tackling an unruly Peer to the ground. Duncan heard that two tackles sent a Peer back to the Edith Bay's prison.

For the first lesson in carpentry, Mr. Lawry pulled him aside from the other Peers. Duncan expected a discourse about safety and precautions, but the introduction turned out to be about the business of acquiring and delivering materials. The lesson centered on three principles Mr. Lawry considered fundamental to all exchanges: acknowledging the person with Name, Sir, or Ma'am; inciting humility in the self with Please; and acknowledging indebtedness with Thank You.

Every exchange of tools, materials, or services was to be accompanied by one or more of these words. Mr. Lawry made clear the practice was mandatory. It was not about parlor manners but about human consideration, dignity, and gratitude—a grace that encompassed all the others, espoused Avery Lawry.

What Duncan considered real carpentry began when he learned to rip boards, plumb joints, and calculate the depths of dovetails. He learned how to use brushes and mix paints to create specific effects, to define the benefits and detractions of specific finishes. He made joint after joint until each turned out perfect.

Other lessons, most untaught in classes, mysteriously seeped into him along with woodworking. Those had an incessant quality that continued at night, first with an acidic loneliness that etched holes through him as he waited to fall asleep and continued during sleep in the form of nightmares. A year would pass before he could work himself into a full night's sleep.

Unable to release the hope that his father would accept him again if he could right himself, he constructed a model of redemption that addressed his father's sensibilities. From the readings and discussions, he borrowed the idea of mandating the best from the things he could control: what he did and the things he made.

Oneself was the only controllable element in any situation. One could control oneself better than one could control weather or what others did. And one had to maintain oneself under control no matter how turbulent the environment. Thus espoused Avery Lawry.

Overflowing with effort, Duncan buried himself in the details of craftsmanship, and almost overnight, his skills exceeded the capabilities of Mr. Lawry's worn and mediocre tools. He took to the lathe so well that Mr. Lawry persuaded a patron to donate a new, more substantial one. One week later, a new set of chisels appeared. While Peers constructed sturdy posts of simple lines, Duncan turned posts that resembled twisted candy canes, strings of pearls, spirals, and coils.

Then, under a pile of hay and scrap wood, he discovered a steaming contraption for bending wood. Overnight, he abandoned the lathe and, with Mr. Lawry's permission, cleaned out the area, reconditioned the steamer, and began to bend wood. For months, he made everything with bent wood to exploit all the possibilities of the technique.

For his first practical project, he made a set of wheels for Mr. Lawry's chair that were an inch wider than his usual wheels so he could roll across soft surfaces like grass more confidently. Duncan experimented with steaming wider strips of wood until he found he could bend thin panels over a curved frame and make domes like the ones he'd seen in etchings of Russian and Persian palaces. After this discovery, he lost no opportunity to incorporate a dome in every project, including a hamper Mr. Lawry asked him to make for dirty kitchen rags.

Then he discovered books with scrollwork patterns and became fascinated with them. He abandoned the steamer and began to explore the scroll knife and saw. The Peers used the scroll saw for cutting gross curves, but Duncan jiggled and tweaked the blades until he was able to cut complex, lacelike patterns that dappled sunlight and astonished everyone.

Soon, he began to receive commissions from customers who discovered his ability to work with wood. They didn't come directly to him but to Mr. Lawry who then called him into his office to offer him the work.

Commissions became the only evidence he had that he existed to anyone outside I of C because he never received letters from anyone. The lack of personal letters sometimes felt so devastating that when the monthly the mail wagon arrived, Duncan went to any corner of I of C where mail was not. There he would work through the break Mr. Lawry gave the Peers because none of them could concentrate on anything until after they read their letters.

One mail day, he came close to rejoicing when a guard appeared and invited him to step into Mr. Lawry's office. In the office, Duncan waited eagerly before he noticed Mr. Lawry was holding up a pale gray envelope addressed generically to The Institute of Craft. Duncan did not recognize any aspect of the envelope.

"Please sit down, Mr. Sassure," Mr. Lawry said gravely.

"Thank you, sir." He began to worry someone had complained about his work.

"We should pray for your father, Mr. Sassure," said Mr. Lawry.

Duncan leaned forward. "Sir?"

"Your brother has written that your father has passed into the good Divine, Mr. Sassure. I am very sorry."

Mr. Lawry pushed the gray envelope across the desk. "And your brother has requested that you not keep the family name. You do not *have* to change your family name, sir. That is entirely your decision, not your brother's." Mr. Lawry took a breath before continuing. "Please forgive my bluntness, but there is no good way to deliver such news. You have my condolences, Mr. Sassure. I am very sorry this has happened to you. Please, the letter is for you to keep."

Duncan clutched the chair's arms as if stricken with paralysis. He had formed an entire inner life on the hope that his family would forgive him. Now his father was gone. Who knew what his mother thought because he had not heard from her in years. And his brother did not even want to acknowledge he was part of the family.

He sat in Mr. Lawry's office as disoriented as if he were falling through air without knowing if he would ever land. Each time he looked at the letter, his anxiety doubled. He wanted to read it but was unable to bring himself to even touch the envelope, much less pull the letter out of it.

Mr. Lawry waited without speaking or pressuring him to

leave. He just waited, hands folded against his chest, not even doing paperwork.

Eventually, Duncan stood and lifted the envelope off the desk with two fingers as if handling a shard of glass. "Thank you, sir."

From Mr. Lawry's office, he walked to the House and sat on the front steps, disseminating silence like a stifling mist. He was still sitting on the steps when night fell. Mr. Lawry brought him indoors and led him to the side of his bed. Duncan intended to crawl in and fall asleep, but in the morning, he was still sitting on the edge of his bed, fully dressed and staring at the floor as if he had lost his sight.

His soul curled into a little ball so tight it would not let him speak for months. His vocabulary consisted of nodding or shaking his head. Questions requiring more complex answers generated such anxiety in him that he could not form sounds. Sometimes he just stood still and concentrated on breathing so he would not die on the spot.

He threw himself into woodworking to prevent wild panics that came over him when he was not distracted. Hoping to shave away his grief layer by layer on the lathe or cut little bits of it out with the scroll saw or bend sorrow with the steamer into something he could tolerate, he set about making "The Great Gazebo," as the Peers took to calling it.

The gazebo called for turned spiral pillars, lace-like walls of elaborate fretwork, arched openings for doorways, and the biggest, most complex dome he had ever attempted. He worked sunup to sundown, or until someone came to get him for meals or told him to go to sleep.

When he finished the gazebo, he painted it a brilliant white that made it resemble marble in the sun. Mr. Lawry, the Guards, and Peers gathered around it and gave him a spontaneous round of applause with cheers.

He did not feel any of it. He dropped the brush into a bucket and walked away to wash at the pump, like a man who created without knowing he existed.

Without a pause, he moved on to a series of lesser projects not quite fully emerging from this state of clouded quietude. Over time, he developed the dense, protective silence and the exquisite craftsmanship that became his trademarks. None of it registered with him. He just created so he would not have to exist.

DUNCAN REMAINED at I of C long after Peers who had come to the Institute after he arrived were released. By then, he had outgrown all the I of C's instruments made for men who would never progress beyond rough carpentry. With the same tools, he did work patrons said virtuoso cabinet-makers had not yet conceived.

His frustration with the lack of tools necessary for finer craftsmanship was only one vocabulary for his qualms about his life. Every once in a while, he frightened himself to the bone by contemplating that he had reached the only destiny he would have, that he would die at I of C trying to teach fumble-fingered men who had little capacity for or interest in absorbing subtleties.

Occasionally, he touched on the fact that murderers were never released and recoiled like someone touching hot iron. He reconsidered how not being hanged had unantici-pated consequences because a dead man does not suffer. Perhaps that had been his father's intent—to keep him alive and suffering.

In addition to teaching other Peers, Mr. Lawry assigned him to work on the buildings, bought him more books, and put him in charge of repairing and rebuilding tools. Of all the tools, the lathe broke down most frequently, occasionally from a Peer's misuse, more often from his overuse.

When he took apart the lathe for the umpteenth time to recondition it, he could see the wear on the bearings was extensive. Bearings were expensive, and each time he told Mr. Lawry the lathe needed a new bearing, he felt he was telling him he had destroyed the old one himself. He mourned the broken lathe because he could not bring himself to mourn his broken life directly.

Duncan was relieved to abandon the lathe when a guard came into the workshop and asked him to please step into Mr. Lawry's office. He hoped whatever new project Mr. Lawry had for him would not involve using the lathe so he would not yet have to mention the worn bearing. In the vestibule, he remembered mail day was a week away and began to experience inner turmoil as he realized Mr. Lawry was not calling him in to assign him a new commission.

The guard opened the door to Mr. Lawry's office but remained outside after Duncan stepped in. Mr. Lawry gestured that he could close the door before rolling himself forward.

"Good afternoon, Mr. Sassure. Mr. Staples, please meet Mr. Duncan Sassure. Mr. Sassure, may I introduce you to Mr. Staples. Please sit down, Mr. Sassure."

Mr. Staples smiled and mouthed *How do you do* but did not offer to shake hands.

"Sir," Duncan said.

He knew exactly who Mr. Staples was—the Bird Cage Minister, as he was scathingly called by the Peers. He was the director of the Edith's Bay penal system and had the power to move prisoners within it like pawns. Everyone knew the Bird Cage Minister's official powers were greater than Mr. Lawry's, although Mr. Lawry was packed with unofficial powers to perform miracles. The Bird Cage Minister's presence at the Institute never boded well for anyone. Duncan developed a queasy stomach as he realized he was firmly in the man's scope and would soon be in his grasp.

"Mr. Sassure," said Mr. Lawry. "It has come to Mr. Staples's attention that no Peer has exhausted the offerings of I of C as profoundly as you have. That is extremely commendable. Extremely. Mr. Staples and I both agree that a man with your intelligence and depth of soul needs to be challenged properly."

Duncan was not deceived. Mr. Lawry always began conversations with praise, even those conversations intended to rectify wrongs. Through Mr. Lawry's praise, all he heard was that Mr. Staples was here to remove him from I of C because he had exhausted its offerings. He closed his eyes. His stomach began to churn.

He would not go back to the prison, an annex of hell for those who were so condemned they needed to start living in hell before they died. A tiny tap with a chisel against his wrist would leave him dead in minutes. He would not die in prison. He would not live there either.

Mr. Lawry rolled forward and placed his hand over his arm. "Mr. Sassure. Please forgive me for making you suffer. I have not made myself clear in my silly attempt to compliment you. I've brought you in here to tell you that Mr. Staples is releasing you. You may begin living as a free man as soon as the paperwork goes through, sir. I suspect within the week."

Duncan clenched so tightly he might not have been able to move had someone set him on fire. The Bird Cage

Minister looked mystified while Mr. Lawry nodded placidly, leaned back in his wheelchair, and folded his hands over his chest.

Duncan had to clear his throat several times before he could speak. "Thank you, sir."

He stood, immediately becoming occupied trying to overcome the lightheadedness from the relief. He nodded to the Bird Cage Minister and opened the door to leave.

To his surprise, the guard was no longer outside the door when he stepped out. He took it as the first trust given to an almost free man. He walked back to the Barn alone, still struggling to believe what had just happened. Nothing seemed made of reality.

At the sight of the disassembled lathe on the floor in the barn, he experienced a revelation that made him stop mid step with prickles running over his skin. The Bird Cage Minister didn't know him from a peg on a wall, much less what he had done or not done at I of C. It was Mr. Lawry and his arsenal of unofficial powers that had set him free.

Duncan drew a breath as refreshing as water to a thirsty man. Hard convincing it must have taken to get the prison authorities to release someone convicted of murder and bank robbery. But when Mr. Lawry believed in the truth of something, few things deterred him. Duncan picked up the broken bearing and vowed to die without ever breaking Mr. Lawry's faith in him—whatever that was made of.

14

THE DUEL

The day Duncan left the Institute of Craft, he shook Mr. Lawry's hand with a tense calmness that stretched tautly over a riot of feelings. He accepted from Mr. Lawry a standard change of work clothes —a pair of pants, two shirts, and sundries—a set of essential woodworking tools in a toolbox, a collection of sterling references from patrons for whom he built pieces, and a substantial amount of money that Mr. Lawry had saved for him from commissions. Mr. Lawry then gave him two gifts that filled Duncan with a sense that Mr. Lawry understood a part of him: a set of expensive chisels with German blades and a book about Japanese joinery.

He walked away from the I of C after almost a decade into a world full of possibilities that made him anxious. Nothing in his life was now guaranteed, not even the familiarity of the place he had lived in as a home but had longed to leave. Even his habits, always a source of comfort, had been stripped from him with the unpredictability of freedom.

Down the road a bit, a wagon from the penitentiary

came to deliver a new Peer, probably as wild as he had once arrived. As it rolled past, Duncan could not help feeling displaced and astray in a way he had never experienced.

After several hours of walking, he found himself across the street from his family's brownstone. He stood in front of it for a long time, taking comfort in its familiar form and mustering the courage to knock on its door. He rehearsed what he would say and tried not to invest too much in the hope that he would not be turned away like an inconvenient salesman.

Just as he was about to step off the curb, a young nanny wheeling a baby carriage came out of the front door. The nanny aimed the carriage to cross the street but reoriented it when she saw him. She stayed on the opposite side of the street from him and began pushing the carriage quickly as if to avoid a menace.

With one foot suspended from the curb, Duncan realized his family no longer lived in the brownstone. They had moved—to where they had not told him—having allowed years of mail days to pass unused.

At that moment, he realized his hope would change nothing. He abided by his brother's wishes and took his mother's maiden name to become Duncan Shay. Perhaps those who knew the family genealogy would recognize the name and be able to find him. If they ever chose.

He began to walk, stumbling through the night because he knew he would not sleep. Around daybreak, he found himself crossing the center of West Edith's Bay, a town he wasn't even aware existed. He continued up the hill on the only road that seemed to lead out of the town and stopped only when the road opened into an orchard fragrant with apple trees.

Surprised at how abruptly the road ended, he remembered looking across the field of apple trees into the dense, black forest that edged the orchard. He was calculating his chances against the forest when a man asked if he had come to pick apples. Knowing he did not have the strength to traverse the forest because no one awaited him on the other side, he nodded and began the day as an apple picker at the Cobb Farm.

UNTIL THE DAY Mary Corwal announced to the world that he was a thief and murderer, he lived in West Edith's Bay without incident. Some knew about his past but hadn't seemed bothered.

Then the slow chill began to follow his steps as it became fashionable to shun him. At church, people began refusing to sit in the same pew with him, and frequently, an entire family with fussing children stood in the back of the crowded sanctuary for the entire sermon while he sat singly in a pew, suffocating in the humiliation of his repudiation. One Sunday, while fully dressed to go to services, his shoes stuck on his floorboards and refused to let him go. He never went again.

He did not expect the resilience and unity of the town's inhabitants to be stronger than his ability to cope, but it proved so and he conceded fitfully. He gathered the insults, slights, and subtle cruelties as a mason gathers stones to build a wall and mortared them with a self-sufficiency and a self-imposed isolation that was as unforgiving of them as they were of him.

He redirected his woodworking away from the town toward Edith's Bay and watched appreciation for his craft flow in as money. And he did it secretly, denying the town any knowledge of his success or worth.

He told himself he continued doing town chores because Avery Lawry always demanded doing what was right in all situations, and a local carpenter had to do town chores, even if he could earn ten times more as a master cabinetmaker. Besides, town chores had sustained him while he set up his cabinetmaking business, and for that, he had to be grateful. He consoled himself with knowing his repairs were more finely crafted than the things that required repairs.

In truth, he feared that if he did not do town chores, no one would ever acknowledge him. Despite his strenuous efforts to become insular, he could not rid himself of his need for personal contact and belonging.

Why he did not leave West Edith's Bay became a question he asked himself daily when he left his shop to walk invisibly among the town's inhabitants. He could not return to Edith's Bay to live near the bank where he had gone to ruin so many lives. He could not go back and risk encountering a family member who would not acknowledge him after having stood by him as his brother or his mother for so long.

Even making business trips to Edith's Bay required several days of gumption building, and he was always ill at ease when he was there, wanting someone to find him while fearing being found. Walking through Edith's Bay was like wandering through a haunted house with tilted hallways.

At least in West Edith's Bay, he raised a shop he considered home. It was a place people could find him, if they chose. He could not go to his family in Edith's Bay—if they still lived there—but perhaps they might someday come to him if he was not too far away. And bring forgiveness.

He had invested most of his savings and hard-earned money from assorted jobs and apple picking in first-class, cast-iron shop machines: lathes, bench saw, joiner, scroll, not to mention an extensive collection of hand tools he needed for his trade. He could not make a living without them. He would lose money if he sold them. He would need a fortune to move them and to where remained a mystery.

And to complicate matters, Old Dog showed up one day, as dirty and underfed as he was affectionate. Duncan could not stuff Old Dog into a portmanteau or put him out to be shot because Wilkes considered the wandering dog a nuisance. In the end, he decided to stay with Old Dog and his tools. They were the only support he had, paltry as they were.

In his well-equipped shop, he indulged in making beautiful things, a work that gave him some sense of inclusion in the world. He could change his shirt without having everyone stare at him and ask for the history of his disfigurements. Home was the only place where he knew where everything was and could slip into a bed in which one hundred men had not previously slept. Those contentments, small but wholly his, were so comforting he was loath to give them up to move to another place where he might never be found—if anyone chose to find him—or where the same shunning would take hold.

But when Leah stepped out of the carriage, something about the way she rested her hand on the coach master's arm to steady herself made him long for touch, not only on his skin but in his soul. In that moment of distraction, he let the chisel slip and gouge his palm, releasing years of anguish in spurts of blood. What he felt then might have brought him to his knees had the urgency to save his hand not ruled over him.

He rushed to Dr. Haloway's house, but Dr. Haloway was not home. With visions of losing a finger, bleeding to death, or dying from gangrene and having no one care, he made his way into the general store to save his hand himself.

There, he found a stranger who calmly tended to his injury as if he were just another respectable fellow. In a professional gesture, she slipped his arm between her arm and torso, fully intuiting he had the decency to remain respectful. In that moment, he received more kindness, respect, and trust than he had in years. He knew then that the walls he built could keep others out forever but were too weak to keep him in. In that very moment, he discovered the fragility of his strength.

Leah had not even thought to fear him when she retorted to his misguided offense and laughed compassionately (in retrospect) at him, as if acknowledging the perfection of his humanity was in its frailties. Then in a continuing flow of reckless kindness, Leah continued to tolerate his approaches, even after she had been "informed"—a privilege he had not had in years.

When she chose him over Cory Baines to dance, Duncan thought he had been the less despicable of her two choices, but while dancing within Leah's vibrancy, he realized Dr. Leah Maays would not have danced with either one of them had she not wanted. She chose him because she wanted to dance with him, another privilege he had not had in years—to be wanted. Leah not only had the courage to confront him about murdering a man, robbing a bank, and being provoked by womanhood, but she also had the courage to believe his answers and to behave accordingly.

With these moments tucked into his soul, Duncan placed his hat on his head and began to walk up the hill to the Cobb farm while Leah worked in the general store.

Martha might not be as brave as Leah, but he still owed her the respect of clarifying matters.

Avery Lawry taught that respect was something to give freely, even when you could not presume to receive it, even when you deserved it. Giving and taking were seldom equal among humans, and you had to work with what you had to make the situation fair in both directions. Because, Avery Lawry espoused, the fairness would someday come back to you in ways you might not even recognize.

DUNCAN ARRIVED at the orchard and made his way to the canning kitchen, a tight, practical, gray stone building that contrasted against the forest flurry of autumn leaves. The clattering sounds of Martha's labor filled the building. He knocked on the doorframe as Martha was lifting a tray heavy with mason jars full of apple butter.

She cried out when she saw him and tumbled back with jars clinking and sliding on the tray. By a miracle, she missed backing into the fires under the copper kettles and braced herself against a wall as the jars continued to slip back and forth on the tray.

"Need a word with you, ma'am," he said.

He stepped forward and lifted the tray from her hands just as she was about to drop it. He shoved it onto the nearest shelf, one that Martha was unlikely to reach without a step stool. Martha skittered to the other corner of the canning kitchen.

Duncan repositioned himself in the doorway. "Need a word with you, ma'am. Now, if that be fine with you. Ma'am."

"I'm busy now!" shouted Martha, bursting into tears.

"Just take a moment. Ma'am."

Martha grabbed the yard-long wooden stirrer from one of the kettles and held it like a staff across herself, dripping apple butter over her shoes and on the floor.

"Strikes me, ma'am, you're not happy about Dr. Maays befriending me," he began, calmly reciting the opening he had practiced as he walked up the hill.

"You be ruining her!" shouted Martha, now standing in a small puddle of apple butter.

"That's not true, ma'am. Dr. Maays can't be ruined. By anybody."

Martha shook the stirrer at him.

"Truth be told, ma'am—if you didn't know much about me except what you saw now, you'd be fine with me, just like you were fine when I picked your apples and built you your porch." He paused, trying to lean against the doorway, but the stiffness in his spine would not allow him. "But there're other truths that can't be ignored, and they are needing clarification. One truth is I killed a man. The other is it was an accident."

"Witnesses said you killed in cold blood!" Martha shrieked, backing into a rack of empty mason jars. The rack swayed until a jar fell and smashed on the stone floor. Martha yipped and hopped away from the rack. A new batch of tears gathered in her eyes.

"They. Are. Wrong. Madam. They are wrong! No witness can see the inside of a man. I was sixteen—*sixteen*—when they busted through that bank door and scared me half to death. I pulled that trigger in front of four witnesses and killed that poor man because I was so scared my hand spasmed. The pistol was halfway down when they come busting through that door, and if they had just been but two seconds later—two seconds—I would have shot a hole in the floor."

Duncan stopped, aware his chest was heaving. To calm himself, he picked up a jar of apple butter and turned it in his hand. He put it down when Martha threw a hand across her face as if she expected him to throw it at her.

He forced himself to speak more calmly. "Sounds real pathetic, now, doesn't it? Ma'am. Boy in search of manhood killing a man on account of jitters. Can't get more pathetic than that. Didn't find my manhood. Lost everything instead. You can despise me, ma'am, but not more than I despise myself."

He paused, evaluating whether Martha was listening at all and found her staring at him with the uncertainty of a child listening to a ghost story. He continued as evenly as he could.

"Just so you understand, ma'am, I don't blame the guards because they busted through the door at the wrong time. I don't blame the man I shot because he didn't get out of the way. I was the one who killed him, for whatever reason. Without me, nobody would be dead. Not looking for your sympathies, ma'am. Just want you to understand what really happened so you can empty your head of all the falseness in it."

He sighed deeply. Then he steeled himself and looked straight through Martha's tears into her eyes. "You're probably thinking remorse comes easy after they haul you off to prison in chains, and you're right. But you need to understand my remorse started before I even saw the guard. It started right when I set foot in the bank, acting on a stupid bet. A stupid bet! I knew I was wrong right then, even before the opportunity to take anything or kill anyone showed itself."

Duncan swallowed and continued. "But I didn't have the courage to stop and do right because wrong can suck you in like a whirlpool, and I was afraid of being called a coward. Took me years—years!—to understand the reason it all happened was because I put myself in that position. Wasn't bad luck in the alignment of the stars. Was me thinking I could rob a bank with nothing going wrong."

Duncan paused, not sure he could continue, but he knew he had to because Martha could not ask. "And I got consequences, ma'am. More consequences than I bargained for. You have some idea how many deaths I died when I saw that guard bleed to death in front of me? His breath leaving his body faster than his blood? Probably not enough deaths for you, ma'am, because I'm still alive. But I tell you, I died a million deaths right then and still more when I think about it now.

"When I shot that man, I made his family go without him. That was plenty clear right then. But I also made myself go without my family because they all walked off in shame and never spoke to me again. It all happened with the same damned shot at the same damned moment. Would have been better off if I'd shot myself. At least someone would have mourned me. Do you know my father died without forgiving me? Do you know the weight of that? Do you know what it's like to live with that?"

Duncan paused to control his breath, which was making him gasp despite the pumping in his chest that almost hurt. "I'm no cold-blooded killer, ma'am. Was once a fool and hope I'm not one now. I'm no danger to Dr. Maays or anybody anywhere. Because there are two truths I live with every day, ma'am. They're rooted in my soul tighter than your apple trees are to the earth. One truth is I killed a man, and the other is it was an accident. There's a requirement that you know the first and believe the other because I can't have Dr. Maays contorting herself to shelter me from you because you think I plan to kill everything I look at."

As his words emptied out of him, the overbearing sounds of trickling water, bubbling sauce, snapping fire, and swishing wind filled his hollowness. He hadn't said it exactly how he planned to say it. It came out however it came out. He was still expecting lightning to strike him for using his deplorable doings to demand anything of anyone, even for a thing he might die without. After all, the man he killed had not had time to make demands for anything, not even for his own life.

Duncan looked out the window where the horizon stretched in a thin line, seemingly unattached to earth or sky. Anything he had ever revealed to Leah about his past he had encapsulated in one- or two-word answers as if handing her individual words from a history tome. The unfairness of his answers always pained him, but until this moment, he had not been able to speak about the entire account, not even to himself, without falling face first into the hell of it.

Much to his surprise, having told the story allowed some of his angst to escape. With a clarity he did not have had before he spoke to Martha, he realized everything was firmly in the past. It might follow him forever, but being followed was not the same as being in the midst. He had come to inform Martha he was more than the worst thing he had done in his life and discovered he, too, had to believe that to go on.

Duncan hadn't anticipated what Martha might do or say, but he was not surprised when she began making moist little sounds with her mouth and lowered the stirrer. Duncan walked away, leaving her amidst the mason jars.

A FEW HOURS LATER, Duncan was again sitting in front of the drafting table with his head in his hands. He'd been sitting for hours, having lost all sense of time. Only when the shop door rattled open did he step into time.

"Duncan?" Leah's smile dropped as she approached him. She placed her hand on his cheek as if she thought he was running a fever.

He wondered if he looked as ghastly as he felt and pressed his forehead against her hand to take in her tender warmth. Wrapping his arms around her, he placed his hand against her face as if to shield her from all things terrible. Without saying a word, he slipped on his hat and opened the door for her so they could walk to the orchard.

Despite his determination to tell Leah the entire story of his fall, Duncan was grateful she did not pepper him with questions about what ailed him. He didn't yet know the outcome of the risk he'd taken with Martha, and Leah was already in the middle enough. He did not want her to think she had to choose between him and her family. Nothing between him and Martha was her fault.

When they arrived at the farm, the canning kitchen was abandoned. An eerie quietude haunted the orchard. Even the squawks of crows seemed to belong elsewhere.

"Sit on the porch?" Leah suggested, tugging gently at his sleeve.

Duncan looked through the window into the dining room, where an oil lamp was lit like a beacon. Martha the Insurmountable was scuttling around, placing plates and bread on the table. He held Leah's hands as if her fingers were little flowers, kissed each one, and departed.

THE ORCHARD RETAINED an eerie quiet for days. Leah knew Utterance was in on whatever ailed the household but was not discussing it with her. Utterance had to know because Martha told him everything, and Leah could see the angst on Martha's face.

Every time she left a room, it filled with troubled whispers that ceased the moment she returned. At night, she listened to their murmurs through the bedroom wall, unable to make out the words. All she heard was Martha's high-pitched bleating followed by the brief rumble of Utterance's voice. Espousing wisdom, Leah hoped.

And Duncan. He had not been the same for the same several days. Each time she touched him, he leaned into her as if to keep himself alive and warm. He had all but stopped speaking as if his mouth had somehow broken. Every time he approached the porch, he looked at its emptiness with a trepidation she could not begin to fathom. Duncan, who considered the likes of Cory Baines and Sheriff Wilkes as gnats, who could shove anyone across a room with a stare, was terrified of something here.

Then one evening, Leah came into the clearing with Duncan to find Martha sitting on the porch, wrapped in several shawls against the evening's chill. She stood as they approached, twisting and retwisting the fringes of the shawls together. Her aunt and Duncan looked each other over like two figures in a duel waiting for the other to fire first.

"Why dun you come in for dinner?" squeaked Martha.

Leah gasped. She looked back and forth between Martha and Duncan. Her heart beat so hard she thought it was going to skip across the orchard.

Duncan opened his mouth, but no sound came out. He cleared his throat with a soft cough and answered with the full expanse of his best courtesies.

"Thank you, Mrs. Cobb. I am mighty grateful."

"We be havin' pot roast."

Leah thought Duncan might collapse when he shifted his weight from one leg to the other. She placed her hand on the small of his back and felt him steady himself against her touch.

"Thank you, Mrs. Cobb," he repeated with a nod.

That evening, Martha set the table with a plenitude and copiousness she usually reserved for holiday meals. Utterance sat in silent consent, and every time Leah considered speaking, he frowned and shook his head.

In silence, she watched Martha practice a kind civility with Duncan that was supreme and Duncan return it as if they had never had a troubled past. They worked out their peace by saying *please, thank you, welcome, sir,* and *ma'am* and by passing back and forth salt and pepper, jam and bread, butter, onions and peas, cauliflower, potatoes, gravy, meat, beets, and cider and coffee.

For most of the meal, only the tableware conversed in little clatters, and conversation consisted of offering and accepting food. But the more Duncan and Martha shifted plates and condiments around, the more the tension between them eased, as if in the mild domestic activity they found a way to forge a sense of ease. Pie was served during the first comfortable silence.

With great tentativeness, Leah spoke her first words of the meal with a voice that sounded to her as if it belonged to another person. "Another slice of pie, Mr. Shay?"

"No, thank you, Dr. Maays."

"Uncle?"

"Oh no. I be full to bursting. Auntie sure outdun herself."

"Auntie, there are no takers for the last pieces. Where shall I put them?"

"Mr. Shay can take it for breakfast, if he wants." Martha reached out for the plate, awaiting Duncan's reply.

Duncan nodded once. "Would appreciate that, ma'am. Pie was mighty fine. Thank you."

Leah ran her hand across Duncan's shoulders as she handed the pie pan to Martha. He had yet to smile, but the soft lines on his face revealed an internal calm with a strength that might be life changing.

15

THE AFTER-HARVEST GATHERING

As far as Leah could recall, the Cobb After-Harvest Gathering was the last celebration of each year before winter settled in. Depending on how the apple trees behaved, the gathering took place in the last two weeks of October or early November.

She had not intended to abandon Duncan at the yearly Gathering, but she fell prey to being a hostess and found herself in charge of a house full of napping toddlers and babies. Keeping one ear bent for crying, she stood on the porch, waiting for someone to relieve her. She could not just abandon a house of sleeping children, but all someone had to do was step on the porch, and she could step off it.

She counted about forty people milling around the orchard, guests and farm hands who had not yet departed for the season. Most adults were gathered around tables decked with potluck offerings. Children were running among the apple trees, shrieking as they played hide and seek and chased one another.

She took a while to find Duncan in the crowd. He was

holding his own with people who tolerated him without fuss—Henry Moore, Dr. Haloway, Hoburn, and Utterance. Other men had also discreetly gathered by the corral to hear the dirty jokes Andy Jenk the blacksmith was famous for delivering.

Leah smiled to herself. The politics of prejudice were highly idiosyncratic. Dr. Haloway would rather stand side by side with Duncan than be within a mile of her.

Always cautious, Duncan stood a little outside the circle, resting one arm on a railing. Andy casually stepped back to open the circle. After some hesitation, the other men followed Andy's lead and realigned themselves to include Duncan.

Duncan had infinitely more presence than the other men, exhibiting a languid sophistication in a well-proportioned body. With supreme delicacy, he held a cider cup by the brim between his thumb and middle finger, swaying it gently as though experimenting with its balance. Leah was drawn to the slight motions of his fingers. How a man who frequently unloaded cartloads of wood boards singlehandedly could handle a tin cup with such finesse...

Andy Jenk began gesticulating wildly, a sign he was about to deliver a punchline. The men tossed back their heads and guffawed so loudly Leah heard them from the porch. Some even slapped their knees and hopped around, spilling cider on themselves.

Duncan's gestures were, as usual, reserved. His shoulders shook a little. He tucked his chin, grinned, looked over the tops of his eyes that now gleamed with amusement. As a grand finale, he shifted his weight and bounced one knee a bit.

Perhaps she could get Duncan to tell her some of the

dirty jokes, although he might clam up at the suggestion. She usually heard dirty jokes from Martha, who got them from Utterance, who got them in town. But only the mildest, most diluted ones survived the various forms of censorship on their way to her ears.

The circle broke, and Duncan strolled toward her, pacing himself to remain a short distance behind two mothers who were returning to the house to check on their children. Leah stepped off the porch the moment the mothers entered the house.

With an impulse to hug, she moved toward him, but Duncan, who feasted on affection in private, kept his distance from her in public, lest wrong assumptions be made. Compromising, Leah let her fingers casually brush against his face under the guise of smoothing his collar. He sighed and lightly bit one lip, then buried all expression under a poker face.

"Are you having a fine time, Duncan?"

"Yes, ma'am. Thank you. And you?"

Leah nodded. "I saw you were listening to jokes. Any good ones?"

"Not sure I can tell you one without getting embarrassed. Cider, Leah?"

Leah smiled at his controlled nervousness. Unused to being in social situations, Duncan had been on edge all day. No one was standing by the cider pot, which was probably why he suggested going there. At the pot, he bought himself a moment of solitude by stoking the fire and stirring the cloudy gold fluid before resting the ladle in the pot.

"Have you visited the whiskey cow?" asked Leah.

Duncan raised one eyebrow. "Your uncle is mighty brave keeping a whiskey cow in the barn with your auntie around."

"Well, it only makes whiskey on the day of After-Harvest. Or so I hear."

"Likely story, Leah. I'm sure your uncle appreciates a good shot once in a while. Even heard a bunch of ladies giving Mrs. Cobb their sympathies, then taking tastes from their husbands' cups."

Leah laughed because that happened every year, and Martha never caught on. "I believe the contract is that if everyone stays sober, Auntie allows the whiskey cow to stay for the day."

"Mighty fair compromise. I suppose everyone flocked to the whiskey cow when Emma Groth showed up last year."

Leah wrinkled her nose. "Uninvited too. She was better than rain for clearing out the guests."

"Heard this year a committee formed to keep her from coming. Heard they left a trail of chocolates past Edith's Bay into the ocean. That's how we got high tide today, with all her sleeves."

Leah laughed, making Duncan grin triumphantly. They lost all interest in the cider and stood with the pot between them, smiling idly. Duncan was still impeccable, and Leah grew self-conscious about the many stains on her apron.

"Dr. Maays! Mr. Shay!" Dr. Elliot waved as he scampered not quite steadily toward them.

Leah leaned toward Duncan. "I take it your secret committee did not find him enticeable with chocolates?"

Duncan grimaced. "Might have drowned, ma'am."

"How fortuitous your uncle is inciting these festivities while I am visiting," declared Dr. Elliot by manner of greeting. "It has been most convivial. Your hospitality is unparalleled. I have been made to feel like an honorary visitant."

Leah gave Dr. Elliot a subtle once over, taking in the

man's flushed cheeks and the slight slurring of his impressive vocabulary.

"Staying until when, sir?" asked Duncan.

"On Monday I take the carriage to Edith's Bay. From there I return to Boston, where I have been engaged to deliver several lectures about venereal epidermal lesions."

Duncan nodded. He poured a cup of cider and guided Leah away from Dr. Elliot when he placed the cup in her hands.

Dr. Elliot pulled out a silver hip flask. "Allow me, Mr. Shay."

"No sir. Thank you."

"Of course, not for Dr. Maays."

Leah restrained herself from poking her finger into the lusty twinkles in Dr. Elliot's eyes.

"Neither for me, sir. Thank you," said Duncan.

"Really? Why, I calculated you would enjoy imbibing."

"Calculated. Wrong. Sir."

An invisible brick wall seemed to fall out of the sky between Duncan and Dr. Elliot. Leah wondered if someone put Dr. Elliot up to the task of offering Duncan whiskey. She looked around and saw a small cluster of men observing them from a distance.

"Well, perhaps I shall..." Dr. Elliot backed away under Duncan's formidable stare. His heel caught on a tree root, and he jerked his arm up to restore his balance, causing the cap of the flask to flip out of his hand. Dr. Elliot flailed like a tightrope walker losing his balance before landing on the grass. A stream of yellow whiskey arced from the flask and landed on Duncan's sleeve with a splat.

Duncan hopped back and flung his arm away from himself as if to throw it across the field. He fixed a look on Dr. Elliot that could have withered the grass around him.

Dr. Elliot began patting grass like a blind man for the flask cap. "I am... I am certain that will...will wash out."

Duncan pointed to the cap in the grass. "Over there. Sir."

Without taking his eyes off Duncan, Dr. Elliot groped in the direction Duncan pointed until he touched the cap. Duncan walked around him and headed toward the house.

From the corner of her eye, Leah saw Utterance standing, his attention fixed on Duncan. She sprinted behind Duncan to the house and, in the kitchen, stood by him as he rubbed a bar of soap over his sleeve with a force that might have ripped the cloth. She slipped a little scrub brush into his hand, and he continued his vigorous scrubbing with it.

"Don't relish stinking of spirits in front of your auntie, Leah."

Leah remained silent. No matter how innocent the spill, someone would be sure to turn the scent of liquor into some epic tale about how Duncan got drunk at the Cobbs'. Perhaps even about how he decked Dr. Elliot for spilling whiskey on him. Worse things had been said about Duncan. Almost all manner of vile actions had been attributed to him.

She despaired the gossip was inevitable, if it was not already happening. Duncan, most likely aware of what awaited him, rubbed the brush hard against his sleeve. Leah pulled the brush out of his hand before it left a raw streak on his skin. She poured a cup of water over his sleeve, patted his arm dry with a dish towel, then sprinkled baking soda on the cloth. Perhaps that would further minimize the smell.

Knowing that touch settled Duncan as nothing else did, she slid her arms around his waist. Duncan abandoned his cleansing and drew Leah close.

His tenor rumbled bass-like through his chest. "Mighty

grateful you being so concerned about me, Leah. Mighty grateful."

Leah wondered what possible comfort he could take from her twiggy arms around his torso. She closed her eyes, wanting to melt into the dry warmth of his body. Duncan tugged her to the kitchen table, where he sat and pulled her between his knees. He rested his head on her shoulder and sighed deeply into her neck, becoming still except for his shallow breathing and the slight rise and fall of his shoulders.

His heartbeat resounded within her body as she stroked the velvety stubble on the back of his neck from his day-old haircut until he arched his body. Duncan mumbled softly, clenched around her as if to absorb her through his pores. He slipped his fingers into her bun and bunched her hair in his fist as he pressed his lips to hers, tugging them with the slight suction of kisses until he kissed her with an open mouth.

Suspended in the microscopic world they had just created, Leah startled when a ruckus of clacking heels and whooping laughter came rolling down the hallway, gathering momentum like a bowling ball toward pins. In a scramble, she pushed Duncan away just as the kitchen door swung open and in charged Martha, leading a gaggle of her quilting companions.

A half dozen ladies swarmed into the kitchen, chattering and laughing over one another, each engaged in multiple, simultaneous conversations. They swept through, asking, telling, pointing, mandating, giggling. From the volume they generated, Leah thought there would be several times as many of them.

Calling instructions, Martha turned to open the pie cabinet and came face to face with Duncan, whose passions were now fully doused. Martha's rare sense of jocularity died on the spot. The other ladies, sensing the change in their hostess, simmered down.

"What happened to your shirt?" Martha asked, her nostril quivering with tiny sniffs.

"Spill, ma'am."

He was the picture of respectability as he opened the cabinet door for Martha. Across the kitchen, Leah finished folding a dishtowel, hoping no one would infer anything about the strands of loose hair from her bun.

"Heared you ain't a drinker," Martha announced loudly as if to justify Duncan's presence in her house.

"Not often, ma'am."

All conversation came to a standstill.

"So, how's the quilt? When do you think you'll finish it?" asked Leah generally to all the ladies.

The ladies started up again, all of them chattering and gesticulating at once. Duncan nodded genteelly to Martha and waited for her to remove and distribute as many pies as she needed before he closed the cabinet door and slipped out of the kitchen.

Leah coughed into the dish towel so the quilting ladies would not see her smiling the way she wanted to smile— with a joyous sensuality she had not felt since the first time Titus held her in his arms. Titus. Leah wondered sadly whether he would have liked Duncan, although surely not if she enjoyed being in Duncan's arms.

She sighed. The day had been one of deprivation. She had spent little time with Duncan and eaten almost nothing in the process of helping Martha and Utterance run the gathering. And now, after this last encounter, an intense need to be with Duncan overcame her.

She went outside to look for him and was pleased to see

him at the nearby banquet table with Utterance. After she extracted herself from a conversation with the quilting ladies, she made her way to the table, now led by her stomach, which was grumbling with hunger.

By the time she got there, Utterance was offering Duncan a slice of cheese. "Nice round of cheese you brought."

Duncan hesitated before peeling the cheese off the knife. "Thank you, sir. How'd you know that's one I brought?"

Utterance tipped the cheese on its side to reveal a cutting board made from several unusual woods. "I be thinking if you made the board, you brought the cheese on it."

"Figure Mrs. Cobb can use an extra cutting board, sir."

"Better tell her it be for her. Else she be running all over creation trying to return it to someone who dun exist tomorrow. She be all irksome you ain't told her on time it be hers."

"I'll mention it, sir."

Utterance held a tin plate out to Leah. "We got you, Haloway, and Elliot all here. With all you doctors, I figure we can resurrect anybody who dies today."

"You have resurrection powers, Dr. Maays?" asked Duncan.

Leah laughed. "I wouldn't put it to the test, if I were you."

"You dun think the others got resurrection powers?" Utterance asked Duncan.

Duncan almost smiled. "Think Dr. Elliot would rather dissect the body, sir. Dr. Haloway might not notice someone died until tomorrow."

Utterance chuckled. "Heared the lame start walkin' to get away from Dr. Elliot. Well, if anybody got resurrection powers, it be Leah. Ain't for lack of trying."

"Dr. Maays is no ordinary woman, sir," said Duncan as he eyed her.

Utterance looked Duncan up and down. "Leah likes challenges. She dun do nothing simple."

Duncan did not acknowledge the implication. "Might be so, sir."

"Heared you dun drink," said Utterance.

Leah turned somber, anticipating Utterance was going to begin asking questions Duncan might find difficult to answer.

"Drink beer sometimes. Like sherry on winter eves. Not averse to something stronger now and then. Sir."

Utterance selected a pickle and a bit into it. "Smoke?"

"No sir."

"Like cards?"

"Just Old Maid, sir."

Utterance snorted. "Wipe your feet before going in a house?"

Duncan hesitated. "If I remember, sir."

"Ain't you got no vices?"

Duncan seemed to sink into himself. "Used them all up early, sir. Not allowed more."

Utterance chewed through the rest of the pickle. "We be starting a game of horseshoe, if you be innerested."

"Play horseshoes like you play checkers, sir." said Duncan, recovering from Utterance's gentle inquisition.

"Best we partner up, then. Cain't stand losing."

Duncan glanced at Leah. She smiled while trying to imagine how sparse Duncan's life was for him to be so startled by a casual invitation to join a game.

Utterance began to walk away. "You a-coming?"

"Yes, sir."

By the time Leah finished loading up a plate with food,

Duncan was well integrated into the game of horseshoes. She arrived in time to see him toss a shoe with such force the iron peg tipped out of the ground when the shoe struck it. Duncan held his pose, knees bent with his arm extended, his rolled-up sleeves revealing stupendous forearms. The horseshoe swung around the peg and dropped to the ground. An admiring murmur riffled through the onlookers.

Leah exchanged looks with Utterance, who shook his head at the skill of the throw. Duncan played hard when he needed to win.

Dusk and the distant rumble of thunder inspired the great cleanup to begin. Martha whisked herself and her friends into the canning kitchen to wash and put away the tin picnic plates. Other women began packing leftover food, while children were put in charge of putting dirty tablecloths in baskets and carrying dirty plates to the canning kitchen.

Duncan joined the men in disassembling banquet tables and dragging them into the barn. They hoisted the tables into a pile and covered them with what had once been an old sail. The men bid one another goodbye and left to gather their families. Impressed by how efficiently the mess of the After-Harvest Gathering was turning back into a tranquil orchard, Duncan petted one of the horses to grab a moment of quiet before going out in public to look for Leah.

He found her in the kitchen, the place where all lost persons eventually reappear. Mary Corwal was slipping her sleeping youngest into Leah's arms. Sitting in a chair was Mary's three-year-old, all boogery and tearful with a scrape across his forehead.

Mary began to wipe the boy's face. "Ain't I told you not to

climb the trees? And in the dark! Serves you right, you falling. What you think Mr. Cobb be thinking when he sees that tree next summer and it ain't got a branch? He be thinking of you, Silas!"

Duncan turned his attention to Leah, whose back was to him as she cradled Mary's youngest in one arm. In the light of the kerosene lamp, her dress looked starkly colorless, as if carved from stone. Almost imperceptibly, Leah began to sway until bit by bit, Duncan came to understand she was rocking not the child, but herself.

Leah once showed him a picture of her with her late husband, who held an infant. She and her husband had stethoscopes draped around their necks as indications of their profession. The swaddled baby looked like a loaf of bread. Behind them, in the distance, stood some blurry elephants that had been more interesting to him than the portraits. After he expressed his condolences, she thanked him with a quiet politeness he had taken for serenity.

At the time, he marveled at how efficiently Leah had processed such a devastating history, folding it neatly into a little box and finding a quiet place in her soul to keep it as she worked her medical practice with a fervor that seemed to exclude everything. He was convinced her grief had ended as he watched her begin to charge through the town, ministering to people between managing the cloth counter and conducting inventory at Hoburn's.

"... now, I catch you in them trees again, you be spending next year sitting on the porch by yourself while everybody else be playing. You understand that, Silas? Now you get with our things. We got be going home."

Mary stood the boy on the floor and landed a slap on his rear. The child ran blindly into Duncan's leg before pushing open the door and running from the kitchen, screaming, more from exhaustion than from the slap. When Mary saw Duncan, she turned toward Leah to collect her youngest and leave.

Without opening her eyes, Leah held up one hand. Mary backed away as if pulled back by a cord.

Duncan could feel the grief pulsing through Leah in her shaky little nods, as if she were convincing herself to give up the child. He wondered if she was prepared for what he sensed was coming. Sorrow of this magnitude had impetuous powers to come flapping out of tidy boxes barely sealed with time. This kind of sorrow had a wildness that could never be tamed, an unpredictability that could not be controlled. For that matter, no grief could ever be fully buried.

Only when Mary's child shifted in Leah's arms did Leah open her eyes. Thick, glass-like tears distorted the dark blue before rolling down her cheeks. She opened her arms and let Mary take the child from her.

"I'm sorry, Dr. Maays. I plum forgot about your baby. I should've never asked you—" began Mary.

Leah slipped out the back door with the quickness of water through a crack, leaving the room dense with her grief. Only when the door slammed shut did Duncan register she was no longer present.

He brushed by Mary to go after Leah. On the porch, he found her incoherent with hoarse coughs and tremendous sobs that heaved her ribs. Duncan slipped one arm around her, experiencing the turmoil of comforting a woman who was grieving for another man. He slipped his handkerchief into her hand, although he knew she was far beyond the realm of handkerchiefs.

Leah clutched the handkerchief and pressed her fists against his chest. "They just died. They just died and died and died! Everyone died! It didn't matter what I did. They just died. All of them!"

Duncan wrapped his other arm around her, knowing no words could comfort such deep, recurring sorrow. This he knew too well. But he also knew grief's paths led into the past while love's paths could lead into the future.

16

THE ILLNESS

Cold usually settled in weeks after the After-Harvest Gathering, pressing people to make last-minute visits to Edith's Bay before inclement weather paralyzed the town. Duncan was no exception, and when he went off to conduct business in Edith's Bay, time stopped making progress in Leah's mind. Inside her head, she awaited him in perfect stillness, although as she flew from one corner of the general store to the other like a hummingbird, no one would think any part of her was ever still. Yet every moment seemed identical to the one before it.

Waiting was so very tedious. Leah put on her apron in the back room while she tried to snap out of the mood that ailed her. She cracked open the door and peeked into the front room of the store, where a few patients were waiting to see her. On the crates Hoburn had rearranged for their benefit, sat a woman with a bile-colored child, a man she remembered once treating for itchy feet, and another woman with maroon shadows under her eyes. No emergencies.

If the carriage arrived early enough, she might still see

Duncan before going home. Tired as he might be, she knew he would insist on walking her home. Leah opened the door of the back room and stepped out smiling like an actress walking on stage.

She faced the small audience of miserable people. "Good afternoon. Who's first?"

In answer to her question, Henry came tripping into the store, clutching a handful of envelopes and shouting like a banshee, "Dr. Maays! Dr. Maays! Come quick! Come quick!"

Hearing the emergency in his screech, Leah grabbed her cloak and black bag. Before she even knew where she was heading, she was in the middle of the street, shivering in the cold, with her cloak still tucked under her arm.

She twirled around. A person could bleed to death in minutes. "Where to, Henry? Where to?"

Henry pumped his arms up and down until a word fell out of his mouth. "Duncan!"

Duncan! His name suspended her in disbelief. Surely Duncan could not be hurt. Leah bolted toward the shop.

Henry shouted, "Back room! Back room!"

She veered without breaking her speed into the alley that led to Duncan's living quarters. With her shoulder, she crashed into the door and collided with the table in the center of the room. Behind her, Henry tumbled in.

A sensation of slow disembodiment overcame her when she saw Duncan's lavender fingertips poking from under a blanket. She rested her hand on the stove. Cold. Her breath come out in a little puff. How long Duncan had been back? Preparing herself for what lavender fingers could mean, she approached the bed slowly and, mumbling a plea into the universe, snatched back the blanket.

A white cloud of breath swirled out of Duncan's mouth when he turned his head away from the light. She placed her fingers over his lips as if to stop the cloud from escaping and lowered herself onto the edge of the bed with an inebriating sense of relief that Duncan was alive. On his forehead, she felt the fever that flushed his sallow skin with purple.

"Henry, fire, please." Her thoughts were so suspended, she could not speak in sentences. Disregarding Henry, she addressed Duncan familiarly. "Duncan? It's Leah."

Duncan winced at the sound of her voice.

"Let me have a look at you. Duncan, please open your eyes." Leah stroked his cheek to see if he would open his eyes on his own. When he did not, she gently pulled up one eyelid. Duncan turned his head away.

"Does your head hurt?"

He squeezed his eyelids, a bare scrap of an answer that Leah took to mean yes. She pulled down the blanket and pressed her hands against his abdomen, in search of swollen organs. Duncan moaned and pushed her hands away.

"Henry, please boil two inches of water in a clean pan."

"Is Duncan going to be all right?" asked Henry, grabbing the first pot he touched.

"Not to worry. Surgery is not required." Leah slipped on her stethoscope and busied herself so she would not have to answer Henry's questions. She noted how every sound grated on Duncan and how he could hardly bear to be touched, even by her.

When the water in the pot began boiling, Leah pulled a leather box out of her black bag and placed the pieces of a disassembled syringe from it into the water. She prepared a solution of morphine sulfide before pulling the pieces of the syringe out with silver tongs and draining them on a linen towel.

Henry began to look queasy. She often forgot how terrifying a syringe could look to a lay person.

"Henry, are you going to faint?"

Henry gulped. "Oh—um—no. I'm fine. Yes."

"What made you come looking for Duncan?" Leah asked to distract him.

"I saw smoke in his chimney last night, but he didn't come for his mail this morning. He always comes for his mail first thing in the morning when he's been away. Figured when he didn't come by noon, maybe I should look in on him."

"I am very glad you did, Henry." Leah pressed the cork plunger until bubbles came out of the needle.

Henry stepped back.

"Henry, please sit down. This is not for you."

"Oh... I know..."

She walked toward Duncan, holding the syringe behind her back. Henry might pass out, but she didn't want Duncan to panic if he saw it. She pulled down Duncan's sleeve and swiped his upper arm with gauze. When she slid the needle under Duncan's skin, Henry jumped. Leah answered Duncan's protestations with sympathetic cooing until, bit by bit, he relaxed. Leah pulled out the needle.

"Henry, does anyone have a carriage or a wagon we may borrow? I am going to take Duncan to the farm. He cannot be here alone."

"Maybe Hoburn? Andy Jenk?"

"Anyone's will do. Get one. Please."

Henry sprinted out of the room, and by the time he returned with Hoburn's surrey and horse, she had trousers on Duncan and was tying the laces on his boots. Duncan was stretched out on the bed, marvelously sedated and seemingly immune to pain and cold.

"Come, Duncan. Let's sit up," said Leah.

Duncan rolled his head to one side without opening his

eyes. Leah considered she might need Hoburn's horse to move him. She cajoled him with a sweet banter until he sluggishly gathered himself and let his legs slip over the side of the bed. His eyes became slits as he almost fell forward. Leah caught him, letting him to rest against her body.

She waited until he seemed steadier, then raised her head and almost sang in a whisper, "Come on, come on. Time to go to the orchard. Come along, Duncan."

She beckoned Henry to get on the other side of Duncan. Together, they dragged him to his feet and laboriously began the shuffle to the surrey.

"Is Duncan going to be all right?" Henry asked as she arranged the carriage blanket around Duncan.

Leah cupped her hands over Duncan's ears, "Can you drive? Let's be quick."

"Why are we whispering? What's wrong with Duncan?"

She put her arms around Duncan. "He has meningitis. His head hurts."

~

From the guest room where Duncan lay muttering and fretting in semi-consciousness, Leah braced herself when she heard Martha thumping up the stairs. The night before, Martha asked Utterance if every sick person on earth was going to end up at the house.

Well, the house was Martha's, Leah conceded. But the life was Duncan's. At least Martha had not said anything to her directly. Leah wasn't sure she would have the patience to answer gracefully or gratefully.

Martha stuck her head into the room. "Mrs. Groth's a-coming. She just pulled up."

They listened to Mrs. Groth bark a series of orders while

her driver opened the carriage door. Martha took off. Leah realized she had not changed her clothes since yesterday because Duncan had been delirious all night long with fever spiking until his eyes rolled into his head when he had convulsions.

She had not even dared leave him to work at Hoburn's and sent a message down with Utterance. She rolled the bedsheets she had just changed and Duncan's nightshirt together and took the bundle to the porch around the time Mrs. Groth was making her way up the steps.

"Good morning, Dr. Leah. How is our patient?" Mrs. Groth asked as she brushed the lapel of a fur coat that made her look as if she might not fit through the doorway. The coat matched her hat, which seemed made from a stack of beavers.

Leah dropped the dirty linens into a basket in the corner of the porch. "Fine, thank you."

Mrs. Groth squinted with piqued interest at the cuff of a nightshirt among the pillowcases. "Is Duncan Shay accepting visitors? Not that I would disturb him."

"Mr. Shay is asleep."

Leah turned and went back into the house, feeling Martha's fitful stare on the back of her head as Emma Groth asked, "How does your niece bathe such a big man? Does she do it by herself or does she engage your help, Mrs. Cobb? That is, providing your husband permits such a thing."

The question with all its innuendos had no correct answer, Leah knew, but poor Martha would give it her best. At the top of the stairs, she paused to listen to the tones in the conversation as if it were discordant music seeping from under a closed door. Mrs. Groth's pointed question. Martha's bleating answer. Mrs. Groth's hard punch. Martha's indignant, hopeless, tongue-tied silence, followed by brief babbling. Then the cycle began again. It would go on for the entire visit.

Such outrageous disrespect, thought Leah, transported to the single time during her residency when the head resident addressed her as Dr. Maays. His friends in the office all kept straight faces while he relegated her to bedpan patrol in the most affluent language possible. But they began to snicker before she could even close the door behind herself. In a state of shock, she went ahead and emptied all the bedpans in the infirmary, as she had been assigned to do. Relegating Mrs. Groth to Martha was the same as relegating a trained physician to bedpan patrol.

Leah turned and walked back to the parlor. At the doorway, she stood and waited for their undivided attention, recalling how she scraped the contents of all the bedpans into a single one and left it under the head resident's desk, where he promptly stuck his foot into it the following morning when he sat. No one ever again asked her to go near a bedpan.

"I trust everything is going well, Dr. Leah," said Mrs. Groth as she tapped her thumbs. "I hear you've taken to bathing Mr. Shay. By yourself. Behind closed doors."

"Mrs. Groth," said Leah, "your visit is inopportune. We are busy, and no one is available to attend to you. Auntie, please see Mrs. Groth to the door and join me as soon as you can."

Mrs. Groth's body made an odd sound as she turned sideways and almost knocked Martha over with her bustle. Leah opened the front door, letting a blast of cold air into the house.

"Good day, Mrs. Groth. Auntie, please remember to close

the door after Mrs. Groth leaves or we shall lose all our heat. And we would not want that."

As Leah made her way up the stairs, she could not find anything within herself that cared about what Mrs. Groth thought. When she got into Duncan's room, she could hear Mrs. Groth making the great commotion she always made while getting into or out of her carriage. Leah sighed with relief. She had not been sure the woman would leave, even if asked.

She knew Martha could not hide her disapproval of having her niece bathe Duncan Shay alone. What a feast for Mrs. Groth! But Leah knew she could not condemn Martha to a lifetime of tact and discretion if she saw the scars on Duncan's torso. And Duncan would die if word got out—he who ordered his work shirts tailored with extra gathers of thick cloth so no shirt would ever inadvertently stretch against his back. Taking comfort in Duncan's steady breathing, Leah settled into the wing chair and closed her eyes.

She must have fallen asleep immediately because the next thing she heard was, "Leah, you got a hard face! You know no bounds. She be telling everybody now how we booted her out of the house!"

Leah jumped up. She grabbed Martha by the arm and pulled her into the hallway so not to wake Duncan. "Auntie! She tortures you with her malice in your own parlor, and you let her. This is your house, Auntie. Don't let her in! Tell her you are not accepting visitors when she comes. Do you truly believe she'll be nice to you because you're nice to her? Just last week she told everyone your coffee tasted bad because Uncle had a bad crop and you were reusing old coffee grounds!"

Martha creased her brow until her eyes were almost crossed. She lowered her head between her shoulders, looking as if she might hiss. But she shook her finger at Leah. "We need her for the church roof, Leah. We can't just go insulting her. She might just declare us heathens and not give money for the roof! Then it'll be on us."

Leah flapped her hands with exasperation. "The church roof? The church roof! Do you think everyone will put up with a leaky church roof without ole Mrs. Groth? Do you think she is the savior of everything that requires money? Auntie, she doesn't give to help people! She gives to be admired. And to lord her gifts over people's heads. There is no kindness in that woman."

Martha's eyes filled with tears. Leah had not expected such a reaction. She put her arms around Martha, wanting to bite off her tongue for being so sharp.

"Auntie, I'm sorry. I meant well. I am sorry." She pulled a handkerchief from her pocket and gave it to Martha, who sniffled and snorted into it none too delicately.

Martha wiped her tears and smiled bravely. "Leah, I know you be tired, that's all. You bin workin' hard."

Leah began to laugh. She was almost hysterical from lack of sleep topped with the stress of Mrs. Groth's visit. And from knowing Duncan might be dead when she went back into the room.

17

THE GOOD DOCTOR

Duncan's fever continued strong, even after a week. In search of any medical procedure she might have overlooked, Leah humbled herself and asked Dr. Haloway for his opinion.

"Mrs. Maays, a tepid enema is my best recommendation to reduce a high fever," he said, complete with condescension.

An enema! She was shocked at how outdated Dr. Haloway's medical knowledge was.

"I am very sure that is your best recommendation. Thank you," she responded and left.

Still desperate, she wrote a letter to Dr. Elliot, who was not incompetent and had contemporary medical knowledge, but was better at research than at working with patients. She held on to the letter for a day before she tossed it into the woodstove, fearing Dr. Elliot would arrive and begin conducting experiments on Duncan. After all her humbling and letter writing, she was still alone in battle.

She cringed to think what could happen to Duncan if she were not around. She might not be the most brilliant physician in the world, but at least she was competent and up to date on current medical practices. The pickings for medical care in West Edith's Bay were slim to non-existent, even with Dr. Haloway. She imagined if Duncan died, town folk would not realize how in danger they also were.

By now, she was desperate enough to consider moving Duncan to Edith's Bay Hospital. What stopped her was having to transport him in Utterance's work wagon in below-freezing temperatures and possibly snow. Duncan might not survive the trip, or he might arrive at the hospital with pneumonia. Or weakened as he was, he might catch something else at the hospital, which, by definition, was full of infections. Every option required worry.

By the time Duncan's daily convulsions finally ceased for twenty-four hours, Leah no longer trusted her touch to determine whether his fever had gone down. For the most part, Duncan spent the day napping uneventfully, but he was still very warm. The critical moment Leah had so eagerly awaited had arrived, and she was too exhausted, too reluctant, to form hopeful conclusions or rejoice.

She rose from the wingback chair and looked in the dresser mirror to brush her hair, noting she had reached the point during an intense illness when the doctor begins to look like the patient. She forced her mouth to smile and watched the curve of her lips mean nothing. Well, nothing was over yet. Duncan still ran a significant fever.

Having given up on buns for the time being, she braided her hair and stood by Duncan, waiting for him to call or open his eyes. Wanting to caress him but afraid to wake him, Leah convinced herself he was sleeping peacefully and headed downstairs, looking forward to a hot meal and conversation.

"Who be you?" asked Utterance as she came into the dining room. "You live here?"

"I am a spirit come to visit." Leah held her arms stiffly in front of her as she shuffled to her chair.

"Pale 'nuff for one," said Martha, handing her a plate. "Sit down and eat before you disappear like one. How's he doing?"

"Stable for now, Auntie. Stable."

Leah surveyed the table. Sausage. Cabbage. Potatoes. It all turned her stomach, but she sat, longing for something simpler like oatmeal. She yawned before nodding to Utterance to begin saying grace.

"Dear Lord, we are—"

"Damn you to hell!"

Martha gasped at the profanity as she had been doing for days. They looked up in the direction of Duncan's room as if to see through the ceiling.

"Let go... No!"

Leah rose from the chair, moving swiftly but calmly, as she had learned to move in front of her medical colleagues— swiftly to arrive in time to be of help, calmly to inspire confidence and hide her panic. When she climbed enough steps to know she could not be seen from the dining room, she lifted her skirts with both hands and jumped the steps in pairs.

In the bedroom, she found Duncan fighting with the blankets for possession of his arms. She pulled the blanket off his chest. Duncan waved his arms.

"Duncan, it's Leah." She approached cautiously, having once been flung across the room by a frail, delirious woman with a postpartum infection. Duncan could fling her into the barn.

"Damn you!"

"Duncan, it's Leah. We're at Utterance's."

"Leah? Leah!" he shouted, trying to sit up.

Leah pushed him back onto the pillow. "I'm right here. No need to get up. I'm right here."

"This isn't a place for you, Leah."

"We're at Utterance's. The orchard." She stroked his temple. Sometimes the gesture comforted him.

Duncan grabbed her wrist. "No..."

"It's Leah. Leah. Shhhh... You're at the orchard."

Duncan settled back into the pillow with a moan. She pulled her wrist from his grip, hoping he had tired himself out. The fever wafted in waves from his body, and in a moment he was drenched in sweat. He turned his face toward Leah's hand and became still.

Please, no more convulsions.

"...said it was an accident..."

"It's Leah. Leah." *Please, no more convulsions.*

She reached for the leather bit on the night table as the perspiration seeped through Duncan's nightshirt, dipped the bit in water, and slipped it into his mouth to keep him from biting his tongue. Duncan threw back his head as his shoulders rolled off the bed. His back arched sharply just as his arms began to thump uncontrollably against the mattress.

Only when he stopped bucking and thrashing did Leah recognize the seizure was over. No matter how short the seizure, it always left her weak with fear.

She tugged the bit out of his mouth. "It's Leah. You're at Utterance's. At the orchard."

She raised his head and gave him as much water as he would drink, then closed the door to bathe him and change his nightshirt. She and Martha had been washing nightshirts daily because she would not let Duncan rest in clothes that had been saturated with sweat. Sometimes she changed him into nightshirts with seams that were still damp from having been washed. When Leah finished and opened the bedroom door, Utterance was patiently waiting in the hallway with a plate of food in hand.

"See you found yourself better dinner company," Utterance said, holding out the plate. Everything was cut into small pieces so she could manage with a fork.

"The fever spiked again." Leah tried to put a compress on Duncan's forehead, but he pushed it away.

Utterance pressed the plate into Leah's hands and pointed to the wingback chair. "Eat. He'll be fine for five minutes."

"Thank you for bringing dinner, Uncle."

"You going pull him through?"

"He'll pull himself through. He's quite strong. He just needs some help."

"Ropes of love—if they dun strangle him, they'll pull him through."

Resenting Utterance's clarity about sentiments that still made her uneasy, Leah responded evenly. "Such talk, Uncle."

"Well, he dun let no one near him, 'cept you."

"He knows I'm his doctor."

"You telling me a feverish feller calls out your name 'cause he be lookin' for a reliable doctor?"

Leah looked away.

"Used to be I was worried 'bout you. Now I be more in favor for worrying 'bout him. Man like him dun trust just 'cause. You be responsible with him."

Leah looked despairingly at the cold food.

"Eat up. He needs you strong. Pointy's saddled, if you need me to go to town. Wake me if you need me. Auntie's dispensable, too, you know. She flaps around a bit, but she always be useful."

"Please say good night to Auntie for me."

Utterance left without saying anything else. Leah forced the food into herself while she listened to Duncan breathe. She felt the way her stethoscope on the dresser looked, sprawled like a depleted creature.

IN THE COLD stillness of the night, Leah contemplated Duncan dying. He could very well die. Surviving meningitis was not common.

In Ghana, she never once imagined Titus or William dying, not even at the peak of their illnesses. Until their ends, she believed she could preserve them with good practices. At the very moment William died, his death seemed the most improbable. She had difficulty even comprehending he was gone. William—born of two physicians dedicated to curing—should have been exempt. He was only a baby.

And Titus. There had been no reason for him to die either. Titus, who prepared his life to better the lives of others, who continued working at the quarantined infirmary even after the rash manifested on his skin, even as he could see his fate in those he tended.

To have thought she could prevent death in the sick when it was natural in the very healthy! Leah wanted to feel scornful at her naiveté, but even now she still counted on it being possible.

She struggled to believe her efforts were valid despite the brutal, insentient forces of a universe that plundered human experience. To accept she had no say in the end, except perhaps by influencing how people died, was like swallowing a behemoth whole. And that night, Leah refused to swallow. Duncan might be better off with her care than without, no matter what the outcome, but knowing this did not comfort her. She wanted him to live.

Duncan's death could happen. It would be permanent. Without her say. Despite her efforts. Without her permission. Or forgiveness. The insentient universe could drench her with new sorrows without ever being aware of her old ones.

She took inventory of her paltry offerings. The syringe, her lancet against the dragon. The pestle and the mortar, her staff and orb. Sterile water from a decanter, her elixir. Herself, ready for the rescue, carrying hope in a worn, black-leather bag with her initials on a small brass plate, her shield. Duncan's was the very death she had to accept, even as she worked and worked to keep his life with hers, using every practice, technique, and medicine she knew.

Leah rolled up her sleeves, preparing to perform the last procedure she learned in Ghana for the fevers from the pox. The procedure had not worked for any patient there, and she did not count on it working for Duncan either. But as everything she tried that could have worked had failed so far, she was left only with what might work, and she was willing to try that now.

Leah approached the bed, steeled herself to clear her mind of random thoughts that might distract her. Then she renounced her arrogance and begged the sentient things in the universe for Duncan's life.

～

Just before dawn, Leah thought she heard Duncan call her name but, stuck in the midst of sleep, she was not sure. He called random people randomly, in various states of delusion and consciousness. She listened carefully and heard him rustle, mumbling something that had the basic sounds of her name.

She slipped out of the wing chair, feeling a twinge in her neck and a throb in her lower back. Duncan was shivering. Leah placed her hand on his forehead, which seemed remarkably cool and dry. Not yet ready to believe, she slipped her hand over the back of his neck.

The fever had greatly reduced, perhaps even broken. Leah felt again, this time across his cheek. He was downright cold. She kissed his forehead, feeling him trying to curl under her for warmth.

She gathered the blankets he had kicked onto the floor and layered them on him, but he continued shivering. She grabbed her stethoscope and listened to his heart. Then lungs. No congestion anywhere. But his hands. They were trembling. Now what? She was resting her hand against his forehead again. No fever. But constant trembling. She couldn't bear the thought that the high fevers had left him with palsy.

"How's he doing?" asked Martha from the door. Leah heard the clink of a belt buckle from Utterance getting dressed in the other room. They were starting the day. Hers was continuing from the night before.

"I think the fever broke, Auntie."

"Well, what you moping for? You dun good, Leah. You brung him through!"

"Can you make some tea, Auntie? For Duncan, please."

Martha leaned forward to look at the tremors in

Duncan's hands. "Tea! That man's hungry. That's why he be shaking. He ain't kept nothing down for a week."

"We'll start with tea, Auntie," said Leah firmly. If he couldn't keep it down, it would be only tea.

"I'll warm him up some broth too, just in case."

Leah stroked Duncan's arm over the blanket. "Tea's fine, Auntie. Don't get elaborate."

But Martha came up with a mug of warm cider and a mug of beef broth into which she mashed a bit of potato. Leah was too tired to argue. Duncan was conscious but barely awake.

She held the broth to his lips, and he drank evenly and quickly. When she pulled it away, the mug was empty except for some lumps of potato on the bottom.

Leah handed the mug to Martha. Duncan turned on his side and closed his eyes.

"I guess it was hunger, Auntie."

"Everybody know when a man shakes all over after a fever, it be 'cause he be hungry 'cause he been too sick to eat. Dun they teach that in medicine school?"

"They don't teach wisdom anywhere, Auntie. Thank you. I'll take the mugs down."

"Drink the cider. I'll take the rest down myself. You can go sleep in a bed now. He be fine."

"Thank you, Auntie."

Leah reached under the covers to touch Duncan's hands, which were still cold but no longer trembling. In a few minutes, Duncan was asleep, his body a half-moon around her as she sat on the edge of the bed.

Leah settled into the wingback chair as she listened to the mug rattle on the tray while Martha went down the stairs. She wrapped her hands around the mug of cider to warm herself and looked at Duncan, silver-skinned in the morning light. Even now, she did not trust the insentient forces to not take him.

AFTER NEARLY THREE weeks in the guest room, Duncan's boredom overcame his lack of stamina. He wove his way down the stairs wearing the only clothes he could find in the room, a nightshirt and a pair of work pants. The house was empty, and he sat in the parlor rocking chair to wait for someone to appear. Feeling chilled, he draped Leah's shawl over himself and after taking a moment to breathe in her scent, promptly fell asleep. He wasn't sure how much time passed before Leah's voice flowed into his consciousness.

"Auntie has been feeding Duncan so much chicken broth, I think he's going to start laying eggs."

Henry's laughter followed, which meant Leah was home from work because Henry had been walking her home. Henry treated Leah as if she were his mother's best teapot. The voices fell quiet as footsteps crossed the parlor and made their way to the kitchen where they resumed, slightly muffled, behind the door.

"You look in the parlor?" asked Utterance.

"We did not miss a thing," said Leah. "How long has he been out there?"

"Hour, maybe?" answered Martha. "When I come back from the coop, there he be. Sound asleep like a cat stuck on a branch. Dint even hear me come in. Dun know how he ain't fell off that rocker."

"Who put the shawl on him?" asked Henry.

Utterance chuckled. "Now, he must have thought of that himself. Don't fancy being the one who dresses him up like a woman when he be napping."

Now they all laughed loudly and shushed one another for his benefit, but Duncan was already awake. He considered slinking up to the bedroom, but the mood in the kitchen seemed so jovial, he could not bring himself to walk away from it.

Utterance, the only one facing the kitchen door, was the first to see him. "You feelin' good 'nuff to go to town dressed like that?"

Duncan realized he was still wrapped in Leah's shawl. Theatrically, he flung one corner of the shawl over his shoulder. "Town needs a fashion statement, sir."

Utterance snorted into his coffee and put down the mug.

"Curious thing, Mr. Henry," Duncan began as he slipped into a chair at the table. "Seems like I've been an object of conspiracy. Seems somebody hid my shirt to prevent me leaving that bed modestly. Looked all over for that shirt. There's nothing in that room a man with arms can wear."

"Least they left you pants," said Utterance.

"Utterance!" scolded Martha before addressing Duncan. "Good you feel good 'nuff to come down."

"I escaped, ma'am!" Duncan said with mock indignation, surprised to cause a new wave of laughter. He tipped his head toward Leah while addressing Utterance. "Got me so used to reclining, I got winded coming down your stairs, sir. That's why I had to take that nap." He continued his soliloquy in Martha's direction. "Be needing your protection, ma'am. Think Dr. Maays plans on being the cause of my sudden death on account of me being out of bed today."

In the middle of a laugh, Henry pulled a wad of Duncan's mail and slid it across the kitchen table.

Duncan abandoned his theatrics. "Mighty grateful, Mr. Henry. Also mighty grateful you walking Dr. Maays home."

"You staying for dinner, Henry?" asked Martha.

"Wish I could, Mrs. Cobb, but I have to get back."

"Well, let me pack you a little something for later."

Martha began filling a mason jar with chicken soup. The others at the table drifted back into their activities. Utterance to sipping coffee and reading the newspaper; Henry to explaining to Leah why packages from New York sometimes took longer to arrive than those from Philadelphia.

Duncan draped the shawl over Leah's shoulders, knowing she would never ask for it even if she were cold. He wondered if Leah ever demanded anything for herself. Only now was he beginning to appreciate that she had single-handedly saved his life with an exquisite combination of clinical care and tenderness that inspired him to want to live —really live, the way people who were not as tarnished as he was did. He reached for her hand under the table, taking in her smile when he squeezed and held it as she continued her conversation with Henry.

Duncan leaned back in the chair, drawing a deep breath of the kitchen smells—chicken, onions, apples, coffee, bread, soda wash, soap—and withdrew into his thoughts. When Martha placed a bowl of soup in front of him, he thanked her and continued to luxuriate in the richness of the moment.

18

THE COMMISSION

By the time Leah deemed Duncan sufficiently healthy to return to his shop, spring was nudging winter out of the way. Granted, on some days, spring was almost indistinguishable from winter in temperature, but the chartreuse buds on the trees were making good promises.

Duncan still felt somewhat depleted, especially on days when men came to his shop armed with town chores. None of the broken things was ever interesting. Charlie Hunt deposited seven fruit ladders with broken rungs before leaving. Piled in the corners were broken milk stools seemingly by the hundreds, pitchforks and shovels in need of handles by the thousands. Andy Jenk dragged in a mail-order kitchen chair with a cracked splat. Hoburn stepped in, probably to request new bins for his store—one of the few reasons he came to the shop. Duncan clenched his jaw.

The clatter of a carriage entering town made everyone look out the window. Judging from the number of bells on the horses, anyone could imagine a delegation of royal dignitaries was entering the town, but Duncan knew the sound was coming from Emma Groth's carriage.

The carriage stopped directly in front of his shop. It was well known that Mrs. Groth did not walk far, and his shop door was closest to her carriage door. She would have stopped her carriage on the shop porch if she could have.

"You ever seen this?" asked Andy, observing the spectacle of Emma Groth getting out of her carriage in her flamboyant attire taking over the street.

"I should sell tickets. I'd make a fortune," said Hoburn.

Duncan did not find any of these comments amusing. Emma Groth, who spent her life dispensing rumors about his shop's sordidness, was finally coming in for a firsthand look. This did not bode well.

Hoburn and Andy shuffled into a corner, becoming spectators to what was about to happen. In West Edith's Bay, anything could become theatre.

For once, Duncan was grateful to be running town chores so he could have witnesses when Emma Groth was in his shop. He did not trust her to not spread rumors that might cause people to burn down his shop if he and she were alone. He took the measurements for a potato bin Hoburn handed him and fortified himself by sketching a proposal.

By the time Mrs. Groth made her way to the counter, he had sketched out an annex for the general store with all kinds of miraculous storage arrangements. He circled the pragmatic potato bin tucked among the drawings and slid the paper to Hoburn, giving Mrs. Groth a chance to position herself in from of the counter and fume with disdain.

Hoburn pulled the sketch to the end of the counter and made a show with Andy of pondering over it. Duncan took his time putting away the pad and pencil before looking up at Mrs. Groth, wishing she would turn into sawdust and stop plaguing everyone.

"Help you, ma'am."

"I wish to have this walking stick repaired."

Mrs. Groth slammed the silver-handled cane on the counter with a whack that made Duncan jerk back. He waited for the sound to die before picking up the cane. He turned it in his hand without taking his eyes off Mrs. Groth. When he touched the split that ran along the grain, he ran his fingernail inside the crack. He looked down the length of the walking stick as if evaluating a pool cue. Then he replaced it on the counter with a tiny tap.

"It's sound, ma'am. Doesn't need fixing."

"But it has a crack," said Mrs. Groth.

"A check, ma'am. Doesn't affect the strength."

"I don't trust it. I want a new one."

"Sorry. Don't have one on hand, ma'am." Duncan turned to Hoburn to indicate the matter was settled.

"Then fit the handle with a plain stick of wood until I can get another one!"

Now he really wanted to strangle her. He set his jaw. "No piece of wood leaves this shop plain. Ma'am."

"Make me a new one, then."

"Don't make them for handles. Ma'am."

Mrs. Groth rolled her eyes and bobbed her head side to side, her nose stretched like a peacock's neck amidst the feathers of her hat. "Then make one without a handle."

Duncan braced himself. Everything the woman said was a trap. He settled on his strategy. "Be over a year before I get to it. Backlog. Ma'am."

Mrs. Groth sighed with exaggerated exasperation and turned to Hoburn and Andy. "I say, I always thought thieves were more motivated than murderers, but I'm afraid this extreme lack of ambition proves me wrong."

Duncan forgot about Hoburn and Andy as he fixed a look on Mrs. Groth. Her self-righteous smirk faded. Worry lines in her face indicated she was realizing that if he killed her right then, he would be arrested, but she would be too dead to enjoy the moment.

Without giving warning, he grabbed the cane and flicked it through the air at a speed that produced the hollow whooh of a whip. He landed its tip on the counter with enough force to produce the tight, sharp snap of a whip against a horse's flank. Mrs. Groth staggered back, glistening with perspiration.

He let the sound sink into her before resting the walking stick back on the counter with a barely audible tap. "The cane's sound. Ma'am."

Beneath the sheen of sweat, Mrs. Groth's wrinkles quivered. For a moment, she looked as though she might leave. Instead, she shouted, "I shall wait the year! How much is a walking stick here?"

Duncan locked his jaw and reached under the counter to pull out a group of letters from Farrar's with the store's distinguished gold letterhead. On a scrap of paper, he wrote a sum from one of the letters and shoved it in front of Mrs. Groth.

Mrs. Groth did a double take at the sum, just as he had anticipated. "Surely, you are delusional. This is a ridiculous price! I can buy three walking sticks for this amount. With silver handles, all of them!" She crumpled the paper and threw it on the floor.

"Try Farrar's. Ma'am. In Edith's Bay," he said as if Mrs. Groth had never heard of the luxury department store. "They got canes with silver handles maybe you can afford."

Mrs. Groth's eyes bulged with massive indignation. For a moment he thought she would keel backward from his insult.

Hoburn lurched forward, shoving the bin drawings in front of Duncan and burst out speaking architectural and structural gibberish. "Yes. I figure something exactly like this is what I need, but a little different in some respects. For example, this detail about this cupola might require some augmentation and definition..."

Andy hung one arm around Hoburn's shoulders, appearing to listen with unwavering interest. Occasionally, he piped in with, "See yeh point, yeah. See yeh point. Needs betterin'."

Duncan locked eyes with Mrs. Groth until Andy raised his voice and slapped his palm on the counter. "Hey! Eyes here. We be talking to you 'bout this."

Mechanically, Duncan shifted his sight to the sheet. Hoburn drew a breath and began a second round of intelligent-sounding nonsense.

Mrs. Groth, left without an audience, snatched her walking stick from the counter and stomped to the door. At the door, her bustle snagged on one of Charlie Hunt's ladders, starting an avalanche as the first fell on another, which fell on another and another like dominos. Duncan, Hoburn, and Andy scrambled forward to stop the falling ladders from destroying themselves and everything else in the shop.

When they finished leaning the ladders less precariously against a wall, Duncan wiped his forehead with his cuff and muttered, "Mighty grateful, Mrs. Barn Bustle." To his surprise, Hoburn and Jenk burst out laughing.

The moment they left, he wiped down the counter as if Emma Groth had left her spittle on it. He flipped the Open sign to Closed and withdrew into his living quarters, where he sat in a chair, cursing Emma Groth for absconding with the comfort he so carefully cultivated for himself in his shop, as if she had released a shoebox full of roaches.

HENRY DIDN'T THINK anything of Mrs. Groth coming into the post office to mail a letter to Farrar's because she was always doing that. But a week later, when he received a telegram for Duncan from Farrar's commissioning a walking stick, he stopped what he was doing to have a long, hard think.

Duncan had told him about Emma Groth's visit to his shop. He'd even sworn, something Henry had never heard him do. Hoburn and Andy had also told him individually about Emma Groth's visit, both expressing surprise Duncan hadn't beaten her to death with her own cane.

Farrar's telegram offered a price with an additional bonus if Duncan could deliver the cane within thirty days. The price was so exorbitant Henry telegraphed back, asking for a resend. Farrar's telegrapher responded by spelling out the price of the walking stick and of the bonus. Henry then suffered from stomach troubles until he figured out a way to convey this telegraphic event to Duncan without abandoning his duty to confidentiality, which included pretending he knew nothing about what anyone's telegraph revealed.

The next dawn, when Henry saw the first lights in Duncan's shop, he walked across the street to deliver the telegram from Farrar's. Duncan was crouched behind the counter, muttering to himself as he sorted through boxes of hardware. More to the point, he seemed to be ransacking the shelves.

"Cannot believe this, Henry. Order six. Get six. Can't find but four. Got to be here…"

"Duncan—" said Henry.

"Joey's coming at any moment. Can't ship it missing two handles."

"Duncan—"

"Had them made especially for this desk. Designed the whole front around the handles." Duncan sneezed. His hand came up and patted the counter for a rag that was on it.

Henry stuffed the rag into Duncan's hand. "Duncan, I have a telegram from Farrar's for you."

"Mighty grateful, Henry."

Henry rolled his eyes. Duncan was barely paying attention.

"Ah! Aha! Aha! Knew they'd be here. Hiding in that other box…" Duncan's hand reached over the counter and slapped two drawer handles on it.

"Duncan, I have a very important telegram from Farrar's for you. Someone wants a walking stick really quick."

The shuffling ceased. Duncan rose from behind the counter, first the disheveled hair that resembled a magnificent sculpture of salt marsh hay, then the creased forehead, then the penetrating brown eyes. Duncan stood from his crouch, gave his belt a tug, and joined Henry on the other side of the counter.

"That so, sir?" Duncan said under his breath, although no one else was in the shop.

Henry handed him the telegram. Duncan took the paper to the window and read it in the burgeoning light. His eyes grew wide at the offered price, then wider still at the bonus that almost equaled the price. He frowned at the proposed delivery date after consulting a calendar on the wall. Then he folded the telegram in half and looked out the window as if checking for rain as he ran his fingers over the crease in the telegram.

"Why you suppose they want one in such a hurry, Henry?"

Henry squirmed, unable to say what he wanted to say because that would mean he knew about business that wasn't his business to know. "Farrar's is very accommodating. Maybe someone needs a replacement real quick? Maybe because they think their old cane is cracked? Most people can't tell the difference between a crack and a check like you can."

"See," said Duncan, nodding as he continued to look out the window.

Henry thought he might be safer if he volunteered some information rather than have Duncan come up with another question. "If haste's involved, then probably a woman ordered it."

Duncan continued nodding. "Mighty grateful, Henry. I am mighty, mighty grateful, sir."

He thrust the note into his shirt pocket, then gave Henry a slap on the shoulder that made his glasses skip down the bridge of his nose. Duncan gathered the handles and went off to select a screwdriver.

Henry pushed up his glasses and grinned. Duncan had heard everything he had not said.

Henry went back to the post office and twitched with anticipation until eleven o'clock, when he began walking to the window between customers to see whether Duncan was heading his way. When Henry saw him coming, he rubbed his palms together and sat down in front of the telegraph.

The price being offered for the walking stick was exorbitant, but the amount was not inordinate compared to other prices Duncan could pull out of people. Henry was certain Duncan would fire off a superbly succinct and diplomatic note, which, when read carefully, simply said "No." It would be a delight to tap it into the wire.

At eleven twenty-seven, Duncan swung open the post office door. He sauntered in and sat in the chair across from Henry, pulling out his replies as if nothing unusual was pending. Henry watched Duncan shuffle through the papers. The telegram from Farrar's, with its gold letterhead, ended up on the bottom of the pile.

Fastidiously, Duncan sent a telegram to each of his customers. Then he came to the paper with the gold letterhead. He unfolded it and slowly smoothed it over his knee before dictating his response as if it were any other telegram. Henry could barely keep his finger steady against the telegraph key as he tapped each word into the wire.

"Address to Mr. Emery Farrar, Farrar's Incorporated, please. Price doubles on cane commission."

Henry fumbled against the key.

"You didn't just ruin that message, did you, Henry?" asked Duncan.

"Heck!" swore Henry, looking at his hand as if his fingers had fallen off. "I'll send that again. Don't worry." He looked at Duncan, completely undone. Henry had a rule never to ask anything about the messages people sent, but now he wrestled with the urge to break that rule.

"Not everybody's lucky like us, Henry, to have such a confidential operator," said Duncan, releasing Henry from his temptation with the compliment. "We are very, mighty fortunate."

"Of course! Yes! Always, Duncan," said Henry. "Never a word to anyone. I'll resend it right now."

Duncan winked. He rose from the chair and walked out

of the post office like a man with a superb sense of mission in his head and a plan in his pocket.

Henry sent the telegraph again, then did some math in his head. He divided the current price of a silver-handled walking stick into the amount Duncan was charging and concluded Duncan would be getting ten to twelve times the going price.

Henry stiffened with revelation. But of course! Emma Groth would tempt Duncan into submission with money, then humble him in public with his own creation. She would pay anything to stroll around town with a Duncan Shay walking stick that Duncan refused in public to make for her. Of course!

Emma Groth might back down because of Duncan's asking price. But if she did not, Duncan would have to make a stupendous walking stick to maintain his reputation with Farrar's after charging such a price. No piece would ever match Emma Groth's expectations, but if the cane did not match Farrar's expectations, Duncan could be discredited. And Duncan did not need more discredit.

The cane would have to be beyond magnificent in case Emma Groth claimed it was not good enough for what she paid. Henry wasn't sure making a walking stick of such caliber was possible. After all, a walking stick was still only a walking stick.

19

THE WALKING STICK

Within a week of beginning to work on the walking stick, Duncan found himself amidst a flurry of attention. Leah went into a frenzy every time she saw a new nick on his hands, despite having seen almost every malady and infirmity under the sun. Utterance began pestering him about getting an assistant to do the town chores so his workload would ease. To his surprise, Martha went on a rampage of hearty cooking and sent him meal baskets that sometimes included a little something for breakfast that he usually ate in the middle of the night. Henry continued to do what he did best, which was to pretend he didn't know anything about anything.

In the dead of night, while he turned and whittled a once-plain column of wood into a walking stick, he often felt the progress come mystically, neither from his head nor his hands. The cane seemed to use him as a tool to carve itself. Sometimes he wondered whether it was his creation at all. Although he could see the intricacy and crispness of his carvings, he could hardly believe such a small thing had taken him a month to make. He wasn't even sure where all his effort had gone.

As he turned the cane in his hands after polishing it, a pernicious doubt began to form. By now, all he could see were little imperfections and things he would have done more adeptly. He began to question its quality. Uncertain of his effort, he packed the walking stick in the box he made for it and went to see if Henry could afford him some perspective.

Duncan made his way across the street with the long, thin box of heavily grained ash that housed the cane thumping against his hip. He avoided looking at anyone because lately some had taken to engaging him in conversations to determine whether what they'd heard about the walking stick business was true. Duncan kept his answers ambiguous, although he liked that town folk knew his work sold at Farrar's and only by commission. Henry, who apparently was waiting for him to arrive, opened the door and braved the early spring chill in his shirtsleeves.

"Got a moment, Henry?"

"Of course! Yes. You need to send that? I can get it ready right now. But it'll go out tomorrow morning. The last carriage just went."

"Mighty grateful, sir. Need Joey to take it in because I'm short on time. But I need your opinion, Henry, if you don't mind."

Duncan placed the long box on the side table. He flipped open the cover, pleased by the scent of resins and waxes that gave the cane a subtle sheen. In the box, it looked stunning, and he wondered why he thought he had to worry about its quality. He reached in and began to pull it out. Behind him, the door latch clicked. Duncan slammed down the box lid and turned around. Leah was standing in the doorway with Utterance.

"Mr. Shay! We saw you crossing the street," said Leah.

"Be walking home with Leah, but you be welcome to come for dinner, if you're up to walking with us," said Utterance. "You, too, Henry."

"Oh, um..." Henry looked at Duncan.

Utterance peered at the box, as if to look through it. "That be your special creation? Figure you be done by now. You sending it by mail?"

Duncan pressed his hand against the box as if the walking stick were struggling to get out. "Carrier. Sir."

"What's the matter? Dun you trust us?" asked Utterance.

Duncan's eyes flickered over Leah. He felt as if he had just been caught without pants in the middle of the street. "Not sure it's proper. Sir."

"Nonsense!" said Leah. "Let me see. It surely is not so bad."

Duncan drummed his fingers on the box. Going against Leah never went well. He hesitated before flipping open the lid, pulling out the walking stick, and holding it at arm's length for everyone to see.

Leah, Utterance, and Henry leaned forward, then back, wide eyed and open mouthed. They ogled the central shaft of blood mahogany he held, around which wrapped a grotesque snake carved from ghostly butternut with irregularly curved coils.

The coils on one side suggested two thin, pendulous, flat breasts sagging over a scrawny belly. To counterbalance, the coils on the opposite side suggested dimpled buttocks shaped like a bustle. The head arose from a scaffold of chins, and in the snake's face, thin lips pursed primly into a condescending scowl. The eyes—small, beady bulges of black onyx—glared with regal pomposity and entitlement. The net effect was a combination of snake, woman, and naked mole rat.

The silence gathered weight. Duncan rested the walking stick in the box and looked away. He had not expected to show it to Leah, much less in front of Utterance and Henry. He certainly had not expected such incredible silence as a response.

Henry was the first to speak. "Good heavens. That Mrs. Groth will have a stroke when she sees that."

Leah pressed a kiss on Duncan's shoulder. "You are brilliant! Absolutely brilliant!"

"You got some idea how potent that thing is?" Utterance chimed.

Leah took the walking stick and ran a finger up and down the contours while laughing. Duncan jerked forward when she began to wrap her hand around the handle, but he was not quick enough. When Leah's eyes widened with shock, he looked away as the burn of embarrassment took over his body. He never imagined Leah seeing the cane, much less handling it.

The rounded head, whose carved hair suggested a slight crease with a dimple on the forehead, was collared with angled chins that did not require much imagination to be seen as phallic. This feature, however, became obvious only when someone grasped the handle of the cane.

Sobered, Leah thrust the stick at Henry, who almost dropped it while trying not to touch any of the private parts, which seemed to be everywhere. Duncan wanted to slip under a rock and never be seen again.

Leah began giggling. "Mea culpa, Mr. Shay. I should have listened—but it was worth it!"

Andy Jenk barged through the door. "Figure since you're still holding court, I'd slip in and get a stamp—" He stopped speaking when the stick of wood full of pale bulges in Henry's hands caught his attention.

"Gooooood Looooord!" Andy let out the words as if someone were squeezing them out of him.

He reached out and took the walking stick from Henry. Andy turned it around and around. When he figured out it was a cane, he put one end on the floor and wrapped his hand around the snake's neck. He shouted the moment the obscenity became obvious to him, but his shout was more of a battle cry than laughter. He looked at Duncan with fresh admiration, then at the snake's head protruding between his thumb and index finger, and began to laugh so hard he slid, as if deflating, into Henry's spare chair.

"I got to piss!" Andy announced, raising his head like a howling wolf.

Not knowing how to take Andy's announcement, Duncan unclenched his fingers from the walking stick and took it back.

"Cain't move 'til I piss!" Andy crossed his legs and slapped his thighs, unable to stop laughing.

Duncan said the only thing he could think of. "Mighty grateful for your opinion, sir."

"You be brave imagining what she look like under them things she wears," said Utterance.

Leah asked, "Can Emma Groth harm you at Farrar's?"

Duncan bowed his head. He had gone over this question frequently, and even now gave it serious consideration.

"Mighty grateful, you asking, Dr. Leah. Mr. Lawry didn't leave much unsaid when he took my work to Mr. Farrar. And Farrar's hasn't said who this cane is for, so it shouldn't be a problem. Besides, from what I hear, Mr. Farrar'll prob-

ably dance around it for a day before he sends it to her."
More confident now, he tickled the mole snake's collection
of chins as if daring it to bite him.

"You know," said Utterance, "ain't likely that stick'll ever
see the light of day."

Duncan replaced the walking stick into the box and
closed the lid. He raised one eyebrow and grinned. "Mighty
expensive kindling, sir."

MARTHA WAS furious she had not been shown the walking
stick, although Leah and Utterance kept reassuring her it
was for the best. Neither described it much except to say
that it looked a bit like Emma Groth. Martha tagged along
when Leah went to work the next afternoon to glean what
she could from town talk because apparently no one at
home was capable of describing a simple walking stick.

Word about the walking stick was all over town, and by
the time Martha entered the general store, everyone claimed
to have known about it. Andy Jenk was describing it to
Hoburn as tactfully as he could in public. Hoburn was
snickering and wheezing so hard his eyes overflowed with
tears. Even Mrs. Hoburn could not conceal an occasional
titter as she pretended not to be listening from behind a
shelf.

"He searched high and wide to get the right trees, and he
found 'em," said Andy. "Give 'im credit. But I tell you, try as
he might, he didn't find a tree that wore a dress!"

Martha gasped as she deduced that the Emma Groth on
the walking stick was not properly attired. She wondered if
Duncan Shay was in the habit of imagining Leah as a
walking stick.

"Dr. Maays, tell them! It's true, ain't it?" called Andy when he saw Leah.

Leah put her arm around Martha and announced, "No, Mr. Jenk. We have not seen a thing. We do not know anything either. None of us do. Please be advised that none of us know anything. At all. Therefore, we must not speak about anything to anyone. Let it be a surprise."

Martha could not believe her ears. Was Leah trying to say that no one was to mention the walking stick that everyone knew about? She could not help but smile at the thought of Mrs. Groth receiving what sounded like a scandalous gift as a surprise. She looked around, trying to evaluate the crowd. Her hope that people would not chatter came from never having heard of anyone confiding in Emma Groth. Most people ran away when they saw her coming.

The buzz of speculation filled the store until the shop door swung open to reveal Mrs. Groth blocking the doorway like a giant cork. Everyone seized up and looked away except Martha, who was caught in the beam of Emma Groth's demanding stare.

"Good afternoon, Mrs. Cobb," greeted Mrs. Groth, her eyes flashing.

"'Noon," mumbled Martha.

"And how is your Mr. Shay? I imagine he misses being bathed by Dr. Leah. All in the name of medicine, of course," said Mrs. Groth. "I hear he's working on something very important. Now what could that be, Mrs. Cobb?"

"Dunno," said Martha, gauging the people around her. Everyone seemed absorbed in inspecting whatever random piece of merchandise was within reach. No one was revealing a thing.

Mrs. Groth looked terribly unsatisfied with the answer,

and she pursed her lips into a frown. "I was just in his shop the other day—not a suitable place for a lady, although Dr. Leah visits it often, but I was desperate. Thank goodness I had my driver to protect me. I was searching for a new walking stick. That man didn't care that mine has a crack and is a danger to my health should it break."

"Now, now, Mrs. Groth," said Hoburn. "Mr. Shay offered you one at fair market cost, and you fussed at the price."

"Fair market cost! I can buy a dozen walking sticks of the finest quality for that price. With silver handles! That man is disgraceful. Thieves in any way he can."

"Well, now..." mumbled Hoburn.

Mrs. Groth swished her hand in front of herself. "So, Mr. Hoburn, did Dr. Leah take care of that problem you had down there?"

Mrs. Hoburn's indignant gasp could be heard from behind a shelf, followed by several bottles tipping.

"Further down, Mrs. Groth!" Hoburn bellowed. "I have rheumatism of the knee. Besides, he said there wasn't anything wrong with yours—your walking stick, I mean."

Sputtering, Hoburn moved to the far side of the counter and began sorting boxes while Mrs. Groth leered as she looked around for another victim. Several people rushed out of the store when Andy opened the door for Duncan, who came in with a cumbersome bin. He put it down on the first clear spot and nodded his thanks to Andy. Duncan pulled some papers from his shirt pocket, handed them to Hoburn, and left.

Martha squinted at Duncan, speculating he must have come to gauge Mrs. Groth's awareness because the store was packed and even now he rarely went anywhere that was packed with people. Much less to a place that was packed with Mrs. Groth.

She moved away from Mrs. Groth, who was gloating to herself. She waited for the moment Mrs. Groth looked directly at her and, with an air of supreme satisfaction, met her gaze, pushed her bustle out of the way, and marched out of the store.

20

THE MAIL-ORDER CHAIR

The doings with the walking stick reduced Duncan's patience for town chores even more, and he shortened the hours he was open to the public. After hanging the Closed sign on the door early one afternoon, he swore he would work on nothing else until he completed all the town chores and got them out of his shop.

But when he looked at Andy's mail-order Windsor chair, which he had not touched since the business of the walking stick began, it spoke nothing to entice him. He was annoyed that it was even in his shop. He would rather make a new chair for Andy than fix the uninspiring one in front of him.

Despite the Closed sign on the door, footsteps came up his porch. An older man in dusty clothes was making his way up the steps. The man was stout, although he seemed fit. His hair, pitch black where it was not speckled with gray, complemented his gray eyes. He looked sore, probably from having walked from Edith's Bay like many of the men who had applied for the position of Carpenter's Assistant.

The man ignored the Closed sign and rattled the door open. "Mr. Duncan Shay in?"

"That'd be me, sir."

The man stepped into the shop and planted both feet firmly on the floor. "I heared you got need for an assistant."

"Your qualifications, sir?"

"Got 'em right here." The man opened his horseless saddle bag and pulled out a plain box with a few drawers.

Duncan took the box from him and turned it, noting the man's hands and face were freshly washed, although most of him was still dusty from the long walk. The box was the man's résumé. Every joint and side was made differently to display the medley of his skills. Duncan ran his thumb over the veneered diamond on the top. He studied the alignment of the grain and the smoothness of the varnish. He slid the drawers in and out to test whether it and the slots were true. The box was sturdy and neatly constructed to demonstrate a noteworthy level of skill but few aesthetic qualities.

He shook his head and held the box out to the man, but the man was not looking at him anymore. He was squatting before a chair constructed from bent strips of wood, tracing one of the bends with his finger and slowly taking in that the chair was made from one continuous curve without beginning or end. The back, the legs, the platform for the seat—they were all part of a single, winding curve.

"You make this?" he asked.

"Yes sir."

"That's real good!"

"Mighty glad you think so, sir."

"I heared there be only one man in the world who can do work like that, and he already been born. Wasn't me. I can say it be the truth, now that I witness this here chair. Damn 'em curves! I cain't do nothing like that. Not me. Me, I'm more like this chair." He pointed to Andy Jenk's mail-ordered Windsor with the cracked splat. "I can fix that and do wagon wheels, and I do real good rough work. Measure twice, cut once. Hardly no waste with me. Plus boxes and drawers and the like. I got limitations, suh, but I be number one otherwise. Yes suh, I am."

Duncan stared at the man. Most applicants attempted to get the job by inflating their few virtues, but this dolt sought employment by exalting his ineptitudes.

The man added one last flourish to his speech. "And I heared you be real finicky. Pretty sure I can keep out of your way real good."

That was it. Duncan drew himself up to his full height and prepared to boot the man out of his shop.

But the man held his ground and threw a question at him. "You happy fixing ladder rungs, suh?"

Duncan stopped short.

The man took a step forward. "What makes you think 'nother one of you gonna be happy fixing ladder rungs? How often this world turn out one of you? Plenty of me's. It takes four wagon wheels to get one of your chairs to town. More me's. One you. Works out perfect."

Duncan installed a poker face and mulled the mathematics. There would always be more town chores and rough work than pieces he liked to make. He looked at Andy's Windsor with the cracked splat. "Your name, sir?"

"Cyrus Olinks, suh. Test me out for free. I'll fix that chair for you right now."

Duncan pointed to the plain, square piece of maple that rested on the chair seat. "Tools be in the barn. Be compensating you for this one labor, sir."

"Only if you like it, suh." Cyrus rubbed his palms together with gusto. "There we go. Heh! Here, gimme that 'fore I lose it." He grabbed his sample box from the counter and dropped it into the saddle bag without anxiety for its wellbeing. Then he picked up the Windsor chair and the board and headed to the barn.

An hour passed with all kinds of industrious sound coming from the barn. Just as Duncan decided an hour was enough uninterrupted solitude for someone he really didn't know, the carriage from Edith's Bay pulled in front of the post office to deliver the mail. Barely a minute later, it pulled away and turned around in the middle of the road to head back to Edith's Bay.

When the dust cleared, Duncan saw Henry standing by the post office doorway next to a few boxes and a canvas bag full of mail. He was also holding a very long and narrow box wrapped in Farrar's distinctive gold paper. Unable to control himself, Duncan stepped out of his shop. Henry grinned and held up the box triumphantly.

Duncan forgot Cyrus Olinks on the spot. He went back inside and paced, unable to make himself do anything. Another half hour passed before he heard the jangle of horse bells and the furious clopping of hoofs coming down the road. The moment of truth had arrived—in a carriage, no less.

Word was already all over town, and people were gathering by the door of the general store. Duncan heard a soft tap at the door and saw Hoburn politely observing the Closed sign. Duncan waved him in, assuming it was important because Hoburn rarely came to the shop. To his surprise, Hoburn took a seat on the bent wood chair. A moment later, Andy Jenk slipped in and sat by Hoburn.

"Shop's closed," Duncan said, but nobody left.

He glared at the men, which would have normally cleared his shop in seconds, but his look had no effect. Andy threw open the window to hear more clearly, letting in the smell of the horses on the street.

The little man in blue velvet livery jumped off the carriage and ran into the post office, exiting seconds later with a pile of magazines, a few pieces of correspondence, and the thin, gold box from Farrar's. He was in and out so quickly Duncan understood Henry had everything ready to go. The driver opened the door to the carriage and handed all the items to Mrs. Groth.

Henry stepped outside and casually locked the post office door. He began to saunter across the street, but when Emma Groth's voice rose to a shriek and her carriage rocked in place until the horses became skittish, Henry hightailed across the street as if chased by a pack of wild boars. He slipped into Duncan's shop and slammed the door shut behind him.

Intrigued by the shrieks that were becoming words, Duncan moved to the window.

"The devil's dick on fire! That bastard murderer! Unnatural acts of Moses! He'll pluck ass hairs in hell! Why, I'll leave him bagless. They should have hanged him! Should have hanged him twice! That murdering thief..."

Duncan pulled himself away from the window after absorbing Emma Groth's hatred in the torrent of words. He had done what everyone in town wanted to do to Emma Groth in some way or another, and the price was to hear what everyone in town thought of him from her.

Andy slammed the window shut with disgust and poked his finger into Duncan's chest. "You s'posed to keep windows shut when it rains horse piss. Dun you know that?"

Duncan nodded, relieved that the verbal assault had been muffled. "Yes sir. Mighty grateful, Mr. Andy."

They looked out the window again as the little blue driver scrambled onto the carriage seat like a monkey in a circus. With a cry and a slap of the reins, he urged the horses into a quick start. The carriage whipped around the road and past Duncan's shop, swerving and almost colliding with the shop wall, sending everyone inside rushing to the opposite wall, tripping over buckets and milking stools.

The carriage transmogrified into a cloud of dust and bouncing pebbles. After the grit settled, the people on the street were still cringing in terror against the walls of buildings, many with their hands over their children's ears. An abandoned horsewhip lay in the center of the street.

Duncan pulled up a stool and half sat on it. He rubbed his face as the silence filtered out the tension of the foul language. Then he began to shake with nothing less than glee, overcome with a need to laugh.

Henry was the first to applaud, hooting and dancing around the shop as if someone had just handed him a bag of gold. To Duncan's surprise, Andy and Hoburn joined him. In the commotion, Cyrus slipped into the shop and handed him a well-scrolled splat with evenly tapered and sanded ends.

Despite the eruption of glorious hymn singing, Duncan inspected the splat carefully by eye and feel. He checked its symmetry. The new splat nested perfectly against the old one, guaranteeing that the curve matched.

"Mighty fine splat, Mr. Olinks. Rest of your work like this, sir?"

"Eh?" said Cyrus, as he observed the men who were babbling about walking sticks that looked like a snakes without dresses. "Better, when I ain't so nervous, suh."

"Mr. Olinks, maybe end of this month, we figure a more permanent arrangement, if we still get along." Duncan handed back the splat.

"That be real good, suh. I'll wait to send for my wife and boy, 'til then."

"Not expecting a mess in my barn, Mr. Olinks. Can be mighty finicky about that."

"Won't be no mess in your barn, suh. I sweep when I get done."

Duncan nodded, incorporating in his gesture the expectation that Cyrus was free to leave, and was glad Cyrus took the hint. The history of this moment was so intricate and delectable he was not up to putting it into words.

Henry came over, slapped him on the arm a few times, and pumped his hand, followed by Hoburn, then Andy. The three kept laughing and hooting and slapping one another as they left the shop. They continued shoving one another with camaraderie even as they straggled into the street.

Leah was the first to step out of the general store, and the men briefly convened around her as she crossed the street. More people poured out of the general store, clapping as if they were in an audience at a show. At the sight of Leah crossing the street, Duncan bolted across the shop to flip the Closed sign to Open.

Leah half ran, half skipped into his shop like fresh air swirling into a vault and threw her arms around his neck. "You don't know what you've done, do you?"

Duncan kissed her before raising one eyebrow and saying with relish, "Got her good, didn't I, Leah?"

21

THE INVISIBLE INFIRMARY

Since the doings with Mrs. Groth's walking stick, Leah kept hearing spontaneous outbursts of loud laughter and limericks about dress-less trees coming from the blacksmith's shop. Everyone could hear them because Andy opened his windows when the summer warmth joined forces with the heat of his forge to make his workshop unbearably hot.

Hoburn could not hear the songs without becoming incensed at how Emma Groth shamed Duncan in his own shop. He often said that if Duncan Shay did not beat Emma Groth to death on that day with her own cane, as she so deserved, chances were good he might now qualify for sainthood. Hoburn's brief tirade caused Leah to contemplate what made a person become like Mrs. Groth. Perhaps the woman would take Duncan's slap as a hint for self-reflection and fix herself.

Leah climbed the steps to the general store but stopped short when Duncan came dashing out of his shop and sprinted toward her across the crowded street. She pretended to inspect the contents of her black bag to give him time to reach her.

"Dr. Maays," he said under his breath as he shook out a flyer from his shirt pocket. "Would honor me greatly if you attended this summer's dance with me."

She looked over the advertisement for the annual church dance and promptly responded, "I shall be delighted, Mr. Shay, but please be advised my uncle has already reserved a dance with me."

"Hmmm..." Duncan displayed his best smile. "Isn't he old and married, ma'am? May need to have a word with your auntie about him."

"Well, you can always dance with Auntie and make him jealous." Leah lowered her chin and batted her eyes.

She turned when a man's deep cough interrupted their flirtations. Wheezing heavily, an elderly man slipped into the general store.

"Please excuse me. I must attend to someone," she said with eyes on the man.

"Yes, ma'am."

Leah took a moment to study Duncan as he headed back to his shop, more clouded than when he first crossed the street. Duncan could change moods at a moment's notice, although he tended to do so only when something was troubling him.

She turned her attention to the flyer and fingered the buttons on her high-collared blouse. She wanted a new dress for the dance. In Edith's Bay, low necklines were all the rage at balls, but at a West Edith's Bay church dance, a low-cut dress might cause a riot. And Martha would want to help make the dress, an instant impediment to a low-cut anything. Deep down, Leah knew, Martha was still in favor of burlap veils for unmarried women.

A scoop neck would be a suitable compromise. Yes. No one could complain about a modest scoop neck. With puffed sleeves and bows on the shoulders.

She opened the door and stepped into the churning chaos of Hoburn's. Mrs. Hoburn was by the cutting table, failing to keep skeins of yarn from falling off pegs. Hoburn was running back and forth behind the counter, attempting to fulfill everyone's needs simultaneously.

Leah waved to Mrs. Hoburn, signaling that she would be available after she tended to Samuel Elson, the old man with the cough. These days, she rarely walked into the general store without finding a patient waiting for her.

She held the backroom door open and beckoned Mr. Elson inside. In the room, she dragged a sack of onions to the end of the table to make space for the old man, who was now coughing uncontrollably. She listened to the congestion in his lungs with her stethoscope, although she could hear it plainly in his cough. The fever and his answers to a few questions confirmed her diagnosis.

"You have bronchitis, Mr. Elson, but not to worry, we shall make it go away. Please lie down. Can you please unbutton your shirt? I am going to put a compress on your chest to loosen things," she said as she folded a towel to put under his head.

Leah drew a blanket over his chest before looking over the contents of her medicine shelf for medications. She was now ordering the contents on this shelf, ensuring she could keep the profits, but the real money-making medicines were still on the shelves in the main store, and Hoburn kept the profits from those.

She decided to prepare a nebulizer with a steaming concoction that would make Mr. Elson cough up some of the mucus. If she could dry out his lungs before the bronchitis turned into pneumonia, he would do well. This meant using the nebulizer several times a day.

Removing the sack of onions from the table before Mr. Elson accidentally kicked it off, Leah felt a slow build-up of resentment that she could not yet offer her patients better accommodations than a hard table to be shared with a sack of odorous vegetables. Surely an old man with bronchitis deserved better than a threadbare towel under his head for a pillow.

She placed the onions in a corner, wondering how patients were deciding between her and Dr. Haloway, who was fully equipped with real pillows and an examination room. Perhaps some chose her because she often did not charge as much as he did, depending on the patient's resources, though some patients came to her without concern about her fees.

Mary Corwal continued to bring her children, even when Leah began charging her the same fee Dr. Haloway charged. John Corwal was not wealthy, but his humble potatoes kept all his children in shoes, and Mary usually wore dresses that were not overly faded.

Mr. Elson was awake, although snoring laboriously to pull air through the mucus in his lungs. Leah mixed a concoction for the compress while waiting for water to boil.

She was tempted to ask Mr. Elson if he had gone to Dr. Haloway first but decided to remain professional and not take the risk. She already knew whatever Dr. Haloway might have suggested was likely to make her roll her eyes in despair. Even if Dr. Haloway was completely competent, he was still very old, putting West Edith's Bay on the precipice of being left without a competent doctor with proper facilities.

She yearned for her own examination room, her own

practice. She visualized the entire topography of West Edith's Bay while a question pounded in her head, demanding its answer: *How can I make this happen? How can I make this happen? How can I make this happen* here?

The feeling was as potent with possibility as it was cruel with obstacles. As a shopgirl she would never raise the money to establish a practice. Her savings were almost nonexistent, having been consumed by her trip back from Ghana. The number of her patients was too low for self-sufficiency.

If her practice remained small, she could never leave Hoburn's back room. If she outgrew his store with her patients, Hoburn would ask her to leave. The purpose of his shop was not to support her practice. The purpose of her practice was to support the shop. Never had she taken so many correct actions to remain so unrewarded. In West Edith's Bay, nothing would ever be hers.

IN HIS SHOP, Duncan kept thinking about Leah and her practice at Hoburn's. The medicine shelf in the store's main room had quadrupled in contents with medications no one had heard of until Leah arrived. Hoburn was making a small fortune through her while paying her shopgirl wages.

Dr. Haloway was scornfully calling Hoburn's back room "Miss Leah's Infirmary." After years of having a perfectly impersonal relationship with Dr. Haloway, Duncan was beginning to dislike him. Word around town indicated that Leah had a wider repertoire of cures—some of which hurt less, many of which were more effective, some of which cost less, all of which were applied with invariable expertise. A patient could do fine by her, if he could tolerate her being a woman, although not everybody did.

Duncan ran his fingers through his hair, wondering where she would practice next. He had visions of Leah appropriately established in more suitable environs like Boston, where she had studied. Dr. Elliot was in Boston, and they still wrote to one another. Every time he came to West Edith's bay to visit Dr. Haloway, he offered her a position as his assistant. It was just a matter of time before she accepted it. Just a matter of time.

Duncan envisioned a porcelain plaque in the window of a sophisticated brownstone, Leah Maays, M.D., and people entering a proper waiting room with wallpaper and a secretary before being seen. Even Edith's Bay would be better than West Edith's Bay for her, and the most logical next step. Edith's Bay had practices she could join—if they would have a woman doctor.

Duncan took a moment to look in on Cyrus, who was diligently rounding square walnut posts for table legs. He was working out just fine, even after a few months. Already he was taking great pride in running the town chores as if the endeavor were his own business. This was fine with Duncan, who hadn't done a town chore in over a month and whose shop was gradually emptying of pitchforks, buckets, stools, and ladders. Cyrus was perfectly content doing things that made Duncan insane, and his garrulousness and solid workmanship was attracting enough customers to almost cover his wages.

As a bonus, Duncan discovered that Cyrus, who could not design a toothpick on his own, could duplicate most things to perfection. And Cyrus stayed out of the way. After only a few incidents, he remembered to replace tools exactly where they used to be so no supposedly finicky person became irritated trying to find them later.

In the pause between looking in on Cyrus and preparing to plane the surface of a dining table, the church bell tolled the hour, and Duncan realized another three would pass before he would see Leah again. A peevishness descended upon him that made him feel in need of her presence.

He brushed off sawdust and shavings from his clothes with an impatience the gesture did not merit. He was yearning for Leah's little touches that released a plethora of chills in him and left him feeling a wreck. But he would be happy to catch a smile and a word from her. He left his shop and walked across the street.

At the general store, Mrs. Hoburn was attending the cutting table. Leah was nowhere to be seen. As if responding to the question in his head, Mrs. Hoburn said to one of the lady customers, "I know we have some in the back room. Can you wait a few minutes? Dr. Maays will be out in just a minute."

Taking his place in the line by the counter to kill time, Duncan scanned the jars of penny candy. The cinnamon jawbreakers he liked had been replaced with uninteresting mints. Dissatisfied with just about everything, he stepped out of line. Planning to leave empty handed and empty hearted, he heard something heavy falling and Leah's unmistakable voice wavering with the effort of a struggle, "No! No! Stop! Please!"

Even Hoburn paused behind the counter to eye the door to the back room. Duncan took no chances. He leapt over sacks and barrels and walked through people to get to the door. He burst into the room, stopped only by a stench of something sweet and putrid.

Before him, Leah was arched over a shirtless Andy Jenk,

who was stretched out on the central table. Half his chest and one shoulder were bloody raw and covered with translucent yellow blisters from burns. Duncan looked away, not knowing what to do with such an image stamped into his mind.

"Is someone ill, Mr. Shay?" Leah asked.

"No, ma'am." To declare he was missing her terribly would sound absurd.

Leah turned her attention back to Andy, whose writhing was about to slide him off the table. He tried to touch his chest, but Leah blocked his hand. "No! Stop. Do not touch."

She slipped her arm under Andy's neck and began to center his body on the table with brute assertiveness. "Mr. Jenk, put down your knee so you do not push yourself off the table, please. I cannot do that for you."

Andy winced and wriggled all over the table, struggling to make his legs go straight, but doing so stretched the skin on his torso, and the pain sent tears running down his face. He was on the table only because Leah was balancing him. She continued to shift him until he was safe from falling, then released him. He clenched his eyes and began taking quick, shallow breaths.

Leah grabbed a pad of gauze she had soaked in something medicinal and stretched it over Andy's chest and shoulder. Andy let out a string of uncensored words that would have knocked most women over and stunned many men. She struggled to keep him from pulling the gauze from his chest. As the extrusion of vile words tapered to loud groans and whimpers, Leah held his hands so he could brace himself against the debilitating pain. Eventually, Andy settled, finding some relief from the compress.

Leah turned to Duncan. "Are you seeking my assistance, Mr. Shay?"

"Thought you might need mine, Doctor."

"Thank you, Mr. Shay. Mr. Jenk is doing the best he can. Please close the door when you step out." At once her attention was back on Andy.

Duncan stepped away and closed the door behind him as instructed. He leaned against a shelf, acknowledging that no one who saw Leah tending to Andy in that brief moment could doubt she had an arsenal of competencies. Her ability to juggle treatments while keeping Andy under control without once losing her gentleness was wondrous. She seemed nothing short of wondrous, a gravely underappreciated healer.

Hoburn approached when the activity at the counter subsided. "Haven't seen your Mrs. Groth for weeks."

"Won't last forever, sir."

"Help you find something?"

"Thought Dr. Maays was needing help, sir."

Hoburn chuckled. "Wouldn't count on her needing help at all. She's made all sorts of grown men cry by now. Ain't needed help with any of them. Gets them all to cooperate real nicely."

"That so, sir?"

"She's got a steady stream coming in these days. Had to put out these crates so they can sit and wait for her. Last week she wrapped Celia Ash's ribs. Her own milk cow almost done her in. Yesterday she took a look at Cory Baines's black eye. Now she's got Andy Jenk in there. Real bad burns." Hoburn puffed out his cheeks as if repulsed by the thought. "Can't believe he walked himself here by himself."

"Cory's black eye..." Duncan began keeping inventory.

"Dr. Maays sure handled him real good. Hmmm. She did, indeed."

Duncan waited, thinking there might be more to the story, but Hoburn did not elaborate.

"What about Dr. Haloway, sir?"

"Oh, I suspect he'd rather die than see Dr. Maays. Not that he's sick, mind you. Lots still go to him though, have no doubt. But I hear he mostly prescribes enemas these days. Seems Dr. Maays has less humiliating ways of treating things. Also doesn't seem cuts and things get infected so much with her. Children like her."

"Children like her..." Duncan repeated to himself.

The back door opened, and a blanched Andy wobbled out wrapped like a mummy in bandages and reeking of some slimy ointment oozing from the edges of the bandages. His eyes were glazed with the effects of morphine. Duncan was now sure Andy felt very little when Leah tended the burns.

Leah attempted to sit Andy on a crate, but stopped when it became apparent he could not bend at the waist. She leaned him against Hoburn's counter as if he were an ironing board and said, "I see your wife, Mr. Jenk. She is almost here."

Mrs. Jenk swept into the store, out of breath from running down the street, and went into a state of jitters when she saw how much of her husband was bandaged. Leah put her arm around her as if Mrs. Jenk were the patient and murmured reassurances until she calmed down enough to listen to instructions.

A moment later, Leah tapped Duncan on the arm. "Mr. Shay, will you please assist Mr. Jenk in getting to his house? He must not fall."

Before he could nod, Leah slipped something into his hand and walked toward Mrs. Hoburn, who was frantically calling her name. Duncan found two cinnamon jawbreakers in his palm. He intended to thank Leah for thinking about him during her unceasingly hectic day, but she was already helping a customer at the cutting table.

With one hand wrapped around Andy's waist to keep him upright, the other on his good shoulder to keep him steady, Duncan crossed the street. Mrs. Jenk was babbling without taking a breath, although Duncan was not sure whether she was talking to him, her husband, or, for that matter, herself.

Leah watched through the window as Duncan and the Jenks crossed the street while she cut cloth. Mrs. Hoburn brought her attention back to the shop by charging across the floor speaking loudly enough for everyone to hear.

"Mr. Jenk has quite the mouth, Dr. Maays, doesn't he? I am certain you were as appalled as I was."

Leah pretended not to hear her and engaged a customer in a discussion about what lace best matched a cloth. Mrs. Hoburn's statement died from lack of attention.

When Mrs. Hoburn turned to attend to another customer, Leah glowered at her. Did Mrs. Hoburn think she would let any person who was not blistered like a pork rind and crazed with pain speak that way in her presence? Did Mrs. Hoburn think she, a physician, should publicly complain about the behavior of patients, reducing their undeserved agonies to the level of social improprieties? Andy Jenk, it was known, was uneducated and roughhewn, but he was always decent in his actions. Leah wished she could stare down tactless, ignorant people the way Duncan did.

She knew Duncan had heard the stream of Andy's filthy

curses. He had heard plenty, both in person and through gossip, but he had yet to say a word against her practicing. She still wasn't sure what Duncan had done or said, but one day when she left him standing in the store to slip into the back room with a patient as Mrs. Maays, she found that when she stepped back out, almost everyone was calling her Dr. Maays.

Yet a little distance had slipped between her and Duncan in the last few days. Something unspoken. A tension. Leah wondered whether Duncan was yielding to the town's talk about her carnal intentions with half-naked, married men whom she allowed to curse freely without redress. Mrs. Groth was not the only one who liked to think of her in those terms. Dr. Haloway encouraged all of them with his smirks and tacit nods.

Leah had hoped that having more and more people come to her for medical attention in the general store would have improved her relationship with Dr. Haloway, but it had antagonized it. On a bad day, he tried to intimidate her patients by claiming that anyone who went to her was bound to die from something she would fail to cure. On a good day, he dismissed their going to her as coincidence or because she charged less, being unqualified to charge fully.

Now she had Duncan to worry about. She hoped his thoughts about seeing her with Andy would reveal themselves in conversation and provide an opening for discussion. One part of her was defiantly waiting to see how Duncan rose to the occasion. Another part of her despaired that he would ask her why she wanted to be a doctor when it prevented people from seeing her as a proper woman. If he did, she might just fold up and die from disappointment that he played along without really understanding.

WHEN THE GENERAL store closed for the day, she headed to Duncan's shop, feeling no less settled. Duncan was tallying the day's earnings from Cyrus's town chores. He looked ill-humored, but then he always did when he worked with ledgers. Not that Leah wished on anyone what Duncan had gone through to land in his profession, but she often wondered whether he would have been stuck balancing ledgers for his father had he not found opportunities for his artistry in carpentry.

Duncan mumbled to himself as he added a column of numbers and scribbled down the sum before arching back and stretching his arms over his head. "You clairvoyant, ma'am?"

His whimsy made Leah laugh. "Apparently not enough to know what you mean."

"How'd you know I like cinnamon balls, ma'am?"

"You've been buying them all week."

"See, ma'am. Can't buy cinnamon balls in secret anymore."

"Well, I have special reasons to spy on you."

"What reason's that, ma'am?"

"You are intelligent, genteel, talented, and very, very soothing for tired eyes—" Leah broke off, laughing at the red rising in Duncan's cheeks, then persisted. "You are the finest of fine cabinetmakers—"

"Now, you stop that, ma'am," said Duncan, but a grin escaped him.

"And so charming! Do you get goose bumps when you look at yourself in the mirror? I certainly get goose bumps when I look at you."

"Be needing wider doorways for my swollen head, if you

don't stop that, Leah." He now had a grin Leah would pay to make permanent. He abandoned the ledger and skirted the table to put his arms around her. "You making house calls, ma'am?"

"I'll be seeing Mr. Jenk tomorrow. Probably daily for several weeks. That poor man."

A dense silence fell on Duncan when he reached into a box and began to rummage. Leah braced herself. What was bothering him? The house calls? The inappropriateness of a woman in the medical profession? Had someone told him Cory Baines tried to kiss her when she looked at his black eye? Had Duncan figured out she had seen Andy below the hip bones to assess the burns and bandage him?

Duncan pulled out a handful of lollipops from a box and tossed them next to her black bag. "Not good form to be without them, Doctor."

"Oh!" cried Leah. She threw her arms around him with such force he took a step back to keep his balance. "When did you get those?"

"Hired Henry to buy them on my behalf, ma'am. Seeing the general store's full of spies these days."

"And here I am thinking you had some objections to my tending patients."

Duncan cocked his head back and blinked at her. "Don't know how much of you would be Leah if you took the parts that like to heal away. Don't think you'd ever be happy." And just as quickly, Duncan became slightly distant. He looked at the ledger.

"Duncan," Leah said, trying to find an opening. "You cannot be honorable about what is bothering you. You understand I touch people as a doctor. Many people. In many places. It is not a very dignified profession when you think about it, although some people think it is. But when a woman does it, it seems disgraceful. Women doctors are not common. People talk about us in unfair ways."

"Be familiar with that, Leah. Not like you haven't cared for me and caused me some embarrassment. Not like I don't know what it's like to have people assume wrong about a person."

"Well, yes." She waited, feeling Duncan receding again. He could not be rushed into revealing anything.

Duncan reached for his hat. "Walk you home. Ma'am."

Leah rested her hand on his. "What is bothering you?"

Duncan rested his hand over hers. "Leah, you held me through a fever when I wasn't making sense. Remember you comforting me—"

Leah snapped her hand from him. Backed away. Glared. Looked away. Now she truly had nothing. She turned so he would not see her eyes begin to tear, but she could not prevent her voice from becoming laden with sorrow, even as she spoke in a heated whisper.

"Do you think Dr. Haloway is intimate with every woman whose child he delivers? You of all people, Duncan."

For a moment they stood in silence until Duncan gripped her shoulders and turned her around. He lowered his head to look her in the eye.

"Leah, I know damn well you're not into anything with anybody. I was misspoken for whatever I said. For that, I am truly sorry. But if a practice in Edith's Bay needed a doctor, how valuable would that be to you? Would you run over there? Would you go back to Boston? Would you go work for Dr. Elliot? New York? Back to Ghana? Not like I don't know what it takes to have a practice. Not like I'm some dolt who can't see your requirements and how nothing meets them here. Leah, I cannot abide Edith's Bay!"

He released her, and in the void of his touch, Leah stood

astonished. Duncan rarely said so many things at once. He stood before her, demanding her answer with his silence, but she was not sure what his question was.

She sifted through the blast of words that addressed many topics, none of which revealed the nature of the small, disturbing silences that kept cropping up between them. She ran the statements back and forth in her head until she finally alighted on the core of Duncan's concern, deeply tucked in the plenitude of his worry.

Her fury folded its wings and landed with a thud inside her. She was the one who betrayed Duncan with her insecurities. She was the one who invested poorly by fearing town talk about herself they both knew was false. She took a moment to consolidate her feelings and take care with her words.

"Duncan, a woman doctor is seldom accepted anywhere without tribulation. Practicing elsewhere would spare me nothing. I came here thinking I would leave again, but I now know I belong here—with my family, with you, in this place that holds my history, serving the people I care most about. Home is where you feel you belong, however you belong. The truth is, I need West Edith's Bay as much as it needs me. I know they will accept me in time. And if I ever have to leave, it will never be to a place you cannot tolerate, my dove."

Duncan seemed monumental, towering before her, feet apart, hands on his hips. She watched his expression evolve from exacting to startled, then to the sternest she had ever seen.

"You mighty sure about that, ma'am? Got many things against me."

"I am certain, Duncan. I love you with all my being."

When Duncan still did not budge, Leah wrapped her

arms around him as if she were hugging flower petals. She rested her head on his chest and listened to his breath as she waited for him to collect himself. A moment later, he leaned against the drafting table and stretched one leg on either side of her as he put his arms around her and held her against his chest.

"Never thought I could love this hard, Leah. Mighty terrifying thing, it is."

Leah listened to their hearts beat in counterpoint within the warmth of the safety they created when they stood in one another's arms. She nodded to acknowledge what Duncan did not say explicitly: The most terrifying thing about love was not the commitment it required but that it could be taken away without a moment's notice.

22

THE DANCE

At the annual dance in June, Leah rediscovered she needed to move her feet quickly when she danced with Utterance because his dance moves had no relationship to the music. Despite dancing so stiffly that he could waltz in a three-by-three-foot box without bumping elbows against the walls, he always managed to step on her feet.

Over her uncle's shoulder, Leah smiled at Duncan, who was moving across the dance floor with Martha, making her square-footed aunt glide with grace. In her moment of distraction, she let down her guard, and Utterance nailed her toe.

"You best be watching he dun abandon you for my girl," said Utterance while she hopped until the pain subsided.

"Oh, I have much to fear, Uncle. Auntie leaving you for another man!"

"Well, that one there be a good-looking one."

"Ah. That must be why Auntie was packing her bags this morning."

Utterance gurgled with laughter and stepped on Leah's

foot again. "Dun know where he gets his valor—asking your Auntie for a dance after all she put him through. Won't be forgettin' the look on her face when she figured she had to say yes."

Now they both laughed so hard they had to stop dancing. When Utterance took the lead again, he started on the wrong beat. Leah stepped systematically, watching him mouth one-two-three repeatedly to himself without realizing he was off by one beat and dancing to two-two rhythm. Leah laughed again, this time not only at Utterance's disastrous dancing but also because she was happy.

When the waltz ended, the fiddler quickly foretold the upcoming squares with a few raspy bars before resting his fiddle against a wall and going in search of punch. Couples left the dance area and regrouped on the sidelines to make alliances with others for the upcoming squares.

"Mighty sharp stepper, ma'am. Mighty grateful for the honor," said Duncan as he returned Martha to Utterance's side. To Utterance, he added, "Most appreciative, sir."

Martha, pink from exertion, patted her face with her handkerchief. She pulled Leah aside and whispered, "Dun know how you keep up with him. Like dancin' with a crab. Legs all over creation. Watch you dun catch your death in that immodest thing. Dun know where you'll ever wear that again."

Leah did not respond to Martha's comment. The scoop neck revealed, at most, her collarbones, and she'd been hearing about catching her death since she modeled the dress a week ago.

"See you still walk like you got ten toes," Utterance was saying to Duncan. "More than I can say for Leah."

The fiddler distracted them from their small talk by rasping another few bars to call people into squares. Utterance and Martha left to join a square on the invitation of another couple.

Duncan turned to Leah. "Catch my breath, ma'am?"

"Of course."

Leah did not acknowledge the pretense. Duncan could dance all night without pausing. He could dance holes through the floor, but many couples would still leave a square if he stepped into it. For Duncan, any scene would be intolerable.

As they walked toward a cluster of chairs, Leah checked the attendees. Everyone in town appeared to be there except the Haloways, who were visiting their new grandchild in Edith's Bay. Emma Groth sat quietly in a corner with her old walking stick. Cory left after Sheriff Wilkes shooed him out for drunkenness. Leah had not yet seen his sidekick, Ogden.

Duncan seemed happy in a way she had not before seen. He was choicely dressed in black pants and a gray, striped waistcoat, all presence and elegance without any awareness of it.

As they settled in chairs, Henry jaunted up to them and stood in front of Duncan, looking him over from head to toe with mock dismay. Duncan raised an eyebrow, waiting for Henry to play out his ruse.

"Feeling old?" asked Henry, a little loudly as if Duncan were deaf.

Duncan cupped his ear. "Pardon, sir?"

"Said, if you're feeling old."

"No more than you, Mr. Henry."

"Well, I see you sitting out like some old man when we be short a couple for a square."

Duncan sat up and looked around. Leah stood, trusting Henry to not put Duncan in a precarious position.

"Step lively, Mr. Shay," said Henry. "You need to get there before the music starts."

They followed Henry to a square just as the fiddler began to warm up. Henry yielded the position of first head couple to Duncan and Leah and took the position of first side couple with one of the Pawlry twins, the other of whom was in another square. Cyrus Olinks and his wife were in the same square. Duncan and Leah slid into position and when they looked up saw John and Mary Corwal as the second head couple.

Duncan withdrew into himself so quickly he almost created a vacuum. The room quieted, under the pretense of waiting for the fiddler, but Leah could feel everyone watching their square. The fiddler started playing. They waited motionless for the first call.

Please, no scene, prayed Leah.

"Honooooor yooour paaaartner! Honooooor yooour cooorner! The two head couples, forward and back! The two side couples, forward and back—"

Duncan and Mary marched into the center of the square and back to their original positions, Duncan looking over Mary's head and Mary looking through Duncan's chest. Neither made eye contact.

Then of all calls the fiddler could have chosen, he sang out, "Two head Ladies Chain! Yea! Gents, promenade your ladies round!"

Please, no scene, prayed Leah because a Ladies Chain left a woman dancing with the man opposite her, who would then walk her around the square in the promenade. At the end of the move, John Corwal would promenade her as his temporary partner, and Duncan would promenade Mary. Leah looked to Henry but could not catch his eye.

Beginning the Ladies Chain, Leah stretched her hand to

Mary, who seemed so jittery she wandered into the center of the square without keeping rhythm. On intuition, Leah squeezed her hand. Mary focused on her. Leah smiled. Mary smiled back and nodded.

Mary's husband positioned Leah for the promenade. Duncan began to walk Mary around the outside of the square, touching Mary just enough to guide her. In another few calls, the women returned to their original partners.

Then it happened. With one deliberate nod, Duncan accepted the apology Mary spent years trying to deliver. Mary's body slumped with relief, and she smiled just before she and her husband do-si-doed according to the caller's new instructions.

"Swiiiing yooour paaartner!" sang the caller, closing the entire move.

Duncan circled Leah's waist with his arm and swung her off the floor, smiling majestically. She tucked her chin. When Duncan was happy, he was simply too handsome to look at.

The fiddler finally took another break four squares later, and Leah was truly ready to sit and catch her breath. Her feet hurt, although she swore she would walk on crutches for a week rather than miss a dance. She sat in the first chair she came across, knowing she had little time to recover before the last set of waltzes began. Duncan sat across from her, and they indulged in the draft from the side door that was braced open with an old folding chair.

Duncan leaned back. His eyes glided over Leah. She visualized all the cowlicks rising through the frizz of her hair and wondered if she looked like Medusa.

"Pardon," said Duncan, slapping his hands over his eyes. "Don't let my foolishness distress you, ma'am. Not often a man gets to dance with the loveliest woman on earth." He parted his fingers and playfully peeked between them.

"Oh, you'll be wearing glasses like Henry before long!" Leah pulled his hands from his face, not caring that people were watching them.

The back door swung open, and in strutted Cory, with Odgen at his side. A few steps behind, Sheriff Wilkes followed. He stopped short beside Duncan when Cory blew a kiss at Leah. Duncan straightened his back, glaring at Cory, who sauntered away. Sheriff Wilkes opened his mouth to speak, but Duncan was on his feet before the sheriff could utter a word.

"Fresh air, Dr. Maays?"

"Thank you, Mr. Shay."

She wove her hand through Duncan's arm, and they walked outside to the side steps of the church, where Duncan began a fit of silence, the great barometer of his inner turmoil.

Leah stroked his arm in an attempt to comfort him. "Duncan, West Edith's Bay is a very small town. It's full of people with very tiny experiences."

"That so, ma'am?" Duncan remained distant.

Leah leaned against his arm. "Yes. They have never had the forces of life destroy everything they value. They think all they have to do is raise their voices and puff out their chests to be in control. It has not occurred to them that some things are not survivable. They have never been tried as you and I have been."

Duncan slipped his arm around her. "Never considered it like that before, Leah. Think you're probably right. Not that I wish it on any of them."

"I am going to put Sheriff Wilkes on the list," Leah said, nodding with determination.

"What list, ma'am?"

"Why, the list of people I am going to clobber on your behalf!" Leah burst out laughing.

Duncan's shoulders shook with amusement. The fiddler sent out the call for the last set of waltzes with a few raspy strokes. Duncan offered his hand, palm down. Leah placed her hand over his, and they walked to the dance floor.

WHEN THE DANCE ENDED, they all stood in agreement that Duncan would be foolish to walk Leah to the orchard when Utterance and Martha were going there in a wagon. Under Martha's scrutiny, Duncan bid Leah goodbye by placing his goodnight kiss on the back of her hand, then sneaking another on her wrist.

As the wagon wobbled up the hill, he waited in the middle of the road, hands on his hips as if he were a lord surveying as his land. He drew a breath and exhaled with satisfaction before heading to his shop.

A mighty fine evening, Duncan concluded. Even the dealings with Cory and Wilkes hadn't put a dent in it. Leah always looked past Cory as if the man didn't matter because he didn't. But then, Leah wasn't Cory's target.

And Emma Groth never wandered out of her corner. He hadn't expected his walking stick to humble her so much, but apparently it had. Even people who hadn't seen it, which included most of the town folk, were claiming to have seen it. The people at Farrar's were probably still laughing about it.

Duncan thought briefly about Mary's apology, doubting it would change anything in his life by now, but it had value nonetheless. Acknowledgements of wrongdoings always had some value. Thus espoused Avery Lawry. Besides, he felt better now that he could look Mary in the eye instead of scorning her. Only now did he wish he could have forgiven her before she figured out a way to apologize to him.

He smiled as he recalled Utterance and Leah stepping all over one another when he took Martha out for a dance. Martha babbled incoherently when he asked her, but she agreed, much to his relief. If he had to do it over, he would first mention his intentions to Utterance so he could prepare Martha. Leah told him Utterance remained straight faced until he saw them take their first steps, then broke down laughing so hard she threatened to lock him in a closet if he didn't stop.

Duncan could still smell Leah's perfume—or thought he could. He felt her hands like an imaginary force still pressing against him—one against his shoulder, one against his palm as when they danced. Leah could waltz. Yes, for sure she could waltz. He would never get any sleep if he let his thoughts meander in that direction.

On a whim, he leapt up and slapped the bottom edge of his Carpentry and Fine Cabinetmaking sign, making it swing with a creak. Life should always feel like this. Sharp. Vibrant. Full. Unconstrained with misery.

When his feet hit the ground, someone uncorked a bottle of champagne. Duncan stood still, thinking he had imagined the sound, for nothing of it remained. Recalling his conversation with Leah about the smallness of West Edith's Bay, he wondered who in town would even have a bottle of champagne.

Two horses still tied to the rail by the general store whinnied when a figure came barreling through the alley between the store and the post office, knocking into the walls and tipping over stacks of empty crates. The flash of uncoordinated motion, all swinging lanky arms and legs, ran across the street and blindly thumped against Duncan's chest before staggering back in an effort not to fall.

"Haloway! Dr. Haloway!" Ogden shouted, his eyes darting all over the place. "Get Dr. Haloway!"

Without waiting for Duncan's response, he took off toward the doctor's house. Duncan moved swiftly into the alley, just barely making his way around the discarded barrels and crates. When he came into the courtyard behind the general store, he tripped over something doughy and heard a human sound.

His senses became almost too acute to bear. The hair on the back of his neck stood, sending a chill through him. By his feet, he made out the silhouette of Cory's body sprawled on the ground with a glistening halo of blood around his head. Duncan jumped back, crashing against the chicken coop and sending the birds aflutter. He could not bring himself to touch Cory to see if he was alive, but Cory rolled his head to one side, revealing an even bigger pool of blood under his head.

"Going for help, sir." Duncan mumbled, more to keep himself organized than to inform Cory. "Going for help, sir."

Duncan sprinted out of the courtyard, bashing against the crates just as Ogden had done. On the street, he took a step toward Dr. Haloway's house and, hearing Ogden banging on the front door, recalled Dr. Haloway was in Edith's Bay, meeting his new grandchild. His panic bubbled, but he felt momentous relief when he saw Cory's saddled horse in front of the general store. He unhitched it and leapt on it to gallop toward the orchard to get Leah.

~

Sheriff Wilkes was already in bed when he heard the gunshot. He did not take kindly to dangerous noises like gunshots, especially after he had taken off his pants for the night. Muttering a string of curses, he slid out of bed and threw on clothes.

Even as Wilkes hustled down the steps to the first floor of the jailhouse, he could hear Ogden making a racket. Everything was looking like drunken and disorderly conduct with illicit use of firearms until Wilkes got near the door and heard Ogden wailing.

"Dr. Haloway! Open up! Cory's shot!"

Wilkes ripped open the door and slammed it against the wall with a force that cracked the plaster in a thin line clear to the ceiling. Running into the street, he spotted Duncan Shay spurring Cory's horse into a gallop. Wilkes drew a breath and put two and two together.

As Duncan gathered speed on Cory's stolen horse to escape, Wilkes jumped up to drag him off the saddle. The effort proved difficult. Duncan Shay was strong and he clung hard—even swatted and swore at him—but Wilkes tightened his grip on Duncan's belt and tipped him off balance enough so when the horse bucked, the rest of Duncan's body followed in a tumble.

"Where's Dr. Haloway?" shouted Ogden as he ran toward Wilkes.

"At his daughter's, you damn fool," Wilkes shouted.

"Cory's shot! In the head! We need a doctor! Where's a doctor? We need a doctor!"

Wilkes looked at Duncan, who was fumbling into consciousness on the ground and scowled. Ogden was running around in circles.

"Fetch Utterance's niece. She might know sumthin'," Wilkes said.

Ogden finished his circle and began running toward the orchard.

"Take the horse, you stupid ass!" Wilkes shouted.

With his arms outstretched, Ogden took several single steps in many directions before spotting Cory's horse a few yards away in the middle of the road. Now with a clear vision of how to accomplish his mission, he jumped on it and raced it up the hill, substituting "Dr. Maays" for "Dr. Haloway" in his cries, as if Leah might hear him from the center of town.

23

THE ARREST

Leah rode Cory's horse back into town, straddling the saddle, her skirts and petticoats gathered around her hips. With her abdomen, she pressed her black bag against the horn to keep it from falling. The lantern in her hand swung so wildly it was almost useless. She had abandoned Ogden, leaving him to come down the hill on foot the moment he told her Cory had been shot in the head.

Both the general store and the jailhouse hosted milling crowds at their fronts, and she didn't know where to go until she saw Hoburn calling and waving to her. Leah dismounted, stuffed the reins into someone's hand, and pushed her way through the crowd and into the general store.

She followed Hoburn's lantern through the shelves to the back room, where Cory presented an exotic sight. He was paler than fresh snow as he lay on the table, although the towels Mrs. Hoburn had wrapped around his head resembled a red turban.

"Dr. Maays, he doesn't look good at all," Hoburn said.

Leah paused by the doorway to catch her breath and compose herself. She dismissed Hoburn's comment. She could always be of help if the patient wasn't dead. Mrs. Hoburn's eyes quivered with anxiety as she draped another towel around Cory's head. Leah took the lantern from Hoburn and raised it, relieved that Cory's eyelids twitched whenever the light shone across his eyes.

"Mr. Baines? Cory Baines?" Leah moved the lantern back and forth before his face to test his reactions. Cory squinted predictably. At least he could distinguish light from dark. She took his pulse, which she found to be sluggish but steady. His hands began to twitch and his legs to shuffle as he regained consciousness.

"Mr. Baines?" she repeated.

Cory made some coarse sound. The Hoburns, now huddled in a corner in each other's arms, mumbled encouragements to themselves, but Leah remained cautious in her expectations. Brain injuries were complex. A person with one could be fabulously articulate and whole, then shudder and drop dead.

She hung the lantern on the hook over Cory. After unwrapping the saturated towels from his head, she felt his skull with her fingertips, moving methodically through his matted hair from the crown to the base of the neck. On the lower right quadrant, she felt a long, soft welt, but it seemed unrelated to the source of blood.

When she pulled her hands away, they were covered in blood. Hoburn gagged and turned. Mrs. Hoburn patted his back. Leah wiped her hands on a towel and felt Cory's head again, still unable to locate the wound. A bullet would make a very small hole when it entered and a bigger, highly detectable hole only if it came out. The bullet had to be lodged in Cory's head.

"Og…" mumbled Cory.

Leah nodded to Hoburn to fetch Ogden. "He is coming, Mr. Baines. Can you open your eyes? Come, now. Open your eyes. Look at me."

Cory drifted back into unconsciousness. Leah pressed the towel against the side of his head where an interminable supply of blood was oozing from a mysterious source. The bullet had to have entered there.

She pressed the towel hard against Cory's head and did a double take when she saw the wound. Leah brushed his hair out of the way and bent her knees to be eye level with the wound. Blood flowed freely, obscuring the opening almost immediately. She dabbed the towel and examined the wound before the blood hid it again.

"Mr. Baines," said Leah dryly, for the benefit of Mrs. Hoburn, who was beginning to look ill. "You have shot off your earlobe."

Mrs. Hoburn quaked as she lowered herself onto a crate. "His earlobe, dear? Just his earlobe? Are you sure?"

"Just his earlobe, Mrs. Hoburn," said Leah, continuing to dab and look, although by now she was certain.

Hoburn opened the door. Ogden ran into the room, flipping over Mrs. Hoburn's lap and landing in a pile beside the table. He half rose to his knees and stared over the edge of the table into Cory's pasty face.

"Cory!" Ogden whispered as his eyes began to tear. "You alive?"

"Ruffle," mumbled Cory.

"Oh, you shoulda took them shot out 'fore you practiced!" wailed Ogden. "Ain't I told you so?"

"Wheh da hell's mah ruffle?" mumbled Cory.

"Sheriff's got it."

Cory tried to sit up, sending a stream of blood dribbling

down his neck and back. Leah took another towel from Mrs. Hoburn and pressed it against his ear as she guided him back onto the table. "Lie down, Mr. Baines."

"Damn sheriff!" cried Cory, still trying to sit up. "He ain't keepin' my new rifle!"

"I'll buy you 'nuther one," promised Ogden, crushing the crown of his hat with both hands.

"Mr. Baines, what happened?" demanded Leah, pushing Cory back on the table.

"He been practicing twirling 'round his rifle like we seen at the rodeo circus in Edith's Bay, when it go off on him," explained Ogden, wide eyed with misery.

Cory pushed Leah's hands off his chest and began to sit up. Leah grabbed his shirt and swayed him forward and back a few times until his eyes began to roll into his head.

"Lie down," she commanded.

She released him and watched him fall back onto his elbows before letting himself slide onto the table. He touched the side of his head. His eyes and mouth became perfect O's when he saw blood cover his hand like paint. He began to form a scream.

Leah pressed a towel over Cory's mouth and stooped down until she was not more than six inches from his face. "You have shot off your earlobe, Mr. Baines. I am going to put in stitches. If I hear. One. Peep. Out. Of. You, I shall leave the needle in your ear and walk away. Do you understand me, Mr. Baines? Not. One. Peep."

Cory closed his mouth and swallowed, then lay perfectly still, not even daring to whimper when Leah began suturing. Without further incident, Leah bandaged, tidied up, and sent him home under Ogden's care.

"Expect a bill, Mr. Baines," were her parting words. She had long ago taken to charging Cory the full city price for her care in an effort to dissuade him from using medical care as a means to pester her. Mrs. Hoburn allowed her to tack her fees to his credit, so Cory always needed to pay her if he wanted to continue buying at the store.

For a few minutes, Leah and the Hoburns loitered on the street in front of the shop, simultaneously exhausted and wide awake. The thing to do now was to drop into a bed and fall asleep, but Leah was too jittery. They watched as Ogden led his and Cory's horse in one hand while Cory staggered in a zigzag a few feet away.

"Next time, take the shots out like I said!" snapped Ogden.

"Shaddup, Og."

Leah looked toward Duncan's shop, not inclined to wake him and ask him to walk her home. Perhaps Hoburn would volunteer to take her home in his surrey. Most likely, though, Utterance and Martha were on their way back into town to investigate the troubles, and she would go home with them.

The crowd in the front of the store was now moving to the front of the jail house. Sheriff Wilkes was struggling to keep order as the crowd increased. Why was Wilkes not waiting on the store steps, officiously rubbing his palms together at the prospect of arresting Cory?

"What's happening at the jail house?" she asked.

The Hoburns looked at each other. After much throat clearing and mumbling, Mrs. Hoburn said, "I think Duncan Shay's been arrested for shooting Cory."

Everything in Leah's stomach turned into a clump. She blinked rapidly, as if she could understand better by looking more clearly into darkness.

"Oh no, honey. It was all that blood. Let me help you. Here, sit down, dear," Mrs. Hoburn cooed maternally.

"Ogden!" called Hoburn. "You talk to the sheriff?"

"Wha' for?" Ogden called back.

"Come on, Og. Let's go," pressed Cory.

"You have to tell the sheriff what happened, Ogden," called Hoburn as he trotted after the men.

Ogden called something back, but Leah did not hear. She broke away from Mrs. Hoburn and elbowed her way through the crowd to get to Wilkes, who was trying to make Henry Moore go away.

"And I'm telling you, Sheriff, I saw him standing unarmed in front of his shop when the gun went off! Unarmed, I tell you. He was nowheres near that Cory Baines—"

"Sheriff Wilkes," interrupted Leah. "I am a physician, and I am here to see Duncan Shay."

"Ain't nothin' wrong with him," Wilkes barked. "Go home."

"But I am a physician, and—"

"I said go home! And take him with you. Almighty!" Wilkes shoved Henry into Leah. "Everybody go home! Or you all be arrested right now!"

Unconvinced, the crowd jeered and continued to mill.

Comprehending she could not bargain with Wilkes, Leah grabbed Henry's arm. "Come with me."

Henry followed as if tethered to Leah's waistband and rolling on casters. They slipped to the back of the jailhouse, where Leah looked at the wall. She sighted the window she knew had to be there, above her head as she had suspected it would be.

"Step back," she said to Henry and began turning in circles, holding the medical bag at arm's length as if preparing to throw a discus. She released the bag with a force that made it smash through the window on the first try.

In response to Henry's ghastly expression, Leah patted his arm. "Be strong, Henry."

"You're not breaking Duncan out, are you, Dr. Maays?"

"Give me a lift, Henry."

Henry wove his fingers into a stirrup. With one foot in his hands, Leah rose to the window, swaying and shaking and fully aware Henry was on the verge of dropping her. She jiggled the stiff frame and slid open the window just before she began to list in one direction. Henry lowered and caught her before she fell over.

She grasped Henry's hands and made him jump. "Henry. Go back and tell the sheriff his trouser buttons are undone."

"Dr. Maays!"

"It shall not be a false statement. Tell him in front of the crowd, and while he's occupied fixing the problem, which I assure you will happen immediately, tell him Ogden Lapp has definitive information about who shot Mr. Baines."

"He does?" cheeped Henry.

"Hoburn is fetching Ogden now. Please help me up again."

Henry clasped his hands into a stirrup again and lifted Leah to the window. She hoisted herself and slid inside with a loud crash, much banging, and the tinkling of broken glass.

"You all right, Dr. Maays?" Henry called.

Leah waved from the window. "Sheriff. Tell the sheriff."

In the utility room, she groped around until she felt a doorknob and opened the door attached to it. Outside, a loud metallic clanging rang through the dry air. Frightened to her bones, she walked along the walls of the unfamiliar hall toward the sound.

DUNCAN WOULD HAVE RIPPED out the iron bars of the cell with his teeth if he could have. With his hands still cuffed behind his back, all he could do was leap into the air and slam the heel of his shoe against the cell door, hoping against all realities that it would fly open and he could step outside the cell.

That the cell wall was barred and not solid stone made no difference. The claustrophobia of being handcuffed and in a cell was choking him. Even being in skin felt claustrophobic. He needed to get out. Of everything. From everywhere. He gasped for air in short, jagged breaths.

He was about to throw another kick when he saw Leah walking toward him. Losing his balance, he stumbled back in horror until his back slammed against the stone wall. A prolonged shudder overtook him with such force he had to press himself against the wall to stay standing. The last person he wanted to see him behind a set of cell bars was Leah. He wanted to die.

"Didn't do it, Leah." His voice came out so hoarse he barely understood himself.

"I know, Duncan, I know." She lunged forward and reached through the bars for him.

"I did not do it!" he shouted into the universe and flung himself against the bars, shoulder first, not even feeling pain.

"I believe you, Duncan. I believe you!"

The noise in his head had grown so loud he could barely hear her. He swayed as his world shrank even more and became constrained to a pair of handcuffs.

"Haven't done it, Leah."

"I believe you, my dove. I believe you. Come here. Right here. Beside me."

The blinding rage and fear was rising in him again, threatening to disintegrate him. As static increased in his hearing, pain that could only come from a migraine was building as if someone were driving a spike through the back of one eye. His vision blurred.

"Duncan! Come here. Right now."

"Haven't done it!" he shouted back. Gray blotches partitioned his sight. He gasped to get air into his lungs.

"Get yourself here, Duncan. Right now! To know the truth."

"Truth is I haven't done it!" Now he could barely hear or see. His world was becoming smaller, more and more gutted with panic and pain.

"There is more truth, Duncan. Come here and hear the rest of it."

Duncan stumbled forward, trying to breathe through his anxiety. He could barely see where Leah stood. Her hand, like a mystery, pulled him forward by his shirt. Pressing one eye against one of the cold, iron bars to find relief for the pain in his head, he forced himself to look at Leah.

"Haven't done it, Leah." A whisper was all he had left in him. He was going to die in jail. In front of Leah. For something he hadn't done. His heart was pounding its way up his throat.

Leah clutched his shirt more tightly and stood on her toes to speak into his ear. He forced himself to quiet down so he could hear.

"Cory is alive. No one has killed him. He is alive."

Comprehension felt like lightning shooting through him. Then the panic took over without respite. A lesser charge.

Horse theft. Didn't matter. Both charges involved prison time and— and— loss of Leah. Loss of his shop. Loss of everything. Utterance would never speak to him again. Martha would charge through town saying she'd been right all along. If they would not believe he hadn't killed a man who wasn't dead, who would believe he had not stolen a horse?

"Duncan, Ogden is vouching you haven't done anything. Then they will release you."

Duncan's legs gave out. He slid against the bars until he was on his knees in despair. Ogden was to be his savior? And Wilkes would believe Ogden, Cory's personal idiot? Nothing was made of reality. He felt the nausea of hopelessness.

Leah kept talking, although he couldn't understand her. She wrapped her hand around some of his fingers. Sometimes he heard that everything would be all right, but he could not believe.

At some point, Wilkes strutted into the jailhouse, flanked by Henry and Ogden. Henry was shrieking at Wilkes like a wet cat.

"Shut the hell up!" Wilkes shouted at Henry. He did a double take when he saw Leah and demanded, "How'd you get innear?"

At the sound of Wilkes's voice, Duncan staggered to his feet, swaying and dispersing fury into the air. He stepped away just far enough so Leah could not touch him, the only way he could insulate her from what was happening to him, if he even could.

Wilkes shook out his keys. "Dun want a word from nobody. Unnerstand? Nobody!" Wilkes stood in front of the cell door. "This be my mistake, but you be coming out of there real calm or not at all. Unnerstand?"

Duncan did not move. The noise in his head was

becoming unbearable again, and he was having trouble understanding Wilkes. People were now shifting blurs.

"You git by Dr. Maays real calm, before I open that door and let you out. You act up, you dun come out. Unnerstand?"

Leah's voice cut through his mind's chaos. "Duncan, please come here."

Duncan moved guardedly within the cell. Nothing was believable anymore, least of all that he was in jail for having killed a man who wasn't dead. Through the bars, Leah grabbed his sleeve when he drew close to her.

"Real calm. Unnerstand? Real calm. There be ladies present," said Wilkes.

Duncan raised and lowered his chin in a barely perceptible nod, not quite clear about what he had just agreed to do. He could barely see. He could barely hear. He could barely breathe. He couldn't even think. Wilkes swung open the cell door and stepped back. Feeling the cell bars with his shoulder to find his way, Duncan stepped out, twitching with self-restraint.

"Dr. Maays," said Wilkes. "You take this here key and undo them cuffs on Mr. Shay for me. Mr. Shay's gonna stay real calm for you. Real calm, Mr. Shay. You hear?"

He felt Leah's hand on his arm. "Duncan."

The noise in his head broke like a cloud at the simple way she said his name and allowed a breath into his lungs.

"Please be still while I undo the handcuffs. It's important. Sheriff Wilkes is setting you free. You can go home afterwards. But you have to be still now."

Duncan nodded, feeling a rivulet of reasonableness flow through him. Leah's hands were now on his wrists, undoing the cuffs. He felt her kiss between his shoulder blades as she wiggled the key in the lock.

When the cuffs snapped open, Duncan sprang forward

with a stomp to keep his balance. Wilkes and Ogden skittered back. Henry stepped forward to catch him, but Duncan stayed upright. He jiggled the cuffs off and threw them across the room into the jail cell, where they bounced off the stone wall and slid into the iron bars with a scrape that could make teeth hurt.

Wilkes began to babble. "Mr. Shay, I'm gonna be issuing you a public apology right now. Right on the front steps of this jailhouse right now. All you got to do is stand there. I'll be posting one in the general store tomorrow, for them who missed it. But right now, I'm issuing you a formal apology."

Half blinded and stumbling, Duncan allowed Wilkes to herd him with the others to the platform in front of the jailhouse. At least the platform was outdoors in air he might be able to breathe normally instead of in short breaths that could be measured in teaspoons. But the crowd, substantial for the late hour, closed around the platform like rising water, making him feel as though he might drown.

At least Henry pulled Leah into the crowd so she would not have to be part of what was happening to him. He couldn't stand the thought of Leah being part of it. She'd never been part of it. What right did he have to pull her into the things that ailed his life?

On the platform, Duncan acknowledged no one as he rubbed his wrists and tried to roll the tension out of his shoulders. His entire body felt so contorted he wondered if he had turned into a gargoyle.

"I be here to announce Mr. Shay ain't dun no wrong. He ain't kilt nobody, and he been erroneously arrested," shouted Wilkes into the crowd.

"Thief and murderer!" Emma Groth's throaty voice boomed from the crowd. "Thief and murderer!"

Duncan's throat closed, forbidding breath. In a single

leap, he flew over the wooden steps of the platform. The tightly knit crowd split to clear a circle for his landing and continued parting to form a path for him. He ran across the street and headed toward his shop.

"Thief and murderer!" Mrs. Groth's voice rang in the night as she waved her silk handkerchief. She was in her glory.

"Shut the hell up, you stupid woman!" shouted Wilkes.

Duncan ran until he turned into the alley behind his shop and stumbled through its ruts. He shouldered the door to his living quarters, almost falling into the room. Behind him, someone knocked on the door.

"Duncan, it's Leah. May I come in?"

He did not answer as he swept the tabletop clean with one swipe of his arm. Screwdrivers bounced against the wall. Sketchbooks fluttered through the air. Drawing pencils skittered across the floor like escaping spiders. The gesture absconded with the last of his strength, and he grabbed the edge of the table with both hands to support himself. His entire body quaked as he breathed through his mouth, each breath shooting out as quickly as he pulled it in.

"Duncan, I love you."

He swept blindly toward the sound of Leah's voice until he bumped into her and wrapped himself around her. Into her hair, he lowered his head, silently mouthing her name over and over. Tremors gathered into shudders so powerful they seemed to rock the room as well as his body.

The door squeaked open, and Utterance stuck his head into the dark room. Leah held up her hand. Utterance backed out. "Hold your horses, Martha. We ain't knocked yet."

Leah stroked Duncan's temple and combed his hair with her fingers. She kissed him on the cheek.

"Duncan, please sit down."

He tried to release her, one quarter inch at a time, as if his joints had rusted in place. Leah pushed his arms apart for him.

"Please sit down. Sit down for just a moment and let me have a look at you."

He stumbled into the chair by the table, almost missing it entirely in a spasm of shudders, and clutched the edge of the table to keep the room from bobbing. Leah knelt beside him. She stroked his cheek. His head was pounding.

Seconds later, Utterance knocked properly, and Martha pushed her way into the room, asking, "Everything fine?"

No one answered, not even when Martha almost tripped on something in the darkness. Utterance located the lantern on the chest of drawers. He patted around for the tinderbox and lit the wick.

The lantern's glow landed on Duncan like a spotlight. He slapped his hands over his wrists to hide the bloody bruises from the handcuffs. Disgrace poured over him like dirty oil. He knew this feeling well. No longer throwing his rage and fear against the universe, he felt absolutely destroyed, a pile of ashes after a catastrophic fire. He pulled his legs under the chair, trying to disappear. Another shudder shook him.

"He all right?" Utterance asked Leah.

Leah shook her head. He barely felt her touch, even as he gripped her hand. His entire body was clenched to the point of pain, releasing only long enough to shudder. Leah began to stroke his back. Her fingers bumped over the scars, which made him feel everyone was looking at them, but he needed her touch.

The shudders eventually ceased, first in intensity, then in frequency. He was sitting only because Leah had her arms around him. Someone poured a glass of water, and Leah handed it to him, keeping her hands over his so he wouldn't drop it. He took a gulp and pushed away the glass, afraid nausea would overcome him.

Utterance's voice flowed into him. "Seem this all be Sheriff Wilkes's fault. Dun blame you for getting upset. Listen, you ain't fit to be by yourself like this. Best you stay the night up at the farm."

To these words, Duncan opened his eyes. He drew a breath that was so labored and uneven Leah slapped one hand over his heart. He thought he might pass out.

Utterance squatted down and placed a hand on his shoulder. "You a-coming?"

"Won't take me long to make up the guest room bed," said Martha.

Through the blur that was now his sight, Duncan squinted at Martha. An opening in his mind let in that Martha was standing by him. Utterance was standing by him. Leah was standing by him.

Duncan closed his eyes to steady himself. A moment later, he pushed himself to his feet, reeling with a dizziness that made Leah, Martha, and Utterance sweep forward to steady him.

Yes. He was going. To the orchard. With people who were standing by him.

24
———

THE PRACTICE

The morning after the dance, Duncan awoke uncertain of his whereabouts. He recognized the room when he saw the wingback chair by the side of the bed. It looked odd because he had seldom seen it without Leah sitting in it, waiting for his fever to break. He rose, systematically washed and dressed, and wandered through the Cobb house into the kitchen where people were talking.

Martha was chopping something with a cleaver. "Eight thirty! Half your day's gone. You all right?"

Duncan looked around. His head was hollow. He had no thoughts.

Leah came to him and put her arms around him as she whispered, "Breakfast?"

Duncan looked away. He had no hunger.

"Not even toast?"

She ran a finger over the dark patches under his eyes that made him look like a raccoon. From the concussion, Leah explained last night. They would go away on their own.

"We got eggs. Saved you bacon," said Martha, her voice unbearably strident.

"We'll start with coffee, Auntie," Leah said.

"It's a fresh pot. Leave some for Utterance. Your uncle be back soon."

Duncan shuffled to the kitchen table and slipped into a chair. All of him was sore—from being pulled off the horse, the kicking in the jail cell, perhaps even from the dancing. Remnants of the migraine still lingered. Resting his forehead in the palm of one hand, he closed his eyes until Leah placed a mug of coffee and a little cup with a yellow liquid in front of him.

"It's good for pain," she explained in a whisper.

Disregarding Martha, he pulled Leah's arms around him as if she were a blanket. He clasped her wrists together and took a sip of the infusion, grimacing at its sourness.

"We have sugar," offered Leah in another whisper, but he downed the liquid like a shot of whiskey and pushed the cup away, locking his body against the sourness.

He looked up when he heard the front door open and a pair of voices grow louder as they came toward the kitchen. Utterance's voice was full of raucous indignation. The other voice carried long pauses and indistinct, concurring mumbles.

Duncan shrugged Leah off his shoulders when Sheriff Wilkes and Utterance came into the kitchen. Without taking his eyes off Wilkes, he slipped forward to the edge of the seat and waited motionlessly like a cat about to pounce.

He'd done no wrong. He thought that had been settled, but he couldn't bring himself to believe anything happening around him. He waited for the worst to happen. At Utterance and Martha's house. In front of Leah.

Utterance pulled out a chair for Wilkes in a way that

clearly mandated the sheriff to sit on it. Wilkes slipped into it, resembling a bulldog as he accommodated his feet flat on the floor and his hands evenly apart on the tabletop. He looked at his hands as if he had scribbled notes on his palms.

Martha placed a cup of coffee in front of Wilkes. Duncan waited. The Bird Cage Minister flashed in his mind.

"I come to apologize, Mr. Shay," said Wilkes. "Man to man. Not official-like. Figure you be in a better mood to hear it now than you was last night. Talked to Mr. Lapp and Mr. Baines. Mr. Baines dun remember much after he shot his ear off, but Mr. Lapp made it clear you ain't had nothing to do with it. Also, Mr. Moore swears you wasn't near Mr. Baines when it happened. Said you was heading to your shop."

Duncan kept silent.

"Want to make it clear I also know you was going for help for a man you don't much care for when I pulled you off his horse. I dun you wrong on that, and hope you'll be accepting my apology for that too. And for accusing you of stealing the horse. And also for thinking you killed a man when you was going for help for him. Formal written apology's been posted at the general store and in the post office. Other spots too. All been taken care of."

Wilkes drew a breath that made his nostrils flare like a horse's. He shifted on the chair to continue the business. "Had a talk with Mr. Baines. He been fined and his rifle been confiscated 'til further notice. You can be sure he be thanking you for trying to save his a-a-ah—"

Wilkes's eyes flickered over Martha and Leah before continuing to address Duncan. "Also, had a word with Mrs. Groth 'bout the legal consequences of her behavior in public last night. Guarantee she be all set too."

"What's that mean?" asked Martha.

Wilkes glared at Martha. "Means I told her I'd throw her in jail if she said sumthin' in public that might can incite a crowd. I believe you be all set, Mr. Shay. Ain't nothing out there against you. And I apologize again for what happened and for impinging on your character."

Wilkes paused with a new bout of unease before he concluded, "Like Mr. Cobb said, we all been so suspicious of you doing wrong, we ain't noticed you been living righteous these days."

Wilkes's last sentence caught Duncan off guard. He slid back into the chair in slow motion and set his sight on Utterance with such profound gratitude that Utterance turned red and looked away. Duncan swallowed and returned his attention to Wilkes. He nodded to release him from his obligations in a way he could not have fully done before.

Wilkes looked at Utterance, who nudged his chin toward the kitchen door and moved to walk him out. When the kitchen door closed behind them, Martha resumed chopping vegetables, and Leah slipped into the chair next to him.

Duncan closed his eyes, spent beyond exhaustion. He sought to focus, resting his thoughts on the actuality that no one would ever accuse Utterance of stealing a horse. Much less drag him off one and throw him in jail on a mere assumption. Everyone would have to sit and think ten times before assuming Utterance had murdered someone found in an alley. And as important, no one would make Martha crawl through a broken window to see him.

"This belong to the sow," announced Martha as she walked out with a bucket of vegetable trimmings. Duncan clenched to shut out Martha's gratuitous announcement.

He opened his eyes when Leah pulled Wilkes's

untouched cup of coffee toward herself and spooned sugar into it. No one had apologized to her or thanked her or offered to look after the cuts on her hands. Not even him. What right did consequences meant for him have to impose themselves on her? Would she forever be a victim of what was meant for him? What right had he to make Leah a part of something that happened before he even met her? Even after so many years, he never imagined his guilt would be so pernicious as to be of such detriment to affect other people's lives.

As Leah stirred the coffee, Duncan's thoughts slipped to Mary Corwal. She, like Wilkes, had succeeded in apologizing. Henry told him later he asked the caller to arrange a Ladies Chain so no one would have any doubts Mary Corwal was dancing with him.

Mary had endured his rebuffs for years. She could have decided she no longer had reason or desire to apologize. Or that he was not worth her efforts. But the desire to redeem herself for her transgression remained in her because some transgressions could rub a person's soul like fine sand forever if not resolved. That she retained her remorse for so long made him see her in a new light. He knew too well that even tiny amounts of remorse could cripple.

He found himself envying Mary's and Wilkes's apologies with such passion his stomach seemed to fold. He knew about apologies inside and out because he could not deliver them.

How could he apologize to anyone for his folly and get his moment of divine relief? Who was left? The guard he shot dead? The guard's widow, who probably descended into poverty with her children? His own father, who died from disappointment in him? His family, who crawled away in shame into oblivion? What apology could possibly compensate for any of that?

Not even the forgiveness of others would undo his wrongs, and deep down, this is what he wanted his forgiveness to entail: the ability to unturn a wooden spindle until it became a living branch again. Unyielding, like a man who does not compromise about forgiveness, he held himself to this goal, only half believing what his intellect accepted readily: that such a goal was unattainable. No amount of apology or time or deprivation could reverse what he had done. He simply had to live with it.

He thought of Avery Lawry, who devoted his life to guiding men who could not undo their actions and whose victims could not hear apologies. Every day, Avery Lawry found a way of saying that the way to apologize when no one could hear you was to do no harm. Do no harm when your hands are tied. Do good when they are not. Practice The Practice until it becomes your life, and forgiveness will find you.

Every day, Avery Lawry promised doubting men with hollow eyes that the world would one day wake up to their unspoken apologies, like winter changing into spring, slowly but assuredly. Duncan never quite believed the promise, but in wretched fear of never being forgiven, he developed the habit before he understood its depth.

The first flower of the spring emerged so slowly and unexpectedly he did not recognize it. That had been Henry, who sought him out, enticing him with sweet buns like someone trying to entice a wild bird with crumbs, and holding steady until he was able to accept the friendship.

Now Utterance, a veritable pillar of the community, suffered a fit of righteous indignation over the injustice of last night's events. He had all but dragged Wilkes up the hill by his ear to apologize. And Martha, whose concerns about him he had never dismissed as foolish, finally welcomed him into her kitchen.

Surely these people would not have permitted him the luxury of being in their lives if they did not in some way see qualities in him that met their standards. Clearly, they believed he was more than the worst thing he had done in his life. He still could not entirely accept he merited the sea change, but he felt overwhelmed with gratitude to have it.

He took Leah's hand, careful not to run his thumb over the fresh scabs on her knuckles. Her love had a way of quelling uncertainties within him and making everything seem possible. He once thought of her as the one spot of light that he followed through the tunnel she excavated for him, but now he felt himself emerging on his own into a broader sunlight, able to abandon a life in shadows and claim his place among the thriving.

For the first time ever, Duncan held this sense the way he could hold a stone in his fist. He felt a tingling lightness, a strange effervescence of amazement and gratitude. Overcome with an intense sense of Leah's immense, understated power, he leaned forward and kissed her.

"Mighty grateful, Leah, you bringing me into this house."

Leah's eyes turned soft with kindness. "You are always welcome here, Duncan."

25

THE RIVER STONES

Not that Leah expected Duncan to bounce back immediately after the trauma of being falsely arrested, but not even she anticipated he would remain somber for so many weeks. She could almost feel him trying to become invisible when he clenched his jaw each time he left his shop.

Riding seemed one of the few activities that shook the unease out of him and left him a little brighter, so they took to riding almost every day until two weeks of nonstop, torrential rains put an end to all but the most necessary outdoor activities.

Martha or Utterance began to pick her up in the buggy so she would not have to walk home in the dreaded downpours. Leah suspected Duncan would have isolated himself in his shop had she not taken to visiting him every day after work. Most of the time, the shop sign was turned to Closed, but knowing she was always welcome, she would flip the sign to Open when she entered to conform with the propriety that the shop had to open to the public when she was present.

The general store, like other shops, remained mostly empty during the rains because people left their houses only under duress. Duncan usually brought her his umbrella as an excuse for him to visit her at the store and for her to visit him when she returned the umbrella. In a small town, propriety was everything.

From the back room where Leah was bringing ledgers up to date, she occasionally looked up and out the front window to see whether Duncan was coming. Eventually, she spotted him battling the rain and winds to open the store door. The fierce wind pulled the door handle out of his hand and slammed the door shut before turning his umbrella inside out. He slapped his hand on his hat to keep it from blowing away while struggling to fix the umbrella.

She laughed at his almost comic attempts to open the door when another gust ripped a brittle apology notice off the door and plastered it against his chest. He peeled it off as if pulling off a leech, then spun around and headed back to his shop, crushing the notice in his fist.

Leah stood up. She had not expected a reaction like that. She abandoned the ledger and walked into the front room.

Hoburn shook his head. "Can't figure your Mr. Shay out, Dr. Maays. Seems like he'd be all kinds of happy about those apologies. Sheriff says he don't intend to ever pull them down."

Leah stood with her fingertips against the windowpane until, without offering an explanation, she grabbed her cloak and bolted out the door into the rain. From tree to tree and door to door, she hastened, plucking off every apology notice she saw. Within minutes, not a trace of the notices remained except for a few yellowed corners here and there. In the general store, she threw the apologies into the wood stove and watched them turn to ashes.

Of course. Why had she not seen this before? The apology notices were casting Duncan as an institution he did not want to be, as surely as if he had been dipped in bronze and placed on the common like a statue. No wonder he could not walk past a notice without feeling drenched in all the assumptions people made about him. If he removed them himself, he would be accused of being ungrateful and disrespectful to the sheriff. No wonder he instead reduced his presence in town to mere sound as he hammered and sawed like a madman enslaved to a demon. Cyrus Olinks said he could barely keep up with him.

Within the hour, Sheriff Wilkes arrived, looking none too pleased. He went into the back room and parked himself in front of Leah, hands tucked in his armpits, arms folded over his chest, elbows resting on his belly.

"Seems I be having trouble 'membering if I authorized taking down them apologies, Dr. Maays."

Leah remained unimpressed by the sheriff's stance. She toyed with the idea of offering the pragmatic man a yellow lollipop, which they always had in surplus because no self-respecting child chose a yellow lollipop if any other color was available.

Putting her musings aside, she spoke gravely, giving the impression of respecting the sheriff's commandeering manner. "It was indicated to me that they became a source of discomfort."

Wilkes's forehead scrunched up like an accordion. "Discomfort? Who said that? They was put up to provide justice, that's what they're there for."

"Could it be that one man feels like a spectacle because others need to apologize?"

"Mr. Shay say that?"

"Mr. Shay is very gracious. He would never complain

about anything on his behalf that is well intentioned. He understands the power of apologies and guilt."

Wilkes ran his tongue over his teeth and into his cheek. He wrinkled his forehead again, nodding while frowning.

Leah swung her arm straight out as if it were on a spring and held a yellow lollipop out to him. "Please accept this on my behalf for your generous intentions, Sheriff Wilkes. Rest assured the apologies have been very much appreciated. It is now time to put the incident aside."

Leah went back to making notes in the ledger before Wilkes could engage her again. She continued scribbling as Wilkes walked away until she heard him open the store's front door and say while sucking the yellow lollipop, "Afthernoon, Mither Ay."

She looked up in time to see Wilkes open the door for Duncan to step in out of the rain. Wilkes pulled the lollipop out of his mouth with a smack and wiped his mouth with the back of his wrist.

"Seem Dr. Maays be intent on giving everybody one of these today. It dun matter if you ain't sick."

"Sir." Duncan stepped aside to let Wilkes exit the store.

Wilkes touched the brim of his hat as a courtesy. He popped the lollipop back in his mouth as he stepped out.

Leah sighed with relief. At least the encounters continued to go well, even if they were a bit mechanical. Most likely, Duncan's curtness made the conversations easier because it kept them brief.

She smiled when Duncan placed his grocery list on the counter under the observation of the Hoburns' averted eyes and made his way to the back room. He tapped on the door, although it was open, and stood before her after placing the umbrella on a crate.

Across the table, he slid a thin sliver of a wood shaving

shaped like a heart and glistening with a little oil that brought out the natural yellowish pink of fresh cherry wood. By now, Leah had such a large collection of these little hearts in various woods she bought a mason jar to keep them safe.

She slipped the wood shaving into her apron pocket from which she pulled out a lollipop and slid it across the table to Duncan. A brown one. Sarsaparilla. Duncan's favorite. With a hint of a smile, Duncan tucked the candy into his shirt pocket and looked up at her.

I love you, he mouthed.

The surface of the table seemed to expand like a vast desert between them. Every part of her wanted to traverse the vastness to touch Duncan and absorb some of his magnificent strength to do whatever was right, even at discomfort to himself. Leah blew a kiss, knowing that if they touched at this moment, she might never want to be a separate being again.

THE RIVER TOOK weeks to recede after the heavy rains and left behind a mess. As soon as possible, Leah returned with Duncan to the river's side opposite the hills of Utterance's apple trees. Almost immediately, they discovered the ground was still too wet, and after a short, unpleasant ride that splattered them with gobs of mud, they turned back, wet and bespeckled.

A safe distance from the mud flat, they dismounted and stood on a knoll, watching the rapids froth. In another few weeks, the water would subside, and the stones that caused the rapids would be visible for the summer.

Duncan wore his silence like a moat. After the disappointing ride, he seemed just as tense as he had been before they headed out. Leah put her arms around him, glad when he enveloped her in the flaps of his coat, an arrangement that warmed them both.

She could almost hear him thinking, gearing up to speak. This was the place where he was most likely to share his most intimate thoughts, where he was most likely to speak about past events and air future aspirations.

"Uncle caught some fish for dinner," she prompted, tracing the buttons on his vest.

"Did he, Leah?"

He said nothing more as they took in the interplay of rushing waters and stoic stones refusing to budge from their intentions to remain. In time, Duncan pulled her onto the ledge and sat beside her.

By the gentleness in his eyes, she knew he was going to speak about his plans, perhaps about his designs for a new cabinet or a new way of expanding his business. She could see his lips moving, but to her disappointment, what the hoarse roar of the river did not mute, the wind stole in a gust.

She leaned toward him, placing her hand behind one ear by way of asking him to speak louder. In response, he abandoned words and lowered his head to nuzzle into her shoulder. The warmth of his breath against her neck convinced her that, even with its occasional patches of muddy coldness, spring would arrive.

UTTERANCE SQUINTED out the kitchen window when Leah and Duncan came out of the barn and began making their way to the house. They were quite animated as they plucked little patches of dried mud off their clothes and flicked them at each other. The mud patches mostly disintegrated in the air, but that didn't stop them from hopping out of the way as if they were flinging rocks at one another.

"They be a right mess," said Utterance.

Martha continued stirring butter into a bowl of turnips. "I warned them. Riverbed ain't that dry yet."

Utterance was about to slide the fish on a platter when Duncan swung Leah out and pulled her against himself. Tight against her body but at quarter pace because the grass was wet and sticky, he danced with her between the dormant vegetable beds until they arrived at the back porch, and he kissed her.

Martha crossed her arms over her chest. "Dun think I dun know the reason a man wants to dance in a muddy garden without music is to put his hands all over a woman! Shame on them, carrying on like that."

"Well, cain't blame a man for wantin' to kiss a pretty girl." Utterance leaned over and kissed Martha on the lips.

"Oh, you!" Martha giggled and nudged him with her shoulder, apparently forgetting her grudge.

Utterance wasn't sure if Duncan heard Martha's comment through the window because the Duncan who entered the house had a completely different demeanor than the one who danced in the back yard with his niece, having become deadly serious the moment the door latch caught behind him. By now, Utterance didn't find Duncan's quiet disturbing. He knew Duncan's silence could be as expressive as an outburst of words. Leah was better at reading him than he was, but she walked into the house and plunged into getting food on the table, barely saying hello to anyone.

In an effort to explore Duncan's extreme shift in mood,

Utterance asked him to say grace when they sat to eat. Without fault, Duncan recited his version of grace—the Godless grace, Martha once called it because it didn't mention God directly. At least Duncan ended the prayer with the traditional *Amen.*

After that, everyone lunged for food as if they were heathens. The mood swing, after so much pious gratitude, never failed to amuse Utterance.

Not that Duncan was never part of that lunging. For that matter, he rarely took the first serving from a platter without first offering it to someone else. Utterance amused himself by thinking Duncan developed that habit to make sure Martha couldn't poison him.

Today, Duncan did not even seem that interested in eating... A rare thing in a man who'd just come back from horseback riding. He sat so straight he looked as if his back ailed him.

"You fine in that chair? Fall off your horse today?" asked Utterance.

"Sir, need a word with you after dinner. If you have a moment. Please."

Utterance nodded. Duncan was as direct as a train on tracks when something was important to him. Utterance glanced at Leah to see if she could interpret Duncan for him, but she seemed determined to not look up from her plate, although sometimes she quivered as if she'd swallowed a bag of something that squirmed.

"Give you advice now, if you be desperate. Won't even charge you for it," said Utterance. *Dun look like they been quarreling after all that dancing in the vegetable garden. Sumthing's going on.*

"Thank you, sir, but I can wait. Mighty fine fish, ma'am."

"Now, why you always say fine fish to my girl when I be

the one who pulled it out of the river? Wasn't for me, wouldn't be no fish to be fine," said Utterance.

"You cook it after you pulled it out, sir?"

"Dint clean it either," muttered Martha.

"There you go, sir."

Utterance chuckled. He often set himself up to be the brunt of Duncan's dry, deadpan humor—masterpieces of understatements.

"You clean fish?" asked Martha.

"Yes, ma'am. When asked."

"You want to try fishing next week? They're bitin'," said Utterance, as if prodding an unidentified object with a stick to figure out what it was.

"Thank you, sir, but I'm going to Edith's Bay."

"Ain't you just come back from there recent?"

"Yes. Sir."

"You out of wood already?"

"Can always use more. Sir."

Utterance knit his brows at the tight silences cropping up between Duncan's words. He stretched one arm and tapped his fingers on the table in a fidget. *Sumthing's off.*

"Want turnips?" Martha held out the bowl to Duncan.

"Yes, please. Thank you, Auntie," said Duncan.

Utterance pressed his lips together and blinked slowly as an epiphany began expanding within him until he jolted in his seat. He gulped the food in his mouth and leaned toward Duncan.

"Well, Farrar's might have better prices than that other feller there. I ain't gone in, but his window tells me he wants arms and legs for rings. Always amazes me what they want for a little ring."

Duncan almost choked in mid chew. He waved away the turnips Martha was offering and looked at Leah.

Leah exploded with laughter and fluttered her hands with an air of futility. "It's no use, Duncan. Uncle knows everything. You cannot slip anything by him. He probably knew before we did."

Utterance pointed his fork at Duncan. "Ha! Got you. You called my girl Auntie. Figure, there be a man tryin' shoes on for fit. Ha! Who's got the milk?"

"Ring!" cried Martha, almost tipping the bowl of turnips.

Duncan took the bowl from her before the buttered roots slid onto the tablecloth. Martha's eyes shifted wildly between Leah and Duncan.

"You 'member when we got engaged?" asked Utterance. "Ain't never regretted most of it. That's the honest truth. Pass me the milk, girl."

"Engaged!" Martha gripped the tablecloth.

Leah reached across the table and handed the creamer to Utterance. He poured milk into his coffee as slowly as he could so he could begin to sort what life had just thrown at him. He'd spent more time discouraging Leah from being with Duncan than he had doing just about anything else. And Martha outright declared war on Duncan. And here he was trying to become a relative.

Utterance stirred the milk into his coffee with enormous diligence. All his concerns about Duncan resurfaced. And there were plenty. Plenty. Starting with murder and bank robbery. And who knew what else because the man never talked about himself. Some of his silences were like boulders to block his past from coming into the present. Leah knew about some of those past things but wasn't telling either. Apparently, she didn't think they mattered.

But now... Utterance had to admit there was nothing much wrong that he could point to, although some things about the man required handling with tweezers. Still, others commanded blunt respect. Utterance stopped himself from sighing out loud. His shoulders slumped as he again faced that he could never bring himself to dislike Duncan, despite everything.

Well, if everyone else chewed on their courage and dared be honest for a minute, they'd have to admit Duncan pretty much kept himself righteous on his own because for years no one talked to him. Surprised he hadn't gone crazy in his shop by himself for so long. At least Duncan Shay had enough solid stuff in him to make a living honestly, and that was more than you could say for most with his background. Had his quirks, yes. But was otherwise, well, solid. More like Leah than anybody else, in fact.

Utterance cornered his conclusions and spoke to Leah as he looked at Duncan. "Mighty fine feller you catched yourself, Leah. Decent. Works everything hard as you. Real hard."

The stiffness drained out of Duncan's posture, and he looked as if he might slide out of the chair. He closed his eyes and released a thick breath as he put down his silverware with a clank against his plate like a man collapsing after being shot.

Utterance chortled as he addressed Duncan directly. "And you catched yourself a handful. You be busy keeping yourself out of the sanitarium with Leah."

"I'll manage, sir. Thank you."

"You still needing to talk to me after dinner? For my permission?"

"No sir. Seems settled. I am mighty, mighty grateful, sir. Thank you."

"I figured that be it."

"Figured right, sir."

"When?" asked Martha.

"Duncan plans to pick up the rings next week at Farrar's, as Uncle has so cleverly deduced," said Leah.

"When you gettin' married?" shouted Martha.

"Oh!" Leah looked at Duncan. "We haven't set a date, have we?"

"Soon as possible, ma'am. No sense waiting."

Utterance grinned. "Now there's a determined feller."

Martha turned to Leah. "Wedding rings from Farrar's... You need get something modest. You ain't got no house yet."

"We haven't even thought about a house," said Duncan as if he had just found out married people lived in buildings.

"Duncan, I doubt we shall need to live in a hollow tree."

"Can build you one. That's no problem. But if you want an infirmary—don't think my lot's big enough."

"You be getting a teeny, tiny ring if you make him build you some fool infirmary," said Martha.

"I don't need an infirmary, Duncan. An examination room will do just fine. Although it should be big enough for small surgeries. Hmm... It couldn't be on your lot anyway. You and Mr. Olinks can give any sound person a headache with all that hammering."

"Dr. Haloway might sell to us. He's right in town. Heard he's leaving for Edith's Bay."

"Dunno," said Utterance. "He been sayin' that for years."

"A good house offer'll get him going..." Duncan muttered to himself.

"His examination room is extremely ample," said Leah. "Imagine! Setting up practice in Dr. Haloway's house. What fabulous revenge."

"Leah, you need to get cloth for the dress. Or you ain't thought of that yet?" said Martha.

"Oh, Auntie! Soon enough."

"Well, you cain't leave a wedding dress to the last minute. Hoburn dun carry cloth for that. You be needing to get that in Edith's Bay. Best to see it in person. Don't order it by mail. Never know what you'll get."

"Auntie, stop worrying. We have not even set a date—"

"Is that cake in the kitchen good for celebrating, ma'am?" asked Duncan, raising his voice just enough to distract.

Utterance nodded, slowly easing into a new level of comfort. A man so endowed with tact should have no problems handling marriage—or in-laws.

"That be Leah's chocolate cake," said Martha. "I ain't got patience to make it."

"Yes," said Leah. "I used the cocoa powder you gave Auntie."

Duncan looked down the length of the table at Utterance, who began to clear his throat and wipe his mouth.

"Believe you told me Dr. Maays cooks as well as she plays checkers. Sir."

"Uncle!"

"I did say that, dint I?" Utterance began to laugh.

"Duncan, Uncle didn't say that to you, did he? It's not true, you know."

"Got you good, dint I? Well, consider it a nice surprise, seeing you was willing to take Leah without the cooking."

Duncan raised one eyebrow. "Think I got you better, sir."

He lowered his head and chuckled into his chest, first silently, then softly. With clenched eyes, he wrapped his arms around his torso and shook until he tipped back his head and laughed deeply and soulfully. His reaction was so robust everyone sat open mouthed until they also began to laugh.

Dint know he ever laughed out loud, thought Utterance.
Learn something new every day.

LEAH WAS NOT pleased when she overhead Martha asking
Utterance how anyone expected to get married if Duncan
refused to go to church. She knew the question was meant
for her to overhear because Martha seldom confronted her
directly.

Discussing going to church with Duncan would require
great delicacy and tact, although she suspected even
Duncan expected to get married in a church. Propriety held
that she could visit Duncan at his shop only when the shop
was open to the public, and Duncan had been known to flip
his Closed sign to Open at the mere sight of her on the
street. Even then, she would have to bide her time, especially now that Cyrus worked at the shop and she could not
often catch Duncan alone.

Leah waited until Martha was in front of her on the
church steps before looking toward Duncan's shop. Nothing
within twenty feet of the shop was moving. Always diplomatic, Duncan would appear at the orchard an hour after
church let out.

Leah entered the church and filed into a pew with Utterance and Martha. She had made them take vows of silence
about the engagement. It was such a delicious bit of knowledge that she was loath to release it into the rumor mill
where it would immediately become crimped and soiled.

Leah rested her hand against her chest over the chain
that held the wooden ring Duncan turned and carved for
her until he could buy the gold one. No ring felt more real
than the one Duncan made for her. It was like a priceless

gem against her breasts. When he returned from Farrar's with gold rings, the secret would be over, and word would travel swiftly through the town.

In front of her, Henry turned and whispered, "Congratulations, Dr. Maays!"

Leah glared at Martha, who was busy thumbing through the hymnal. Utterance would keep a secret to his death.

"Congratulations!" Henry repeated, a little louder. Some people now turned to look. "Duncan told me yesterday! I think he slept on Dr. Haloway's front steps waiting to ask him if he would sell."

"Dr. Haloway?" whispered Leah. She hadn't asked Duncan to keep their engagement secret. He was so private, she just assumed he wouldn't tell anyone.

Henry lost some of his color. "Did—Did I break a confidence?"

"Oh no," Leah said because she couldn't think of anything else to say.

She looked at the Haloways, whose eyes were on her. A few pews down, the Hoburns were also staring at her and whispering.

Leah sighed. The secret never had a chance. "Oh, Henry! Tell everyone. Let everyone rejoice. Thank you."

"Then why you making me keep it secret?" hissed Martha.

"Please stand for the opening hymn, number eighty-six," Parson Mills instructed the congregation.

Mrs. Bluette, the pianist, began the prelude as the congregation flipped through the hymnals and rustled into standing. The doors of the church opened as the Corwals and their children slipped into the church, filling the sanctuary with the sounds of whispering children and shushing adults. They were always late, which is why they were tactfully given the very last pew by the door.

Mrs. Bluette frowned like a frog at them. She played more loudly until they settled into their pew. But even after they were seated, commotion continued. Mrs. Bluette looked up and did a double take. Her fingers fell on the wrong keys, and she banged out a bar of garbled dissonance until she jerked her hands from the keyboard. Everyone turned around to see the cause of her discombobulation.

Under the scrutiny of the entire congregation, Duncan stepped into the soft light of the interior and let the door close behind him. A uniform murmur rose, followed by a silence in which only babies mewed and old men coughed.

Leah began to step over Martha, who urged her in whispers not to make a spectacle of herself. After a battle of whispers, Utterance placed his hand on Leah's arm, and she relented. In his eyes, she saw he already knew what to do. Utterance always knew what to do.

Leah held her breath as Duncan stood in the center aisle, still as a pillar. She scanned the congregation, hoping it would be kinder to him than it had been in previous years. She would not put it past him to turn and leave at any sign of intolerance.

Sheriff Wilkes turned at the first rustle from Emma Groth's pew and delivered a look that made her snap her mouth shut and settle back into the hard seat. In contrast, Henry waved to Duncan and pointed to the seat next to himself. Andy consulted with his wife, and they pressed deeper into their pew, making another space but not drawing attention to it. Mrs. Olinks scrunched against her husband without a second thought to make room for another person. Hoburn looked at his wife, who looked away.

Utterance stepped out into the aisle and pointed to the pew as he called gently, "Duncan." The name filled the building.

Duncan walked forward, his footsteps muffled against the pine boards. In front of Utterance, he took the hymnal already opened to the relevant page and whispered his thanks. He slipped into the pew and acknowledged no one as he looked into infinity with eyes that saw nothing, clutching the hymnal as if it might wiggle out of his hands.

"Hymn eighty-six, please," prompted Parson Mills.

Mrs. Bluette wiggled into a renewed state of self-importance on the piano bench and raised her hands theatrically before banging out four bars of introductory music. The congregation began singing as it always did, loudly and out of tune. Leah followed the hymn silently while she listened to Duncan's voice rise with the others. He, too, sang with a lack of musicality, his voice raspy and cracking like the voice of someone who had not sung in years.

After singing an entire verse, he looked at her, his eyes settled with the strength of someone who arrived at a place he never thought he'd see. Leah smiled with a swell of love, concluding that despite the imperfections in his voice, he carried the tune quite well. She looked at the upcoming verse in the hymnal and took her place in the community just as forcefully by joining in the cacophonous singing.

HISTORICAL NOTE

Addressing People During the Victorian Era

In *Song of the Wooden Sparrow,* Duncan and Leah address each other in a variety of ways: Dr. Maays, Miss Leah, Leah, Mrs. Maays, Dr. Leah, Mr. Shay, Duncan. They call one another Mr. Shay and Dr. Maays in public while addressing one another as Duncan and Leah in private. Because both Duncan and Leah were familiar with the addressing traditions of the upper and lower classes, they often switch between or amalgamate traditions.

Victorians had a gift for social complexity that today we deem unnecessarily formal and overwhelming. The higher and more educated the social class, the more rigid and complex were its social traditions. Duncan and Leah would have been familiar with these protocols for addressing people.

People in the lower classes, such as tradespeople, servants, and farmers, addressed one another more or less as we do today. First names were acceptable in mixed company, although men commonly used surnames instead of first. Children addressed elders as Mr., Mrs., or Miss Surname. Employees and employers would address one another by surname.

In contrast, people in the upper classes seldom referred to anyone by first name, except immediate family members and very close friends, and only when alone. The upper classes used these distinctions partly to distinguish themselves from other classes.

For upper-class Victorians, addressing someone in public was a complex endeavor by which one's social class and relationship to the person being addressed could be assessed. "Public" was defined as more than two people present. For example, if a married couple was having a conversation and their five-year-old walked into the room, they were then in public. In some houses, the presence of servants constituted being in public, while in others not so much because servants were meant to be invisible.

The mode of address depended as much on the social context as on the personal relationship. In an informal public setting, such as at tennis game, men from the upper classes addressed one another other by their surnames without the title of Mr. A man could call the same man Smith during a tennis game, Mr. Smith in a business setting, or John if they were close friends or brothers and they were in private. Being on familiar terms did not soften the discipline of addressing someone in public.

Upper-class women frequently used first names in informal settings where men were not present. If the company was mixed, the use of first names depended on whether the women were on familiar terms with the men, and the men usually added a Miss or Mr. to the first names, as in Mr. Henry or Miss Mary. More often, men would address a woman as Miss Surname. For example, "I am most honored to make your acquaintance, Miss Smith." Usually, if one person was called Mr. or Miss Surname, everyone else also shifted to calling everyone Mr. or Miss Surname.

In public, married persons were always addressed by surname, even by their spouses. For example, Mr. Smith might say to his wife in front of their family, "Good morning, my dear Mrs. Smith." To do otherwise was considered extremely rude to the spouse. In (very) private, a husband could address his wife by her first name ("I am very happy you do not have a headache tonight, Jane."). Parents could also call their adult children by first names when in private.

Male children were addressed formally as Master First name, as in "Master Teddy." Female children were addressed formally as Miss First name, as in "Miss Sarah." Otherwise, children were addressed by their first names. Servants were required to add Master or Miss to the child's first name. Depending on how long the servant had been at the house, the tradition of calling a child Master or Miss First name might persist into the child's adulthood.

Male servants were addressed by their surnames without titles like Mister, as in "Jeeves, let's have some light here." Female servants were usually called by their first names only or Miss First name, even if they were married. The exception was the cook and sometimes the head housekeeper, who was usually called Mrs. Surname, even if she was not married because Mrs. was considered the greatest title to which an American Victorian woman could aspire, just as marriage was expected to be her greatest accomplishment.

BOOK CLUB QUESTIONS

Song of the Wooden Sparrow

1. What is your first impression of Leah? Of Duncan? Of the community members? How does this impression change as you linger in West Edith's Bay?
2. What do Duncan and Leah have in common?
3. Duncan and Leah have both lost their immediate families. Why does Leah heal from her grief and Duncan does not?
4. Duncan blames himself for being abandoned by his family. Do you think he is solely responsible?
5. While Utterance and Duncan are playing checkers, what does Martha do that might make her more sympathetic to Duncan when he later speaks to her in the canning kitchen about when he killed the guard during the bank robbery?
6. Discuss the nature of apologies as presented in *Song of the Wooden Sparrow*.

7. What is Leah's realization about death?

8. What does *Practice The Practice* mean? Do you or someone you know *Practice The Practice*?

9. What does Mrs. Groth's walking stick reveal about Duncan?

10. What characteristics does Duncan have that make people open up a little to him?

11. Do you think Utterance seriously considers refusing to give Duncan permission to marry Leah? Why or why not?

12. Do you think Duncan forgives himself by the end of the book? What is forgiveness?

13. How would you feel if Duncan wanted to marry into your family?

14. Who's your favorite character in *Song of the Wooden Sparrow*? Why?

15. Leah claims she wants to find West Edith's Bay exactly as she once left it. Is West Edith's Bay the same? Is this good or bad for her?

16. How do Leah, Henry, and Duncan express courage? What about Martha? Are there characters who do not have courage?

ABOUT THE AUTHOR

Isabel Tutaine writes about ordinary people who summon the courage to take control of their lives. She is Cuban by birth, American by citizenship, Cuban-New Englander by culture. She lives in midcoast Maine where she listens to what the ocean has to say, then runs home to write it down.

When not writing, she rescues porcupines and makes yarn the old fashioned way on a spinning wheel. However, she hates knitting and thinks it should be outlawed.

BestLit Review 2018 selected her as one of the ten best prose writers in midcoast Maine based on an excerpt from one of her novels. *Blanket Sea* nominated one of her pieces for *Sundress Publications Best of the Net 2019.* She is a member of The Authors Guild, Women's Fiction Writers Association, and Maine Writers and Publishers Alliance.

Check her out at **IsabelTutaineAuthor.com**

www.ingramcontent.com/pod-product-compliance
Lightning Source LLC
Chambersburg PA
CBHW022009310726
48972CB00006B/1581